...Bright Futures is a cautionary tale of parental anxiety run amok in the high-stakes world of elite college admissions. I loved this wild ride of a novel, brimming with truth, mischief, and consequences. It's a smart, provocative debut that will keep you turning pages until the riveting end."

—Tara Conklin, *New York Times* bestselling author
of *The Last Romantics* and *The House Girl*

"The road to college admissions is paved with good intentions—and many bad ones, too. *Girls with Bright Futures* is an audacious, chilling, thrilling look at what happens at an elite private school when the two collide head-on, the casualties multiply, and secrets pop out like beach blankets on a quad."

—Meg Mitchell Moore, author of *The
Admissions* and *Two Truths and a Lie*

"*Girls with Bright Futures* is a scandalous and timely story of three women who will do anything to secure their daughters' future in a winner-take-all world. An engrossing mix of satire and thriller."

—Andrea Dunlop, author of *She Regrets Nothing*

"Wickedly paced and devilishly clever, *Girls with Bright Futures* is a serious case of moms behaving badly, perfectly showcasing the dark side of ambition in the cutthroat world of elite college admissions. For those who enjoy mischief and mayhem in an urban, ultra-competitive private school setting, this smart and riveting debut is a wildly entertaining read."

—Christina McDonald, *USA Today* bestselling author
of *Behind Every Lie* and *The Night Olivia Fell*

"*Girls with Bright Futures* is a dark and wild trip into the cutthroat world of college admissions, placing vicious, out-of-control parents under a harsh and unforgiving light. Dobmeier and Katzman have cranked up the volume on Varsity Blues–type scandals in this gripping novel packed full of escalating surprises."

—Amy Poeppel, author of *Small Admissions* and *Musical Chairs*

"A scintillating deep dive into a college admissions scandal and the terrifying lengths parents will go to in securing their children's futures. Propulsive and shocking."

—Robyn Harding, internationally bestselling author of *The Party*

Girls with Bright Futures

a Novel

TRACY DOBMEIER
WENDY KATZMAN

To Van Katzman and Eric Dobmeier, the original KatznDobs

Published by Sourcebooks Landmark, an imprint of Sourcebooks
P.O. Box 4410, Naperville, Illinois 60567-4410
(630) 961-3900
sourcebooks.com

Library of Congress Cataloging-in-Publication Data

Names: Dobmeier, Tracy, author. | Katzman, Wendy, author.
Title: Girls with bright futures : a novel / Tracy Dobmeier and Wendy Katzman.
Description: Naperville, Illinois : Sourcebooks Landmark, [2021]
Identifiers: LCCN 2020001705 | (trade paperback)
Subjects: GSAFD: Suspense fiction.
Classification: LCC PS3604.O23 G57 2021 | DDC 813/.6--dc23
LC record available at https://lccn.loc.gov/2020001705

Printed and bound in the United States of America.
SB 10 9 8 7 6 5 4 3 2 1

HOME OF MAREN AND WINNIE PRESSLEY

FRIDAY, OCTOBER 29, 11:30 P.M.

IF THE DROOL AT the corner of her mouth was any indication, Maren's attempt to stay awake until Winnie got home from her babysitting gig was, as her daughter would say, an epic fail. Maren took in the laptop still perched on her chest, which had similarly slipped into sleep mode. With a quick tap, the web search she'd started before falling asleep flooded her retinas.

Out of sullen curiosity, she had Googled the unusual name of the professor she'd met earlier in the evening when she'd dropped by her boss's house unannounced to deliver their tuned-up espresso machine. As the longtime personal assistant to Alicia Stone, one of the most powerful women in tech, Maren met celebrities and power players all the time. This Boston professor didn't seem to be anyone special—likely just another pawn in Alicia's elaborate scheme to secure admission to Stanford for her daughter, Brooke. But with the early admission deadline now just three days away, he served as yet another reminder that Stanford was off-limits for Winnie, just in case Maren had missed all the previous warnings.

Stretching her neck, which was stiff from dozing off at a weird angle on the couch, Maren slammed her laptop shut and jammed her hand between the couch cushions in search of her phone. The last thing she remembered was Winnie's text saying she was heading home, but when she fished out the phone and unlocked the screen, Maren saw it was already eleven thirty p.m. Winnie's text had been over an hour ago. Had she come in already and gone to bed without saying good night?

Maren was just about to check Winnie's bedroom when the doorbell rang, followed by insistent knocking—and suddenly Maren realized it was the sound of the doorbell that had jarred her awake in the first place. With a smile playing at the corners of her mouth, Maren pictured Winnie on the doorstep, keyless once again. For such a smart kid, her daughter was ridiculously forgetful. As Maren strode the few steps to the door of their tiny bungalow, she called out, "OK, OK! Coming!" She turned the doorknob and prepared to greet Winnie with a classic motherly look that said, "I'm happy you're home safe, but what the heck?"

But her wry grin faded the instant she threw open the door. It wasn't her daughter; not even close. At the sight of the uniformed police officer standing under the dim, dead-bug-filled porch light, Maren instinctively closed the bulky cardigan she was wearing over her threadbare pajamas. "Hi, Officer. Can I help you?" Despite having been raised to believe the police were the world's best helpers, Maren's only real interaction with the police years ago had left her with an altogether different impression.

"Good evening, ma'am. I'm Officer Wilson. Are you Mrs. Pressley?"

How did he know her name? Maren's nervous system switched into high alert. "Yes?"

"Is Rowan Pressley your daughter?"

No one ever called Winnie by her full name. "Yes," she said with a growing sense of dread.

"Ma'am, I'm sorry to tell you this, but your daughter was in a serious accident."

"No," Maren said, shaking her head. "Are you sure you have the right person?" She wanted to slam the door shut and disappear back into her nap or her confusion or even her bitterness toward Alicia. Anywhere but here.

"Ma'am, is this your daughter's cell phone?" Officer Wilson held out an iPhone with a familiar pink case. It looked silly in his large palm, and Maren almost said so, like if she could muster a wisecrack, that would somehow prove the phone wasn't Winnie's. As if in slow motion, Maren saw her hand reaching for the phone. The glass was badly cracked. She turned it over, hoping against hope not to find the most obvious identifier, the unique PopSocket designed to look like a salmon sushi roll that Winnie had splurged on with some of her babysitting money. Fear surged through Maren. "Oh my God...is she OK?"

"As I said, she's been in a serious accident. On an electric scooter," Officer Wilson said. "She's been taken to Memorial Hospital. I'm sorry, but I don't have any information on her condition."

"But she's alive, right?"

"They didn't share any details with me. I was only asked to notify her parents and bring them to the hospital." Officer Wilson shifted his weight and appeared to peek over Maren's shoulder into the house. "Is Winnie's father home?"

"No. It's just me. Just the two of us."

He nodded. "You're going to want to follow me to Memorial now, ma'am."

Maren was frozen in place.

"Ma'am?"

"Yes, OK. Just give me one minute." As she closed the door and turned to change out of her pajamas, a black cloud of panic engulfed her. She leaned back against the door and squeezed her eyes shut for a moment, willing her vision to clear and her legs to stop shaking. With one hand steadying her against the wall, she took a few steps toward her bedroom but was stopped cold by the photos lining the hall. Though she passed these pictures every day, she only rarely registered them. Now she couldn't tear her eyes away. Winnie's goofy grin on her fifth birthday showing off the gap where her bottom two baby teeth had once resided. Winnie and Brooke as ten-year-olds in matching Stanford T-shirts with their arms wrapped tightly around each other on the beach in front of the Stones' San Juan Island cabin. Back when they were still best friends. Last year's junior prom, with Winnie three inches taller in heels than her normal five feet seven inches, wearing a soft blue dress that highlighted her natural beauty without flaunting it. And the most recent picture on the wall—of Winnie's induction into the National Honor Society just last month—in which she was almost the exact age Maren had been when her life changed forever. Maren remembered thinking as she snapped that photo that all she wanted was to preserve her daughter's happiness and keep her safe. Winnie was all she had. She cast a tearful glance upward and begged an omniscient being she'd long since given up on: Please, please, please, let her be OK.

———

Maren followed the flashing lights of Officer Wilson's squad car in front of her as they wound their way down the side streets of her modest neighborhood, one of the few left in Seattle's tech boom landscape, and onto the arterial that would deliver them to Memorial Hospital. She tried to focus on keeping the appropriate space cushion between their cars, but her mind refused to cooperate, and she shivered uncontrollably as her fears bombarded her one after the other. What if Winnie died before she got there and she never got to say goodbye? What if she was paralyzed or brain-dead? And though she knew this was the least of her worries, how would she ever manage the astronomical medical bills no matter what happened to Winnie?

Despite working for Alicia for more than ten years and outlasting every other household employee, health insurance had never been part of the deal. Maren had looked in to getting them covered this past year, but even the subsidized rates available on the state healthcare exchange had seemed too daunting. She'd gambled on their good health and diverted the money to replace her car's transmission instead, knowing that they just had to get Winnie to college, where at least Winnie would then be covered by a more affordable university plan. Would the hospital even treat Winnie? Should she text Alicia? As a member of the Memorial Hospital board, Alicia could ensure that Winnie received whatever treatment she needed. Alicia had always claimed to love Winnie like another daughter. Before all the college madness of the past few weeks, Maren wouldn't have hesitated to ask her for help. But now Maren hoped that was a call she wouldn't need to make.

After a sloppy parking job in the first available spot, Maren sprinted through the automatic sliding doors of the ER and approached the desk clerk, desperate for information. The clerk consulted her computer. "Your daughter's in surgery right now. As soon as the doctors can, they'll send someone out to update you. You can have a seat in the waiting area."

Surgery already? "What kind of surgery?" Maren's voice cracked. "That means she's alive, right?"

"I'm sorry, but I don't have any more information. A doctor should be out soon," the clerk said. "Oh, wait. Mrs. Pressley? It looks like we don't have your daughter's insurance information in the computer. Do you have that with you?"

"Uh no, I don't. I left my house so fast." Maren made a show of patting her pockets. "That won't affect her care, right?"

"No, but I'll need that information when you have a chance."

"Yes, of course," Maren said. "I'll take care of that as soon as I can." It wasn't exactly a lie, even if it was more aspirational statement than concrete plan.

Maren scanned the waiting area. There was a young family with three children running wild, a disheveled bearded man who was either homeless or hipster, and a woman sitting across the room wearing a black puffy coat and a baseball cap. Maren found a solitary seat, far away from the others, with a clear view of the "Unauthorized Entry" doors, and proceeded to wait.

A half hour passed, and Maren again pleaded with the desk clerk for information, studying her facial expression for any sign at all that Winnie would be OK. But there was still no word from the surgeon, and neither the clerk's words nor her body language revealed anything. As she wandered back to her seat, Maren noted that the young family and homeless/hipster guy had been replaced by new anxious faces, but the woman on the far side of the room continued her own lonely vigil. Maren wondered what her story was. Who was she waiting for? Maren had the feeling the woman was sizing her up too. She tried to take comfort that she was not completely alone with her worry, but it was no use. She sat down and dropped her head into her hands.

There was simply no way a chance accident on a stupid neon electric scooter could mark the end of their story. Winnie's life had begun as the ultimate heartbreak for Maren. But over time, with Winnie's inner light to guide her, Maren had managed to chisel away most of the ugly parts. Now all she could think about was the past three weeks. They'd argued more than they had in all the years of Winnie's childhood combined. If the worst came to pass, how would Maren be able to live with herself, knowing one of her last acts as Winnie's mom had been to torch her dreams? Their story was supposed to be one of triumph, with Winnie graduating first in her class from Elliott Bay Academy and heading off to Stanford, not fighting for her life inside an operating room. With the sleeve of her sweater, Maren wiped away the tears on her cheeks. Lately, she'd begun girding herself for the intense loneliness she knew she'd feel when Winnie left for college. But losing her daughter to college would be nothing compared to being swallowed whole by grief—again.

PART

1

1

Maren

**THREE WEEKS UNTIL STANFORD EARLY
ADMISSION APPLICATION DEADLINE**

MAREN PRESSLEY HAD WALKED the halls of Seattle's Elliott Bay Academy multiple times per week for the past six-plus years, though ordinarily, she did so in her role as Alicia's personal assistant, fulfilling the multitude of volunteer commitments her boss had no intention of doing herself. In fact, Maren could probably count on two hands the number of times she'd appeared on campus simply as Winnie's mom. Unlike most of the other EBA moms, Maren had precious little free time, and when she did manage to carve out a few minutes for herself, she was loath to spend them sticking her nose in Winnie's academic business. Her daughter had that well under control.

But at seven this morning, Maren had received an urgent summons from the college counseling office. It was a request—or was it a demand?—for both Maren and Winnie to meet that morning with Winnie's college counselor. EBA moms frequently speculated that the school's seven college counselors had virtually unchecked power to sort students into elite universities. At Back to School Night, Maren had over-heard a group of parents swapping stories about dropping everything when the college counseling office called, no matter if they were titans of tech in the middle of negotiations, doctors performing routine sur-gery, or even, almost unbelievably, a wealthy divorcée undergoing a labia resurfacing procedure. (Being essentially invisible at EBA had its amusing perks.) So Maren figured she owed it to Winnie to show up this morning. Checking the clock on the way into the office, she hoped that whatever the reason for the meeting, it could be dealt with quickly so she could get to work on Alicia's massive to-do list for the day.

When Maren walked into Ms. Lawson's office, Winnie was already there, sitting on the edge of her chair, her long blond hair pulled back in a messy bun. Maren noticed Winnie staring at the wall with longing in her eyes and followed her gaze to the array of college posters and pen-nants that formed a patchwork mural of leafy quads, Gothic architecture, and earnest students of all shapes, sizes, and colors. "Hi, Ms. Lawson, I'm Maren Pressley. We met last spring." Maren shook the counselor's hand and slid into the open seat next to Winnie.

"Right," Ms. Lawson said with a growing smile. "I still can't believe you're old enough to be Winnie's mom." She turned to Winnie. "You're so lucky. My mom had me when she was forty-three, and people always thought she was my grandma. So embarrassing! I mean, other than the way you two dress, you could totally be sisters."

"If I had a nickel…" Winnie laughed.

At thirty-five, Maren was well aware she stuck out at EBA: the elite prep school version of a sore thumb. In high-income Seattle, most moms her age were still nursing babies or chasing after toddlers. Although Maren tried not to call attention to herself, the comparative youthfulness of her skin set her apart from fellow moms of EBA seniors, most of whom were a generation older. But whatever small advantage Maren gained with her natural glow, she lost a hundred times over with her glaring lack of any of Seattle's subtle signifiers of status. Electric luxury vehicles. Athleisure clothing paired with designer handbags. Prestigious professional degrees useful for dropping into casual conversation, preferably in shorthand ("My marketing professor at Kellogg used to say…") or, even better, in acronym ("When I went to HBS…"). Maren could hardly wait until the coming spring, when Winnie and Brooke, Alicia's daughter, would graduate from EBA and Maren could watch this place recede in the rearview mirror for good.

Ms. Lawson twisted the cartilage piercing in her ear. "So hey, yeah. So…I've been charged with delivering some, ah, difficult and pressing news."

Her defeatist tone struck Maren as incongruous with the we-make-your-dreams-come-true ambiance of the college counseling office. "OK?" Maren tucked her calloused hands under her thighs and pressed her clipped nails into the tasteful wool slacks she'd scored at Value Village last year while dropping off a gigantic load of castaways from the closets of Alicia and Brooke. Though it sometimes took every ounce of her willpower, Maren's policy on hand-me-downs from her employer was strict—as in never ever do it, even for Winnie.

The only time she'd broken this rule was in Winnie's ninth-grade year, soon after she'd started at EBA. Winnie had begged Maren to let her keep one of Brooke's discards with the tags still attached—a cute, pink, and thoughtfully pre-torn sweatshirt. The very next day, she'd worn it to school, but the instant she'd walked in the door after cross-country practice, she'd yanked it out of her gym bag and cut it to shreds. It was around the time Brooke had inexplicably started icing Winnie after years of close friendship. Maren had understood things were not great between them by that point, but she had never known Brooke to be vicious. Apparently, Winnie had been taken by surprise as well.

"What news, Ms. Lawson?" Winnie prompted her counselor.

As they continued waiting for Ms. Lawson while she shuffled papers and avoided their eyes, Maren kept her expression neutral and held her posture in the decorous manner that had been drilled in to her by her mother in the stifling dining rooms of her childhood home and country club, perhaps the only lesson that still served her from that long-estranged relationship.

Ms. Lawson tilted her head up as though consulting a teleprompter on the ceiling. "Well, um, you see…" She pushed up her sleeve, revealing a small black butterfly tattoo on the inside of her forearm. "Four student athletes—an EBA record actually!—have committed to Stanford. Now, I know we've been talking about Winnie applying early to Stanford since last year, and of course the deadline is only three weeks away. But, well, here's the unfortunate part. We've been in touch with Stanford admissions and have learned they only plan to accept one additional student from EBA this year."

"But didn't they take seven students last year?" Winnie asked, her voice rising.

Ms. Lawson nodded. "Yes, but it turns out they're really pushing to increase their public school yield this year, so they can't accept as many kids from top-notch private schools like EBA as they did last year."

"But the whole reason I moved from public school to EBA was to improve my chances of getting into Stanford."

Before Ms. Lawson could respond, Maren jumped in. "That's interesting information, but Winnie's ranked first in her class and also has that first-gen hook, so what does this have to do with her?" Not only was Winnie an academic standout, but they'd also been informed by the college counseling office last spring that Winnie was blessed with an admissions "hook" of special interest to elite colleges: the first-generation college student. Maren had been pleasantly surprised by this, although it sort of felt like receiving a Nobel Prize posthumously. But apparently, she'd celebrated the victory prematurely, because Maren knew exactly what this news meant for Winnie. And she suspected Winnie did too. Nevertheless, if they were going to get the shaft, Ms. Lawson at least owed them the courtesy of copping to it out loud.

Ms. Lawson squirmed in her chair. "Um, yes. Well, of course, under ordinary circumstances, as we've discussed, Winnie would be an excellent candidate for admission. But with the number of remaining spots so limited due to the unusual number of a-MAZE-ing athletes this year, there are other, um, considerations. There might be students who, you know, have even stronger hooks than Winnie's. What I'm trying to say is that while Winnie is free to take her chances, we think she might be better served by applying somewhere with a little less in-house competition. After all, that first-generation hook is golden at any Ivy Plus college."

Ms. Lawson must have mistaken Maren's look of disgust for one of confusion.

"Ivy Plus," she continued, "is the term we use to talk about Ivy League schools *plus* Ivy-equivalent schools like Stanford, MIT, Caltech, and the

University of Chicago. Anyway, unlike Winnie, some other EBA students may have their best hooks with Stanford alone."

Maren gritted her teeth and willed her eyeballs to remain centered. Her well-developed maternal warning system was blaring. It didn't take a genius to understand what Ms. Lawson was really saying: they were clearing a path for either a Stanford legacy or someone with big bucks. Or both. These EBA people were all the same. They all talked a big game about merit and equity, but the instant their sense of entitlement was threatened, they had zero qualms about politely (this was Seattle, after all) manipulating the less fortunate in their orbit to stabilize the applecart.

"But, Ms. Lawson, you said yourself last spring I had the best chance of getting into Stanford of anyone at EBA. Why are you telling *me* to find someplace else and not another student?"

"Winnie, you know I can't talk about other students with you."

"But are you saying the same thing to everyone?" Winnie pressed, her voice quivering.

Maren gently put her hand on Winnie's forearm. "Win, it doesn't matter. Stanford isn't the only great school out there. We'll find another one, and it will be an incredible experience. I promise."

"You know what this is about. How can you just cave like this? This is my future. Why should girls like Krissie or Brooke get a spot over me? Their moms do everything but take their tests for them. I've earned this all on my own."

Ms. Lawson consulted her computer and then looked up with a smile. "Maybe you should look at this as an opportunity, Winnie. Your record is so strong I'm certain we could find you a university that will offer you substantial merit money. What about University of Oregon or

Case Western? They've been extremely generous recently to entice stellar students like you."

"Why do you assume we can't pay for college?" Winnie's tone was biting. She never challenged authority like this. "Just because we're not rich like everyone else here doesn't mean we need charity."

"Honey, that's enough," Maren snapped, sparing the shocked Ms. Lawson an awkward reply. Maren whipped her head back toward Ms. Lawson. "Thank you for letting us know about this development. Obviously, we have some things to discuss, but we don't need to take up any more of your time this morning." With eyebrows raised at Winnie, Maren scooped up her work bag from the floor and stood to leave. And then, like she always did in the privileged community she inhabited only at the extreme margins, Maren smoothed her features into agreeability, bid Ms. Lawson a good day, escorted her justifiably upset daughter out of the office—and took another one up the butt.

———

Winnie followed Maren to the parking lot even though she was already late for second period. The instant Winnie slammed the passenger-side door, tears slid down her cheeks. "It's not fair, Mom."

Damn straight it wasn't fair. Maren's hand shook with anger as she jiggled the key into the ignition. She'd put up with years of being treated as a second-class citizen at this school so Winnie could reach her full potential. But this would be a tough enough pill for Winnie to swallow without adding her own bile to the mix. She needed to be the calm, steady one. "Life's not fair, Win." Maren reached over to touch Winnie's shoulder, but Winnie shrugged her off. "Look. I'm doing the best I can, but I can't control everything. If there's only one spot at Stanford, it's got Brooke's name on it, not yours. If you even apply, I can guarantee Alicia will fire me. We can't risk that." She started the engine, which sputtered and rumbled before coming to life, and waited for Winnie to pull herself together and head off to class.

"But Stanford is all I've ever wanted. They can't take this away from me. I've done everything I was supposed to do. I put up with years of nasty financial aid digs and smiled and kept my head down and outworked all of them, just like you said."

This was the most Winnie had vented about her EBA experience since freshman year when Brooke and all her friends were buying $1,000 bikinis for their winter break trips. In stark contrast, Winnie's vacation plan was to help Maren with her dog-walking clients so she could afford the expensive outdoor gear on the packing list for EBA's community service trip to clean up Pacific Northwest beaches. The irony of scooping dog poop for a week to fund an "opportunity" to pick up even more trash did not escape her.

"Honestly, Winnie, I've never understood why Stanford is so important to you. Any degree will open doors and give you tons of choices. Why is only that one good enough? Isn't it possible you're buying in to a myth?"

Winnie sniffled and glanced sideways at her mom. "You know that Stanford T-shirt I've had forever?"

"You mean the one you still wear even though it's basically a crop top?" Maren kidded.

"Yeah," Winnie drawled. "I still remember the day Alicia brought it back for me after she took Brooke to see Stanford. When we were, like, eight? I remember every detail of it, how she handed it over to me, put her hands on my shoulders, and locked her eyes on mine. She made a big point of impressing on me how Stanford's the best school in the country and if I worked very hard, I might be able to go there and be a success like her. I've thought about that so many times. It's not that I don't totally appreciate your choices, so don't take this the wrong way, but I just want more. I want to be super successful like Alicia and have the respect of everyone."

Maren flinched at the inadvertent insult.

"Not that people don't respect you... Anyway, Alicia always said I was like a daughter to her. Just because Stanford said only one more kid doesn't mean Alicia can't figure out a way around that. I mean, what if she had twins? Do you think she'd let one get in and not the other? She always said it was her dream to have us go there together. Me and Brooke used to talk about it all the time."

"Brooke and I," Maren corrected. "And no, Alicia cannot help with this."

"Whatever, grammar Nazi. This isn't a college interview. It's a con-ver-sa-tion."

"Sorry," Maren said, berating herself for reflexively picking the wrong battle. "We have to think big picture here. I know you feel like Alicia has always been your champion, but you have to understand that nothing— and no one—will get in the way of her ambitions for Brooke."

"If you only knew how Brooke trashes her mom to everyone. It's really harsh. I mean, Alicia's only trying to help her. Brooke doesn't know how lucky she is. And she doesn't even want to go to Stanford. Also, she's got, like, a B-plus average. That should be, like, totally disqualifying."

Maren nodded as Winnie finally paused for air. "Listen, honey. I get why you're so frustrated. But the fact of the matter is we can't risk Alicia seeing you as Brooke's head-to-head competitor. So how about we don't rock the boat? If we can keep Alicia on our side, we can make sure you end up at another great school. Harvard? Yale? Columbia?"

"No."

"What do you mean? No to which one?"

"I mean, N-O. No. As in no effing way. To any of them. You always said I should go after my dreams. Well, that's what I'm gonna do. I don't want to move to the East Coast. I want to go to Stanford. I'll figure out a way, with or without your help."

Maren hunched forward in the driver's seat and rapped her forehead on the steering wheel. "You have no idea how bad this could be for us, poking Alicia like this."

"Please, Mom? I just want my fair shot at Stanford. I've at least earned that right."

Maren ran her fingers through her straight blond hair, trying to collect her thoughts, but her brain was as scrambled as the eggs she'd whipped up two hours earlier for the Stone family. All she knew for sure was that she needed more time. "Look, let's just put a pin in this for a few days. At least give me the weekend to think this through?"

"But apps are due in three weeks! Am I supposed to waste, like, a whole week when I could be working on my essays? That's crazy!"

Maren pictured a decibel meter but for hysteria and watched the needle go haywire. "Calm down, Win," Maren said. "There's no reason you can't keep working on your essays, right? Won't you need them for any school?"

"No. I won't. These essays are specific to Stanford." Winnie huffed. "If you'd pay even, like, one-tenth as much attention to my life as these other moms do, you'd know this. I mean, I'm not asking you to be a psycho like Krissie Vernon's mom, but at least know the difference between the Common App and supplemental essays."

Finally, Maren's temper flared. She smacked the steering wheel. "I don't have the kind of time these other moms have to obsess over their daughters. You of all people know I have an insane full-time job—and three side gigs on top of that—and I still struggle to pay all our bills." Maren rarely raised her voice at Winnie. She glanced out the driver's-side window for a second and tried to temper her tone. "Listen, I've always trusted you to ask for the help you need. And you're never obnoxious like this."

Winnie looked chagrined. "I'm sorry. You're right. I think that was me trying to ask for help and totally blowing it. It's just—I've never wanted anything more than this. Will you please try to see it my way? Dream a little bigger?"

"Just give me a few days," Maren pleaded. "OK?"

Winnie pulled her backpack from between her legs and into her lap and fiddled with the zipper. "I guess," she said with a disgruntled shrug. "Anyway, I gotta get to calculus. See ya tonight."

The jolt of the car door slamming reverberated inside Maren. She watched Winnie dart off to class, her long, lean body accentuated by her standard school attire of a fitted hoodie and skinny jeans with more holes than fabric. Before backing out of the parking spot, Maren glanced in the rearview mirror and noted the dark circles under her eyes. Winnie might not think Maren had dreamed big for them, but her naivete made Maren feel like her chest was going to explode. Maren's entire adult life had been devoted to securing Winnie's future. The last thing she wanted was to deny her daughter the only thing she truly desired, but still, what Winnie wanted was 100 percent impossible. Without Alicia, she would have no income, no job prospects, no safety net. Once Winnie was done with college and out on her own, the power Alicia wielded over Maren would fade. But for now, Maren knew she had no choice. She had to convince her daughter to apply ABS—Anywhere But Stanford.

2

Alicia

WITH HER BODYGUARD LEADING the way, Alicia Stone exited
through the service door and slid into the back of a waiting black Lincoln
MKT town car. He shut the door, climbed in the front passenger seat, and
gave the driver the signal to begin maneuvering down the tight alley. The
public relations rep sent along to chaperone Alicia at the evening event
was already buckled in, head bent over her phone, thumbs flying. What
was her name again? Sienna? Savannah? Why couldn't everyone just wear
a name tag? Life would be so much easier. The young woman flashed a
nervous smile as Alicia clicked her seat belt. The car merged into traffic,
and Alicia tipped back her head against the smooth leather seat, closing
her eyes for just a moment to summon strength for tonight's panel on
women in tech at the 92nd Street Y.

Alicia had become CEO of Aspyre, a visual lifestyle technology company, after the company's founder and CEO was ousted over multiple
sexual harassment charges. A woman had been the logical choice to rehab

the company's image. And since she was the only woman on the senior management team, the job had gone to Alicia. Never mind that she'd spent the last several years as vice president of business development, negotiating the hundreds of deals that had put Aspyre on track to be the hottest IPO of the past five years. But the job was all-consuming and exhausting. Today had been no different. She'd fended off attacks over her company's abysmal quarterly earnings report and a recent data breach affecting all three hundred million users.

What the hell was she thinking, closing her eyes? Thirty seconds of productivity swirling down the drain. Alicia yanked her phone from her Goyard tote and began firing off texts to her personal assistant, Maren.

Alicia: Replace the batteries in my noise-canceling headphones. Will blow my brains out if I have to listen to Bryan bingeing his stupid ninja wrestling show

Maren: No problem

Alicia: Check my work calendar for Thursday, send me photos of three outfit options with accessories

Maren: Will do

Alicia: I like that Korean avocado moisturizing mask. Get more!

Maren: Already ordered. Will be on your vanity waiting for you when you return

Alicia: I'm low on Ambien—did u refill?

Maren: New bottle in the top drawer of your nightstand

Alicia: Good, also—

An incoming call interrupted Alicia's wants-and-needs dump to Maren. Normally, she'd let it go to voicemail, but a call from Elliott Bay Academy's head of school in the fall of her daughter's senior year? Ted Clark couldn't be ignored.

"Ted, to what do I owe this pleasure?" Alicia said.

"Alicia, I hope I'm not catching you at a bad time," he said.

"No, not at all." Alicia gazed out the window at the passing buildings of Manhattan and briefly entertained thoughts of how different her life might have been if she'd accepted the Goldman Sachs job out of Stanford business school instead of joining Microsoft. With that fateful decision, she'd traded leisurely brunches and weekends in the Hamptons à la *Sex and the City* for hiking, mountain biking, and kayaking in the Pacific Northwest. And of course, she'd met Bryan, a former University of Washington baseball player and avid outdoor enthusiast. Alicia had been instantly attracted to his rugged good looks and sense of adventure, the confident "guy's guy" who swept her off her feet. She'd admired Bryan's work ethic and that they were starting out on equal footing. No country clubs, trust funds, or multigenerational homes for them. They would build their lives together from the ground up. She almost laughed out loud at how far they'd veered from those early years as a young married couple before Ted's throat clearing brought her back to the conversation.

"Well, I'll get right to it." Ted paused. "I understand from Ms. Barstow that Stanford is still at the top of Brooke's list?"

Top of her list? Why was this even a question? Alicia had made it clear to Ted during Brooke's junior year that Stanford was the *only* school on her daughter's list and that she expected Ted to direct Ms. Barstow and the rest of the college counseling team to proceed accordingly. "Yes, of course Stanford is still her choice."

"Well, in that case," Ted said, clearing his throat again, "I need to pass along some information we received from the Stanford admissions office."

Alicia massaged her temple. She'd spent enough time around Ted to know his incessant throat clearing was a prelude to bad news.

After waiting a beat, Ted continued, "As you know, we've had a lot of success with EBA students gaining admission to Stanford in the past. You may have heard that four EBA student athletes in this year's senior class have already committed to continue their athletic careers at Stanford next fall. It's the most in EBA history."

Kelly Vernon, whose daughter Krissie was also applying to Stanford, had breathlessly kept Alicia apprised of each student athlete's Instagram announcement over the past several months. The woman was a syco-phant, but her information-gathering skills about all things college rivaled those of a government intelligence agency operative. All Alicia had to do in return was call her up for a cup of coffee now and then and slip her some gossip about one of the many local tech zillionaires. "You must be so proud after all your efforts to make athletics an institutional priority at EBA. But what does this have to do with Brooke?"

Ted cleared his throat yet again. "EBA will only be allotted one more spot this year."

"Interesting," Alicia said, noticing a small chip in her polish on her left thumbnail. She'd need to remember to tell Maren to schedule an extra manicure to fix it as soon as she got home.

"They're doubling down on their commitment to inclusivity and diversity," Ted said. "They want sixty percent of this year's class to come from public schools."

"I'm familiar with the statistics, Ted. I am on the Stanford board of trustees, remember?" Alicia held the phone between her ear and shoulder as she dug through her bag for a nail file. If she filed the nail just a little, no one would see the chip. The car pulled into an alley and idled next to another service door entrance. PR Girl pointed at her wrist, signaling that it was time to wrap up, but the bodyguard remained motionless in the front seat as he waited for Alicia to complete her call.

"You know, Alicia, given Brooke's academic achievements and extra-curricular activities, she may want to—"

"Ted," Alicia interrupted, forgetting her nail and pressing the phone to her ear. "Are you actually suggesting I need to worry about Brooke getting into Stanford?"

"Well, it's just that she may want to consider other options."

"Other options?" Alicia said, brushing lint from her pantsuit. "I just can't think of what other suitable options there might possibly be. Brooke is a legacy, after all. And while we haven't announced this publicly yet, you should know I recently made a $15 million donation to Stanford's Computer Science Department."

"Oh, I wasn't aware of that," Ted said.

"I'm just curious—other than our very talented athletes, how many other EBA students will be applying early decision to Stanford this year?"

"As always, there's a lot of interest. We're guessing some students who had Stanford as their early admission choice—"

"You know, it's really neither here nor there." As far as Alicia was concerned, the biggest, or rather only, obstacle to Brooke's admission was getting her to finish her application. "Ted, I'm sure we can agree that Stanford is the perfect choice for Brooke and that you'll do absolutely everything in your power to support her application. After all I've done for EBA, not to mention your career, I can count on you for that, can't I?"

"Well, of course," he stammered.

"Wonderful," Alicia said, ending the call and tossing her phone into her tote. What an idiot, wasting her time with such a frivolous call.

"I'm really sorry, Alicia, but we need to head inside," PR Girl simpered. "The meet and greet starts in five minutes. Here," she said, extending a tube of Trish McEvoy Wild Rose lipstick, Alicia's signature color, and a tissue.

As she applied the lipstick, Alicia finally remembered the girl's name. "Thank you, Samantha," she said. She removed her readers and returned them to their case. Alicia detested wearing them, but at fifty-two, she found readers to be her inescapable and constant companion. At least the other dead giveaways that she was a perimenopausal, middle-aged woman—her graying hair, the loosening skin around her jowls, the cellulite that persisted no matter how many lunges and squats she did—could be disguised by throwing gobs of money at personal trainers, stylists, expensive clothes, smoothing undergarments, and cosmetic dermatology. As if this battle against age wasn't hard enough on her self-esteem, Alicia almost always found herself in the company of younger women such as this Samantha girl or even Maren. Maren wasn't as young as Samantha, but her stubbornly bland style only seemed to emphasize her effortless beauty, just as her shapeless clothes somehow drew attention to the enviable figure she didn't even need to work at maintaining. It was so unfair.

The bodyguard opened the door for Alicia as two more guards moved into position to escort her into the building. Alicia glanced at her watch as she strode from the car and saw that it was nearly five thirty p.m. She performed the mental calculation that she repeated a hundred times a day when she traveled, which felt like all the damn time. Seattle was three hours behind New York, so Brooke would still be in her last class of the day, or at least she was supposed to be there. Alicia had received two emails this week alone notifying her that her daughter had missed several classes. For reasons that remained a mystery, Bryan, the parent not running a billion-dollar company, never received these emails. She of course covered for Brooke—cramps! doctor's appointment!—and apologized for forgetting to alert the office—you know how chaotic traveling is! Alicia tamped down on the bubbling resentment for her husband, who couldn't be counted on to make sure their daughter did the bare minimum of attending school.

But now wasn't the time to be distracted by the inevitable future fight over college essays and cut classes. Alicia needed to be on her toes. The moderator of tonight's panel was one of the toughest but most respected journalists in tech. Time to smile and inspire the eager, striving young women who had paid their $75 to learn how they too could reach the C-suite and have it all.

———

"Hey babe, how's the Big Apple?" Bryan asked as he bit in to something crunchy.

Alicia pulled the phone away from her ear and switched to speaker-phone. She drew back the fluffy comforter and slid under the crisp white hotel sheets. "Fine. Is it just you, or is Brooke home yet?"

"She went out to dinner after the game. Senior girls' dinner or something."

"Damn. The game," Alicia said, berating herself for forgetting Brooke's soccer game. She liked to text Brooke good luck before each game even if she was rarely there to see her play. "How'd they do?"

"They won 2–0, still undefeated."

"Maybe they'll have a shot at winning state this year." Despite nearly ten years of travel soccer, weekly private coaching, and even a summer training in Spain, they'd been told by a soccer college consultant at the end of Brooke's sophomore year that she had no chance of getting recruited by Stanford. Brooke had promptly quit her travel team, and now she just needed to get through the season with the captain's badge on her sleeve as a symbol of leadership for her Stanford application—and a state championship wouldn't hurt. Lucky for Brooke, it was EBA's policy to give a captain's badge to every senior on a varsity team.

"Ya miss me?" Bryan asked in what Alicia immediately recognized as his phone sex voice.

She rolled her eyes, wanting nothing more than to watch a half hour of crappy TV and fall asleep. His sexual desires and demands seemed to have increased in direct proportion to her rise in power and prominence. Whether she was in the mood or not, Alicia often acquiesced to avoid the petulant behavior that typically followed any perceived slights to his manhood. And she had to admit that once they got going, it was usually pretty rewarding. But it wasn't going to happen tonight.

"Check your phone," he said.

Alicia looked at the screen and saw the notification with the small picture. She didn't bother to open it. "Really, Bry? Looking at a picture of your junk is so not a turn-on. What if this got out?"

"So what? You're my wife. And anyways," he said, lowering his voice, "I'm hung like a horse."

Alicia sighed and waited. She could hear him whipping a ball against a wall. Imagining the mark the ball made with each thwack pissed her off. "Ted Clark called this afternoon."

"What'd he want?" Bryan asked.

Alicia could hear the surliness in his voice because she failed to play along. "Surprisingly, he didn't want anything," she replied. "He called to let us know that Stanford will only be taking one more student this year because a record four student athletes have already committed. Diversity, inclusion, more kids from public schools, blah, blah, blah. He even suggested Brooke might want to consider another school for early decision. Can you believe that? After everything we've done for EBA?"

"Who else is applying?" Bryan said.

"I'm sure Krissie Vernon. She's a double legacy as Kelly reminds everyone every chance she gets."

"What about Winnie? She worships you. It seems like she's wearing that Stanford T-shirt every time I see her. When you got it for her, it came down to her knees like a nightgown, and now it barely covers her rack." Bryan guffawed at his own observation.

"Maybe Winnie thought she was going to apply to Stanford, but not if they're only taking one more student. She's a smart girl. She'll know she needs to find another school." Alicia broke off a square of the dark chocolate Maren arranged to have next to her bed every night when she traveled. It was Alicia's one consistent concession to her sweet tooth. "The spot is Brooke's for the taking," she continued. "She may not be anywhere near the top of the class, but with my pull at EBA and Stanford, she should be fine. If Stanford can accept four dumb athletes, they can accept Brooke too. But all this is moot if Brooke doesn't finish her damn application. What's the status on the essays?"

The ball throwing stopped, and she heard a long exhale on the other end of the phone, which was all she needed to confirm that zero progress had been made since she'd left yesterday morning with strict instructions to both of them that essays were their top priority.

In an effort to avoid precisely this situation, Alicia had directed Maren to enroll Brooke in last summer's EBA essay boot camp, but as insurance, Alicia had also hired Cynthia McIntyre, the supersecret college admissions whisperer who flew around the country providing her services to the progeny of America's ultra-ultra elite. Alicia had been lucky enough to secure Cynthia for three hours (for $25,000) the weekend before the boot camp to select Brooke's essay topics and provide guidance for completing her activities résumé. The plan was for Brooke to have all her essays wrapped up with a bow by the first day of senior year. What Alicia hadn't counted on was Brooke finishing the boot camp with the sweeping declaration that all her essays sucked and she would just deal with it in the fall. With Stanford's early admission deadline three weeks away, the essays were mission critical, but still Brooke rebuffed Alicia's every status check. It mattered not one iota how Alicia raised the topic. The cheerful, nonchalant sneak attack ("So, honey, you spent a lot of time in your bedroom this weekend; I bet those essays are really coming along…") yielded the exact same result as the direct approach ("Where are your damn essays?"): deflection and disgust, and not necessarily in that order.

"For God's sake, Bryan," Alicia snarled. "Her app is due in three weeks. Why is she out with her friends tonight? She should be grounded until the essays are done."

"You know, Leesh…" She could hear him stretching. "Maybe this

Stanford news is a blessing in disguise." Now he was probably scratching his balls. "Brooke isn't exactly enthusiastic about Stanford. You know that's why she's been giving you such a hard time about the essays."

Alicia could hear Bryan turn on the TV, his less-than-subtle signal that he was checking out of the conversation. "You're kidding me, right?" she said. "This is just like sleepaway camp. Remember the stink she made about that? Now those are her best friends in the world."

"She was ten when we sent her to camp. She's seventeen now."

"And your point is?" Alicia took a slug from a chilled bottle of Perrier, also courtesy of Maren. She traced a finger down the outside of the green glass bottle, drawing a line through the condensation. Sometimes it felt like her whole life was courtesy of Maren and that without her, it would all fall apart. Indeed, she was so indispensable that Alicia had made the conscious decision years ago to overlook the yearning expression on Bryan's face whenever Maren was around.

"If she gets in, everyone's going to think it's only because of you," Bryan said. "And what if she gets there and can't cut it? It's gonna be hard for her to live up to everyone's expectations of being your daughter."

Alicia set down the Perrier and grabbed her own remote control, pointing it at the TV. She too was rapidly losing interest in this conversation. Oh, the hardship of being Alicia Stone's husband or Alicia Stone's daughter—a lament favored by both of them. Yet when it came to living in their fourteen-thousand-square-foot home in Washington Park, flying on private jets, belonging to five golf clubs, vacationing in the most incredible places on the planet, or having an American Express black card it didn't seem quite so bad.

But even if Bryan wasn't the most hands-on father, having one parent physically present most of the time at least assuaged Alicia's guilt about all the travel her job required. When the first dot-com bubble burst in 2001, taking Seattle's commercial real estate market and Bryan's career with it, Bryan had struggled to find purchase. To save her marriage and her sanity, Alicia cashed out her Microsoft stock and bought several rental properties around Seattle for Bryan to manage as investments. They'd since acquired a vacation property on San Juan Island, a condo in Telluride, and a beach house in Del Mar as well as several more rental houses and small apartment buildings scattered throughout the city. Bryan enjoyed fixing up and flipping some of the properties, though generally he played the role of rent collector and occasional fix-it man. But his real estate endeavors left him with a lot of free time, which he spent playing golf (two hundred and fifty rounds last year, he bragged to anyone who would listen), drinking with his college buddies, working out, playing video games, and watching porn. And in theory being a stay-at-home dad.

"The only thing Brooke wants right now is *not* to write her goddamn essays," Alicia scoffed. "She's just doing this to upset me. Or embarrass me. She'll thank me once it's all said and done."

"What if we're just setting her up for rejection? With only one spot left, maybe we should think about another school," Bryan said. "You know she'd probably love Michigan if you'd let her consider it."

Alicia bit her lip. As he'd no doubt intended, Bryan's mention of Michigan flooded Alicia with memories of her older brother, Alex. His sandy-brownish hair, always buzzed short and bleached out. The smell of chlorine. His habit of teasing her and throwing her over his muscular shoulders. Alex had died just six weeks before he was supposed to follow in their parents' and grandparents' footsteps and head off to Ann Arbor on a full-ride athletic scholarship to swim for the Wolverines. There was never a question after that of where Alicia was going to college. The

University of Michigan was the only option. It was the Harvard of the West—or at least their whole family had T-shirts that said that.

As much as Michigan was part of her family's multigenerational legacy, the idea of Brooke going there was too painful to contemplate. Alicia had established a scholarship in Alex's memory after Aspyre's IPO as a gift to her father. The family attended a small ceremony to honor the first scholarship recipient, but that was the only time she'd set foot on campus since graduation, and she'd needed two Valium to get through it.

"You know damn well Michigan isn't an option," Alicia said. "The balls on you to bring that up right now. Ted's phone call today changes absolutely nothing. Why do you think I donated the $15 million?"

"Fine," Bryan said, emitting an audible sigh. "I'll talk to her tonight."

"That won't be necessary," Alicia said. "I'll be taking over the essays now because, once again, I have to do everything." She ended the call and tossed the phone across the king-size bed. If Brooke wasn't going to write her damn essays, then it was time to take matters into her own hands. Alicia opened her laptop and scrolled through the college folder in her email. During an executive retreat she'd attended in Sun Valley last year, a colleague had been complaining about the college admissions process over dinner. His daughter had become so stressed that he'd hired an English professor from a highly selective college to interview her and write her essays. Alicia had been taken aback by this brazen admission. At the time, she couldn't imagine stooping so low, but she had nevertheless emailed her colleague the next day for the professor's contact information and filed it away—in case of emergency. Apparently, it was time to break the glass. She clicked on the professor's email address and started to type.

3

Kelly

KELLY VERNON SAT FUMING in her car outside the College Bound Tutoring Center as she waited for her kids—Calculus II for Krissie, her senior; AP Chemistry for Katherine, her sophomore; and English for Kaleb, her seventh grader. She'd purposely chosen her exercise clothes this morning so she could spend this hour after school walking the trail behind the tutoring center. Between driving, sitting in volunteer meetings, and stress eating, Kelly was painfully aware that her butt was growing larger by the day. But the call from Ms. Barstow, Elliott Bay Academy's powerful director of college counseling, just before school pickup scuttled her plans in more ways than one. Upon learning from Ms. Barstow that Stanford would only be accepting one more EBA student this year, suddenly Kelly's fat ass was the least of her grievances. There was no mistaking the tenor of the call: Ms. Barstow was clearly signaling Krissie should step aside in the Stanford competition. But to make way for whom? Winnie Pressley? Brooke Stone? Yeah, right. There was no fucking way Kelly was going to snatch defeat from the jaws of victory after she'd sacrificed so much to support Krissie, which involved planning every goddamn EBA meeting, potluck, coffee, and party over the past six years. How dare they not support Krissie's application after all the time and energy Kelly had donated to the benefit of literally everyone at EBA?

Obviously, there was no time for a walk now. Instead, she dug in to the protein snacks she'd brought along for the kids and flicked through all her social media feeds (and logged in to check Krissie's too), looking for any clue as to who else might be applying—the critical question Ms. Barstow had refused to answer in their call. Failing to turn up any new nuggets, Kelly brushed aside the empty wrappers on her lap and opened the Notes app on her phone, in which she'd been recording her findings about each of the one hundred students in the EBA senior class for the past year. She tracked legacies (parents were only too proud to brag about that), college visits (kids made it so easy with those location filters), who was taking which AP classes, test scores, class rank, who attended which on-campus college sessions (it wasn't spying if the PTA office was just across the hall), and updates on sports recruiting websites. She also estimated parental net worth based on home values (thank you, Zillow) and Securities and Exchange Commission stock sale filings to determine who might be in a position to make large donations to "facilitate admission" (as opposed to outright bribery) and had identified the few lucky bastards on financial aid who might get to go to college for free.

Kelly also recorded the detailed maneuverings of the EBA moms who, like her, had few other options except to throw their precious resources at building their kids' college résumés and pray they were enough. There was the mom who'd started a nonprofit to teach kids to knit in Kathmandu and named her daughter president. There was the mom who'd sent her son kicking and screaming to Oxford last summer to take a crash course in Latin and Greek mythology to augment his classics cred. There was the mom who'd stalked a Harvard biology professor for internship opportunities for her budding scientist every summer since seventh grade. But Kelly really had to hand it to the enterprising mom who'd turned her daughter into an Instagram influencer with more than six hundred thousand followers and the ability to command upward of $5,000 per post, which would probably pay for a hundred years of college.

All this cyberstalking was time-consuming, but Kelly firmly believed it was the school's fault for promoting a culture of secrecy. At last fall's junior year college kickoff meeting, Ms. Barstow had made clear that the school's "community values" required parents to refrain from talking to other parents about their students' college lists because of some nonsense about how the students were deserving of their privacy. Kelly had been gobsmacked by this—how were you not supposed to talk about the only thing on everyone's mind? She had thought it might be a joke, but Elliott Bay Academy never joked about anything. In the wake of Ms. Barstow's edict, the main goal of every interaction between increasingly edgy and elusive moms became trying to ascertain where other kids were applying without giving away any of those same details about their own kids. The "Big Brother" effect didn't actually shut down the college gossip mill; it merely forced the whole enterprise underground.

Kelly's phone chimed.

Diana Taylor: Just heard Robin Riley shouting from the rooftops that Alexis got a likely letter from Harvard.

Kelly: No big surprise there, but still, athletes. So annoying. Taking all the spots.

Diana: Tenley said Greer went to the Whitman admissions presentation today. Think Augusta knows? Is it possible Greer might not get into Vanderbilt?

Kelly: Augusta said Vanderbilt told all legacy families not to count on getting in early. Must be hedging their bets.

Diana: Well, Vandy IS the new Yale, right?

Kelly: Have you heard of anyone applying early to Stanford? Besides Brooke Stone, of course.

Diana: Nope. But I did hear Graham told his mom he wants to go to UCLA or UVA.

Graham was a strong student who took AP math and science classes and had scored a 33 on his ACT (according to his ex-girlfriend, a junior, who was only too happy to spill the beans after he dumped her). What a relief to know he was not in the Stanford mix.

Kelly: That's nuts! Why wouldn't he aim for Ivy Plus with his GPA and test scores? But at least he's not going for Brown or Stanford!

Diana: True...GTG!

Kelly reflected for a moment on how much her friendship with Diana had evolved over the past year. Last spring, with a straight face, Diana had delivered to Kelly what was obviously a stock college deflection line: "We just happened to find ourselves in the middle of Rhode Island, so we thought we might as well check out Brown." But Kelly had known the truth. Tenley had already let it slip to Krissie that her mom had taken her on a forced march to twelve East Coast schools over spring break, and Brown had been Tenley's favorite by far. Kelly had been relieved she didn't have to worry about Tenley applying to Stanford, especially since Diana's husband, Michael, was a successful venture capitalist who could write a large check to the school of Tenley's choice. Once it was clear there was no direct competition between their girls, Kelly and Diana had happily joined forces as college gossip coconspirators.

With her phone still in hand and no one there to bear witness, Kelly pulled up the website she craved daily, like a digital Xanax: Stanford Undergraduate Admissions. Yup—the early admission deadline was still November 1, the same as it was yesterday...and all the days before. Twenty-one days to go. But only fifteen minutes before the kids finished up. Kelly gathered up all traces of her illicit snacking and brushed away the crumbs as she hoisted herself out of the car and walked across the street to Subway. Another family dinner to be eaten in the car on their way to the next round of extracurricular activities: fencing practice for Kaleb and an oboe lesson for Katherine while Krissie got started on her homework.

———

"Wow, honey, you really went all out tonight," Kevin Vernon teased his wife as he stood at the kitchen island and unwrapped the meatball marinara sandwich she'd brought home for him. "How was your day?"

Kelly uncorked the bottle of "Two Buck Chuck" from Trader Joe's they'd started the night before and poured them each a generous glass. "Well, Ms. Barstow called. I haven't told Krissie yet," she said, taking a large gulp of wine, "but apparently Stanford is only taking one more student this year because of all the athletes who've already committed."

"Wow, really?" Kevin said between bites. "Does Barstow think Krissie still has a chance?"

Kelly rolled her eyes. "Obviously she *was* a terrific candidate before this breaking news or Ms. Barstow wouldn't have approved her plan to apply in the first place. But surprise, surprise, today she suddenly changed her tune."

"Other than Brooke Stone, who else is applying?" Kevin asked as he crumpled up his sandwich wrapper.

"Last week, I heard from the mom of a girl Winnie Pressley tutors that Stanford's still her top choice. But that was before this news. With Stanford only taking one more kid, I can't imagine Maren doing anything to upset Alicia. If I were Alicia, I'd fire Maren in a heartbeat if I thought Winnie was going to try to take my kid's spot after I so generously funded her education all these years. I certainly wouldn't pay for her college too. And I know for a fact Maren works at least three other jobs besides Alicia's—catering, party planning for Diana Taylor, and dog care—so I don't know how she thinks she'd pay for Stanford on her own, even with a generous financial grant." Kelly poured the rest of the wine into her glass and dropped the empty bottle in the recycling bin.

"Yeah, even the plane flights back and forth are expensive," Kevin agreed.

"But if Winnie's still applying, it's definitely a little worrisome. She is first in the class, even if she's just barely ahead of Krissie, and she's taken all AP classes and is editor-in-chief of the paper. But then again, as far as I've been able to figure, Winnie has no special hooks." Cheered by this, she took a sip of wine before continuing. "I mean, just look at her. She's a white, blue-eyed blond girl, so not exactly part of an underrepresented minority group. And there's no way she could be a first-generation student—I have no idea where Maren went to college, but Alicia would never hire an assistant without at least a college degree. And Winnie hasn't done any of the college-level STEM work Krissie has. Also, let's not forget, Krissie is a double legacy at Stanford." Kelly swirled her wineglass.

"Not that her double legacy is going to do her much good," Kevin said as he hunted in the pantry for something to supplement his sandwich.

Kelly almost laughed aloud at how naive they'd been, thinking their double legacy at Stanford would carry the day for their kids. But at their twenty-fifth reunion, Kelly and Kevin had eagerly attended a meet and greet hosted by the director of admissions, only to learn that legacy status was far from a guarantee of admission (unless of course it was accompanied by a very generous donation). OK, they hadn't said that last part, but it wasn't difficult to read between the lines.

Ms. Barstow had all but confirmed this conclusion during their first college counseling meeting early in Krissie's junior year. Even with the double legacy status and Krissie's outstanding grades and test scores (and applying early to her top choice as all EBA students were advised to do, a strategy most public school students weren't adequately counseled on), she'd informed Kelly that Krissie would need another hook if she wanted a reasonable chance of not being rejected by Stanford. And by reasonable, Ms. Barstow estimated a 91 percent chance of rejection instead of the much-publicized 96. The EBA college counselors always quoted rates of rejection rather than rates of acceptance in what seemed to Kelly to be a naked effort to bludgeon any inflated parental expectations around college.

Ms. Barstow had then gone through the list of the most meaningful hooks at elite colleges, including recruited athlete, first-generation college student, man in humanities, woman in STEM, and of course the development priority (à la Brooke Stone). "You know, Kelly, I wonder if Krissie wouldn't be better served using her early admission opportunity for a more attainable school," Ms. Barstow had finally suggested.

But Ms. Barstow had severely underestimated Kelly. She had promptly calculated that woman in STEM was Krissie's best, and probably only, available option short of a sex change operation. Initially, Kevin had mocked Kelly's campaign to turn their daughter into a woman in STEM, but he hadn't interfered with her extensive efforts, which had included convincing Krissie to switch into AP math and science classes, bribing her with a new iPhone to take a computer science class at the local community college to make her stand out above all the poor schmucks settling for EBA's high school–level version, securing an internship at Alicia Stone's company, and creating a day camp last summer so Krissie could teach coding to the young girls of the neighborhood. That had turned out to be glorified babysitting, but no one reading Krissie's activities résumé would ever know.

Kelly cut a hunk of cheese and balanced it on a cracker. "I hope being a woman in STEM is enough to go up against Brooke Stone and their high net worth." She shoved the whole thing in her mouth.

"Kudos to you for manufacturing a science and engineering hook for a girl who loves history and hates math." Kevin raised his glass.

"Yeah, but it only matters if it trumps the other applicants' hooks. It's not just Krissie against some hypothetical kids around the country anymore. Now it's Krissie against Winnie and Brooke specifically—and any other EBA kids who might be applying."

"I'll talk to Steve Masterson and see if he'll write Krissie a letter of recommendation. I wanted to avoid that, but it sounds like we need to pull out all the stops."

Steve had been a friend of Kevin's at Stanford, and he was now in the enviable position of Stanford trustee. He was also Kevin's biggest client, and Kelly knew he didn't want to lean on the relationship, but she was relieved Kevin understood they were now operating under extraordinary conditions. "I think you should definitely ask Steve," Kelly said, cutting off another slab of cheese. "But I also think we should hire a private consultant to review Krissie's essays. And maybe add another weekly tutoring session. Winnie's GPA is only one one-hundredth of a point higher than Krissie's. Her first-quarter grades might be what puts her over the top."

"Kel, no. Look, I want Krissie to get into Stanford every bit as much as you do, but we are absolutely stretched to the limit right now. I mean, we're already paying $100,000 a year in tuition for the three of them." The vein in his forehead started to throb. "We definitely can't afford any more tutoring. And why would we pay someone else to read her essays? For what we pay in tuition, they should be writing her essays for her."

Kelly stared into her wineglass and sighed. The m-word. Everything always came back to money. Kevin was a partner at a Big Four accounting firm, but everyone knew that even a big-time CPA no longer came close to the top of the food chain in Seattle. Today's masters of the universe worked in tech and finance. If only she'd stuck it out a few more years at the start-up where she'd been working when Krissie was born. They wouldn't be Alicia Stone wealthy, but if she'd waited for her options to fully vest, they definitely wouldn't be having conversations like this one. Those people were no smarter than Kevin and Kelly, but they were certainly a whole lot wealthier. It filled Kelly with a toxic stew of envy and regret whenever she encountered these arrogant idiots who had made tens of millions of dollars just by being in the right place at the right time. Meanwhile, she and Kevin still had to put Katherine and Kaleb through EBA and all of them through college and pay the mortgage, ever-increasing credit card bills, and healthcare premiums as well as figure out how to squirrel away something for their retirement.

Against Seattle elite society norms, Kelly had been driving the same Volvo SUV for the past eight years, they'd dropped their swim club membership, and they'd embraced hiking and camping in the Pacific Northwest as their preferred vacations to afford private school tuition for three kids. They'd calculated that the sacrifices would be worth it in the end. In an increasingly competitive and inequitable world, graduating from EBA, earning a degree from Stanford, and gaining access to these exclusive networks would give their kids an edge and maybe a shot at hitting it big or at least earning a decent-enough living that they might be able to send their own kids to private school.

What Kelly had failed to comprehend when they'd first decided on EBA was that sending your kids to a competitive private school in Seattle meant mixing with the elite of the elite. While ostensibly a leader of this prestigious community, Kelly often had the sense she was on the outside looking in. Her children enjoyed invitations to over-the-top parties Kelly could never dream of reciprocating. She'd developed quasi friendships with some of the uber-wealthy moms like Diana Taylor and Alicia Stone through their kids or volunteering, but these never turned into meaningful relationships (although Kelly consoled herself with the knowledge that her kids benefited indirectly from the obscene financial support these women and their husbands provided to EBA). But Kelly simply didn't have the pay-to-play kind of money for girls' nights out at the hottest new restaurants, spontaneous shopping trips to New York on someone's private jet, or a palatial home where she could host the next cocktail party.

Waiting in line at school pickup provided constant reminders that she didn't quite measure up. Even if she could have afforded weekly blowouts and color touch-ups every five weeks like the other moms, her limp dishwater-blond hair would still refuse to cooperate. She admired the skill of the other moms with makeup but ended up looking like a clown when she tried to mimic them, so instead she clung to "natural" as her signature look. And her "vintage" Volvo stood out in the parade of new top-of-the-line luxury hybrid SUVs. She had taken pride in her one Kate Spade bag, even if it was six years old and woefully out of date, until Diana Taylor had shown off her purse collection while giving a tour of her stunning lakefront home during a volunteer coffee last year. One peek at Diana's gigantic purse closet, and all Kelly could think was that those bags alone could probably fund college for all her kids.

In any event, Kelly had quickly figured out that she couldn't compete on the money front, so she'd worked hard to develop her own valuable currency: information. While information didn't allow her family to spend spring break skiing in Gstaad like the Wayland family or hire the $50,000 college consulting service that whisked applicants around the country on a private jet with a team of college admissions experts on board to provide briefing packets and wooing tips for each school the way Lydia Peters had for her daughter, Felicity, when it came to any topic related to EBA or college admissions, Kelly knew more than anyone. And whenever possible, she used that information as a weapon to advance the goals of her kids the way others wielded their checkbooks. Maybe she just needed to look at the glass as half full and see this single Stanford spot as an opportunity. After all, wasn't it vastly better to know exactly whom Krissie had to beat as opposed to worrying about Stanford's other forty-thousand-plus applicants?

Kelly drained the remaining contents of her wineglass and placed the empty glass in the sink. "You know what? You're right about hiring the essay consultant. Ms. Barstow always says the transcript is really the most important component, and Krissie seems to have everything under control," Kelly said, placating both her husband and herself. She moved around the island and put her arm around his waist, which she self-consciously noticed lacked the extra fat tire currently encircling her own.

"I'll give Steve a call tomorrow and get the letter going," Kevin said, giving Kelly a kiss on the top of her head. "It can't hurt."

"Thanks for doing that." She hoped Steve's reference would be enough. "I'll talk to Krissie to confirm we're all on the same page."

"Great," Kevin said, grabbing a beer from the fridge. "I'm gonna catch the end of the playoff game."

———

As Kelly climbed the stairs past photos from their college graduation, their wedding in the Stanford chapel, Stanford football games, and camping trips with their college roommates and their families, she recalled Ms. Barstow's parting words to all the parents at the end of that fateful junior year college kickoff meeting: "Applying to college is not a team sport. Do not use the royal we, do not usurp your student's independence, and do not make this journey about the bumper sticker on your car." But if Ms. Barstow truly believed her own words, then why had she called Kelly this afternoon and not Krissie to deliver the "difficult and pressing news" about Stanford? What a bunch of hypocrites.

She knocked on Krissie's door before opening it and peeking her head in. "Hey, honey, how's it going?" she asked, sitting down on Katherine's twin bed opposite her daughter.

"Just reading through my supplemental essays again." Krissie was twisting several strands of her long brown hair and staring at the screen propped up on her lap. "Ms. Barstow had a few comments, but she said they were fine and ready to submit. I wasn't aiming for *fine* though. I wanted her to say they were fantastic or amazing."

Ever since Krissie was a toddler, she would become hysterical if her carefully arranged dolls or books or shoes were even the slightest bit out of place. She overdid just about everything in her quest for perfection. Setbacks, such as a B-plus, were shattering and left Kelly struggling to put Humpty Dumpty back together again. "I can read them again if you want, but I thought they were fantastic the last time I read them," Kelly said. "Speaking of Ms. Barstow, she called today. They heard from the Stanford admissions office—"

"I know," Krissie interrupted her mom. "They're probably only accepting one more student because of all the athletes."

"Oh, you heard?"

Krissie nodded. "I stopped by her office to ask some clarifying questions about her comments on my essays, and she told me." She looked up from her computer screen and, with a shaky voice, continued, "What if I don't get in? Stanford's all I think about. I'm so tired of EBA. I feel like none of my friends get me. Everyone looked so happy at Stanford the last time we toured. I picture myself happier there. I really do."

"Don't worry, honey. It will all work out," Kelly said. Last year, as the college admissions mania took hold of their community, Kelly privately agonized over whether Krissie could withstand the pressure of applying to Stanford. But Krissie was adamant and pushed herself to study harder and longer. And then she started pulling out her hair. Kelly hadn't noticed at first. It was the woman who cut Krissie's hair who'd alerted her to the problem. Their pediatrician diagnosed Krissie with trichotillomania (which Kelly at first thought was the foodborne illness caused by undercooked pork), prescribed a low-dose antidepressant, and encouraged Krissie to exercise. Krissie's mental health became a top priority, with Kelly vigilantly monitoring her medication, eliminating unnecessary stress like household chores, and doing absolutely everything in her power to figure out how to help her fragile daughter achieve her dream of getting into Stanford without going to pieces in the process. They were so close now. Kelly leaned over and gave Krissie a hug. "Once you're into Stanford, you'll feel so much more relaxed. You're in the homestretch. Just hang in there a little while longer."

"I know," Krissie said. "I just can't wait for this to be over."

"Me too," Kelly said. "Other than Brooke, have you heard anyone else mention they're applying?"

Krissie rolled her eyes. "You're not the only one who swore your kid to secrecy."

Kelly had made Krissie promise not to share their plans to apply early to Stanford to hedge against a bad case of groupthink suddenly sweeping through the EBA senior class. After all, the competition for a top-tier college like Stanford was stiff enough without it being crowned this year's "it" school. Last year, in a cautionary tale, there'd been a crush of EBA kids— thirteen in all—who'd applied to Dartmouth thinking it was their best bet for an Ivy since Dartmouth's admit rate had been as high as USC's the year prior. They hadn't counted on so many other fellow students thinking the same way, though, and ultimately only two were admitted. Unfortunately, Krissie's Stanford ambitions were a badly kept secret, as everyone knew it was Kelly and Kevin's alma mater. In any case, Kelly had figured it was better to keep 'em guessing than to stick a cardinal-red target on their backs. In light of today's revelation, though, it occurred to her that she might need to revisit this strategy. "I just thought with the early admission deadline coming up, people might be talking about it. Has Winnie said anything?"

Krissie shrugged her shoulders, and her eyes returned to her laptop. "I don't hang out with her."

Kelly recognized the signs that she'd reached her allotted question limit. She stood up and leaned over to kiss her daughter on the top of her head. "Don't stay up too late. I love you."

———

Kelly climbed into bed, her mind churning. She watched as her right thumb reflexively tapped the Facebook icon on her phone and scrolled through her news feed, which lately was flooded with the anxious college musings of friends and acquaintances all across the country. At least this was evidence that college insanity afflicted parents everywhere, but unfortunately, this was not a misery-loves-company situation.

Eleanor McHenry: Pomona! Williams! Bowdoin! Oh my! Those final college visits were such a blast! But now where to apply… the early admission deadline is coming up so fast!

Ginger Park: I heard applications are already up 20% at University of California schools this year.

Trina Finney: Facebook friends, urgent advice needed! Do you think Sophia needs more than three alumni recommendations for Amherst? Not sure about the advice we are getting from the private college counselor. He says one is enough. Is there such a thing as too many?

Astrid Collins: Moms of college-bound teens beware! I just wasted six hours on the message boards of CollegeAdmissionsSecrets. com. Serious question: How do any non-superhuman kids get into college? There go our Georgetown dreams…

Gemma Smith: Woohoo—go Bailey! State fencing champion! Team MVP! And just in time to beef up his Common App awards & honors. Phew!

Lindy Lewis: October ACT finally here—shooting for perfection! Fingers crossed third time's the charm! After 40 hours of astronomical private tutoring, it better be…hahaha!

But the biggest gut punch of the night came from one of Kelly's Stanford roommates who now lived with her family in suburban Chicago and also had a college-bound senior:

Angie Swanson: Ella just submitted her Stanford application. *Woohoo!* Hope our girls will be roomies just like we were, **Kelly Vernon**!

Kelly could feel her blood pressure skyrocketing and her competitive instincts shifting into overdrive. Three days earlier, the *Seattle Times* had published a list of the EBA students who had been named National Merit Semifinalists. Krissie had made the list, along with Winnie, but Brooke's name had been conspicuously absent. Even though the college counselors told parents the National Merit Semifinalist award meant nothing to colleges, EBA parents still strategized over how to attain the honor for their children...just in case. Without hesitation, Kelly had ponied up for that insanely expensive PSAT boot camp both freshman and sophomore summers, but she had resisted the urge to post anything about the award on social media, abiding by the college counseling office's gag rule. But why shouldn't she post something? With today's news, it now seemed important to stake her public claim to Stanford—and let everyone know she was playing to win. After a half hour spent crafting a caption, Kelly selected the picture she'd snapped the other day of Krissie holding a copy of the *Seattle Times* and sporting a mile-wide smile. The newspaper headline read: "Elliott Bay Academy Tops Washington State High Schools with 27 National Merit Semifinalists." She added her carefully worded caption, "Couldn't be more proud of my brilliant girl! Palo Alto–bound? Yes please!!!" and hit Post.

4

Alicia

"ALICIA, YOU HAVE TWENTY minutes until your biz dev status meeting," her assistant, Charlotte, said, breezing into Alicia's office holding a silver tray. She placed it on the sideboard and pulled a gray linen place mat, matching napkin, and silverware out of the drawer. She set lunch for one at Alicia's glass conference table, took a bottle of sparkling water out of the mini fridge, and poured some into a cut-crystal glass. "I made sure they left the onions and cucumbers out of your salad this time. Do you need anything else?"

"I'm good, thank you, Charlotte," Alicia said, her eyes focused on her computer screen, digesting the one-page memo she required in advance of all status meetings. She really wanted to say, "It's about damn time you got my salad order right." Maren would never screw up something so basic. Maybe she should have Maren hire and train her work assistants so that she'd finally get a decent one. Her phone vibrated on her desk, announcing an incoming text. She glanced over and saw her husband's name.

Bryan: thx for the wake up 😜

The combination of her phone sex rejection and her criticism of Bryan's handling of Brooke's essays had resulted in a nearly twenty-four-hour stony silence on his end. He'd ignored her calls and hadn't waited up for her when she'd flown in from New York last night. In a peace-making gesture to restore their household equilibrium, Alicia had woken him up this morning with a blow job before heading off to work for an all-hands presentation, followed by review meetings with three different teams and an interview with some business blog. Bryan was planning to play not one but two rounds of golf, followed by a beer flights tasting dinner with a group of EBA dads.

Alicia: How was your first round?

Bryan: 2 under. Did u c Kelly the Cow's post?

At least he was talking to her again, but she bristled that he was interrupting her at work about a Facebook post.

Alicia: No. Kinda busy. Why?

Bryan: She thinks the Stanford spot is actually in play! LOL!

Alicia picked up her phone and flicked open the Facebook app. She typed Kelly's name into the search bar. She was not about to get sucked down the rabbit hole looking for that pathetic woman's post. As she waited for Kelly's page to populate on her screen, Alicia gazed across the room at her salad. Her board-mandated executive coach had recently recommended that Alicia make more of an effort to eat throughout the day to avoid dips in blood sugar. She intimated that Alicia might be perceived as less bitchy by her team if she wasn't hangry all the time. Charlotte was put in charge of providing Alicia with a steady stream of protein. It didn't matter if the food was healthy. Alicia's body insisted on clinging to every last calorie she put in her mouth. Her husband might be enjoying her "new curves" as he called them, but she had no intention of keeping them and had doubled down on her workouts. Clicking on Kelly's name, she immediately saw the post. "Oh my God. 'Palo Alto–bound'? 'Yes please'? Who does that woman think she is?" Alicia said out loud.

Charlotte appeared in the doorway. "Do you need something? Do you not like the salad? I have an apple and peanut butter."

Alicia looked up from her phone. "What? No. Everything's fine. Can you close my door?" She was stunned that Kelly Vernon, kiss ass extraordinaire and PTA everything, would be so aggressive. This post was a virtual peeing on the carpet to mark her territory. Studying the photo, Alicia had a vague sense that she should have known about this award. She clicked on the link to the *Seattle Times* article Kelly had helpfully included. Well, at least twenty-seven winners sounded like a promising number. The article loaded, and Alicia's eyes scanned down the list, pausing for a second on Winnie's name, but when she got to the S's, there was no Brooke Stone.

Alicia was momentarily disappointed, like she'd been excluded from the guest list of a party. From what she could tell, Brooke's 3.5 GPA seemed respectable enough given EBA's rigorous curriculum, but she'd taken the ACT four times and hadn't yet cracked Stanford's bottom quartile for admitted students. For the first time, Alicia was forced to wonder just how far Stanford would lower its academic floor for the progeny of one of its biggest donors.

Alicia noted the time, put her phone in her top desk drawer, and returned to the memo on her screen. Aspyre had recently signed a letter of intent to acquire a high-flying start-up, but as soon as the team started its due diligence, problems surfaced all over the place. After rereading the same bullet point three times in a row warning of accounting irregularities, Alicia clicked the memo closed and spun around in her chair to face the window. There was no way Ted had defied her and not instructed the college counseling office to tell Kelly that her daughter needed to find another school. Who did Kelly and Krissie think they were, ignoring EBA's directive?

In addition to Krissie being a strong student and double legacy, Alicia knew Kelly had been counting on Krissie's woman in STEM hook to get her into Stanford. Kelly had hounded her last spring about an internship for her aspiring computer scientist, emailing her mousy daughter's résumé multiple times until Alicia arranged an opportunity for her as a business analyst just to make Kelly stop contacting her. Alicia took a small amount of pleasure in the knowledge that while a woman in STEM might be a meaningful hook at other elite schools, she'd learned at a recent trustee meeting that for the first time ever, it was no longer considered an institutional priority. Apparently, Stanford had been absolutely inundated during the last admissions cycle with women in STEM applicants. She'd debated whether she should share this with Kelly and the EBA college counselors. But alas, it had slipped her mind.

Alicia twirled a lock of hair around her finger. She wasn't exactly worried, but she did have to wonder: Might Kelly's public declaration that they weren't backing down embolden others? If that was the case, Alicia had to at least consider the possibility that there was one EBA student who could actually stand in Brooke's way of getting the coveted Stanford spot. And for that, she had no one to blame but herself.

Alicia opened her bottom desk drawer and pulled out a sleeve of salted caramels—her go-to comfort treat when faced with a difficult situation. As she popped the first one in her mouth, she reflected how from the moment Maren and Winnie had come into their lives, Alicia had known there was something special about Winnie. At eight years old, she already had an insatiable curiosity. Her vocabulary and speech patterns made you forget you were conversing with a child. As Brooke's nanny in those days, Maren often brought Winnie with her to work, and Alicia encouraged the friendship between the girls, secretly wishing some of Winnie's intellect and determination would rub off on her own daughter. Alicia even concocted a perverse fantasy: Winnie was the sister she'd been unable to give Brooke. The girls would grow up and go to Stanford together! She bought them matching Stanford T-shirts and talked about them being roommates someday. Alicia had not only planted the Stanford seed, she'd watered it and watched it grow.

Even once Brooke had left the public elementary school they'd both attended for EBA, the girls had remained close. Alicia made sure of this by treating all four of them to a standing mani-pedi date every Saturday morning. However, a rift developed soon after Winnie joined Brooke for high school at EBA. Alicia was never able to pry out of Brooke the specific reason for the falling-out, but it probably hadn't helped that Winnie established herself as a standout student from the minute she'd stepped foot on EBA's campus.

The extent of the schism had become clear when Alicia agreed to host a pre-func for Brooke and all her friends before that fall's homecoming dance. When Brooke pointedly excluded Winnie from the guest list, Alicia had been mortified and almost canceled the entire event but finally relented because she didn't want to be blamed for ruining her daughter's special night, and anyway, it wasn't fair to make Brooke responsible for Winnie's popularity. As part of Maren's household duties, she planned the event, served the food and drinks to the assembled kids and their parents who were on-site to snap pictures, and cleaned up afterward, all without ever saying a word about Winnie's exclusion. In fact, she rarely mentioned Winnie unprompted after that episode.

Alicia worried that the painfully awkward incident would impact her complex relationship with Maren, on whom she relied not only for Maren's unparalleled skills as a personal assistant but also as a prized confidant. Indeed, the more Alicia succeeded at work, the more isolated she felt. It sometimes seemed like Maren was the only person who truly understood her life. So in the end, Alicia had decided to skirt the issue of the girls' deteriorating friendship altogether. But unfortunately, Winnie's Stanford dream hadn't ended along with her friendship with Brooke. It had blossomed as she collected awards, accolades, and attention for her outstanding achievements inside and outside the classroom.

Alicia noticed the paper wrappers scattered across her desk and realized she'd consumed at least half a dozen caramels. Did she feel sick to her stomach because of the caramels or because of the thought, however improbable, of Winnie applying to Stanford? She swept the wrappers into the trash can under her desk. Maren was her longest-serving and most loyal employee, who had lasted so long because she was sharp and knew how to avoid crossing Alicia. Furthermore, she couldn't imagine Maren doing anything that would hurt Brooke. Maren had been like a second mother to her. And after everything Alicia had done for Maren and Winnie, would they really be so ungrateful?

After all, Alicia had been paying Winnie's tuition since she'd started at EBA in ninth grade and had promised to fund Winnie's college education as well. The EBA gossipmongers assumed her generosity was out of the goodness of her heart, and she'd never bothered to disabuse anyone of this falsehood as it was great for her "leading woman in tech" brand. Whatever the reason for Alicia's largesse, Winnie was receiving a top-notch education thanks to her, and Maren was bound by a nondisclosure agreement expressly forbidding her from disclosing anything related to Alicia, Bryan, and Brooke. A single violation was grounds for termination and damages, as Alicia couldn't afford to be too careful thanks to the media's fixation on her and her family.

Clearly, EBA's college counseling team had failed to change Kelly's mind. What if, as a result, Maren and Winnie also came to see this as a "let the best woman win" situation? Pressing the heels of her hands into her eyes, Alicia wished they'd never brought Winnie—the girl who made her daughter look like a dunce in comparison—into their family fold. She ran a quick risk analysis in her head. There was no way Maren would ever dare violate her nondisclosure agreement and reveal the true reason Alicia had been funding Winnie's education, *even if* Alicia were to unilaterally change the terms of their deal. Alicia was a pillar of the community now; no one would ever believe Maren. And Maren would know she was inviting certain financial ruin. On the flip side, if there was even a chance Winnie might apply to Stanford, that was definitely not a risk Alicia was willing to take. Enough was enough. Alicia might have started Winnie's Stanford dream, but now it was time to put an end to it.

5

Maren

MAREN TUCKED A SOCK-COVERED foot under her leg and examined the label of the cabernet sauvignon she held in her hand. It was one of Alicia's castaways, a hostess gift from some unsophisticated dinner guest who wasn't privy to Alicia's house policy that a bottle had to be worth at least fifty dollars to warrant a spot in the Stones' two-thousand-bottle wine cellar. Normally, Maren distributed the "cheap stuff" to the house and garden staff, enjoying their delight as though she had bought the bottles herself, but she had liked this particular label and decided to keep it. Now she was happy she'd had such a visceral reaction to the bright logo.

She took another sip and let the flavors coat the inside of her mouth; though she was no connoisseur, she knew what she liked. She was not typically much of a drinker, preferring instead to stay in total control of her faculties, but the email from Alicia she'd just read for the fourth time today had knocked her off-balance. It was a peculiar feeling of suspended animation, reminiscent of an antsy student wobbling on the back legs of her chair, wondering if this was the time she'd finally tipped back a centimeter too far. If ever the numbing effects of alcohol were warranted, it was tonight.

She set down her glass and ran a hand over the distressed-wood kitchen table as she tried to strategize her response to this latest betrayal from her usual position of vulnerability. Instead, her thoughts wandered back a few years to the night she'd acquired this beloved table. She'd been moonlighting as a dog walker for a persnickety older woman who lived alone in a Capitol Hill mansion and seemed to believe that if one dog was good company, then four were better. At the end of the walk, Maren had taken the dogs through the back alley to toss the eco-waste bags, imprinted with the slogan "Dumps for Trump," into the garbage bin. Maren couldn't help but think the snarky poop bags were somehow emblematic of a town full of liberals in large houses who regularly "composted" enough food to feed four families and who displayed bright yard signs preaching love and tolerance behind their imposing wrought-iron fences. If anything, Maren had come to believe that these Seattle folk were worse than the country club conservatives she'd grown up with in Indiana—just as mean and selfish but a lot less honest about it.

But on that day, she'd been grateful for Seattle's "reuse and recycle" mantra. The handwritten "free" sign in bright red marker was taped to the table and caught Maren's eye as she closed the lid to the garbage can. Approaching for a closer look, Maren was astonished that anyone would throw an item like this away. It was well worn, probably an antique, and beautiful. And someone had literally tossed it to the curb. Maren was good with mental measurements and knew right away it would be the perfect size for meals and Winnie's homework in their rented bungalow if she could manage to get it home.

She punched in the code on her client's locked gate. After wiping every trace of mud and street debris from all four underbellies and six-teen paws, she let the dogs inside, filled their water bowls, and then dashed out the front door to retrieve her car, praying the entire time that her new kitchen table—it was already hers in her mind—hadn't been stolen in the ten minutes that had lapsed. When she pulled into the alley, she pumped her fist in victory and got to work wedging just enough of the table into her hatchback that she was hopeful if she drove very slowly, she would make it the mile or so home without it toppling out into the road. As it turned out, the effort had been worth it. After all, it was right here at this table that Winnie had applied to EBA at Alicia's insistence and where she'd studied for every test and written every A-plus paper of her high school career. And it was here that she would have been putting the finishing touches on her Stanford early admission application over the next few weeks, if not for Stanford's intention to accept only one more EBA student.

But now Maren was feeling stuck in a way she hadn't since her preg-nancy with Winnie. She pulled up the email from Alicia on her phone, hoping it had been a figment of her imagination. But it was still there and still as disastrous as it had been earlier this afternoon.

———

From: Alicia Stone   Today, 12:55 p.m

To: Maren Pressley

Subject: My Mom/Winnie

Hi, M,

Apologies for doing this over email, but I wanted to let you know as soon as possible of a change in circumstances that may affect Winnie's college decision-making process. As you know, my mom has not been well. With Dad too feeble to care for her and her Alzheimer's progressing, I've recently been advised they are in need of twenty-four-hour skilled care for the foreseeable future. The costs for in-home caregivers are simply astronomical, so we met with our financial planner earlier today to discuss our options. I regret to tell you that he strongly urged us to redirect the discretionary funds we'd set aside for Winnie's college tuition and use them for my mom's care instead.

I'm truly sorry if this new situation causes you or Winnie distress, but I figured it's better that you have the information now so you can plan accordingly rather than have Winnie reach for unattainable dreams. I'm quite certain with Winnie's fantastic record, she will have no trouble at all winning merit scholarships, even full rides, to one of the many up-and-coming colleges that would be lucky to have her. And UW Honors is also a terrific option. She could even live at home and commute to school, further reducing your expenses. Whatever you decide, please know it's been our absolute pleasure to support Winnie's education at EBA (as of now, we still plan to make her final tuition payment for senior spring semester).

Happy to be a sounding board as you consider all the fantastic options available to Winnie! As always, I treasure your friendship and am Winnie's biggest fan.

XX, A

―――――

The more times Maren read it, the angrier she got. Alicia Stone, a millionaire many hundreds of times over, needed that discretionary fund about as much as her husband, Bryan, needed a sixth golf club membership. This was nothing less than a shot across the bow to warn Winnie off Stanford. Maren's hands were completely tied, which was exactly what Alicia was counting on. If Maren dared complain about Alicia reneging on the deal they'd struck years ago, Alicia's email made clear she would pull Winnie's spring tuition, which would in turn force Maren to withdraw Winnie from her last semester at EBA. And the NDA Alicia had made Maren sign was no doubt ironclad, not that Maren could afford an attorney to give her an opinion.

In the ten years since Maren had begun working for Alicia, Maren's job responsibilities had evolved substantially. What started out as a contract-based house-cleaning gig had turned into a full-time nanny job and then, as the girls grew older, transitioned into her current role as full-fledged household manager/personal assistant. Early on, Alicia established a fierce grip on Maren's life—and by extension, Winnie's—that grew with each passing year. In the beginning, though, all Maren could see were the benefits.

Maren started cleaning for Alicia when the girls were kindergarteners in pigtails. She could hardly believe her good fortune when Alicia poached her from the cleaning service to work for them directly as a nanny. After living hand-to-mouth to provide the basics of shelter, food, and care for Winnie, she was finally on stable footing with a decent salary. Not only that, Alicia offered as part of the deal to let them live in a small bunga-low the Stones owned at a dramatically reduced rent, which was a giant step up from the apartment they'd shared with a rotating cast of fellow house cleaners in the south end of the city. Their new neighborhood was not only suburban-level safe, but it was also home to the highly regarded public elementary school that Brooke attended, Portage Bay Elementary, a far cry from the dilapidated school Winnie had been attending since kindergarten.

Maren didn't have much experience with children beyond the few she'd babysat or lifeguarded in high school. However, from the time Winnie was a toddler, her intuition had told her that Winnie was wise beyond her years. Maren would routinely climb into bed with Winnie to help her fall asleep but would instead feel her own eyelids succumb to the lively staccato of Winnie's questions. After Winnie switched to Portage Bay Elementary in third grade, Maren's early suspicions regarding her daughter's intelligence were confirmed—repeatedly.

By the spring of third grade, Winnie's teachers at Portage Bay, a much more engaged crew than at her prior school, had urged Maren to test Winnie for the district's Highly Capable program, which was located just a few miles away from Portage Bay. Filled with pride and a budding opti-mism for Winnie's future, Maren scheduled the exam for an upcoming weekend when the Stones were planning to visit friends in San Francisco. She hadn't mentioned the test to Alicia. In fact, it had never even occurred to Maren that it would be any of Alicia's business. Even if Winnie changed schools, the move wouldn't impact Brooke's morning routine in the slightest. Big mistake.

Unfortunately, Alicia had canceled their trip at the last minute due to a work emergency and had called on Maren to accompany Brooke to her Saturday activities. When Maren explained to Alicia why she couldn't step in on such short notice, Alicia lit into her. "I can't believe you would do this to Brooke! How would Winnie feel if Brooke left her behind? What kind of message does that send? That a regular school like Portage Bay is good enough for Brooke but not for her nanny's daughter, who apparently needs a special school to house her very special brain?"

It was a vicious tirade that left little doubt where Maren and Winnie stood in the social hierarchy of Alicia's mind, but it was the fact that she hadn't seen it coming that really shook Maren. Of course, Alicia frequently teased Winnie about being too smart for her own good. "Lay off the brain food—have a Pop-Tart!" "Be careful—none of the kids at school will understand all those big fancy words you use!" One time, she even went so far as to give Winnie a brand-new iPad preloaded with dozens of mindless games and TV shows—without asking Maren for permission. "Hey, little smarty-pants, don't you think it's about time you pulled your nose out of all those chapter books and had a little fun?" Maren laughed off Alicia's comments as harmless banter, especially since they were usually followed by gushing declarations of her love for Winnie and the special relationship the girls shared.

However, in the wake of Alicia's outburst over the Highly Capable test, Maren recognized that she'd been duped. Alicia's digs had always been about kneecapping Winnie's high-achieving tendencies. Nevertheless, Maren was eager to appease her angry boss and repair the damage to their relationship. She'd withdrawn Winnie from the test with regret but without hesitation.

Maren had thought her own mother was the queen of the silent treatment, but Alicia was in another league altogether. It took months for things to get back to normal between them. From that point forward, whenever Winnie's teachers recommended her for testing, Maren politely declined—to their utter incomprehension. Each year, when Maren said no to the opportunities she so badly wanted for Winnie, it took another large divot out of her maternal self-worth, but she came to accept the annual ritual as a sort of employment tax she owed for the job they relied on to survive.

Maren glanced at the ominous email in her palm and now saw with total clarity that Alicia's reaction to Winnie taking the test for the Highly Capable program had been the first of many instances where Winnie became collateral damage to Alicia's ambition for Brooke. And Maren had been powerless to stop any of them.

———

Ironically enough, by the start of middle school, it was Brooke who left Winnie behind when she was admitted to EBA, a grades 6–12 prep school positioned as a pipeline to elite colleges. However, it wasn't until a couple years later that Maren discovered what Alicia had orchestrated to get Brooke into the prestigious school. A scheme that had ultimately changed Winnie's academic career, and Maren's life, forever.

When Brooke was a fifth grader and applying to EBA, Alicia's career was rocketing to stratospheric success. Which was why Alicia had suddenly set her sights on EBA, buying into the "only the best for my family" mentality that dominated her company's C-suite, a place Alicia was determined to one day belong. The only hitch in her plans was Brooke's average academic profile.

A decent student, Brooke was no Winnie. No matter how many hours Maren spent with Brooke on homework, she struggled to perform to her mother's standards. When it came time to prep for the EBA entrance exam, her practice test scores were subpar, and Brooke was falling apart, crying nearly every day in Maren's arms. Maren finally broke down and spoke to Alicia about her daughter's deteriorating mental state, but instead of taking pressure off the poor girl, Alicia pushed Brooke to try harder, offering her outlandish bribes with one hand while threatening to take away everything she cared about with the other, which only sent Brooke into a deeper spiral.

Maren knew Alicia could be ruthless, and she also knew that Alicia was used to getting what she wanted. But Maren always believed that at the end of the day, their deeply entwined relationships would keep Winnie out of Alicia's crosshairs. However, that was until Maren learned the truth behind Alicia's EBA campaign and realized that in Alicia's world, as long as you had the money and status to back you up, every line was made to be crossed.

Around the same time as the EBA entrance exam, Alicia and Bryan were invited to a swanky party thrown by Diana and Michael Taylor, whose fifth-grade daughter, Tenley, played soccer with Brooke. Tenley was also applying to EBA, and Alicia was peeved that Diana had the inside track. All fall on the soccer sidelines, Diana had been gleefully trumpeting her recent appointment to the EBA board of trustees, which Alicia grumbled was directly tied to the fortune amassed over the previous decade by Diana's venture capitalist husband. In an attempt to ingratiate herself with Diana, Alicia had offered Maren's services for the party that night, which had given Maren a front-row view of the no-expenses-spared affair.

Along with the 250 other movers and shakers of Seattle, Diana's guest list included her "dear friend" Ted Clark, who was then EBA's admissions director. Once word of Ted's arrival at the party spread, Maren watched with grim amusement as eager moms of EBA applicants swarmed him, attempting to curry favor or at least stand out from the crowd. As Maren handed him his second glass of sparkling water, she actually felt a little sorry for the guy, but she noticed that he handled the persistent advances like a pro. He must have observed her doing the same, and when she discreetly sidestepped another grabby husband who felt entitled to assume that her fitted catering uniform was an open invitation to grope her, she and Ted shared a glance of *Can you believe these people?* commiseration.

Not long after that moment, Alicia pulled Maren aside and whispered in her ear: "Ted Clark can't take his eyes off you. I'll give you $1,000 if you can get any useful EBA admissions information out of him."

With $1,000 hanging over her head, money that Maren desperately needed to cover medical bills from Winnie's recent bout of pneumonia, she accepted Ted's offer to grab a drink after the party. She was terrible at flirting, and though it pained her to pull one over on him, she managed to get one tidbit from Ted: EBA's score floor on the SSAT exam. Apparently, Brooke would need to score above the 92nd percentile to be considered for admission. Ted had seemed like a genuinely decent guy—with a boyish charm and kind eyes—but their evening had started and ended with one drink, and Maren felt dirty afterward for using her tight blouse and doe eyes to get what she needed. But Alicia had been pleased with the information and paid Maren the cool grand in cash the next morning. Brooke ended up scoring well above the threshold and received her EBA admission letter the following February.

With Brooke officially ensconced in her posh private school, Maren had assumed the admissions craziness was at an end. And with Winnie and Brooke finally out of direct competition, opportunities at Winnie's public middle school were fair game. Which was how, when Winnie was in eighth grade, the truth came out.

One afternoon, Winnie pulled a packet of information from her backpack describing a program sponsored by the University of Washington called Husky Launch, which allowed accelerated high school students to take two classes per semester at the university for college credit while still graduating from their local high schools. Tuition was gratis, and students received a free city bus pass and lunch coupons. All Winnie had to do was submit an application with teacher references and score above the 97th percentile on the standardized entrance exam. Though Maren had misgivings about her daughter venturing out alone on a college campus, she figured there was no harm in letting Winnie sit for the test, so they signed her up for the next available exam.

When Winnie emerged from the three-and-a-half-hour exam, Maren was waiting to take her out for her favorite treat: a red velvet cupcake with cream cheese frosting from the Cupcake Genie. As they dug in to their first sinful bites, Maren asked how the test went. To say Winnie's reply took Maren by surprise was perhaps the understatement of the century.

"Easy. It was just like the test Alicia took me and Brooke to a few years ago."

Maren's antennae shot up. "Oh really? Hmm…I don't remember that. When was it again?"

Winnie's face turned red. "Oops. Now that I'm remembering it, I think Alicia made me promise to keep it a secret."

"Well, it was such a long time ago, it can't hurt now, right?"

"I guess. The dress she got me after the test as a thank-you doesn't even fit anymore."

"You mean that beautiful dress she gave you for Christmas in fifth grade?"

"Yeah, the green plaid one with the black sash? God, I loved that dress."

"It really was gorgeous on you." Maren smiled. "So tell me more about that test?"

"I don't remember much except it was a Saturday and we were in the car for a long time. I thought she was taking us to play laser tag, but then she pulled into some dreary school in a scary-looking neighborhood— the drinking fountains had yellow tape around them and big signs that said, 'Do Not Drink.' We were the only two white kids there. Alicia said Brooke had to take a test, and she asked me to take it with her to keep Brooke company. She said it would be good practice for me for college someday. Anyway, she filled out the forms for us with the lady at the front of the room, and I remember the test was long and boring but super easy."

"Did you ever find out how you did on the test?"

"Yeah, it was weird. I remember asking Alicia a few weeks later how I did, and she said I did fine, almost as well as Brooke, but that was to be expected since Brooke had studied hard for the test and I was doing it just for fun. I think that might have been the only time Brooke ever outscored me on anything!"

Maren understood immediately what had happened. Indeed, part of her was surprised that her normally astute daughter hadn't put it together.

But on another level, Maren saw why. For years, Winnie had worshipped Alicia, and Alicia had actively cultivated Winnie's belief that she was all but an official member of the Stone family, just like Maren was supposedly Alicia's "treasured friend." Alicia didn't just steal her daughter's score that day; she took full advantage of Winnie's yearning to belong to their family and used it all to propel Brooke. It was only because of Winnie that Brooke had been admitted to EBA, and meanwhile, Winnie was left to suffer at a less-than-stellar public school.

Even today, Maren's anger over Alicia's treatment of eleven-year-old Winnie was raw. Until now, Maren could at least console herself with the knowledge that the incident had ultimately paved the way for Winnie to receive the rigorous education she'd been so long denied and, even more exciting, the promise of a fully funded college education on the horizon. Maren had kept from Winnie the backstory behind her move to EBA in hopes of protecting her from the hard truth of Alicia's empty affection. But now everything was about to come crashing down. As Maren sat at the kitchen table preparing to dash Winnie's college dreams and break her heart in the process, she finally understood: where Alicia was concerned, it was pay now *and* pay later.

The tuition deal Alicia was audaciously withdrawing in her email was struck after Maren confirmed the truth about Brooke's EBA entrance test and finally worked up the nerve to confront Alicia—job security be damned. To Maren's surprise, though, Alicia was unfazed. No apologies. No remorse. Alicia had turned a cold stare on Maren and said, "I thought Winnie would be smart enough to remember not to talk about that day. We had a deal."

"Yes, I know. You promised an eleven-year-old a designer dress in exchange for her silence to keep me from ever learning how you used my daughter. I'm pretty sure what you did is illegal, Alicia. And it's definitely wrong. The only reason I'm not quitting and reporting you to EBA is because I know how devastated Brooke would be if she ever found out. But this can't happen again."

Alicia looked momentarily stunned. Maren had never spoken to her so angrily or directly. But Alicia quickly drew on her keen negotiating skills. "Anyway, I've been meaning to tell you that with my vested stock options so valuable now, I've decided I'd like to sponsor Winnie at EBA."

Maren cast a skeptical glance at Alicia but stayed quiet.

"You know what? I'll even throw in tuition for the college of her choice. All you need to do is sign a nondisclosure agreement my lawyers will draft in which you promise never to reveal this minor episode to anyone. Do we have a deal?"

Maren took the deal.

And look where that deal landed us, Maren thought as a venomous, helpless fury coursed through her veins. She poured the dregs of the wine bottle into her glass, hiccupped, and took another long gulp as she waited for Winnie to get home from the EBA football game. Once again, Maren would force her daughter to take a back seat to Brooke. And this time, she wouldn't be able to shield Winnie from her idol's betrayal: a double whammy.

What a stupendous mom she'd turned out to be. More like stupid. Despite working herself to the bone all these years, Maren had been for her extraordinary daughter little more than a pathetic, subservient mom with a shameful past. Winnie had no father and no extended family, and now here they were: backed into a corner with a powerful and unscrupulous woman holding Winnie's college dreams hostage. Fine work, indeed. Maren took another swig of wine and put her head down on the treasured table that was once someone else's trash.

The hollow front door rattled shut, and Maren lifted her head up as Winnie walked into the kitchen. "How was the game?" A loud hiccup punctuated the question. "Oops!"

"Oh my God, Mom. Are you drunk?"

"I don't know about drunk, but I maybe had a little too much wine."

Winnie chuckled. "You never drink. What's up?"

She knew it would devastate Winnie to see for herself that her hero had abandoned her like a dead raccoon on the side of the road. But she needed Winnie to understand. "This is what's up," Maren said as she waved her phone at Winnie.

Her daughter was a speedy reader, so Maren guessed she must have read the email at least three times before finally shoving the phone back.

Winnie turned her head in a patent attempt to hide the tears that were welling up in her eyes. "How can she do this? She promised! This is so messed up!"

"Yeah, I have to agree with ya there, hon." Maren dropped her head back down to the table. "Obviously someone really wants to make sure you don't apply to Stanford."

"You know what? Screw her. It sucks, but it doesn't change anything for me. Stanford is a no-loan school." Winnie stamped her foot. "If anything, this makes me want it more. Why can't you just find another job?"

"You don't understand, Win." Maren sniffled and rubbed her nose. "She's got my tits in a vice grip. If I quit or get fired, I'll never find another job. She'll withhold references or worse. She hasn't achieved that huge success you desire without destroying a few people along the way. Believe me, I've seen the bodies. And I'm legally bound to keep my mouth shut about everything I've learned while working for her, including how she stole your identity to get Brooke into EBA in the first place."

"What are you talking about?" Winnie finally sat down in the dining chair next to Maren.

Maren leaned over and squeezed Winnie's shoulders. She knew she could be in for a world of hurt for breaking her NDA, but what the hell. Alicia had thrown the first punch. Maybe there was a self-defense exception to NDAs? Honestly, she was almost past caring. She was just that tired. Overriding the niggling feeling that she might regret this in the morning, Maren told the truth.

"I really shouldn't be doing this, but I need you to understand who we're dealing with here. You can't ever breathe a word about this to a single soul." Maren stared into Winnie's watery eyes and swallowed down a feeling of nausea. "Do you remember that time when Alicia took you with Brooke to take a 'practice' standardized test in fifth grade and then she bought you that Christmas dress and told you to never tell me about it?"

"Yeah?" Winnie said.

"Well, after you told me about it in eighth grade, I did some digging. I figured out that she drove you girls all the way to an elementary school in Tacoma to take that test so she could be sure she wouldn't run into anyone she knew. Do you want to guess why?"

Winnie shook her head slowly. "What are you saying?"

"I'm saying she swapped your test scores with Brooke's so Brooke could get into EBA."

"Are you serious?" Winnie's eyes widened.

"I wish it wasn't true, but that's why she paid for EBA and why she promised to pay for college. Because I confronted her and threatened to report her. It was the only time in ten years I had the upper hand on her.

But now she's got me—or I suppose us—right back where she wants us, and there's no way out." Maren massaged her temples. Her head pounded like she had skipped the drunk part and moved straight into the hangover. "So how 'bout we find you another dang college before she does something really insane like kidnaps you and hires a surgeon to transplant your brain into Brooke. I'm telling you, this woman will stop at nothing to get what she wants."

"That's just…no, that's just crazy. I can't believe she did that to me." Winnie slumped in her chair, tears streaming down her face. "How can she get away with this?"

"I've been over and over and over it. If we do anything to challenge her, she could also evict us. Remember, they own our house, and we're lucky they haven't raised our rent. If we lost my job and this house, we'd practically have to move to Canada to afford something decent. Or worse, we could end up homeless again. I can't go back to that, Win. I can't do that to you ever again."

"You have to stop blaming yourself. I don't even remember it."

"Well, I can't forget it." Living out of their car, trying to make a home for Winnie who was only three without a bathroom or a kitchen, making it a game to pee in used coffee cups, sneaking into café bathrooms to wash up. Moving the car every three days so she wouldn't get hauled into the police station for loitering. Except for the hours upon hours spent in libraries reading and staying warm, every minute of that hell was seared in her brain. "It's just not worth it. No single college is worth it. Can't you just accept UW as a good enough option? Don't they have a great honors program? Once you get your degree, then we can make our move. Please?" This was a new low for Maren, tearfully begging her daughter to be a doormat. But she couldn't see another way out of this. The devil she knew was the only option.

"OK, Mom. Jeez! Just stop! Fine. I'll do it. I'll be the joke of EBA, staying in Seattle for college after busting my butt to graduate first in my class, but whatever. College is college."

"Exactly. It will set you free, I promise," Maren said and knocked over her empty glass.

"Easy there," Winnie said, righting the wineglass. "I think maybe we need to get you to bed." She helped Maren up from her chair and steadied her on the short walk down the hall to the bedroom.

As Maren fell onto the bed, she allowed herself a small sigh of relief. Maybe she needed to drink more often if that was what it took to get Winnie to see things her way. For years, Maren had vowed she'd get out from under this warped relationship with Alicia. But it wasn't time yet; she had to get Winnie through college first. And, she reminded herself, she'd endured far worse than being pushed around by a bitter, overprivileged, emotionally stunted middle-aged woman. Anyway, if Stanford was filled with people like Alicia and Brooke, people who would do anything to get ahead, wouldn't Winnie be happier somewhere else in the end?

MEMORIAL HOSPITAL
EMERGENCY ROOM

SATURDAY, OCTOBER 30, 12:30 A.M.

YOUR DAUGHTER WAS IN *a serious accident.*

Maren still couldn't believe the police officer's words, even as she sat here in the ER waiting room, eyes glued to the "Unauthorized Entry" doors. As she continued her desperate wait for word of Winnie's condition, she found herself replaying the exchange with the officer at her front door, wondering if she'd missed something in her state of shock. Did he know more about Winnie's condition than he had let on? Had she hit a pothole or swerved to avoid an animal? In Maren's hand was the iPhone the officer (What was his name? Johnson? Truman? Definitely a former president—that much she remembered) had given her at the door.

She'd once checked out a library book describing how people, children especially, used magical thinking to deal with trauma, and she'd instantly recognized it as one of her own go-to coping strategies. If she didn't set the phone down, Winnie would be fine. If she held her breath for twenty seconds of every minute, Winnie would pull through. She tried to make out the time on Winnie's cracked screen to no avail, instead using a wall clock on the other side of the waiting area. How was it possible that just an hour ago, the police officer had appeared at her house and turned her world upside down, and yet it felt like she'd been waiting an eternity to find out if Winnie was OK? She held her breath again and counted to twenty.

From the moment she'd opened her front door and seen the officer instead of Winnie, Maren had been thrown headfirst into a sinkhole of despair the likes of which she'd only experienced one other time in her life. It was bone-chilling to be back in that place after almost two decades spent resisting its pull. Even now, when she spoke to the clerk, she could feel the vibration of words in her larynx, but the sounds that emerged were distorted, like they'd traveled the length of a tuba before emerging from her mouth. To prove to herself she was still connected to reality, she periodically ran a finger over the shattered glass of Winnie's phone until a broken shard sliced the pad of her fingertip. Three fingers and a thumb currently stung with invisible slivers, but at least the pain grounded her in the present.

The sound of footsteps seeped into her consciousness. As she lifted her head, she noted a broad-shouldered man coming her way and rose to meet him.

"Hello, Mrs. Pressley? My name is Detective Davis." His booming voice reverberated through the somber waiting area. "I'm the detective in charge of your daughter's case."

"Hi, I'm Maren." She winced as her sore fingertips made contact with his outstretched hand. "Please, what can you tell me? They haven't told me anything. How bad are her injuries?" Maren shivered. Now that she might finally be getting information about Winnie, she wished she could hide in the not-knowing for a little while longer.

"Ma'am, I'm sorry. I don't have any information on your daughter's health status. That's not my department. I can tell you what we know about the accident, but unfortunately, I have more questions than answers at this point." He ran a hand over his close-cropped hair.

"OK..."

"Your daughter...um, Rowan, is it?" Detective Davis checked his spiral notepad.

"Yes, she goes by Winnie," Maren clarified.

"Got it," he said, making a note. "So it looks like Winnie was riding an electric scooter near Lake Washington Country Club. A witness called 911. EMS arrived within a few minutes. The witness stayed with Winnie until the first responders arrived and told them what she saw, which unfortunately wasn't much. The road was poorly lit, and the witness couldn't provide any details other than she was driving a short distance behind a dark-colored SUV that appeared to be closely following your daughter. She observed a person fly off the road in front of that car. According to the witness, the driver of the SUV didn't stop. When the medics arrived, your daughter was on the parking strip, disoriented and bleeding from a head wound."

Head wound? Maren's breath hitched on the words. "This can't be happening." Her voice sounded high in her ears. "Please tell me she was wearing her helmet?" Like nearly every mom in Seattle, Maren viewed with extreme suspicion the thousands of neon ride-share electric scooters that had swarmed into the city the prior year like a plague of locusts. But Winnie had at least promised she'd always wear a helmet if she ever rented one. Though new, off-the-shelf purchases were not a part of their consumer vocabulary, Maren had made an exception and invested in a top-rated bike helmet for Winnie. She tried to think back to this morning but couldn't *remember whether Winnie had left the house with her helmet dangling from the outside strap of her backpack as it usually did.*

"I'm afraid there was no helmet found at the scene," the detective said as he consulted his notes. Detective Davis looked Maren directly in the eye. "I'm sorry, but I have to ask you this: Did your daughter have any enemies? Anyone threatening her? The witness said Winnie was mumbling about someone following her."

"Oh my God, do you think someone did this on purpose?" Maren froze. Like a sports highlight reel, all the cutthroat jockeying to claim the last remaining spot at Stanford cycled through her mind. Even by EBA standards, the past few weeks had been unhinged. Maren thought back to the night of Alicia's email when Winnie had promised to take Stanford off her list. If only Maren could have frozen time that night, Winnie might not have gone on to break her word and make the decision that may have landed her here at Memorial in a full-blown medical crisis.

But would someone in Winnie's privileged school community risk everything just to secure a spot at Stanford? That it was difficult to imagine didn't mean it was impossible. As Maren knew all too well, given the right set of circumstances, even normal people were capable of heinous acts. And in her experience, Alicia Stone was far from normal.

6

Kelly

KELLY SAT IN THE PTA lounge skimming the wrap-up report from last Friday night's victorious home football game, a satisfying smackdown of EBA's crosstown rival, Olympic Prep. She noted with satisfaction that the PTA sports committee's plans for merchandise sales, food concessions, and this week's spirit surprise—distribution of giant photos of the faces of the starting offensive and defensive lines on sticks for the students to wave around—had all gone off without a hitch. However, with Ms. Barstow's shocking news of Stanford's single spot still ringing in her ears, Kelly was having more trouble than usual caring about the details.

Sipping her lukewarm coffee, she took in the smartly decorated parent hangout where she'd spent countless hours over the past several years (and where she would no doubt still be spending time five years from now when her youngest would finally be a senior) and hoped all her hard work would pay off. She thought back to the new parent welcome coffee she had attended in this same room on Krissie's first day of sixth grade. The PTA president hadn't explicitly said so that day, but the implication was clear: women (it was only women in attendance) in her position (stay-at-home moms who had time to attend parent coffees and could afford to send their kids to EBA but not make huge donations) were expected to volunteer— with gusto. Having given up her career years before to raise the kids, Kelly figured she might as well apply her energy and talents to the betterment of her new school community, so she'd started at the bottom and worked her way up through the volunteer hierarchy.

Along the way, she discovered that the EBA parents who most generously supported the school's annual fund and never-ending capital campaigns were rewarded with secret cocktail parties with the head of school, the tables closest to the action at the school auction, preferred parking, and, eventually, the best college counselors for their lucky offspring. No random lotteries there. Lacking the financial resources to get noticed by the school's development office, Kelly doubled down as EBA's ubervolunteer as an alternate path to earning the same perks.

However, no matter how many hours she devoted to her thankless volunteer positions, it was galling to realize blood and sweat were never valued as highly as financial contributions. Last spring, as Kelly completed her two-year term as PTA president—basically a fifty-hour-per-week unpaid job—she was looking forward to finally getting the recognition she deserved at the annual EBA awards luncheon at a fancy hotel downtown. She'd even bought a new dress for the occasion. But in a shocking turn of events, Diana Taylor was awarded Parent Volunteer of the Year, and Kelly had been caught starting to rise from her seat in the front of the room as the announcement was made. Kelly could not believe her ears. In what had been an obvious quid pro quo, Diana had been appointed chair of the EBA board of trustees that year, a mostly honorary position, after she and her husband had donated $1 million to fund the new gym's snack shack. Apparently, her ego required even more brownnosing from the school.

Instead of the public appreciation Kelly had rightfully earned, her consolation prize for years of exuberantly donated quasi-professional services was her appointment as chairwoman of the Senior Send-off Team or SST, the committee responsible for planning all events for the graduating senior class. She may as well have had "sucker" stamped on her forehead. But she swallowed her pride. She had two more kids to consider. At least she'd been rewarded with the college counselor who was always assigned to the wealthiest families. Plus the new SST position gave her the opportunity to keep tabs on the most powerful families at the school during Krissie's crucial senior year. A fleeting glance at the expensive mid-century modern wall clock, donated by a mom when it clashed with her new Hamptons-style kitchen, confirmed that Kelly was due at the SST meeting in five minutes.

The SST was originally composed of a couple of EBA big donors, including Diana Taylor and Augusta Wagoner, the Southern belle wife of the CEO of Cascadia Airlines, and a few industrious worker bees like Jennifer Tan, Amanda Russell, and Sarah Silver (after all, someone had to be willing to execute the grand visions of the wealthier ladies). It had been Kelly's idea to invite Alicia to join the committee in an effort to leverage her proximity to Alicia for Krissie's benefit. All it took was promising Alicia she wouldn't actually have to do anything.

The unexpected bonus was that Alicia sent Maren in her place to all the meetings. Kelly had never experienced the luxury of a personal assistant, or even a nanny or regular house cleaner for that matter, but as head of the SST, she could almost pretend Maren was her own hire once she, and the rest of the committee, realized Maren could be called on to do most of the work. And now, precisely when Kelly most needed to know where Winnie was applying, it felt like destiny that Maren was trapped under her thumb.

Kelly planned to focus today's meeting on the final plans for College Critter Day, which was scheduled to take place the following week. College Critter Day was a long-standing EBA tradition. Seniors brought their pets to school to alleviate college application stress. Of course, in the spirit of inclusivity, the SST would also be sponsoring a menagerie of animals from local pounds and pet stores to be transported to campus for students without their own portable pets. The question of portability was a controversial topic at the last meeting; after last year's horse manure debacle in the quad, the maintenance staff had issued a rare complaint when the students hadn't bothered cleaning up after their animals, so horses were now officially deemed not portable (i.e., not welcome).

When Kelly opened the door of the Taylor Family Conference Room (named after Michael, Diana, and Tenley Taylor, of course), she was surprised to find Maren already seated at the table looking at her phone. "Good morning, Maren," Kelly said, perhaps a bit more brusquely than she'd intended, as she took her place at the head of the table.

"Hey," Maren said, barely looking up from her phone.

"Maren, while we're waiting for the others, do you mind running down to the office to make sure they're bringing in coffee? I requested it when I booked the room, and I'm not seeing any," Kelly said, making a show of looking around. Kelly hadn't actually ordered coffee service, but the errand would occupy Maren long enough for Kelly to enlist help from the other SST mothers.

"Sure—"

"Good morning, ladies," Kelly sang out, cutting Maren off and turn-ing her attention to Augusta, who entered the room followed by Jennifer, Amanda, and Sarah.

Once the door closed behind Maren, Amanda squealed, "Oh my God, Kelly, we just heard the Stanford news. Are you freaking out?"

"No," Kelly said, prickling at Amanda's brash question. "It doesn't change anything."

Sarah's mouth formed a perfectly round O. "Wow, you're so brave! I would be dying."

In her peripheral vision, Kelly could see Augusta, the only college admissions veteran in the room, smirking. But it was easy for Augusta to minimize everyone else's anxiety when her daughter, Greer, was a shoo-in at Vanderbilt like her two older brothers and untold generations of Wagoners before them. "I'd hardly call it brave," Kelly said. "I mean, Krissie is second in the class with a 34 on her ACT, and she's a National Merit Semifinalist, a double legacy, and a woman in STEM."

"I know, Krissie's so amazing. But if there's only one spot and Brooke is applying too..." Amanda said, her question trailing off as her forehead creased to give the appearance of concern. The women were careful never to talk about Alicia or Brooke in front of Maren, convinced she reported back everything they said. "And what about Winnie? Have you heard anything?"

"I haven't, but maybe one of you can ask Maren?" She looked at Amanda. "You know, so it's not coming from—" Kelly stopped mid-sentence as the door opened and Maren returned carrying a tray with coffee. "That was fast, Maren. Thank you!"

"Well, I have news," Sarah said. "Over the weekend, Hannah finally flipped a coin between three schools. She's applying early to Middlebury."

"Oh, that's great! But gosh, isn't Vermont cold?" Amanda asked.

"Yeah, I'm pretty sure we can afford to buy her a new coat and boots if she gets in." Sarah rolled her eyes.

Maren sat back down at the table, and all eyes turned toward her.

"So, Maren," Amanda started in. "Has Winnie made any decisions about where she'll be applying early?"

"Her plan is UW Honors," Maren said matter-of-factly.

"Oh," Amanda said, raising her eyebrows and directing her next comment in Kelly's direction. "Isn't that great?"

While Amanda's methods were about as subtle as a sledgehammer, she could always be counted on to deliver the goods. Kelly pressed her lips together to suppress a smile. She wasn't shocked that Winnie had decided not to go head-to-head with the daughter of her mom's boss, but she was overjoyed to hear the words straight from Maren's mouth. Winnie had been Krissie's nemesis since arriving at EBA. At nearly every turn, Winnie had edged out Krissie for special honors, awards, and class rank. But those small losses no longer mattered. Kelly's eyes were now locked on the big prize, and Winnie had bailed out of the running. As far as Kelly was concerned, the only outcome worse than Krissie not getting the Stanford spot would be Winnie getting it. Given Kelly's education and commitment to her family as well as all she'd sacrificed to support Krissie and build her résumé, she really didn't want to lose to someone like Maren.

"UW will be so lucky to have her. How 'bout you, Jennifer?" Amanda said, shifting the conversation. "Where is Lily going early?"

Jennifer's face instantly went from smiling to blank. She adjusted her sweater and said, "Well, we've decided to respect Lily's privacy in the college journey."

Dead silence. But really, what could anyone say? Jennifer was merely following the counseling office's guidelines. Nevertheless, there was something about her rehearsed comment that rankled Kelly. Maybe it was her self-righteous tone. Kelly couldn't escape the feeling that Jennifer's closed lips were an indictment of her and the others talking openly about college. But everyone knew Lily wasn't Ivy Plus material, so maybe Jennifer could afford to follow the silly EBA rules.

"Y'all, it's all gonna work out," Augusta reassured. "Every kid is going to end up where they're meant—"

"Hi, everyone," Diana said, bursting into the room holding her small, white fluffball of a dog under one arm. "Sorry I'm late. Miss Fussypants here refused to let me put on her pearl necklace today. I had to bring her. I mean, we're planning College Critter Day after all." Diana held up her dog's face to her own and in a voice several octaves higher than normal said, "You can be the queen of College Critter Day. Yes, you can!"

Ordinarily, Kelly was not an animal person, and she was even less a fan of people who flouted rules, like the "No Dogs Allowed" signs clearly posted on each EBA entry door. And of people who dressed their pets in jewelry. But Diana was her friend now, so Kelly tried to be tolerant. She couldn't help noticing, though, that the dog's pearl necklace looked nicer than the one Kelly's in-laws had given her at the engagement party they'd thrown for her and Kevin years ago. Kelly made a mental note to text Diana after the meeting to update her on the college gossip she'd missed.

"Oh my God, Miss Marigold is so adorable!" Jennifer squealed.

"Look at her matching sweater and booties," Amanda cooed.

Kelly tried not to gag.

With a beatific smile, Diana pulled out a Swarovski crystal–encrusted water bottle, poured water into a matching dog bowl, and set it on the floor for Miss Marigold. After the first time Diana had done this during a meeting, Kelly had been curious and found the water bottle and bowl set online for $500 at Saks Fifth Avenue.

Over the incessant lapping sounds, Kelly said, "Looks like everyone's here. Why don't we get started? Lots to do to get ready for College Critter Day! Jennifer, you're the College Critter Day chair. Where should we begin?"

Jennifer turned in her seat. "Maren, were you able to get those EBA-branded tissue boxes we talked about in case anyone has an allergic reaction?"

Maren checked her notes. "Yes, I ordered twenty boxes."

"Diana, based on all your party planning experience, do you think twenty boxes is enough?" Jennifer asked.

"I already placed the order," Maren said. "If they run out, couldn't the students just use regular recycled tissues?"

"Oh my God, that's disgusting," Sarah said.

"Sarah!" Kelly laughed. "I think what Maren means is generic tissues that are also made out of recycled content, like the EBA-branded tissues. Not previously used tissues." Honestly, sometimes Kelly wondered how bright children emerged from such dim bulbs.

"Whoops! My bad," Sarah said with a lighthearted shrug. "Sorry, Maren."

Maren acknowledged the apology with a nod, but she was, as usual, all business. "I also ordered EBA-branded animal waste bags. And yes, they too are made from recycled content."

"Such good thinking, Maren," Kelly said. "And let me see, do you also have the pet labels for us to approve?"

"Yup. I was thinking B for bites, F for friendly, H for hypoallergenic, W for wash hands after petting," Maren said, reading from her notes.

"What about D for don't fucking touch me?" Amanda said, chuckling at her own suggestion.

"Do you think Double Ass will be OK with that one?" Sarah asked, her eyes wide with concern.

"She's kidding, Sarah," Kelly said. "Those sound fine, Maren. I'll run them by Ms. Richards just to be sure and then let you know so you can get them printed." Ms. Richards was the assistant to the assistant head of school and the faculty liaison for the SST. Augusta, the colorful Southern transplant, had dubbed her Double Ass early on, and the derogatory nickname had stuck, but Kelly refused to use it mostly because she worried she might slip up and say it to her in person.

The meeting proceeded apace with Maren providing updates and the rest of the SST members no doubt secretly thankful to be escaping without any action items. Kelly wrapped up the excruciating meeting, but at least it had yielded important intel. As far as Kelly was concerned, Winnie was mission accomplished. Now she set her sights on Brooke.

7

Alicia

ALICIA LEFT HER ROLLER bag in the front hall and called out, "Hello! Anyone home? Bryan? Brooke?" Her voice echoed through the house. Not even the dog bothered to come greet her. As Alicia walked into the kitchen, she dropped her handbag on an island chair and glanced at the familiar loopy handwriting on the counter.

> A—Cut-up veggies and fruit in the fridge. Found a new brand of dark chocolate called "Wicked Dark"—87 percent cacao—left a piece on your nightstand. Hair at 10 a.m. tomorrow.—M

Maren's terse two-word response ("message received") to the email ending Alicia's yearslong financial support of Winnie's education had been their only communication since Alicia had pressed Send. Relieved to see they were back to business as usual, at least on the surface, she crumpled up the note and tossed it in the recycling bin on her way to the fridge. She stood at the counter munching on a carrot, opened up the cable app on her phone, and turned off the Wi-Fi. A foolproof way to draw out her family.

Approximately eight seconds later, Brooke bellowed, "Dad, the Wi-Fi isn't working! Can you reboot it?" *Bingo.*

"Oh hey, babe, I didn't hear you come in," Bryan said, padding into the kitchen clad in cargo shorts and a faded UW Baseball T-shirt. "I gotta reboot the Wi-Fi."

A smirk played at Alicia's lips. "No need." She held up her phone and waggled it back and forth.

"You turned it off? What the hell? I was right in the middle of something." He ran a hand through his sandy-brown hair, making it stand on end.

"Seems like the only way to get you guys to talk to me."

"Oh gimme a break." Bryan bent down to open the undercounter beverage fridge and pulled out a bottle of beer. He flipped off the cap and took a long swig. "So how was…wait, what city were you in last night?" he asked, leaning against the counter.

"Salt Lake City. And it didn't go well." Alicia closed her eyes and massaged her temples. "My gut is telling me this acquisition might be a huge mistake. The CEO has been tweeting all kinds of crazy stuff."

"Dad, the Wi-Fi still isn't working," Brooke yelled as she clomped down the back staircase that ended next to the butler's pantry in the kitchen. She stopped cold when she saw her mother.

"Hello, sweetheart," Alicia said with all the false cheer she could muster. She was a CEO, not an Academy Award–winning actress, for God's sake. "I brought you back some saltwater taffy." She rooted around in her tote for the package and slid it down the island.

"You know salt water taffy isn't some special treat. They sell it at the grocery store." Brooke was no longer willing to exchange her anger at her mother for a guilt gift, but Alicia couldn't bring herself to stop trying.

"Consider it a treat for working on your essays. How'd the call go this afternoon with Professor Bejamaca?" Earlier that week, Alicia finally reached the professor her colleague had referred her to for college essay assistance. He charged her double given that the early admission application deadline was just over two weeks away, but at least he'd agreed to do it.

"Um, well, he had to reschedule," Brooke said, shooting her dad a conspiratorial look. "Dad said Mr. Clark told you last week that Stanford's only taking one more EBA student. You've known for a whole week. Why didn't you tell me when you got home from New York?"

Alicia glanced at her husband. Why did he insist on making everything more difficult? "If you'll recall, we had other things to discuss that night during the limited window in which you tolerated my presence. And besides, it doesn't change a thing." They'd spent forty-five minutes screaming about the other's ethical breaches—Brooke decrying her mother for hiring someone to write her essays and Alicia firing back that Brooke had no qualms about using her mother to cover up her unexcused absences. What would have been the point of giving her daughter yet another excuse not to finish her application?

"What about Winnie and Krissie? They're both planning to apply."

"Actually, Winnie is planning to apply to UW Honors, which is a terrific program and will be a great fit for her." Alicia swiped a carrot through the hummus with a flourish and relished the text she'd received from Diana relating Winnie's plans.

"Would you say that if I wanted to go to UW?" Brooke asked, nibbling her cuticle. A habit Alicia detested.

Alicia shot her husband an expectant look. On the topic of Brooke not going to his alma mater, they were aligned. For much different reasons, of course, but that was splitting hairs.

"B, you know I'm the biggest UW fan around. I bleed Husky purple," Bryan said, stopping for a sip of beer. "As much as I would love for you to go there, it's really important that you have the chance to go away to college and get out from under the glare of being Alicia Stone's kid."

"And you think going to Stanford, where there will literally be a building with our name on it, will do that?"

Bryan held up his hands. "Hey, it's not me saying it has to be Stanford."

"Why are you both so intent on flushing this opportunity down the toilet?" Alicia snapped. "It doesn't matter how you get in, and it doesn't matter what anyone thinks. To hear a lot of people tell it, the only reason I became the CEO was because some guy couldn't keep it in his pants. Not because I worked my butt off and earned it."

"Maybe, but unlike you, we both know I haven't earned Stanford. Just like I didn't earn my spot at EBA." Brooke crossed her arms and stared at her mother.

"I have no idea what you're talking about," Alicia said.

"Bullshit. I heard you and Dad talking about my shitty eighth-grade report card the summer before high school started. I heard you wonder if you'd made a mistake using Winnie's test scores to get me in. So don't fucking lie to my face. At least have the balls to admit what you did. I'm the one who's had to see Winnie every goddamn day the past three years knowing my own mom wishes she were her daughter instead of me—and worrying that someone is going to figure out I'm a total fraud. Winnie's the one who deserves the Stanford spot, not me. Or even that bitch Krissie. At least Winnie doesn't make me feel like an idiot the way

Krissie does. She never misses a chance to remind everyone she's smarter than me."

Brooke's lower lip quivered, so Alicia downshifted to a softer tone. She reached out to smooth her daughter's wavy dark-brown hair and tuck it behind her ear. "I know you think everything in life should be fair. But it's not. The world just doesn't work that way. Winnie will be fine at UW, and the good news is once you're at Stanford, you'll never have to see her again. And don't worry about Krissie," Alicia said, waving her hand dismissively. "Her mom is operating under the mistaken assumption that her hooks somehow matter. But, Brooke honey, I need you to do your part. Can you just finish your application, for the love of God?"

Brooke broke eye contact first with an exaggerated sigh. "Whatever. Why can't you just snap your fingers and have me admitted? Why do I even need to apply?"

"Don't whatever me, Brooke. Let me make this crystal clear—you will not embarrass me," Alicia said, enunciating each word. "This is about so much more than college. This is about my career. My image. If you can't get into Stanford with all my support, what does that say about me?"

"Alicia, come on," Bryan said, moving toward Brooke.

"Not another word out of you." Alicia pointed a finger at Bryan and then turned to look her daughter square in the face. "If you finish your goddamn application and manage to keep your mouth shut about whatever you think may or may not have happened with your admission to EBA, I will buy you a Range Rover. Do you understand?"

"Yes, I understand perfectly," Brooke said through gritted teeth.

————

Alicia finished her call and relaxed back into her in-home styling chair. Up until the day Alicia's regular stylist had canceled on Alicia and Brooke two hours before Brooke's fifth-grade graduation, Alicia hadn't realized what a wizard Maren was with hair and makeup. But after all the compliments they'd received that day, Alicia had immediately purchased the styling chair and added hair and makeup to Maren's regular duties. She smiled at Maren in the mirror. "Ugh, investors," she said, bugging out her eyes for effect as Maren applied product to Alicia's wet hair and began sectioning it out. They'd weathered bumps in their relationship before, but Alicia was a master at smoothing over uncomfortable situations. "I got Winnie a little gift," she said, pointing at a box sitting on the counter wrapped in paper with a repeating UW logo and a giant purple bow.

Alicia had been waiting in the parking lot when the university bookstore opened earlier that morning. She'd selected a light-gray hooded sweatshirt emblazoned with the words "University of Washington" in purple and a purple block W underneath and paid in cash. No need for rumors that Alicia Stone was seen buying a UW sweatshirt.

"Wow, word travels fast." Maren returned Alicia's smile. "That's so thoughtful, I'm sure Winnie will appreciate it." She turned on the hair dryer.

"Mare," Alicia said over the din of the dryer, trying to catch Maren's eye through the reflection in the mirror. "I never anticipated my mom's health would deteriorate so quickly. You have to understand, none of this is personal."

"I get it," Maren said, her eyes focused on Alicia's hair. "Family comes first."

Alicia stared down at her hands clasped together in her lap. It was clear from Maren's clipped response that she was pissed off, but it wasn't

Alicia's fault Stanford was only taking one more EBA student and that college admissions was not, and never would be, a meritocracy. "Does Winnie have her heart set on UW, or is she looking at other options like, I don't know, something like Arizona State or schools like that with honors colleges and merit scholarships?"

"She's got a couple of those schools on her list. With her grades, we're really hoping she gets some kind of merit scholarship at UW. I want to help her as much as I can, but, man, college is expensive." Maren finally looked up at Alicia. "Even if she gets tuition paid for, there's still room and board, a new computer, books, stuff for her dorm room."

"I'm sure I could help out with some of that stuff when the time comes," Alicia said, hoping her offer would ease the tension between them.

"I'm not asking for a handout, but a raise wouldn't hurt," Maren said, her eyes once again trained on her boss's tresses.

Alicia had lost track, but it had probably been several years since she'd given Maren a raise. She was paying Winnie's EBA tuition, after all, which went up 5 percent like clockwork each year. More than a cost of living adjustment. "OK, how about a 5 percent raise starting with your next paycheck? I'll text my accountant when we're done." She waved her phone in the air. A small price to pay to ensure Maren's continued loyalty.

Maren turned off the hair dryer and set it on the counter. "Thanks, Alicia. That will help."

"Oh good," Alicia beamed as she absorbed Maren's gratitude. The ship had been righted. Equilibrium restored. She grabbed her talking points as Maren moved on to the curling iron to create the beachy waves Alicia's image consultant said made her look powerful yet still youthful. The *New York Times* was flying a *Sunday Styles* reporter into town for a human-interest story. They were doing the interview at Alicia's house to position her as "she's just like us." Today wasn't the first time her PR flacks had taken advantage of her gender and mommy status to burnish the company's image. Soon after she'd been appointed CEO, the director of corporate communications had decided it would benefit the company to establish Alicia's personal brand as a leading woman in tech. Although Alicia hadn't been entirely comfortable becoming the feminist face of working women in tech, she'd been so focused on actually running the company that she'd trusted her PR team. They'd lined up a high-profile *60 Minutes* interview featuring Alicia as the new darling of Wall Street who had it all, including a supportive partner who shared equally in all parts of their home life and an adoring, accomplished daughter.

If only that were even remotely true. The reality was that as Alicia's career had ramped up, Bryan had done less and less around the house. After countless nasty arguments, Alicia had finally given up and backfilled the job, first with au pairs and then with Maren, who oversaw the entire childcare operation and eventually came to manage the housekeeper, the kitchen staff, the groundskeepers, the property managers for their personal homes, and just about every aspect of their lives. While Alicia could never admit it in an interview, in many ways, Maren was the supportive partner who made her career possible.

"Hair's done. Good luck with your interview," Maren said as she put the curling iron back on the dressing table. Spinning the styling chair around, she handed Alicia a hand mirror so she could check the back of her hair.

"Looks fabulous as always, Maren. Thank you. You're the best." She handed back the mirror. "I hope Winnie enjoys my gift. Our girls have such bright futures ahead of them."

8

Kelly

From: Kelly Vernon   Today, 11:05 p.m

To: Alicia Stone, Diana Taylor, Augusta Wagoner, Amanda Russell, Sarah Silver, Jennifer Tan

CC: Maren Pressley

Subject: SST Update

Hi, ladies,

First, congratulations to Jennifer on chairing a fabulous College Critter Day! The EBA-branded poop bags and tissues made from recycled content were right on target with the EBA Sustainability Policy. Yay for our negative carbon footprint!

I can't believe we had two hundred animals on campus! That's two for every senior! Other than the three epi shots the school nurse had to deliver, the two dogs mating in front of the gym, and Jasper Kincaid's potbellied pig giving birth in the quad, it was a wonderful event and no doubt helped our spectacular seniors during this incredibly stressful time in their lives. Making lemonade out of lemons, the Kincaids are generously letting us auction off the piglets. All money raised will support the EBA Sexual Health Awareness Program. The online auction will go live when the piglets are weaned... just in time for the holidays. Anyone want a piglet for Christmas?

Maren, when you get a chance, we would love an update on Snowcoming. It's just six weeks away! Is everything on track? Can't wait to hear who Alicia has in mind for the big surprise!

xx

Kelly

———

Kelly took her triple venti mocha with extra whipped cream back to her chair in the café. She'd given up manicures and her monthly massages, but she was not giving up her overpriced coffee even after her fight with Kevin this morning over their Visa bill. Kelly had been washing her face when he'd stormed into the bathroom waving a printout of the latest charges. One of the perils of being married to an accountant. He carefully monitored all spending in real time.

"We need to talk about this," he said.

"Can it wait until after I'm done getting ready?" Kelly asked, rinsing the last traces of soap from her face.

"There's a $900 charge from College Bound Tutoring." Kevin stared at her in the mirror. "Please tell me that's a mistake."

Kelly reached around her husband for a towel. Unable to afford a larger house in Seattle's overheated real estate market, they'd instead added a "master" bath to their attic bedroom when Krissie started middle school. There was no way they were going to survive five family members (including three teenagers) fighting over one bathroom. Instead of an en suite master bath with separate shower, jacuzzi tub, toilet room, and double sinks like so many other EBA parents had, they'd ended up with a three-quarter bath with a single sink and no counter space. Kevin had to bend his knees to take a shower under the sloped ceiling. Stalling for time, as apparently the conversation couldn't wait until she was done getting ready, Kelly patted her face dry. Even though last week, Kevin had said they couldn't afford any more tutoring, Kelly had added a tutoring session for Krissie after she'd come home hysterical about her upcoming Calc II test. Rather than just have the other kids sit in the car during Krissie's tutoring session, Kelly had figured she might as well add sessions for Katherine and Kaleb, which totaled six private hours of tutoring for the week at $150 a pop.

"I think it bears repeating, Kelly, we're paying $100,000 a year in tuition," he said, his face inches from hers given the lack of space in the bathroom. "I can't wrap my mind around why they all need tutors on top of that. Maybe we should be talking to the school?"

"One-on-one tutoring is so important. Especially for Krissie. It really helps reduce her stress," Kelly said, rubbing in her moisturizer. She knew Kevin would back down if she brought up their daughter's fragile mental state. "And science is always difficult for Katherine, you know that. The tutoring could be the difference between an A and an A-minus in AP

Chem. Kaleb needs as much help as he can get if you don't want to be editing his English papers into college. EBA does a great job teaching the kids to think, but they're terrible when it comes to teaching the mechanics of writing."

"Are you kidding? Why aren't we talking to the school about this?"

"Writing came so naturally to the girls that I didn't realize it was a problem." Kelly dabbed on some foundation. "I've been in to see Kaleb's teacher and the head of the middle school English department, but they don't see a problem with his writing, but that's because either his tutor or I edit everything before it gets turned in."

"Here's a radical idea: don't edit his work so the teacher can see the problem for herself."

"But every parent is doing this. It's not just me." Kelly walked back into their bedroom. "If we don't help Kaleb, he'll suffer in comparison, and the teacher will think he's the one with a problem."

"It sounds like he is the one with the problem," Kevin said, following her. "So what's the IvyPlusorBust.com charge for $2,500?"

"They're reviewing all of Krissie's essays." Kelly looked for her stretchiest jeans. "Last year, they had a twenty-five percent acceptance rate for clients who applied to Stanford."

"Jesus, how do you know they didn't have four clients and one got in? And anyway, we discussed this a week ago, and I said absolutely not. How could you go behind my back and do this?"

"Krissie was freaking out last weekend when you were out of town with Kaleb at his fencing tournament. She didn't think they were good enough, and Ms. Barstow had already reviewed them. I didn't know what else to do," Kelly said as she pulled on her jeans.

"Kelly," Kevin said, slumping on the bench at the end of their bed.

"We can't afford this. And there's no way we can do all this for Katherine and Kaleb. I just filed our taxes and took a hard look at our finances. These are my peak earning years, and the only money we saved this year was what the company deducted for my 401(k). I didn't even max it out. Have you even thought about what would happen to us if I dropped dead of a heart attack or got cancer or something? It happens to people our age. Just look at what happened to the Ropers."

"Oh please. You're one of the healthiest people I know. You go running five times a week."

"Yeah, well, so did Tom Roper. All I'm saying is we have to get our spending under control and start saving something. The last thing I want to do is take out a second mortgage to pay for college, but it's looking more and more like that might be our only option."

"I'm not trying to bring financial ruin on our family, but we're so close to the finish line," Kelly said as she zipped up her hoodie, which she noticed was tighter than usual. "After everything we've sacrificed and spent already, is now really the time to pull back? With Winnie applying to UW, Krissie is—"

"Kelly!" Kevin interrupted. "You're not hearing me. You've got to go back to work. We need the money, but more than anything, it might give you some perspective. If I'd known how much EBA would change our priorities, I might not have agreed to send the kids there." He shook his head, his lips pressed together in a thin line. "I gotta go."

Kevin's indictment stung. On some level, Kelly knew she'd gotten too wrapped up in EBA, but the more she witnessed the workings of that world of privilege, the more she feared her kids would be left behind if she didn't go pedal to the metal to make up for their family's relative lack of resources. In the past, Kevin had taken pains to reassure Kelly that her contributions to the family were valued even though they didn't come with a paycheck. But over the past year, he'd started hinting that maybe she should redirect some of the time and energy she devoted to volunteering at EBA to something that paid. Although he never offered to help more at home if she went back to work. In fact, she couldn't remember the last time he'd folded laundry, gone to the grocery store, fixed dinner, or cleaned the house. Who was going to do all that on top of managing the kids if she went back to work?

For that matter, who would even hire her? The marketing skills she'd honed nearly twenty years ago were hopelessly obsolete now. Once again, Kelly reminded herself it had been her choice to give up eighty-hour workweeks—and lots of stock options—for the privilege of staying home and raising her children, which that morning had already meant cooking three different breakfasts, packing three different lunches, and driving the kids to school. Now she listened to a podcast through her AirPods as she sipped her coffee. A few minutes of hard-earned bliss before heading home to do laundry, scrub the family's two overused toilets, and vacuum out the dryer vent. Why had she thought staying home was the better deal?

The café was hopping. With a fleeting glance, she saw two twenty-somethings take the empty table directly behind her. She instantly recognized one of the women. It was Ms. Lawson, the most junior member of the EBA college counseling team. Thank goodness Krissie hadn't been assigned to her; otherwise, Kelly would've had no choice but to sign up for IvyPlusorBust.com's full plan, which was a whopping $15,000.

Kelly took out her AirPods and strained to hear their conversation. She could only make out a few words here and there, but it was clear Ms. Lawson was talking about EBA. Recalling a trick Kaleb had recently played on his sisters (for which he'd been grounded), Kelly tucked her phone into her purse, which she slung over the back of her chair, grabbed her coffee, and made her way over to the other side of the café. Keeping her eyes down to avoid attracting attention, Kelly slid into a chair and popped her AirPods back in. Ms. Lawson was indeed talking about EBA, and Kelly could now hear every word thanks to a technological glitch—or miracle—that had turned her iPhone into a spyware microphone worthy of the Russian KGB.

"I don't know how much longer I can keep working there," Ms. Lawson said, "especially if things don't work out for this one girl."

"Why?"

"Oh my God, I'll have to show you her essay. It's incredible! It's about her and her mom. They were homeless for a while when she was little. Her mom works, like, three jobs. The girl has been working since she was twelve. She has such a fresh voice. She's actually self-made and so authentic. She doesn't need all the extras like tutoring, boot camps, select sports, and service learning trips to Central America that the other parents fall all over themselves to provide. She's so different compared with the other students I work with. No sense of entitlement. She's all grit and determination. Exactly what the elite colleges are all saying they want."

"She sounds amazing. How'd she end up in a snake pit like EBA?"

Ms. Lawson chuckled. "I don't know for sure, but it probably has something to do with Alicia Stone. Her mom works for her."

"*The* Alicia Stone?"

"The one and only. But that's part of the problem."

"What do you mean?"

"Stanford's been this girl's top choice forever, and last year, I made the mistake of telling her she'd be a terrific candidate and totally supported her applying early admission. In addition to the great essay, she has it all—grades, leadership, test scores. And she'll be the first in her family to go to college."

Kelly's stomach dropped. "That can't be right," she muttered to herself, utterly incredulous that this critical piece of information had somehow evaded her.

"I don't get it. What's the problem? Is it money?"

"Nah, I don't think that's the issue. Stanford is need-blind. But two weeks ago, we found out that Stanford is only taking one more student from our school because we're already sending four athletes. So I was told in no uncertain terms to encourage her to apply early to any other school besides Stanford."

"Why?"

"No one said it in quite so many words, but I think it's because of Alicia Stone. She's a Stanford trustee and a huge EBA donor. She made it clear to the head of school she wants her daughter to go there, but she's kind of a screw-up. I mean, at least compared to the other girl. Please don't ever quote me on that!"

"Oh shut up! You know I'd never say anything," the friend said. "Wait, so what's your student going to do?"

"She absolutely refuses to pick another school. She's planning to apply to Stanford even though—you won't believe this—she told me her mom's afraid she'll get fired if Alicia finds out. Says if she gets in, they'll figure something out. I've got to admire her. She knows exactly what she wants. I'm twenty-eight and still have no idea. She's been telling everyone she's going for UW Honors to protect her mom's job. Only the counseling office knows Stanford's still the plan, but we're not telling anyone anything."

This time, Kelly covered her mouth to stifle her outrage. The balls on Winnie and Maren. Who did they think they were, lying to everyone's face about Winnie applying to UW Honors? And enlisting the school in their deception?

"God, I hear all this stuff, and I'm not sure I ever want to have kids. Are all the parents this bonkers?"

"Pretty much, yeah."

As the conversation took a personal turn, Kelly yanked out her AirPods. She was boiling mad. On top of everything else, Ms. Lawson had never even once referred to Krissie as a viable candidate for the spot. If this was a two-horse race, Ms. Lawson should have been comparing *Krissie* to Winnie. All Brooke had was a meager academic record and a mom with millions. Though Kelly couldn't completely discount Brooke, she still, in her heart of hearts, refused to believe Stanford would be that craven. But if Winnie really had a first-gen hook, that could be serious trouble for Krissie. If Winnie and Maren were willing to lie about applying to UW, she had to wonder: What else were they willing to lie about? To hell with EBA. To hell with this unfair process. Kelly crossed the café, scooped up her belongings, and hightailed it to her car. She had work to do.

————

Kelly clutched the steering wheel as she sped home, triaging everything she'd just heard to determine what she could use to her advantage. While fascinated to learn that Maren and Winnie had been homeless, Kelly knew such hardship would not necessarily benefit Winnie. Even if that nitwit counselor thought she'd written a great essay. A group of college admissions officers from several highly selective schools had conducted an essay writing workshop for EBA parents and students the previous spring. Their guidance had been clear—avoid topics involving death, disease, and disability. And whatever you do, don't make them read another essay about a service trip to Costa Rica. They'd even pointed out that previously compelling topics, like homelessness, were now considered overdone.

For the past several months, Kelly had taken some measure of comfort that Krissie had two hooks from Ms. Barstow's sacred list to vault her to the front of the line, whereas Winnie had none. She'd blithely assumed the ultracompetent Maren had gone to college—probably just a crappy one she wouldn't want to brag about. Now she had to know for sure, and there was only one way to find out.

Kelly pulled into her driveway with three hours before school pickup. Gripped with purpose, she opened her laptop at the kitchen island. In college, Kelly had worked for the school's daily paper. Her biggest reporting scoop had begun with an anonymous tip that the hot new student-run magazine had been faking its own letters to the editor— letters that were supposedly written by students and faculty from universities around the country. After receiving the tip, she'd figured out if she simply called the registrar's office at each university, she could confirm whether the names on the letters actually matched those of enrolled students or alums. Unfortunately, this time, all she had to go on was that Maren had grown up somewhere in the Midwest. She gambled that Maren had stayed close to home for college and started dialing.

It took Kelly two hours and twenty-four phone calls to discover exactly what she was looking for. That one Maren Pressley had enrolled at Indiana University eighteen years ago. *Gotcha.* Winnie would be precluded from leveraging the valuable first-generation college hook.

Now she just had to figure out how to expose the lie those duplicitous

Pressley girls were perpetrating on both EBA and Stanford—without it coming back to bite her.

———

As Kevin wandered into the kitchen trolling for an evening snack, Kelly pulled a pint of ice cream out of the freezer. "So I was waiting for the kids to scatter," Kevin said, glancing back toward the family room. "I finally heard back from Steve. No dice on the recommendation letter. He said he already wrote one for Brooke Stone."

Kelly stopped midscoop. "Are you kidding? Alicia's a trustee. Why would Brooke need another trustee to recommend her?"

Kevin shrugged and sat down at the island.

"Dammit," Kelly said, plopping a generous helping into each bowl and pushing one toward Kevin with a spoon.

"It's not like a letter would have made that much of a difference."

"No, I know, it's just that today I learned Winnie's applying to Stanford after all."

"What happened to UW?" Kevin asked.

"I think Winnie and Maren were lying about UW because if Alicia finds out, they're worried Maren will lose her job."

"Won't Alicia fire her if Winnie gets in?"

"I have no idea, but that's not the only thing she's been lying about," Kelly said, adding another smidge of ice cream to her bowl. "She's also been lying to the school about having a first-generation college hook."

"Are you serious?" Krissie yelled as she stormed into the kitchen. "How am I supposed to compete with all these people lying and cheating their way into Stanford?"

Kelly and Kevin exchanged looks. "What do you mean, 'all these people'?" Kelly asked, wondering how much Krissie had heard.

"You just said Winnie's lying about applying to UW and lying about having a first-generation college hook. And then yesterday, Brooke skipped class and was vaping outside the window of my AP Lang class. I heard her laughing about how her mom hired a college professor to write all her essays. How am I supposed to compete with all that?" Tears streamed down Krissie's face.

"Alicia paid someone to write Brooke's essays?" Kelly wondered how much that had cost. Krissie's essays were fine, but this whole process would have been a lot less stressful if Kelly could have paid someone too. Chalk it up to another perk of being wealthy. Buy your way out of stress and right into college.

"For starters," Kevin said, "you can hold your head up high knowing we did everything on the up-and-up."

Kelly took a large bite of ice cream. Kevin's statement had been technically true until about seven hours ago when she'd engaged in a bit of vigilante justice to punish Maren and Winnie for lying to everyone and to regain Krissie's advantage in the Stanford competition. Specifically, she'd purchased a disposable phone and carefully crafted an anonymous text with two pieces of information about Winnie, one true and one false. She sent the text separately to Alicia, Diana, Amanda, Sarah—and herself as cover. If the plan worked as expected, her fellow EBA moms would spread the rumors far and wide, and Ted Clark would be deluged with irate parent phone calls by morning. After all, Kelly wasn't the only EBA parent gripped by college mania.

"That's just great," Krissie snapped. "But if everyone else is playing all these games, maybe we're just the losers playing by the rules."

"I know you're upset, but sacrificing your integrity is never the answer. You're an amazing person, and Stanford would be insane not to want you over those two," Kevin said.

"Dad's right, and everyone knows Brooke isn't even in your league," Kelly said, wiping away the tears on her daughter's cheeks. "She barely has a 3.5, and I have it on good authority she's taken the ACT four times."

"I know, so once again, the problem is Winnie. It's always Winnie," Krissie said, her voice rising. "All the teachers treat her like she's so special because she's less fortunate than everyone else. I'm so sick of it!" Krissie's left hand flew up to the hair just behind her ear.

"Krissie, please." Kelly reached out to stop her. She prayed this news wouldn't cause Krissie to start pulling out her hair again.

Krissie slapped her mom's hand away. "Stop it. I'm fine. I'm applying to Stanford. And I am not losing to Winnie this time." She stomped out of the room.

Kelly took a step to follow her, but Kevin held up his hand. "Let her go." He dug into his ice cream.

Kelly deliberately maintained a neutral expression. With her anonymous text already making the rounds, she figured Winnie's plans would be toast by the end of the week. If Alicia didn't take care of her, Kelly had no doubt the mob of mothers with kids applying to Ivy Plus schools would. And now she had new information that Brooke was cheating. If she was being honest, the thought of going after the daughter of Alicia Stone scared the crap out of her. But she didn't have to think about that yet. After all, she couldn't contact Stanford to report a fraudulent application that hadn't yet been submitted. She only hoped that when the time came, she'd have the guts to use this new ammunition.

9

Alicia

ASPYRE WAS ENTANGLED IN a shareholder lawsuit over the $65 million payout the board of directors granted to the founder and CEO after he was fired for sexual harassment. The suit had dragged on in the background as Alicia assumed control of the company, and its existence was a constant reminder of the precariousness of her position. To keep her job, Alicia needed the backing of the board of directors, most of whom had supported the decision to award the sleazeball the big payout in the first place. But defending the board's decision put her personal brand of female empowerment at risk. To complicate matters, Alicia herself had paid off one of their tenants who'd accused Bryan of sexual harassment two years ago. Bryan was adamant that the woman was only a victim of her own lack of humor. Apparently, the leggy redhead hadn't found his obviously playful offers of earned rent reductions very funny. If word ever leaked about the settlement, though, Alicia stood to lose everything.

After postponing her deposition four times and buying herself another six months, the judge put his foot down. She'd been locked in a conference room all day with half a dozen lawyers. Exhausting to be sure, but at least the secret settlement never came up. While she waited for the valet to bring her car around, Alicia pulled her phone from her handbag. Her eyes popped at the notification that she had 157 unread texts, surely an all-time record for her. What was going on? She clicked on the most recent message, which was part of a group text with easily two dozen EBA moms. From the looks of it, this chain accounted for the majority of her new messages.

Amanda: Me too!!!!!

Peggy: Me too!!

Kelly: I think he needs to hear from all of us.

Holly: I've already left a message…

Barbara: OMG! So ungrateful!

Diana: This cannot stand. Ted is going to get an earful from me!

Nora: Ted Clark needs to see this. Unacceptable!

Ugh. How can so many women say so little? She didn't have time to get to the bottom of yet another crisis du jour manufactured by a bunch of bored EBA moms; she had actual work to do. After dispensing with a few Aspyre messages, she clicked on a text from an unfamiliar number:

Winnie Pressley is a liar. Her first-gen college hook is bogus. And she's applying to every top 10 college—goal is to run the table to prove she's the best

Are you fucking kidding me? Adrenaline surged through her. Suddenly, it all made sense. She flipped back to the outraged moms and paged up until she confirmed that the flurry of texts she'd dismissed thirty seconds earlier as nonsense was actually about Winnie and Maren. She practically dragged the valet out of her car. As she roared out into traffic, Alicia commanded her phone to call Bryan.

"Hey, Leesh, what's up?"

"I should fire her! That fucking bitch!"

"Whoa, slow down. What's going on?"

"Winnie is applying to every goddamn top-ten school," Alicia shrieked into the speaker. "There isn't a college list in the country that doesn't have Stanford at the top."

"What? How do you know?"

"I got a text! FUUUUUUUCK!" Alicia said, pounding her steering wheel. "Dammit, I thought I took care of this. I even gave her a raise. How could they do this to us? After everything I've done for them. I don't even want to be in the same room as her! Is she at the house?"

"I'm just walking in now," Bryan said. "Her car wasn't in the driveway."

"She fucking lied to my face, right to my face." Alicia slammed on the brakes as she approached a red light, thankful for the fully tinted windows on her Mercedes AMG SUV. The last thing she needed was someone snapping a photo of her screaming in her car like a lunatic. "I can't believe I gave Winnie a fucking UW sweatshirt. Did they think I wasn't going to find out?"

"That's nuts," Bryan said. Alicia could hear him opening the refrigerator.

"Oh, and guess what else?" she sniped. "Professor Bejamaca emailed that Brooke blew off their call yesterday. For the third time! He said he's very busy and we're running out of time so he's not sure how to proceed. I sent you both a reminder text. What the hell?"

"I reminded her," Bryan said. "I assumed she did it."

Alicia ignored the sheepishness in his voice. "Dammit, Bryan!" Alicia said, rubbing her forehead. "It's not like I can ask Maren to do this. Why didn't you watch her do the call? You knew she didn't want to do it. For Christ's sake, she'd already blown it off twice."

"Come on, Alicia."

"What were you so busy doing yesterday afternoon that you weren't around to make sure she did the call? Tell me."

Bryan didn't respond.

"Nothing. That's what I thought. You're fucking pathetic. End call," she screamed.

———

When she arrived home, Alicia blew past her useless husband sprawled on the couch in the TV room off the kitchen. Sometimes she wondered why she stayed married to him at all, but then she'd talk herself down. At least the sex was still great. And the last thing she had time for was a divorce. She ran up the stairs and slammed the door to her home office. Ever since she'd hung up on Bryan, she'd been fixated on the other part of the anonymous text—that Winnie's first-generation college hook was bogus. Alicia vaguely recalled a presentation during the last Stanford trustees meeting touting first-gen as an institutional priority. She'd zoned out, assuming first-gen was a politically correct term for race-based affirmative action. Certainly not meant for blue-eyed white girls. It never occurred to her Winnie would try to use it.

Even though Maren was more resourceful, a faster learner, and a better manager than most of her highly qualified employees at Aspyre, college definitely hadn't come up on the background check Alicia had run when she first hired Maren. And Maren had never once mentioned going to college. Alicia knew she'd gotten pregnant when she was seventeen or eighteen at the oldest. There was just no way Maren could have gone to college.

But the person who sent the text seemed to think Winnie had a parent who went to college. If it wasn't Maren, the only possibility was Winnie's father, whom Maren insisted was a nameless one-night stand. But Maren had lied to her face about Winnie applying to UW. Had she been lying all along that Winnie didn't have a dad too?

Over the years, Alicia had tried to ask Maren about her background and childhood, but the boundaries of their relationship confused her. She'd entrusted the care of her only child to Maren and had invited her into nearly every single aspect of her life, but the intimacy didn't flow in the other direction. Maren volunteered very little about her own life, and Alicia was met with a brick wall the few times she'd fished for details about Winnie's origins. Eventually, Alicia gave up asking. Maren did such great work and was always there when she needed her, so what did it matter? But now Alicia needed to know the truth about Winnie's father. And she had an idea for how she might find him.

Back when Brooke was in eighth grade at EBA, all students were required to participate in the EBA Science Fair. As had become their household habit, Brooke procrastinated until Alicia had no choice but to do her assignment for her. Not long before, Alicia had bonded with the CEO of a consumer genetics company at a tech leaders summit. She emailed her new contact for science fair ideas and received a page-long list of suggestions from the VP of marketing and a discount code for the $200 test on apairofgenes.com. All Brooke needed to do was find a dozen people who would agree to spit in a test tube and take the DNA test, participate in a short survey on their exercise habits, and then, once they received the results of their tests, share whether they had a propensity for building slow-twitch or fast-twitch muscle fibers.

Bryan took Brooke to his gym, and they were home an hour later with several samples. The rest of the samples were provided by the housekeeper, the chef, her personal trainer, and Winnie, who just happened to be staying with the Stones for a few days while Maren was in Del Mar stocking up their new vacation property. Because Winnie was a minor and Maren was gone, Alicia had set up the account for Winnie by pretending to be her legal guardian. Alicia had planned to tell Maren about the DNA experiment but then worried Maren might overreact given their blowup earlier in the year about Brooke's EBA entrance exam and eventually decided it was better left unsaid. In the years since, Alicia had received countless emails from apairofgenes.com prompting her to log in and see updated results or to try its new ancestry DNA offering. She'd never given the emails a second thought. Until now.

She typed "www.apairofgenes.com" into the search bar and hit Return. On the login page, she entered her private email address and was relieved to find she'd saved the auto-generated password. Alicia clicked on the ancestry DNA tab and moved the cursor over the words "Winnie Pressley's Ancestry Match." Her heart raced, and her face was burning up. She lifted her hair off her neck and welcomed the kiss of cool air. Was this a hot flash? Or just good old-fashioned guilt? But what choice did she have? For all she knew, Winnie had a long-standing relationship with her dad and was lying to everyone about her first-generation college hook. Who knew what they were capable of hiding?

Alicia clicked the link. Within seconds, she was staring at a picture of Winnie's father. Familiar big blue eyes stared back: Winnie's eyes. "Chase Alder," she read aloud. "Who are you?" Fingers flying, she brought up his bio on the website of a law firm she'd never heard of. Her eyes skimmed past the boring stuff about his practice areas and clients until she came to the line that mattered. Chase received his BA from Yale University and a JD from Northwestern Law School. Winnie was a legacy at Yale. Why the hell wasn't she applying there? Alicia continued reading to discover that Winnie's father lived in San Mateo, California, with his wife, Naomi, and their two children. He'd included his graduation years (something no woman in her right mind would ever include in a corporate bio). Alicia did the mental math. Oh my God! This Chase character would have been sixteen when he got Maren pregnant.

If Maren and Winnie had any relationship at all with Papa Yale Bulldog, it would blow Winnie's first-gen hook to smithereens. But there was one glaring problem: How could Alicia ensure that EBA knew about this lie without revealing that she—a CEO of a major public company—had conducted an illicit DNA search? Her hands were tied.

———

For the entire next day, Alicia avoided both her husband, with whom she was still annoyed, and Maren. Her outrage over Maren's lies burned brightly, and she didn't trust herself to play it cool while she figured out what to do with the information she'd learned about the identity of Winnie's father. The only person she made an effort to see was Brooke, who had capitulated and done the interview call with Professor Bejamaca under Alicia's watchful eye in an Aspyre conference room. Alicia took a small measure of comfort that Brooke's essays were finally in process, even if Brooke wasn't the one writing them. They were in the homestretch of this college admissions nonsense.

Through meeting after meeting about lawsuits, user data privacy concerns, and possible financial fraud committed by the start-up they were trying to acquire, Alicia was consumed by how to use the information about Winnie's father. Confronting Maren was out of the question. How could Alicia ever explain or justify how she'd come to possess the information? But she was running out of time to block Winnie from applying to Stanford. Not knowing where to turn, Alicia called Ted Clark on her way home from the office to see if she could get anything out of him without giving herself away, but she got his voicemail.

At ten p.m., she popped one and a half Ambien pills. Two hours later, she had to face facts: even a megadose wasn't enough to thwart the sleep-thieving beast that seemed determined to haunt her night after night. Fed up with her restless tossing, Alicia tiptoed across the hall to her office for her iPad. There, she curled up on the couch under a pile of throw blankets, simultaneously shivering and overheating in that way only a middle-aged woman can. Pulling her iPad under the blankets with her, she searched for a show to trick her insomnia into retreat, fare that would distract without enlivening. *The Real Housewives of Beverly Hills* must have done the trick, because the next thing she knew, her Apple Watch was vibrating with a phone call from Ted. It was a quarter after seven.

"Ted?" she squeaked into her wrist.

"Good morning, Al—" he said before Alicia interrupted him.

"Is it true?" Her voice croaked. "Is Winnie applying early to Stanford?" Alicia sat motionless, waiting for Ted's response.

"You know I can't talk to you about another student's plans."

She could hear the annoyance in his voice, but she pressed on anyway. "Ted, I have to know."

"Come on, Alicia."

"Maren told me last week, to my face, that Winnie wants UW Honors. But then I heard that was a lie. Can't you just tell me if she's planning to apply to Stanford? I have to know." The sound of her own voice begging roiled Alicia's stomach. Ted was probably enjoying making her grovel.

"Look," Ted said, clearing his throat. "From what I understand, Winnie's pretty dug in. I think she's planning to apply."

"Let me understand." Alicia moved to the edge of the couch. "Everything she and Maren have been running around town saying about UW is a bald-faced lie?"

"I think she's still applying to UW as a backup, so that's technically true."

"Don't be cute with me," Alicia snapped. "There are a dozen other highly selective schools she could apply early to, and you couldn't figure out a way to get her to apply to one of them?"

"What can I tell you?" Alicia could hear his exasperation. "She really wants to go to Stanford."

"I'm just curious." Alicia paused. "Have you read Winnie's essay or reviewed her application?"

"Her college counselor is handling that," Ted said. "It's not something I get involved with as head of school."

"I see," she said, keeping her voice steady. "Why does Winnie think she's got a chance with only one spot available? Does she have a hook I'm not aware of?"

"Alicia, it's really not appropriate for me to talk about other students like this. Please don't put me in this position."

"What position is that? The one where you deny very basic information to the lead donor of your current capital campaign?"

"Fine," he said, exhaling loudly. Alicia smirked at how quickly he'd caved. "From what I understand, her essay is about her unique life experience."

"Isn't that the point of every applicant's essay?" Alicia rolled her eyes.

"I just meant, you know, surviving a period of homelessness, working multiple jobs. Maren's worked for you for a long time. I assume you know all this, right?"

"Of course I do."

"Look, Alicia, we can encourage and nudge, but we can't control where a student applies. But listen, I don't think you should lose sleep over Winnie."

"Why?" Alicia asked, latching on to what sounded like promising news. "What do you know?"

"All I can say is that while Winnie's an excellent student, no one gets into Stanford these days without at least one solid hook, sometimes even two. If their selectivity trend continues apace, they'll be down to an unprecedented three percent acceptance rate by the end of this admission cycle. Winnie's been counting on a first-generation-to-college hook, but there have been some recent developments that may make it difficult for us to support that hook."

"Wait, what?" Alicia shook her head, trying to clear the Ambien fog.

"Oh good." She relaxed back into the couch. "So you already know about her dad going to Yale. Why aren't you trying to convince her to apply there instead of Stanford? At least she'd be a legacy."

"Yale? What are you talking about?"

"What are you talking about?" Alicia quickly turned the question back on Ted, realizing that maybe they weren't in possession of the same set of facts. *Shit.*

"Well, just that Maren may have attended college. We're looking into it. Did you say Winnie has a dad?"

"Everyone has a dad, Ted," Alicia scoffed. "But it's probably best if we keep that just between us."

10

Maren

AS ALWAYS, THE STONES' huge golden retriever, Cardinal, greeted Maren with an exuberant tackle. When Cardinal was a new puppy in the household four years before, Bryan had made it known to all he would not "break the spirit" of his new little buddy (i.e., put in the time and effort to train him in basic civility). As a result, Cardinal had the manners of a six-month-old puppy in a one-hundred-and-twenty-pound frame. Maren braced herself with one knee up to guard against his paws landing on her chest. She'd learned that lesson the hard way after the time Cardinal managed to stamp two perfect muddy pawprints on her white blouse, one on each breast, like sponge-on tattoos. Of course, Bryan had a field day teasing her about that. "You're such a kink puppy, Maren." "Love the paw pasties. Can you do pussies tomorrow?" Even the fleeting memory of his raunchy comments still repulsed her.

Cardinal finally tired of humping her, which allowed Maren to get through the foyer and make a break for the kitchen. On the way, she peeked in the main floor guest room and caught a glimpse of the ferociously unmade bed, a clear indication Bryan had received another demerit from his perpetually pissed-off wife. What a mess. How did he manage to kick off not just the blankets and sheets in his sleep but even the mattress cover? Was this something all men did? Or just slobs like Bryan?

Bryan was likely already off at one of his country clubs, but just in case, she lightened her footsteps in hopes of getting a jump on her work without having to interact with him. Her first errands were across the lake in Bellevue: dropping off the kitchen knives for sharpening and delivering the super-automatic espresso maker to its routine maintenance appointment at the European coffee gear shop. On the way back, she'd stop to pick up Alicia's newly tailored suits. If traffic cooperated, she'd be back by eleven a.m. and could dive into the pile of bills that awaited her. Peeking in the kitchen, she saw that the coast was clear and made her way over to the storage drawer where the chefs stuck the dull knives until they could be sharpened and put back into rotation.

As she tucked the last knife into the bag with padded sleeves she'd found online for this purpose, a hint of warmth brushed across her neck. She whirled around to find Bryan's face inches from hers, his body bare save for crumpled Brooks Brothers boxers.

Startled, Maren slid a few steps into the coffee alcove. "Oh hi, Bryan. Sorry—I was just about to take the espresso maker in for cleaning. Have you had your coffee yet?"

Bryan moved in again, instantly canceling out her sidestep maneuver. "Who needs coffee when I have you to get me going?" He wiggled his eyebrows.

"Very funny!" She'd come to think of Bryan as her number one occupational hazard, but a bit of lighthearted banter always cleared a path to the exit. This morning, though, he was a little too close for comfort. It was only eight thirty a.m. Was that booze on his breath? "Hey—I forget. Are you taking Cardinal for his morning walk today, or am I?"

"We could just skip his walk and get another form of exercise." He reached out to touch her forearm, but Maren saw it coming and turned away to unplug the espresso machine.

"Don't you have a golf game or something you need to be leaving for?" Maren suggested.

"Come on, Maren," Bryan pleaded. "Alicia's got me sleeping in the guest room."

"Bryan," she said, shaking her head. "When are you going to accept no as my final answer?" She took a step toward the kitchen to grab a rag so she could wipe down the machine, but Bryan remained in her way.

"You know you'd miss me if we had to let you go," he said, grinning down at Maren.

Maren froze. Was Bryan just being his usual audacious self, or was he actually threatening her job? She forced a chuckle. "What are you talking about?"

He abruptly dropped the grin. "Just that Alicia is super pissed about Winnie applying to Stanford."

"What? No, Alicia's got it all wrong. Winnie's applying to UW. I swear! We wouldn't do that to Brooke." Why would Alicia be doubting their intentions? Especially after the crystal-clear missive withdrawing college tuition and putting Winnie's last semester at EBA at risk. They'd have to be out of their minds to cross her under these circumstances.

"I really want to believe you," Bryan said, leaning heavily into her personal space again. "But I don't know, people are talking. And we both

know how ruthless Alicia can be when she doesn't get what she wants."
He made a show of scratching his unshaven chin. "Now, don't you think
I deserve a little thank-you for this heads-up?" Bryan asked in a tone that
was both menacing and whiny, something only a rich white man could
pull off.

Before Maren could respond, Ariana, the beautiful young prep cook,
sauntered into the kitchen, hips swaying. "Hiya, Bryan!"

Bryan swiveled his head and greeted her with an appreciative smile
and a smarmy full-body appraisal. Ariana smiled brightly and returned
the favor. *Saved by the belle.* Bryan was so predictable it was embarrassing, but Maren had learned how to survive in this job by preying on his
allergy to focus.

Snatching up the bag of knives, she dashed out the side door. Her
pulse raced as she got into her car and tossed the knives on the passenger seat. *What was that all about?* Maren hardly needed a heads-up from
Bryan that his wife could be ruthless. And anyway, she and Winnie had
gotten the message loud and clear about Stanford. Why would Bryan
think otherwise? But this wouldn't be the first time Bryan had gotten his
facts wrong.

It wasn't until she was almost across the lake that she realized she'd
left the espresso machine in the kitchen. She'd have to reschedule with
the espresso guru for later in the week. As for Cardinal's morning walk
and crap? Well, Bryan could put on some pants and walk his own damn
dog.

———

From: Ted Clark   Today, 10:20 a.m.

To: Maren Pressley

Subject: Meeting Request

Hi, Maren,

I need to discuss a few things with you about Winnie's Stanford application. Can you swing by my office today at noon?

Ted

———

From: Maren Pressley   Today, 10:25 a.m.

To: Ted Clark

Re: Meeting Request

Hi, Ted,

Your info is out of date. Winnie's no longer applying there. She's going for UW Honors.

———

From: Ted Clark   Today, 10:27 a.m.

To: Maren Pressley

Re: Meeting Request

_____

Please come anyway. I need to discuss a few things with you in person.

_____

"What's going on?" Maren said as soon as Ted closed his office door behind her. Disturbed by their email exchange, especially coming right on the heels of her "heads-up" conversation with Bryan, she was determined to set the record straight.

"Well, hello to you too, Maren," he teased.

"Sorry," Maren said as she shrugged her arms out of her jacket and sat down in the chair facing him. "I sometimes forget not everyone is too busy for pleasantries. Let me start again. Hello, Ted." She cracked a brief smile.

Over the past several years, they'd developed a comfortable rapport through their work together at EBA, with Maren serving as Alicia's representative. Although Ted had asked her out a few more times after Diana's party, she appreciated that he had taken her rejections graciously. She had always felt guilty about using Ted's obvious infatuation with her the night of Diana's party all those years ago to help Alicia and make a few bucks. A part of her had even occasionally wondered what might have happened if they'd met under different circumstances. However, once Winnie got into EBA, the issue was moot anyway. It would definitely be frowned upon for an administrator to date the mother of a student.

Ted smiled back, but Maren noticed he was more disheveled than usual. His polka-dot skinny tie in EBA navy blue and yellow was loosened and askew, and the sleeves of his button-down were sloppily rolled and shoved up his forearms. He squeezed his eyes shut in an exaggerated blink as though to remedy a bad case of dry eye, and Maren could hear the incessant ringing of the office phones in the next room.

"Well, thanks for meeting in the middle of the day like this," he said, clearing his throat. "So, um, this is a little delicate, but we've received some information, and I just need to ask you a few questions about Winnie's family educational history. Please don't take this the wrong way, OK?"

"Ugh, Ted. Really? In the history of humankind, nothing good has ever come after the words 'please don't take this the wrong way.'" Under ordinary circumstances, Maren might have enjoyed the sight of Ted squirming in his chair like a schoolboy waiting for the recess bell, but today a distinct sense of dread drowned out that impulse. Where could he be going with this?

"So I hope you know we all want the best outcome for Winnie. She's really an extraordinary young woman," he said. "And we've been excited to promote Winnie's college applications using the first-generation college hook. But it's come to our attention that the hook may not be accurate."

"I'm not following."

"I've been contacted by a slew of parents," he said, waving a hand in the general direction of the reception desk, where a ringing phone seemed to provide circumstantial evidence in real time, "with concerns about the veracity of Winnie's first-gen hook."

"Are you kidding me? What the hell, Ted? Are other parents really trying to sabotage my daughter?"

"I'll handle the parent community. But I do need to know a few things.

I'm sorry, Maren. First, there's a rumor floating around that you may have gone to college. Is that true?"

Maren crossed her arms. "All the college counseling office ever asked me is whether I have a college degree, which I definitely do not. I was very briefly enrolled at Indiana University, but I had to withdraw before I even finished my first semester due to, you know, um, discovering I was pregnant with Winnie. I never hid anything; it just never occurred to me this was relevant information." Over the years, Maren had become skilled at maintaining a wall between her mind and body, so it came as a surprise to realize she was blushing so fiercely her cheeks felt like they'd passed the fire stage and were already turning to ash. "There's no way me spending less than three months at a university can hurt Winnie's future, right?"

"No, don't worry, Maren. That shouldn't be a problem," Ted said. "You didn't do anything wrong. I just have to do my due diligence. It would be damaging to EBA's reputation if we were to champion a student under false pretenses. The circumstances and timing are helpful to know."

"I don't understand. Winnie should be a lock for UW Honors without the added boost of her mom's underwhelming educational background, right?" Maren checked her watch.

"Uh, yes, so that's the other thing we need to discuss," Ted said, raking his fingers through his hair. "I gathered from your response to my email earlier today that you may be operating under a misconception regarding Winnie's college plans."

"What are you talking—?" Maren stopped midsentence. "Oh no," she said, putting up a hand. "Please don't tell me Winnie is still applying to Stanford?"

Ted pressed his lips together and nodded. "It appears that way, Maren. I confirmed it with Ms. Lawson this morning. She's planning to apply early to Stanford, and if she doesn't get in, she'll go to UW. Apparently, she really wants to stay on the West Coast."

"Dammit," she said, smacking the desk. "I can't believe she's been lying to me! She knows I could lose my job over this." Maren dropped her head into her hands.

"I'm sorry to be the bearer of bad news," Ted said in a tone rife with genuine understanding.

Maren lifted her head. "But wait, isn't this outside your normal head of school duties? Why were you even asking Ms. Lawson about it?" She narrowed her eyes at Ted, who quickly averted his gaze, suddenly fascinated with the paper clip on his desk. "Hmm. Let me guess. Someone just a tad more important to EBA than a charity case like me called you, right? Who was it? Alicia? Kelly?"

"You know I'm not at liberty to discuss specifics, Maren. Suffice it to say, there's significant interest across the parent community about who is applying to every top school, but the competition is especially fierce for Stanford. To be honest, we're regretting ever telling parents about there being just one spot remaining for EBA. We knew there'd be tension— there always is around the elite colleges—but we never expected things to get this heated."

"Yeah right. You mean you're just now figuring out how crazy this place is?" In a perfect imitation of Winnie, she rolled her eyes for effect.

"That's fair," he said with a sideways smile before his face turned serious.

"So are we done here? I need to get back to work—and then I need to have a serious talk with my daughter," Maren said, standing up.

"Look, Maren, I'm afraid there's more."

Maren dropped back down in the chair and clasped her hands on

Ted's desk. "Now what? Perhaps you need the name, rank, and serial number of my kindergarten teacher?"

"Uh no." Ted cleared his throat. "What can you tell me about Winnie's father?"

Maren flinched, every muscle in her body on high alert. "Nothing. Nothing at all." She enunciated each word slowly and deliberately. "Why?"

"Well, we also received information that Winnie's dad is a graduate of Yale. So obviously, that would be pertinent here."

"It's not possible for someone to know that, so whoever told you that is a liar." Maren's voice sounded high in her ears. "This is really crossing the line, Ted."

Shuffling a few papers on his desk, Ted said quietly, "Can you please just explain to me why no one could know that? I'm sorry to pry, Maren. I really am. But I have to cover my bases here."

"Because, Ted," Maren practically spat the words out, "I don't even know who he is myself, so I couldn't have ever told anyone his name. It was a one-night stand the night before I left to start college, and I never saw him again. Are you satisfied? And besides, even if it were true that Winnie's biological father attended Yale, he's been nothing more than a sperm donor. He's not even named on her birth certificate. Jesus Christ, Ted, do you ask lesbian couples like Mary and Julie Morgan if their sperm donor went to college? Of course you wouldn't because it's absurd. Not to mention insulting. And probably illegal."

"Of course not. I understand." Ted looked chagrined. "But I just want to make sure we're one hundred percent clear here for Winnie's file: Winnie has never had a relationship of any kind with her father?"

"Correct." Maren's brittle tone betrayed her. She had to get out of there before she lost her cool. Had someone really learned about Winnie's father? She couldn't imagine how that would be possible. More than likely, this was just some asshole making shit up to mess with Winnie's application. But what if she was wrong? She jumped to her feet. Her hands were shaking so badly she dropped her purse to the floor. By the time she'd picked it up, Ted was standing in front of her, blocking her path to the door. He awkwardly reached out to touch her shoulder, but she recoiled from his touch and took a step back. She knew she looked crazy, and she was suddenly itching all over. This hadn't happened to her in several years, but she knew exactly what it was. Clawing at her arms and torso, she said, "Ted, please step out of my way."

"Oh my God, Maren, are you OK? I think you're having some sort of allergic reaction. Sit down. I'll get you some water. I have some Benadryl in my drawer. I'm sorry. Look, I obviously dredged up something difficult for you."

"You have no idea, Ted," she replied as her body continued to mutiny. Her voice rose with panic. "Please just tell me who is spreading that rumor about Yale."

"It was anonymous, Maren. I really don't know," he said. "The good news is it sounds like we can still support Winnie's hook. Try not to worry, OK? Hang on a sec." He poked his head out the door and asked his administrative assistant to bring a glass of water and waited until he handed the glass across the threshold. "Here, take this." He handed her the water and then rifled through his desk drawer for the Benadryl.

After Ted's fourth futile attempt to open the tamper-resistant packaging, Maren wordlessly held out her hand for the pill pouch and took over.

"Yeah, wow, that thing is really, really childproof—and adultproof. Or at least manproof," he added with a self-deprecating grin as Maren effortlessly popped out the pills. "Impressive work there. So anyway, I'm going to keep an eye on you for a bit until, um, until your reaction, you know, gets better. I mean, goes away."

She knew she must look like hell for Ted to be reduced to such a fumbling, stammering idiot. Maren touched her cheeks and felt the raised rash. "I bet no one's ever broken out in hives in your office."

"You'd be surprised the crap that goes down in this office." Ted tried for jocular, but it was clear he felt sorry for her.

Maren cracked a half-hearted smile and took a deep breath to try to calm her nervous system as the first visible welts on her arms appeared.

"Maren, if you ever need someone to talk to, just say the word."

"Thanks." Maren nodded. They sat in an awkward silence for several minutes waiting for the Benadryl to kick in, until Maren touched her hands to her cheeks again. "How does my face look now?"

"Beautiful—as always," Ted replied softly.

Maren's cheeks heated again—blush on top of hives, no doubt an attractive look. She tilted her head and cast a wistful smile back at him as she rose from her chair. "Well, this has been a fun little interlude, but I think it's time for me to haul my rash-covered body back to work or Winnie won't be finishing out the year at EBA, let alone going to college. Thanks for your help, Ted."

As she drove back to the Stones', Maren churned over her conversation with Ted. Yale? Impossible. She'd always been sure it was Charles Brown. He was all over her that night, and God, was he an entitled pig. He was also scary smart and a rising sophomore at Harvard that summer, and Maren had always thought Winnie's eyes and the shape of her chin resembled those of his mom. But on the off chance her suspicion was wrong, she'd tracked all the boys she remembered being at the club that fateful night. This had become much easier after the dawn of the social media age. She knew where each of them had gone to college. Two had attended the University of Illinois, one had attended the University of Wisconsin, and another had gone to Purdue, but none had gone to Yale.

This had to be a hoax. But what if it wasn't? What if someone got to Winnie before she could tell her the truth? Winnie would never forgive her. She'd always intended to tell Winnie everything when she turned eighteen—which was only a few months from now. Part of her wondered if she should sit Winnie down tonight, but her intuition told her to hold off just a bit longer. The last thing she wanted was to distract Winnie right now, in this critical senior fall semester.

As difficult as it was to reconcile, Maren also had much more immediate concerns in front of her. Winnie had lied to her. And the Stones, as usual, were a step ahead. Maren gripped the steering wheel, imagining Alicia's reaction if Winnie actually applied to Stanford. *Heads-up indeed.* But the fact was Winnie was almost an adult and able to make her own decisions. Would Maren's warnings even matter? Probably not. Like all teenagers, Winnie was both blessed and cursed with a sense of invincibility. Perhaps Maren's best option for the moment was to feign ignorance about Stanford to everyone, Winnie included, at least until she could figure out how to save her daughter—and herself—from this dangerous game of chicken Winnie seemed determined to play.

MEMORIAL HOSPITAL
EMERGENCY ROOM

SATURDAY, OCTOBER 30, 12:32 A.M.

"MA'AM?" DETECTIVE DAVIS'S VOICE gently coaxed Maren back to the conversation.

She must be losing her mind. There was no way Winnie was down the hall in an operating room over something so senseless as a spot at college. She tried to focus on the detective, but her vision was fuzzy.

"To answer your question," Detective Davis continued, "I'm afraid our current working theory based on the witness statement is that your daughter was the victim of a hit-and-run. What we don't know at this point is whether the hit was intentional."

"This can't be happening."

"Mrs. Pressley, if you can think of anything unusual in Winnie's life recently, even if it doesn't seem like a big deal to you, it might help with our investigation. For example, was there a spurned romantic partner? A fight with friends? Cyberbullying? Anything ring a bell?"

Maren gulped in some air. Her breathing felt shallow, her chest tight. "Actually, there have been a few strange things lately. Winnie goes to Elliott Bay Academy with a lot of kids from very wealthy families—not us," she said, dismissing the misimpression before it could form. "There's been all this hubbub over Stanford because there's only one spot and a number of kids, including Winnie, were planning to apply. I'm worried one of the crazy parents or kids from her school could have done this to her. The competition's been insane."

From the disbelieving look on the detective's face, it was clear he'd pegged Maren as the crazy one. Saying it out loud, though, convinced her she was onto something. "My boss's daughter is one of the students applying to Stanford, and her husband recently hinted that I could lose my job if Winnie even applies."

The detective crinkled his eyes quizzically. "And who is your boss?"

Shit. The fastest way to get fired would be to accuse her employer of a crime. But what was the alternative? "Uh, I work for Alicia Stone. I'm her personal assistant."

"The Alicia Stone?"

"I'm afraid so. But it's really sensitive. I'm actually violating my employment agreement just by telling you that right now."

"I see." Detective Davis looked askance. "Mrs. Pressley, I'm going to be frank with you. There's not a police precinct in the country that would investigate a school full of powerful families like the Stones with so little evidence. What you're describing—competition over college, is it?—well, that sounds more like harmless shenanigans than motive for a serious crime. Remember, it's also possible this was just an accident."

"But, Detective, you don't understand," Maren pleaded. "I don't even know if Winnie's going to be OK, but if she is, she might be in real danger. You're not even going to try to figure out who did this?"

"Of course we'll be checking with all the neighbors to see if there's any useful home security footage or if anyone heard or saw anything, but I wouldn't hold your breath. Unfortunately, most cases like this are never solved. But here's my card. Please call me if you think of anything else or your daughter remembers anything more concrete. In the meantime, my prayers are with you and your family."

That was it? The risk of making rich people mad outweighed Winnie's right to health and safety? Unfortunately, Maren knew if she kept pushing him, he might run a background check on her, which would reveal the one stain destined to define her forever—and then he'd never believe another word she uttered. She was almost out of moves. "It's just Winnie and me. No other family." She hoped maybe this information might spark his sympathy, encouraging him to launch a real investigation.

"Well then, my prayers are with you and your daughter, Mrs. Pressley." Detective Davis shook Maren's hand and left.

As the detective walked out the door, Maren stifled the urge to scream in frustration. She caught the eye of the desk clerk, who shook her head in answer to Maren's silent question. Still no word. Turning to take her seat in the waiting area again, Maren noticed that she was the only one there now. Aside from the desk clerk, she was all alone with her darkest fears. There was nothing to say and no one to say it to anyway. Her body hurt in a visceral way, like someone had carved her in half with a rusty bread knife. The only thing that mattered was the one thing she didn't know—whether Winnie would be OK.

11

Kelly

KELLY HAD BECOME OBSESSED with trying to confirm that her explosive information about Maren's academic history had reached Ted Clark and, more to the point, whether he or Alicia had managed to "persuade" Winnie not to apply to Stanford. She'd spotted Winnie in the hallway wearing a UW sweatshirt a couple days earlier, which she took as a good sign. And then just yesterday, Maren had forwarded a detailed plan for the Snowcoming dance for Kelly's approval. If Maren was still working on Snowcoming, that meant Alicia hadn't fired her. There was no way Alicia would let Maren get away with stealing what she considered to be Brooke's spot, so Kelly could only assume (or hope) that Maren and Winnie had realized they were punching above their weight with Stanford.

"Good morning, Sherri," Kelly said, giving the college counseling team's administrative assistant her most winning smile. "I just wanted to drop off a little treat." Kelly handed over a Tupperware container full of homemade chocolate-chip cookies as her eyes scanned Sherri's desk for any useful tidbits, but Sherri had all her paperwork either facedown or tucked into blank folders. EBA seemed to have instituted new CIA-level protocols for handling sensitive information.

"Well, aren't you a doll." Sherri peeked inside. "I'll be sure to put them in the counselors' lounge. Right after I sneak one myself. You parents are so thoughtful. You're the fourth mother today to stop by with treats."

"Oh, that's great. I know how hard you all must be working with early admission deadlines approaching," she said, unfazed by Sherri's implication. "Well, OK then, I'll come by in a day or two to collect the Tupperware." As Kelly retreated, she tried to peek inside Ms. Barstow's office, but Sherri jumped up out of her desk chair and blocked her line of sight. Foiled but not about to give up, Kelly sauntered down the hall to the Taylor Family Conference Room to pretend to work on important SST business while monitoring the comings and goings of the college counseling office. When she pulled open the door, she was surprised to find several other mothers standing around chatting. Clearly, she wasn't the only one skulking around school fishing for college intel.

"Can you believe the nerve of that girl? Applying to every top-ten school? And with a fake hook?" Nora Chapman said as Kelly took her place in the circle. Nora's son, Scotty, was a Princeton double legacy. "I called Ted the minute I heard."

"I know! Give the rest of us a chance. Right?" Kelly said.

"I cornered Ted at the middle school band concert last night, and he was totally evasive," Patti Moore said, shaking her head. "It's so greedy. Bad enough she has to win every award, but now trying to take our kids' spots when they've worked so hard? And for what—bragging rights? I can't believe how far some people will go."

Kelly bit her inner lip hard to keep from snorting at Patti's hypocrisy.

She knew for a fact that Patti had forced her son, Nicholas, to study Arabic starting in eighth grade because she heard from someone in the Penn admissions office that Arabic studies students were an institutional priority.

"Has anyone heard which schools Winnie's actually applying to? I mean, top ten is kinda vague," Amanda said. "Is she using the *U.S. News & World Report* list or maybe *Forbes*?"

"Probably *Forbes* because they rank based on salaries coming out of college," Diana said. "I have to imagine that's important to her, you know, given her situation."

"Do you think I need to worry that she's applying to Middlebury?" Sarah asked.

There was an awkward pause in the conversation.

"I think you're safe." Kelly rested a hand on Sarah's arm. "But, gals, aren't we getting off track? I mean, isn't the most important question not which top-ten schools she's considering but which one she's applying to *early*?"

"In theory, that may be true. But our counselor told us most Ivy Plus early applications get deferred, so that would mean most of us could eventually be pitted against her in the regular decision pool," Patti pointed out.

"This is absurd," Amanda scoffed. "I can't believe Maren was naive enough to think they could get away with lying about her not going to college. As if Alicia would ever hire a personal assistant without a college degree? I'm surprised she doesn't demand her assistants have master's or PhDs."

"If Winnie lies on her applications, that could be bad for all of us if it damages EBA's reputation," Diana said. "As far as Michael and I are concerned, they should expel her. That kind of deceitful behavior shouldn't be tolerated. As chair of the EBA board, I've demanded that Ted launch a formal investigation."

Just then, Ms. Richards (aka Double Ass) popped her head into the conference room. "Sorry, ladies. But I need to clear the conference room now for an admin meeting."

The women dispersed, and Kelly beelined out the doors of the administration building for her car. By the time she reached the school parking lot, she'd worked herself into a snit. The early admission deadline was in six days, and from the sound of it, Ted Clark wasn't doing a damn thing to stop Maren and Winnie from using their bogus hook. As much as she enjoyed the cabal of outraged mothers conspiring to take Winnie down, what the hell did she have to do to get a goddamn answer to one very simple question: Was Winnie Pressley still applying to Stanford?

⸻

The whole Vernon family was home for dinner, which on its own was a special occasion on a weeknight, but tonight it was even more significant. Tonight was the night. Krissie was finally ready to push the Submit button on her Stanford early admission application. For weeks, Kelly had been imagining a meaningful way to mark this momentous occasion, even creating an Aspyre "notebook" with all her ideas. In the end, she'd kept it simple and settled on her two favorite things—a family dinner and a photo. Kelly stood behind Krissie—whose hands were on the keyboard with her dad positioned to her left and her siblings to her right—and leaned forward to rearrange her daughter's hair so that it cascaded down her back. Krissie swatted her hand away, but not before Kelly noticed how strange her hair felt. Had she changed shampoo? Kelly thought better of mentioning it as she knew from experience her subjects would only pose for so long. Finally, she stepped back and pressed the button on her iPhone as Krissie did the deed. This milestone was another bittersweet reminder that her family of five, her primary raison d'être, would soon exist mostly as a relic in her iPhoto library.

After hugs and a few tears, Kelly sent them all to wash their hands for dinner. When she'd hugged Krissie, Kelly had taken the opportunity to run a hand over Krissie's hair again. It felt synthetic. After Krissie's trichotillomania diagnosis, Kelly had read online that some women used extensions to disguise their hair loss, but Krissie hadn't done enough damage at the time to need them. And anyway, once Krissie started on the anxiety medication, her hair pulling seemed to abate. Her gut twisted at the idea that Krissie could be pulling out her hair again and not feeling like she could tell her mom. The end of the stressful college admissions process could not come soon enough. Maybe now that her application had been submitted, Krissie might be able to relax, even if Kelly couldn't.

"Ugh, salmon." Katherine wrinkled her nose as she walked into the kitchen. "You can have mine, Kaleb. What else is there? I'm a vegetarian. Remember, Mom?"

"Yes, Katherine, I remember your recent conversion to vegetarianism. It's you who seemed to forget when you had sushi the other night with your friends," she said, scooping quinoa onto each plate. "This is Krissie's special night, so I made her favorite dinner."

Katherine rolled her eyes.

Kelly didn't mind that one of her daughters was flirting with vegetarianism. It seemed nearly every girl in Seattle tried it on for size at some point. She'd always attempted to model a dietary philosophy of "everything in moderation." Until this year, her strategy had worked. But now,

Kelly was eating everything in sight, and her daughters barely ate anything at all. As Kelly tossed the Caesar salad, she gave thanks that Katherine hadn't put it together that the salad dressing contained anchovies. Morally questionable or not, Kelly had no intention of pointing this out, lest she further complicate her already absurd daily meal-planning contortions. No gluten or dairy for Krissie. No meat for Katherine. Loads of meat and carbs for Kaleb but no slimy tomatoes. No soups or casseroles for Kevin— battle wounds from his childhood with a working mom.

As they gathered around the table, Kevin raised his glass. "To Krissie!" he said, beaming at his eldest daughter. "Your work ethic, your focus, and your determination are a credit to you and our family. You're an outstanding role model."

Kaleb sniggered. Krissie would be leaving big shoes behind to fill, and Kaleb was turning out to be the kind of kid who preferred to stay barefoot.

"It's out of your hands now," Kevin continued, "but you can feel great knowing you've given Stanford your best shot."

"Thanks, Dad," Krissie said, "but I don't want a participation trophy."

Kelly exchanged a worried look with her husband.

"Regardless of the outcome," Kevin said, "we love you and couldn't be more proud of the person you've become."

"Absolutely," Kelly said, reaching out to touch her daughter's arm.

"Whatever," Krissie said, stabbing at her salmon.

"Dinner looks great, Kel," Kevin said. "So anyway, other than Krissie submitting her application, anything newsworthy happen today?"

Kaleb snorted but continued shoveling food into his mouth.

"I got assigned a solo for the winter concert," Katherine offered.

"That's great, Kath," Kevin said.

"Is it your American Protégé piece?" Kelly asked. Last week, Katherine had submitted her oboe audition recording to the prestigious national competition. The ultimate prize was a chance to perform onstage at Carnegie Hall. Kelly was already envisioning how that would look on Katherine's college application in a couple years' time. *College.* Like a Pavlovian dog, mere thought of the word caused her mind to ignore Katherine's answer and swerve right back to early decision. Without warning, she heard herself blurt, "Krissie, any new scuttlebutt about where everyone is applying early?"

Krissie's color rose, and she stared down at her plate. Loose locks of hair framed her face.

"Well, have you heard anything?" Kelly pressed.

"God, Mom. You're, like, the most annoying song ever playing on repeat." Krissie narrowed her eyes. "I submitted my application, like, twenty minutes ago, and we're already back to worrying about what everyone else is doing. Why isn't anything ever enough for you?" She jumped up from her seat and dumped her plate in the sink. "I'm done. Can I please be excused? I need to study. Don't want to blow my grades and ruin my chances with Stanford."

"Krissie, this is your favorite dinner, and you didn't eat anything. And you know you can't just throw your plate in the sink. Scrape your food into the compost bin or we'll get fined by the city."

Krissie scowled at her mother from the sink, scooped up a pile of salad with her hand, and shoved it into her mouth before making a half-hearted attempt to scrape her plate. She left the kitchen without another word. *Lovely.* Kaleb mumbled something about homework, left his empty plate on the table, and followed his sister out of the room. Katherine stayed seated for a moment but must have realized where the conversation was headed and took off after her siblings.

Kelly threw her napkin on the table.

"You just had to go there, huh?" Kevin said.

Kelly cleared the table, annoyed over her family's ungrateful behavior after she'd spent hours preparing dinner. "I was just curious if she'd heard anything."

"What does it matter at this point?" Kevin asked, setting his empty dish on the counter next to the sink. Not waiting for an answer to his semi-rhetorical question, Kevin said, "I gotta catch up on my email. Thanks for dinner."

After the brief and furious dinner frenzy, Kelly looked around at the mess that would take her an hour to clean up. But her irritation over the untidy kitchen was far outweighed by the nagging feeling she still hadn't done enough to get her accomplished daughter into her alma mater. Just because Krissie had submitted her application, that didn't mean Kelly's job was finished. Far from it. Pushing aside several dirty dishes on the island, she cleared a spot for her laptop. If EBA wasn't going to do anything about Maren's deceit, perhaps it was time to dig deeper. With so much already invested in this college endeavor, Kelly didn't think twice as she typed her credit card information into a website promising a comprehensive background check for $500.

12

Alicia

ALICIA DIMMED THE LIGHTS and lit her favorite magnolia-scented candle, allowing the lovely smell to envelop her. A bath was the sooth-ing balm she needed to restore her spirits after another grueling day at the office. She dipped a foot in the water just as she heard the ping of an incoming text. She sighed, turned off the spigot, and ran naked to her dressing room where she'd left her phone. She'd check to make sure every-thing was OK, and then into the bubbles she'd go.

> **Emily Johnson:** Hi, Alicia! It's Emily Johnson. Chloe's mom. So sorry to bother you. I know you must be so busy. I wasn't sure if I should text what with your huge job, but I thought you might want to know.

Good God. Why did Emily have to introduce herself every time she sent Alicia a text? Brooke and Chloe had been friends since they'd started at EBA. Emily, along with most other stay-at-home moms, prefaced every conversation with "I know you must be so busy, but…" Maybe they thought they were being respectful because she really was busy all the time, but nevertheless, it felt like a dig. As if she wasn't an attentive mother because she was busy working.

Alicia: What's up?

She waited, naked and freezing, watching the typing indicator bubbles.

Emily: Brooke is sexting with a boy who goes to Greenleaf. If this is news to you, you might want to check her phone.

If this was news to her? Alicia knew she should be thankful that Emily had the guts to text her directly rather than blast the juicy dirt out through the EBA grapevine (although she might do that too), but it still felt like crap to hear from another mother that her daughter had screwed up. Yet again.

Alicia: Thx for letting me know.

Alicia threw her phone on her bed. Sexting? She pulled the drain plug in the tub. No amount of bubbles could relax her now. Would Brooke really do something this stupid and put her mother's reputation at risk? Unfortunately, Alicia knew all too well the answer to that question was an emphatic yes.

———

Earlier in the day, Brooke had texted that she was having dinner with the soccer team after the game and then hanging out at Tenley's, which Alicia's security detail had confirmed. It was nearly half past ten on a work night, and Alicia was meeting her trainer at six a.m. for high-intensity interval training, by far the most demanding of her trainer's workouts. However, she couldn't deny its effectiveness for weight control, so in less than eight hours, she'd be doing burpees to the brink of puking. As much as she wanted to crawl into bed and deal with Brooke tomorrow, this sexting situation could not wait.

When Brooke finally sauntered in through the mudroom, Alicia looked up from her laptop and removed her reading glasses. "Hey, congrats on the win today."

"How would you know?" Brooke opened the refrigerator.

Alicia kneaded her forehead. "I wanted to be there, but my meeting ran long. Chef Louise made you a Cobb salad. It's on the bottom shelf."

Alicia studied Brooke, looking for clues as to what was going on with her daughter. Lately, she was looking more mature, dressing more provocatively, and wearing her dark hair—newly highlighted ombré purple—in a flowing, tousled style that screamed sexy and rebellious. "So what'd you do tonight?"

"I went to dinner with the other seniors on the team, and then I went over to Tenley's. Like I texted you," Brooke said between forkfuls of salad.

"Can I see your phone?" Alicia asked.

"Why? I'm not lying," Brooke mumbled and chewed, her eyes on her phone.

"I know you're not, but I want to see your phone."

"What the hell, Mom?" Brooke finally looked up.

"Have you been sexting a Greenleaf boy?" Alicia asked.

Brooke dropped her fork. "Who told you that?"

"Does it matter?"

Brooke shrugged. "It was only one picture. Relax."

Alicia leaned across the island and snatched the phone out of Brooke's hand. "This isn't a joke. What was the picture of exactly?" Alicia was struggling to maintain her composure in the face of her daughter's insolence. She needed the full story and wasn't going to let Brooke off the hook until she had it.

"Why are you so mad? It was just a temporary glitter tattoo I got with my Brazilian." Brooke rolled her eyes and looked away.

"Excuse me? You put glitter *where*?" Alicia gripped the marble counter.

"On my vag. Don't be such a prude. It's called a glitter gram, and it was only the guy's initials."

Alicia exploded. "What the hell were you thinking? Do you know what people would say about me if that photo got out? And do you really want to see your private parts plastered all over the internet? I didn't think anything could be worse than your pregnancy test debacle." The empty EPT pregnancy test box retrieved by some enterprising dumpster diver last summer had provided a news cycle worth of clickbait fodder. Brooke claimed the test was a friend's, but Alicia had known she was lying. A quick check of Brooke's texts had confirmed it was hers all right. Thankfully, Brooke hadn't been pregnant, but the experience had resulted in a whole new level of security precautions for the family. And a trip to the gynecologist for an STD check and birth control for Brooke.

"Whatever."

"I'll have my cyber team track the photo down and scrub the internet, but I'll need to give them the phone so we can take care of this," Alicia said, placing Brooke's phone next to her computer. "What's your passcode?"

Brooke blanched at the notion of giving her mother access to her phone, but she was in no position to argue, and for once, she seemed to know it. She wrote down her passcode and went upstairs, leaving her unfinished salad on the counter.

Alicia whipped off a humiliating email to her security lead informing him of his search-and-destroy mission first thing in the morning. Then she picked up Brooke's phone, entered the passcode, and clicked on the texting app to see the ill-advised photo for herself. It wasn't hard to find, and luckily there really was only one. At least Brooke hadn't included her own initials or any other identifiable details. Other than the fact that she'd sent it. As Alicia scrolled through Brooke's many other text conversations hoping to learn more about the owner of the "P.H." initials now artfully rendered on her only child's vagina, one group text in particular from earlier that day caught her attention.

Chloe to Brooke, Tenley, Sadie: Yo bitches—youll never guess what I found in the back of my mom's closet when I was looking for a pair of boots

Sadie: fur handcuffs?

Brooke: whips?

Chloe: haha as if

Chloe: if they had those in the house i guarantee they wouldn't be using them for sex, they hate each other so much

Tenley: giant dildo? anal beads?

Chloe: gross!

Chloe: you guys suck at this

Chloe: ok fine—it's three huge bags filled with columbia gear!!!!

Chloe: i mean WTF? Even if i am 3rd gen I probably won't get in and now the whole goddamn store is stashed in her closet

Chloe: and why would i ever need 17 sweatshirts, 9 hats, 11 scarves and 4 pairs of columbia pjs?

Sadie: maybe theyre planning to outfit u + an entire village of syrian refugees?

Tenley: WTAF!

Tenley: that is so messed up, but don't worry chlo youll probably get in

Tenley: and at least ur mom is excited about where ur applying

Tenley: my parents are all SMH about why i'm wasting my early shot on a loser ivy like brown, like the embarrassment is just too much for them

Tenley: like how could they not have raised a HYPS kid?

Brooke: that sucks Ten

Sadie: wait, what's HYPS?

Tenley: harvard yale princeton stanford

Sadie: ohhhhh…not really my scene

Chloe: but what if i don't get in?

Sadie: then there will just be lots of super educated looking homeless dudes walking around town this spring!

Sadie: and anyway, you think that's bad? My parents are already talking about how it will be ok if i ONLY get into claremont or hopkins bc i can apply to transfer right away

Sadie: they literally told me it's easier to get into a second tier ivy as a transfer and i can just think of all this as "practice"

Sadie: like my whole first year of college is just supposed to be a fucking dress rehearsal until i finally make it to a school they can brag about at cocktail parties?

Brooke: if you think a #practiceyear or a few bags of sweats are batshit try having your famous richass mom donate 15 mil to stanford

Brooke: don't even talk to me about pressure!

Chloe: ouch wow

Chloe: ok thanks i feel so much better now!

Brooke: that makes one of us at least 💩

Brooke: can't wait for this year to be over

Alicia was enraged. The biting comments stung for sure—how could these girls be so ungrateful? But it was Brooke's text revealing Alicia's $15 million donation to Stanford that took her breath away. Brooke was well aware that they were intentionally keeping the donation quiet until after early decision to shield her from the inevitable snarky comments that her mom was buying her way into Stanford. Alicia smacked the phone down on the counter. Now that Brooke had blasted out their secret, her foolish daughter would just have to deal with the fallout on her own.

13

Maren

"HI MOM! I'M HOME!" Winnie burst in the front door after cross-country practice. "Smells good. What's for dinner?"

Maren heard the thump of Winnie's backpack hitting the floor as she pulled their sheet-pan dinner out of the oven and set it on the stovetop. "Chicken."

"Great. I'm starving." Winnie appeared beside Maren and picked a wedge of roasted potato off the pan.

"Careful, that's just out of the oven!" Maren said as Winnie shoved the potato into her mouth.

Winnie spat out the steaming potato into her hand. "Now you tell me."

Maren swatted Winnie's hand away as she reached for a piece of chicken. "Stop that! Let's sit down at the table and eat. How was your day?"

"Fine, I guess. Except for the woman who got on my bus with me and watched me basically the whole way home."

"That's odd. What'd she look like?"

"I don't know. I never really got to see her whole face. She had a baseball hat pulled down and a puffy coat with the collar kind of pulled up over her chin. And black yoga pants, I think."

"Well, that's helpful. You've basically just described the wardrobe of every mom in Seattle." After her conversation with Ted the other day, Maren suspected either Kelly or Alicia of trying to screw with Winnie. As far as Maren knew, Alicia had never set foot on a city bus, so that left only Kelly. "Is there any way it could have been Mrs. Vernon?"

"No way. She was definitely younger and thinner. Plus I would know Mrs. Vernon anywhere. She's like the campus witch, emerging out of thin air—like poof!—to ask where you're applying to college whenever you're alone in a hallway."

"Charming," Maren said. "Maybe the woman just thought you looked like someone she knew."

"Maybe." Winnie sounded skeptical.

It seemed insane, but was it possible that Kelly or Alicia had hired a private investigator to dig for dirt that might disqualify Winnie from the Stanford competition? Maren couldn't totally discount the theory. If that were true, though, it was yet another reason she needed to get Winnie to give up on Stanford once and for all. Then all this madness would go away and their lives could return to normal. Maren gritted her teeth with resolve. It was well past time to put an end to this charade between them. "Listen, there's something we need to discuss." She reached into the cabinet for two dinner plates and passed them off to Winnie.

"Uh-oh, sounds serious," Winnie said as she opened the silverware drawer and grabbed a couple of forks. "Let me guess…you need a fashion intervention? I'm in!"

"Very funny." Maren placed the tray on the trivet and took her seat. "Actually, it is serious."

Winnie filled her plate. "I'm listening.…"

"I had a meeting with Mr. Clark a few days ago."

Winnie's eyes widened for an instant, but she quickly busied herself with placing her napkin on her lap. "And? What did he want?"

"It wasn't so much what he wanted as what he told me." She glanced meaningfully at Winnie. This would be so much easier if Winnie would just come clean. But teenage girls weren't known for wanting to make things easier for their moms. "He mentioned that you're still planning to apply to Stanford. Is that true?"

"What if it is?" Winnie said.

"Well, if it is, I find it worrisome on many levels. First that you would lie to my face about it. And second, the Stones are onto you. Bryan told me Alicia's pissed you're applying to Stanford and all but threatened my job. By deceiving me, you put me in a position where my employer thinks I lied to his face. Can you even comprehend how cosmically bad that could be for us?"

"Bryan's an idiot. I think you're being a little paranoid." Winnie shoveled food into her mouth, conveniently avoiding eye contact.

Not about to be derailed, Maren slapped down her fork and glared at Winnie. "Back to my question about Stanford. I thought we agreed on UW Honors. I need a straight answer from you, and I need it now."

Winnie took her time chewing and wiping her face with her napkin before responding. "Fine. I haven't one hundred percent decided, but I'm most likely still applying. I didn't want to tell you because I knew you'd flip out. And also, I thought it would be better for you with Alicia if you really didn't know the truth. You're a pretty bad liar, you know."

"Oh really? What have I lied to you about?"

"Nothing, because you suck at it and you know I'd know." She raised her eyebrows.

Maren let out what she hoped was an imperceptible sigh of relief that Winnie still wasn't onto her whopper. "Don't you think it's a little too much of a coincidence that you lied about UW Honors and then suddenly my employer is threatening me, I'm getting hauled into the head of school's office, and now it seems like someone was stalking you on the bus? I honestly don't know what these people are capable of, and it's starting to really stress me out."

"Mom, chill. There's no way anyone outside the counseling office could know about my college plans. They're always making a huge deal about how all our sessions are confidential and where we apply is no one else's business. I haven't told a soul other than Ms. Lawson. And also, why was Mr. Clark even sticking his nose in this anyway? Maybe it was just an excuse to get you to come in so he can ask you out again." She shimmied her shoulders.

"I think you're being naive about the confidentiality issue. People don't always follow the rules," Maren said. "And as for Mr. Clark, you can just drop that for good. I'm never going out with him." Maren gave her daughter a teen-caliber eye roll; two could play that game.

"Why not? You should just go out with the poor guy already. Unless you're a lesbian or something? That's totally cool if you are. No big deal. But if you're not, it's been obvious for years that he likes you. And all the girls think he's a total hottie—you know, like in an older man way."

"Stop changing the subject!" Maren took a sip of ice water to cool herself down. "Look, we've been over this too many times. If you really hate the idea of UW so much, let's talk about that. Isn't there another choice that isn't the one school that could cost us our safety net? I just don't get why you have to be so hung up on that one school. You're an incredible student, and Ms. Lawson said your first-generation hook will help anywhere."

"Gee, I don't know, Mom. Unlike every other student at EBA, I haven't had the pleasure of visiting a dozen Ivy Plus schools just to show interest and explore my perfect fit."

That stung. Maren busted her butt every day to try to give Winnie a small fraction of the advantages her peers enjoyed, and Winnie was normally grateful. But Maren also knew a snow job when she saw one. "Oh baloney. There's this super cool invention called—what is it again? Oh yeah—I know, the interwebs? Perhaps you've heard of it? I'm told you can type any college name and voilà"—Maren threw her hands up—"a whole world of fact and fantasy is unlocked."

Winnie set down her utensils and stared at her plate for a moment. "Fine. I also like Brown. It's really good for social justice, and it's on the no-loan list, so it would be free if I got in. But it's also supposed to be really cold, and it's so far away I'd probably never see you. Also Tenley Taylor's been planning to apply early there forever, and she'll probably be super pissed if I apply too."

"Have you done the supplemental essays for Brown?" Maren said, hoping Winnie would appreciate her newfound attention to application minutiae.

"Yes, I did them. Just in case," Winnie said.

"Good. Brown it is then."

"What about Tenley?" Winnie said.

"What about her? Does she own Brown? You have as much right as anyone to apply there."

"I could say the same for Stanford."

"Dammit, Winnie. Not Stanford. Anywhere but Stanford. That's it. These people are not playing around!"

"Jeez, Mom." Winnie stiffened at the verbal assault. She grabbed her plate and stood in one hurried motion, dropping her fork and knife to the floor in the process. "Fine. You win. Brown it is. Happy now? I gotta go study."

"Just so we're clear. No more lying and no more Stanford," Maren said. Winnie dumped her plate in the sink.

"And one more thing. Promise me you'll stay alert when you're out and about, and let me know if you see that woman again. OK?"

"That's two things, but yep. I promise."

Thankfully, Winnie hadn't dug deeper into Maren's meeting with Ted. It was just as well since Winnie was at least half right about Maren's ability to lie. She didn't suck at it in general, but she was pretty awful at lying to Winnie specifically. For years, Maren had dreaded the day she'd be forced to tell Winnie the whole truth about her father, incinerating the only life story Winnie had ever known in the process. Unfortunately, with each passing day, the walls of this twisted EBA community seemed to be caving in on her—in a way that seemed far too reminiscent of the country club community of her youth. But this time, she had even more at stake. This time, Maren had a daughter—her reason for living—to protect.

14

Alicia

IT WAS ONLY NINE thirty a.m., but Alicia was standing in the walk-in pantry looking for something to snack on to quell her anxiety over Brooke's Stanford application. As usual, Brooke had procrastinated, and now there were only three days left before the November 1 deadline. Alicia had just shoved her hand into a box of Cheerios when Bryan surprised her by wrapping his arms around her waist and kissing her neck. "Good morning, beautiful," he whispered in her ear.

"Good morning," she said, releasing the fistful of Cheerios and closing the box.

Bryan massaged her shoulders. "Stressed?"

"Yes." Alicia was irritated that he couldn't be bothered to take on at least some of the burden over this damn application. "Remember, tonight we're supposed to finish Brooke's application and submit it?"

"Hmm," Bryan said, pressing himself up against her back.

She could feel his erection. "I'm worried she's going to try to blow it on purpose."

"I was just going to hop in the shower," he said. "Might help you relax a bit if you joined me." He grabbed her hand and led the way to their master suite.

With the large shower head raining down and the twenty side jets pulsing at them, Bryan reclined on the built-in bench. Alicia ran her hands along his tight abs and mounted him. As she thrust herself onto him, he whispered, "I took care of it for you, babe."

Alicia assumed he was referring to his body, but talking wasn't her thing, so she moaned in appreciation. Several times.

Grabbing her hips and pushing himself deep into her, Bryan locked eyes and said, "I fucking did it for you."

Did what for her? What was he talking about? She closed her eyes and willed herself to stay in the moment. Bryan expertly flipped her around, and as he entered her from behind, Alicia groaned with pleasure. She liked it when he got a little rough. His big hands were massaging her breasts with their favorite coconut-scented body wash, his thumbs teasing her nipples. Alicia could feel herself getting close to the edge when he growled in her ear, "I told her you were onto her."

Her eyes flew open, and she stopped moving. She pushed away from Bryan and stood up, reaching out for the wall to steady herself. Her legs and head were jelly from the sex, but maybe more so from the realization that Bryan was talking about Maren. "What did you do?"

Bryan ran his hand through his wet hair, slicking it back, and smirked. "I just let her know it'd be a shame if we had to fire her. That's all. Come on, that felt so good. Let's finish," he said, reaching out to pull her back onto his still-erect penis.

"What were you thinking?" She wriggled her wrists out of his grasp. She turned off the water, yanking a towel from the warming rack as she stepped out of the shower.

"You were freaking out that Winnie was still applying to Stanford when you called me the other day from the car. I had to do something." He followed her out of the shower.

"My God, you can't come right out and threaten her job." Alicia stopped in front of her sink, wrapped the sumptuous Turkish cotton bath sheet (researched and selected by Maren) around herself, and opened a vial of her favorite age-slaying miracle skin serum (sourced by Maren from a celebrity dermatologist in LA). "What if she quits because of this? Did you even consider that?"

"Gimme a break." Bryan stood with his hands on his hips, dripping water all over the floor. "She needs us a helluva lot more than we need her."

"Really? Are you sure about that? Because I sure as hell don't have the bandwidth to run our lives on top of running a company. Are you going to be the one who takes care of everything until we find someone else who can do the job as well as Maren?"

"Relax, Leesh." His warm hands covered her shoulders. "I was just gently reminding her of her place."

"I was managing the situation," Alicia said through clenched teeth.

"And I was just trying to help." Bryan's erection pushed into her towel. "I actually thought you'd appreciate what I did."

Alicia closed her eyes. The venomous, emasculating insults she'd hurled at Bryan after learning that Winnie was still applying to Stanford came roaring back at her. And his exile to the guest room. However misguided, Bryan had only been trying to make her happy and look out for Brooke. "I had it under control," she whispered and dropped her head to his chest.

"Well, I made sure of it now, didn't I?" He guided her head to his penis, closed his eyes, and tilted his head back as she finished him off.

Earlier in the week, Alicia texted Brooke an invitation for a mother-daughter Friday date night with their favorite estheticians—Trevor and Jules—for a relaxing evening of microdermabrasion facials and Chef Louise's delicious tuna salad Niçoise for dinner. Brooke immediately responded with a thumbs-up and heart emoji. Alicia worried that if she shared her real Friday night plans with Brooke, her daughter might blow her off.

"Wait, where are Trevor and Jules?" Brooke said as she walked into the kitchen to find two strangers seated at the kitchen table. "I thought we were having a spa night. Oh no." Brooke looked at her mom and covered her mouth with her hand. She started backing up. "Is this an intervention?"

Did Brooke need an intervention? Alicia feigned laughter as she got up to fix a plate for Brooke. Chef Louise had prepared tuna salad Niçoise for dinner, so at least that part was true. "Honey, meet your team. This is Professor Bejamaca, who you spoke with about your essays, and this is Deborah. She's a professional proofreader. We're finishing your Stanford application. I told you that last night," Alicia lied. She could see Brooke's eyes darting around the kitchen looking for an escape.

"Come on, B," Bryan cajoled, pulling out the chair next to him. "The sooner you sit down, the sooner we can all be done. Professor Bejamaca over here wants to get home. The Red Sox are playing in Game 7 of the World Series tomorrow night, and he has owner's box tickets thanks to your mom."

Brooke flopped on the chair and pulled out her phone. In one graceful sweeping motion, Alicia slid a plate on the table in front of Brooke and snatched her phone out of her hand. "Professor Bejamaca brought copies of the five essays he wrote based on your interview. Professor, should we all start by reading them?"

The professor nodded his agreement.

"Great. Then we can discuss and vote on which ones we'll use and tweak them as needed." Alicia turned to the proofreader and handed her a folder. "Deborah, I've printed out the individual pages of Brooke's Common App. Why don't you get started on those while we work on the essays? You can use the living room so we don't distract you. Bryan will show you the way."

As Brooke picked at the salad, her anger radiated in every direction. Alicia refused to engage and instead smiled at Professor Bejamaca while they waited for Bryan. She glanced at her watch. He was probably hitting on the poor girl. "Brooke, honey, why don't we just get started," Alicia said. "Writing isn't Dad's strong—"

"Really, Alicia?" Bryan interrupted as he walked back into the kitchen. "Just because I'm not some brainiac professor and I didn't graduate from some superelite college doesn't mean I can't add value here. But you know what? It looks like you've got this covered." Bryan stormed out of the room, leaving the rest of them stewing in an uncomfortable silence. Alicia stared straight ahead, avoiding eye contact with Brooke, but she could feel her daughter's glare boring into her. Professor Bejamaca's head was bowed. What must he be thinking? The sound of the front door slamming broke the silence.

"Why do you always have to be such a bitch to him?" Brooke asked.

"Why don't we start reading," Alicia said, her voice barely a whisper.

Moments later, Alicia heard the front door open again. Relieved Bryan had changed his mind, she turned her head to apologize and usher him back into the fold, but instead she was stunned to see Maren walking into the kitchen carrying their espresso maker. "Oh hey, Maren," Alicia said, going for breezy to mask her shock. "I'm surprised to see you here so late."

"Sorry to interrupt. I had the espresso machine serviced." Maren set the heavy machine down on the counter. "Wanted to make sure you could have your coffee in the morning."

"You're such a peach." Alicia cast a nervous glance at Professor Bejamaca, knowing she had to introduce Maren without letting on the true reason for the professor's visit. Digging her fingernails into her palm, Alicia said, "Professor, this is Maren Pressley, my personal assistant. Maren, this is Professor Bejamaca. He's visiting from Boston, and we're just discussing his fascinating research."

Brooke exhaled sharply at the obvious lie Alicia was trying to feed Maren.

"Nice to meet you, Professor. I'll be back in the morning," Maren said, smiling first at Professor Bejamaca and then at Alicia.

Before the door closed completely behind Maren, Brooke tossed her copies of the essays on the table and said loudly, "These essays don't sound like me at all."

"Without knowing you well, Brooke, it's difficult to capture your voice," Professor Bejamaca explained. "We can work on the tone and edit the language so the essays sound more authentically like you. But we should probably focus first on picking the essays we want to refine."

"But these are all stupid and boring," she said, pushing the papers back toward the professor. "This isn't at all what I told you I wanted to say."

"Brooke, honey, Professor Bejamaca's writing is so crisp and descriptive," Alicia said, putting her hand on her daughter's arm. "And these are the topics your outside college consultant, Cynthia McIntyre, recommended last summer. I'm sure she knows what she's talking about."

"I think I'll just use the essays I wrote last summer at that boot camp you made me go to," Brooke said.

Alicia swallowed. Hard. Brooke had been right about those essays the first time; they were abominations that wouldn't even get her accepted to community college. Alicia mentally tallied up the $25,000 she'd paid Cynthia plus the $15,000 fee she was paying Professor Bejamaca (plus the Red Sox tickets and what it cost her in fuel and pilot time to fly him round trip on her plane). And the $95,000 Range Rover for Brooke. Who spends $150,000 on five fucking essays? Four years of EBA tuition for just over three thousand words. Obviously, money wasn't the issue, but still. Alicia screwed on a tight smile while she collected some more constructive thoughts.

But Brooke wasn't done. "I saw you added babysitting to my activities résumé. I've never babysat for anyone in my life. I feel like you and Cynthia want me to lie on my college application." She crossed her arms and gave Alicia the death stare.

"Brooke, don't be ridiculous. You babysat your cousins the last three summers when we were in Telluride." She hoped her daughter wouldn't fact-check that quasi-truthful statement and further embarrass her. Her cousins had been with them at their house in Telluride, that was true. And they definitely acted like children, even if they were all in college. "Why don't we just pick two of Professor Bejamaca's essays to submit and we can all get back to the rest of our lives? Professor, perhaps you have two you'd recommend?"

The professor adjusted his reading glasses. "Yes, I think the one about being attacked on social media about the pregnancy test and the one about exploring your relationship with religion after spending the weekend at the Vatican with the Pope."

"Those are excellent choices, Professor," Alicia said. "Brooke, don't you agree?"

"Fine, whatever. Does that mean we're done?" Brooke asked, pushing back her chair.

Alicia ignored her petulant daughter. "Professor Bejamaca, it looks like we're all set. Thank you so much for your help," Alicia said. "I'll request an Uber to take you to the airfield. My pilot's on standby. She'll have you back to Boston by early morning. Go Red Sox!" She handed him an envelope containing payment for his services, two World Series tickets, and a copy of his signed nondisclosure agreement.

An hour later, Deborah finished proofreading all the components of Brooke's application. For an extra $1,000, she agreed to make the changes online and upload the essays for Brooke. All that was left was for Brooke to hit Submit. Unlike every other task associated with the entire college admissions journey, Alicia only had to ask her to do it once. And then Brooke held out her hand for the keys to the brand-new, fully loaded, pearl-navy Range Rover she knew was waiting for her in the garage.

MEMORIAL HOSPITAL
EMERGENCY ROOM

SATURDAY, OCTOBER 30, 2:30 A.M.

WHEN THE UNAUTHORIZED ENTRY doors finally swung open, Maren stood, her heart pounding. A man in blue scrubs, clearly exhausted, walked into the waiting room and pulled the surgical cap from his head as he came toward Maren, revealing a mop of curly brown hair.

"Mrs. Pressley? I'm Dr. Grant. Your daughter is in recovery now from surgery."

Relief swept through Maren. She's alive. "Oh thank God. So she's going to be OK? What kind of surgery?"

Dr. Grant rubbed the back of his neck. "When she arrived, she was disoriented with an obvious head wound. We did a CT scan, which is our standard procedure for a head injury. Unfortunately, that test showed an acute epidural hematoma, which is a broken blood vessel in the brain that causes bleeding between the brain's outer membrane and the skull. We drilled a small hole in her skull so we could tie off the blood vessel and stop the bleeding."

"Wait, are you saying my daughter just had brain surgery?"

He nodded once. "It's rare that I can say this in my line of work, but in this case, it sounds worse than it probably is since we were able to catch the bleed so early. It's lucky your daughter was found and transported here quickly, because with a brain bleed, things can change pretty fast."

"Oh my God. Please tell me she doesn't have brain damage." Maren searched Dr. Grant's face for more clues.

"I never make promises, but I expect she's going to do well. We'll be able to assess her neurological function in a few hours once she's out of recovery. When we get her up to the ICU in the morning, you'll be able to see her." He glanced at the clock on the wall. "Why don't you go home and try to get a few hours of sleep?"

"Is there any chance at all I can see her tonight?" Maren asked. "Please. I really need to see her."

"It's possible, but just for a minute or two at most."

Maren tamped down the questions swimming in her head. "Thank you so much, Doctor, for taking such good care of Winnie."

"You know, Mrs. Pressley," Dr. Grant said. "With these rental scooters all over the place, we've seen a huge uptick in head injuries. Kids aren't wearing helmets. Your daughter got extremely lucky this time, but tell her she needs to wear a helmet from now on. Doctor's orders."

"Yes, of course," Maren said. "That's if I ever let her leave the house again."

As she wobbled and reached back for her chair, Maren replayed Dr. Grant's terrifying words: We'll be able to assess her neurological function in a few hours... For Winnie's entire life, Maren's only mission had been *to give her the kind of unconditional love and support Maren herself had been denied. But now, Winnie needed more. She needed a mom who wasn't a coward. A mom who would fight for her. Maren looked up at the sterile square ceiling tiles and vowed, hand to heart: she was done screwing around with Winnie's future. If Winnie pulled through this, first Maren would nurse her back to health. Then she'd figure out who did this to her daughter. Finally, she'd make damn sure Winnie got everything she deserved. It was two days until the deadline, and if her brilliant, beautiful, hardworking daughter wanted to go to Stanford, Maren would not only have her back, she would join the battle.*

PART

2

15

Maren

MAREN WAITED AT MEMORIAL another hour after Dr. Grant left in hopes they might let her catch a glimpse of Winnie, until the nurse finally delivered word that she should go home and come back in the morning. Though she viewed the suggestion of sleep as optimistic at best, she went home anyway to take a quick shower, hoping to rinse off the stale stench of desperation from her body. It was nearly four a.m. when Maren walked in her front door, and she was back at Memorial by six.

Two hours later, an ICU nurse finally led Maren to Winnie's room down a long hallway. She entered the room prepared for the worst, or so she thought, until she laid eyes on Winnie for the first time. Were it not for her thick mane of blond hair, now matted with blood, she might not have recognized her daughter at all. She almost couldn't bear the sight of her but then instantly berated herself. The small shaved section on the right side of her head near her temple, peeking out above the bandages, made no secret of the fact that she'd just had a hole drilled into her skull. Maren grabbed the bed rail and fought off a wave of light-headedness. Then she took a slow, girding inhale and forced herself to study Winnie's face for familiar signposts. It was hard to see past all the swelling and bruising. *Please let her brain be intact. I can handle almost anything, but not that.*

Winnie's blue hospital gown stuck out from the top of the sterile white blanket, and her right arm was in a cast. Searching for a body part she could touch without causing more pain, Maren settled on Winnie's left hand. With her index finger, Maren traced a small heart on the palm of Winnie's hand, their secret code for "I love you" from Winnie's childhood. No response. Maren began talking, hoping her voice might rouse Winnie from what seemed to be a restless sleep. If Winnie could just give her a sign. "Winnie," she said. "It's me. Mom. Please wake up. I need to know you're OK. I love you so much. Please, Winnie?"

Winnie stirred but didn't open her eyes.

"Winnie, please wake up," she pleaded, this time a little louder. "Winnie, honey…you're in the hospital. Can you open your eyes for just a second?" She traced another heart, this time pressing a little harder.

Winnie's head shifted slightly toward Maren's voice, and it appeared she was struggling to open her left eye, just a slit.

"I'm right here, Win. Can you see me?"

In response, Winnie wiggled her index finger and contorted her lips into a hint of the smile Maren adored, and that was enough. Maren burst into tears. A wholesale breach of the seawall. She kissed the top of Winnie's head, dripping no small amount of tears onto her daughter's battered face, but she didn't care as long as Winnie recognized her. "I'm s-sorry, sorry—" she said, choking back her sobs. "But you know who I am, right, Win?"

Winnie nodded.

"Oh thank God. I've been terrified. I love you so much. We'll get through this, I promise."

Winnie winced, her pain evident.

"Win, you were in a bad scooter accident. Do you remember anything?"

"No," she mouthed.

"Anything at all from last night?" she prodded as one of the monitors started beeping. It sounded like a piece of heavy machinery backing up on a construction site.

The ICU nurse rushed in, took one look at the offending monitor, and said, "Her heart rate is elevated. I think she's had enough excitement for now. Why don't you go get some coffee?"

The nurse's brusque tone indicated that this was an order, not a suggestion. Maren felt her face flush. "But I just got here."

"In the ICU, visiting hours are governed by the patient's condition, not the clock."

While she was peeved about being shooed out of her daughter's room, she feared doing anything to set back Winnie's recovery. Nodding at the nurse, Maren said, "Please take good care of her." She grabbed a handful of tissues from Winnie's bedside and wiped her nose.

The nurse turned toward voices coming from the hallway. "On second thought, here comes the team on rounds. You may as well hear what the attending has to say. Stand in the corner over by the sink and stay out of the way."

Maren did as she was told.

"Hello, there, Miss Pressley," announced the attending physician in a cheery voice as he strode in the door flanked by his team of five residents. He was the shortest person in the room, but his presence was commanding, and his eyes were fixed on Winnie. "Let's have a look and see how you're doing this morning." When he noticed Maren standing in the corner, he introduced himself. "I'm Dr. Patel."

"Hi, I'm Maren, her mom. How is she, Doctor? She opened her eyes and responded to me a minute ago. That's a good sign, right?"

"Absolutely," Dr. Patel said, pushing his glasses up on the bridge of his nose. He sat on a swivel stool and reviewed Winnie's records on the computer. "It looks like she woke up during the night a couple of times. She appeared aware of her surroundings and understood she'd been in an accident. She had a neurology consult early this morning, which looks like it went well. All very encouraging."

"Oh thank goodness," she said. "So she's going to be OK?"

Dr. Patel scratched his balding head and clicked through several screens. "All things considered, Mrs. Pressley, your daughter is a very lucky young woman. The fractures in her right arm were evaluated by the ortho team. They were able to set the bones, so that's also good news. All in all, I expect she'll make a strong recovery. We should be able to move her to the general care floor later this morning. Be prepared though. She'll probably be pretty out of it for several days, maybe even a week, until the swelling subsides. The best thing for her now is rest, and that means as little physical and emotional agitation as possible." He nodded at the nurse in the doorway as he led his team from the room.

The ICU nurse turned to Maren. "Why don't you go get some coffee while your daughter sleeps? It'll be the best thing for her, I promise. I'll take your cell phone number and call you when she wakes up."

Maren wrote her number down on the clipboard the nurse handed her. Winnie's eyes were still closed, but Maren gave her a light kiss on the cheek. "It's all going to be OK, Win. I promise. You just sleep." As she ducked out of the room, Maren checked her watch—it was a quarter after eight. The Stones lived only a mile from the hospital, and she could easily dash over there to fulfill her morning duties. With a tsunami of medical expenses now forming on the horizon, Maren needed to keep her job for as long as possible. Because once they pushed the button on Winnie's application to Stanford, all bets would be off. Maren would have six weeks, at most, to develop a disaster plan in case Winnie got in and Brooke did not. In the meantime, she had to figure out how to keep her daughter out of harm's way.

16

Alicia

WITH BROOKE'S STANFORD APPLICATION submitted at last, Alicia awoke on Saturday morning with a looseness in her limbs she hadn't felt in months. No more harping on Brooke. No more worrying about missed deadlines. It was only a matter of time now. As Brooke strolled into the kitchen with her eyes glued to her phone, Alicia glanced at the stove clock. It was one p.m., but she was not about to let her daughter's slovenly sleep habits ruin her good mood. "Hey, sleepyhead."

"Oh my God! Did you know Winnie was in an accident last night?" Brooke asked.

"What on earth are you talking about?" Alicia set her lukewarm coffee cup on the island.

"Maren just posted on Winnie's Insta account. Said she was seriously injured riding one of those rent-a-scooters."

"That's terrible!" Alicia's hand flew up to her mouth. "Is she OK?" She grabbed her phone to check her texts, but the last one from Maren had been Friday morning. Why hadn't Maren texted her? "It must have happened after Maren stopped by last night, but it can't be too bad if Maren was here this morning, right? I had a personal training session at the club and then stayed for a spin class so I didn't see her, but she cleaned up our dinner dishes and made us each smoothies. She even left a note that she took Cardinal out for his walk."

"I dunno, it sounds pretty bad. She's in the hospital." Brooke took her smoothie out of the fridge.

Maren's standard schedule included working Saturday mornings, but her daughter had been in a serious accident and she'd had the wherewithal to come to work anyway? Had Maren come to work because she couldn't afford a day off? Did Maren even have health insurance? Alicia didn't provide it for any of her household employees. At this point, it would be embarrassing to ask.

"But, Mom," Brooke interrupted Alicia's thoughts. "It sounds like it wasn't an accident." She handed her phone to her mom. "Someone tried to kill her."

"What are you talking about? That's crazy." Alicia's pulse quickened as she took the phone and looked at the Instagram post on Brooke's screen. There was a screenshot of a text received on Winnie's phone from an unknown number:

Today 11:34 a.m.

Shame you survived. Maybe next time you won't be so lucky. Take the hint and back off Stanford.

Underneath the photo of the text was a caption that read:

winnie_press2 This is Winnie's mom, Maren. Wanted to let her friends know she was run off the road on a rent-a-scooter last night and is in the hospital. Winnie received the threat shown above this morning. If you know anything about this, please contact me. Stay safe, everyone.

"This is about Stanford?" Alicia said.

"Oh my God. Seriously? Someone tries to kill Winnie and all you care about is Stanford?"

"Oh please," Alicia said. "Did they call the police?"

"I have no idea. Why? Are you worried?" Brooke sassed. "First we find out there's only one spot left, and then someone tries to knock off my competition? Everyone knows you're psycho about Stan—"

Alicia practically sprinted for the basement stairs. She'd never heard Bryan come home after he stormed out during the college application intervention. Now he was camped out watching sports in their home theater—first the UW football game and then later the World Series game that Professor Bejamaca would be attending on her dime. "What the hell did you do?" Alicia stood in front of him, glaring, her hands on her hips and elbows spread wide, trying to block his view, which, given the size of the massive screen, wasn't easy.

"What are you talking about?" He peered around her.

"Winnie." She paused, watching closely for a reaction, but Bryan's face was blank. "She was in a serious accident last night? Someone tried to run her off the road? Sent her a threatening text about Stanford?"

"That sucks. Is she OK?" He tipped back the beer in his hand.

She lowered her voice. "Bry…you have to tell me: Did you have something to do with this?"

"Yeah, right." He chuckled. "After the way you reacted to my harmless comment to Maren, you really think I'd do something like that?" He cracked his neck. "Maybe she'll finally get the message though. I can't wait till we're done with all this college BS. Can you please move?"

"It's not like I want something awful to happen to Winnie. I just don't want her taking Brooke's spot."

"Leesh, we're kicking a field goal—I can't see."

"Oh my God." A wave of nausea hit her as she collapsed into the recliner next to Bryan's. "You don't think that stuff you said to Maren about her job the other day could make us look guilty, do you? Shit. This could get really ugly."

"Relax. No one's gonna think that."

Alicia prayed her husband was right. However, if experience was any indication, the odds weren't good.

———

Alicia peeled off her workout clothes and closed her eyes tight. For a moment, she gave thanks it was Winnie and not Brooke in that accident. She made a mental note to increase Brooke's security. For all she knew, it was that nutcase Kelly or her daughter, Krissie, and Brooke could be the next target on the list. Alicia had barely survived losing her brother, Alex. She wasn't sure what she'd do if anything terrible ever happened to her only child. Her relief that Brooke was safe was quickly replaced by guilt over Maren. No mother should ever have to endure the fear of losing a child.

Forever seared in her memory was the sound of her own mother screaming after the police officer delivered the devastating news that Alex had been killed. He and his best friend, Paul, had been partying with their swimming buddies. They were both drunk far beyond the legal limit, but Paul drove Alex home anyway. So much for all those lectures about not drinking and driving. They were six blocks away when Paul ran a red light and they were T-boned by another car. Alex died instantly, while Paul survived and was paralyzed from the chest down. Two years ago, Alicia footed the bill for construction of a new, more accessible home for Paul in a grand gesture of forgiveness that the media hungrily devoured. But forgiveness and a sterling public persona would never bring back Alex and make her whole again.

Alicia put on her robe and padded back to her dressing room for her phone. She stood there for more than a minute trying to decide what to text Maren. Accidents and threats aside, she was still furious with Maren for lying to her about Stanford and Winnie's father. But in light of the threat Winnie had just received—coupled with Bryan's ill-conceived effort to "help" the other day—Alicia had no choice but to continue pretending nothing was amiss. The last thing she needed was anyone thinking she or Bryan had had something to do with Winnie's accident.

> **Alicia:** Brooke just told me about Winnie. Is she OK? Are you OK? What happened?

> **Maren:** She was riding one of those electric scooters. Brain bleed, surgery, broken arm

> **Alicia:** OMG! I can't believe you didn't call me!!! Is she still in the hospital?

Maren: Out of ICU as of a few minutes ago.

Alicia: Brooke showed me that awful text. I assume the police are involved. Any leads?

Maren: Nothing yet—text sent from burner

Alicia: That's terrible. I insist you take a couple days off. Paid of course. Use my credit card to order groceries. Whatever you need.

Maren: Thx. Really appreciate it. What about SST meeting on Monday?

Alicia: I'll tell Bryan he needs to go.

Maren: Thx—I'll email him all the info he needs by end of wknd

Bryan. She'd been so eager to believe he had nothing to do with the accident that she'd smothered her instinctive emotional response when he asked: "Do you really think I'd do something like that?" The truth was she didn't know what he or anyone else was capable of doing—herself included.

17

Kelly

IN THE FEW DAYS since Krissie had submitted her application, well ahead of the November 1 deadline, Kelly found herself plagued by the niggling sense she'd overlooked some key piece of information. If anything, her college surveillance operation needed to intensify now that the deadline was only two days away. Today, she planned to kill time during Kaleb's Saturday afternoon fencing lesson with another round of social media research to see if she could get final confirmation about who else was applying. For months, she had focused on Brooke and Winnie as Krissie's only competition, but there was always a chance someone else could have flown under her radar. Kelly clicked open Krissie's Instagram account. In the midst of the usual photos of kids partying, dogs, and girls experimenting with filters—and the occasional reference to college, but nothing that raised a red flag—was a post by Maren from Winnie's account. As she read the post detailing Winnie's accident and the threat she'd received, Kelly gasped, causing several other mothers in the waiting area outside the gym to look up from their phones. *Unbelievable!* After everything Kelly had done to torpedo Winnie's application, the threat made it clear: Winnie had still been planning to apply to Stanford.

Ignoring the inquisitive stares, Kelly went out to her car to wait for Kaleb. She pulled out a large bag of Pirate's Booty and feverishly paged through Facebook, Instagram, and Snapchat as the full situation came into view. Setting aside her surprise that all her efforts to deter Winnie had failed, not to mention that Maren allowed Winnie to use those motorized death traps, Kelly worried that her made-up rumor might make her indirectly responsible for Winnie's accident. Her text had swept across campus and had left a path of scorched earth and seething parents in its wake. You couldn't turn the corner at an EBA sporting event, PTA meeting, or parent coffee without a group of adults discussing with vitriol the "Pressley situation" as it had been dubbed. One father of a Princeton hopeful went so far as to shout for Winnie's expulsion outside the college counselor's office, drawing a crowd of faculty and students alike. And each day, Ted Clark appeared more and more harried as he fielded calls and appointments with venomous parents. She'd only wanted to reveal Maren and Winnie as the liars they were, but now it seemed everyone wanted them to pay. Was it possible one of the parents on the receiving end of her anonymous text had tried to mow down Winnie? And what if they were trying to frame Kelly? After all, Kelly had publicly announced Krissie's intent to apply to Stanford on Facebook. Everyone knew there was only one spot left. Oh God. What if people thought she was the one who had done this?

Kelly paused her fretting long enough to thank her lucky stars that such a horrible thing had happened to Winnie and not to Krissie. She couldn't bear the thought of something happening to one of her kids. But then it occurred to her: Maren's signoff had been "Stay safe, everyone." Was Krissie in danger too? Kelly whipped off a text to Kevin to keep a close eye on Krissie until they learned more. But as she pushed Send, the more pressing question, the one she could not bring herself to give voice to, even to Kevin, did cartwheels in the back of her mind: Did Krissie have something to do with Winnie's accident? Kelly climbed out of the car and checked the Volvo three times for body damage, but thankfully none of the scratches in the dark-gray paint looked new.

The accident occurred sometime Friday evening. Kelly had made gluten-free spaghetti with turkey meatballs (tofu balls for Katherine) for dinner, and they'd watched *The Princess Bride* as a family. Their favorite family movie of all time, although that night, she was the only one who actually watched and quoted the movie out loud, while Kevin fell asleep on the couch, Kaleb and Katherine stared at their phones, and Krissie quizzed herself for her AP Microeconomics class. Kelly closed her eyes tight, wishing she could forget that halfway through the movie, Krissie had tossed her flash cards on the coffee table, announced she was going to work out, and grabbed Kelly's car keys. From what Kelly could piece together, the site of Winnie's accident was near Krissie's usual route to and from the gym.

Now Kelly sat paralyzed with fear. She couldn't decide what terrified her the most: that her actions could have been the catalyst for Winnie's accident, that Krissie could be the next victim, or that her daughter could have gone off the deep end.

———

For the rest of the weekend, Kelly monitored Krissie's behavior and social media activity even more frequently than usual, but Winnie's misfortune barely registered for Krissie. When Kelly asked her about it, she shrugged and said Winnie was probably lying about this too. Even to Kelly, that sounded harsh. Out of an abundance of caution for Krissie's mental health and not wanting to derail her before the midterm exams that would determine her final grades sent to Stanford as part of her application, Kelly decided to keep her concerns to herself.

Instead, Kelly lay awake ruminating over all the vicious lies circulating across social media platforms linking her to Winnie's accident. Someone had actually taken Kelly's head from a photo on the EBA volunteer webpage and Photoshopped it so it looked like she was piloting a helicopter and then superimposed that image over the photo of Krissie holding the *Seattle Times* article on National Merit Semifinalists. They'd also done the same thing with Kelly's head in place of a snowplow driver and a bulldozer operator. All the memes were captioned "Palo Alto–bound? Yes please!" Another one was just Kelly dressed head to toe in camo and holding a machete with the caption "Guerilla Moms Take No Prisoners!" and another added, "Bushwhacker Mom!" She was guessing these monikers were considered way worse than a tiger mom, a designation she'd long ago embraced.

It seemed especially unfair that Kelly was the only subject of these memes. After word had spread like wildfire last week about Alicia's $15 million donation to Stanford, people must have assumed the Stones didn't need to resort to attacking Winnie to get what they wanted. But wasn't it just as likely that they were incentivized to protect their investment? And what about all those other parents gunning for Ivy Plus schools? They were equally intense.

Regardless of misguided public opinion, though, Kelly would never apologize for being an involved parent and doing whatever was necessary to support her kids. Without having a ton of money to grease the skids like Alicia or so little money that unearned preferences were magically unlocked like Maren, Kelly's kids needed every edge she could give them. So let the haters hate. She would stay the course. And when she came out on top with that coveted acceptance letter to Stanford, she'd leave all those losers behind wondering how on earth she'd done it.

18

Maren

From: Maren Pressley   Sunday, 7:15 p.m.

To: Ted Clark

Subject: Winnie

Hi, Ted,

FYI—Winnie was badly injured in a hit-and-run scooter accident Friday night. Not only that, but while she was recovering from surgery yesterday, she got a text saying: "Shame you survived. Maybe next time you won't be so lucky. Take the hint and back off Stanford."

I met with the police detective on the case. His name is Detective Davis. I gave him your contact info. He'll be in touch. If you or anyone at EBA learns anything about the incident, please contact the East Precinct immediately.

Thankfully, Winnie's recovering and is resting at home now. I'm hopeful she'll make it back to school in a week or so. In the meantime, I trust you'll make sure her teachers cut her all the slack she needs so her grades won't suffer.

And by the way, I thought you said you were going to take care of the parent community? Just so you know, there's no shortage of speculation about who might be capable of doing this to Winnie. I'm forwarding all the texts and emails I've received from "concerned parents" to Detective Davis.

Maren

———

From: Maren Pressley   Sunday, 7:30 p.m.
To: Bryan Stone
Subject: SST Meeting/Snowcoming

Hey, Bryan,

Thanks for filling in tomorrow at the SST meeting so I can stay home with Winnie. The main agenda item is Snowcoming, which is sort of like a winter prom for seniors. Don't ask me why they need a prom for every season. It's scheduled to take place Saturday, December 5. The committee is counting on Alicia to secure a celebrity to announce the surprise location and theme for the dance. Alicia already knows about this, but I don't think she's gotten to it yet. But maybe don't tell them that, especially if Ms. Richards (you may hear the women refer to her as Double Ass behind her back) is at the meeting—just say it's in progress.

Anyway, thanks again and please let me know what action items get assigned to me and/or Alicia at the meeting so I can follow up.

Maren

———

From: Bryan Stone   Sunday, 7:35 p.m.
To: Maren Pressley
Re: SST Meeting/Snowcoming

Thanks for the info. Think I can handle Double Ass, but I'd rather handle yours.

———

From: Maren Pressley   Sunday, 7:37 p.m.
To: Bryan Stone
Re: SST Meeting/Snowcoming

Please don't do that. It's unprofessional, immature, and never gonna happen.

———

Maren pushed Send on her brush-off email to Bryan and then opened the refrigerator to check on the tray of jiggling raspberry Jell-O beans she'd made at six that morning before going to the hospital. It had been a crazy day, but Maren had achieved her goal of getting Winnie discharged a day early. Probably by being a gigantic pain in the ass. And also by confessing to anyone who came within ten feet of Winnie's room that they didn't have health insurance. That seemed to do the trick. By the time the orderly wheeled her aching daughter to the car, the discharge nurses had speed-talked Maren through fifteen pages of instructions covering her post-op care and a host of possible complications. But at the end of it all, Winnie was home, and Maren was grateful for that.

The Jell-O beans had set. Maren transferred them to a bowl to take to Winnie in bed. She hoped they might perk her up the way they had when she was a little girl. With little money to spare in Winnie's elementary school years, Maren had been perpetually on the lookout for inexpensive treats to break up the monotony of their lives. She smiled, recalling the day she had spotted that red plastic Jell-O bean mold at the specialty baking equipment store while searching for a Little Mermaid cake mold for the birthday cake Maren was charged with ghost-baking on behalf of Alicia for Brooke's party. Of course, that party had taken place long before Alicia's PR team remade her into a vanguard feminist business leader. God forbid anyone should learn today that Alicia had once served a party full of eight-year-old girls such an unwoke dessert. Although if that fact ever did come to light, Maren had no doubt she'd finally receive the baking credit she deserved.

But the Jell-O bean mold—that was Maren's real reward. The joy Winnie had derived from it over the years more than made up for Alicia's pathological need to take credit for Maren's work. Snatched up at the discounted price of $1.99, it was the gift that kept on giving, making an appearance for every cold, flu, and skinned knee visited upon Winnie.

With all the bruising around Winnie's skull, face, and jaw, eating was painful, and the nurses had advised a soft-food diet for the next several days. Maren tiptoed into Winnie's bedroom with the bowl of jiggly red and blue beans and set it on Winnie's nightstand. Standing beside the bed, she stared at Winnie in a fitful sleep and thought about all the times she'd made her this same treat. She'd miss that when Winnie went to college, but for now, she was just relieved to have Winnie asleep in her own bed.

"What day is it?" Winnie murmured, opening her eyes. "How long have I been home?"

Maren perched on the side of the bed. "It's Sunday night, honey. You slept all afternoon after we got home from the hospital. Are you hungry? Do you want a Jell-O bean?"

Winnie shook her head and then blinked hard. "Am I too late for Brown? Or wait—am I applying to UW? I can't remember anything." Her eyes were glassy with confusion.

"Winnie," Maren said firmly, "you need to rest. Doctor's orders."

"But—"

"No buts," Maren interrupted. She gently placed a hand on Winnie's leg. "You need to close your eyes now and trust me on college. OK?"

Winnie didn't respond. She was already asleep.

———

After scooping up Winnie's backpack off the floor of her bedroom, Maren sat down at the kitchen table and pulled out Winnie's laptop. She logged in, determined to live up to her promise to her daughter. She located Winnie's

Common Application account and dug around the site. True to form, all the pieces of Winnie's early admission applications for both Brown and Stanford were totally complete and ready to go. As far as Winnie knew, Brown was their final decision. It would be so easy to hit Submit on the Brown application and put this horrible chapter behind them once and for all. She'd miss Winnie terribly for those four years, but there was no denying it was a great school. Maren's hand hovered over the button. But she couldn't do it. From the day Winnie had been conceived, their life together had never been easy or even particularly safe. Why should she make the safe choice now? Winnie wanted Stanford. Winnie had always wanted Stanford. Fuck it. She clicked over to the Stanford tab and pushed the Submit button before she lost her nerve.

———

The doorbell rang, which really annoyed Maren. Yes, it was Halloween, but she'd taped a sign to the door begging for no trick-or-treaters. She jumped up, eager to prevent the bell from ringing a second time and waking Winnie. She opened the door prepared to shoo away a costumed candy grubber, so she was shocked to find Brooke standing there with Ben & Jerry's Chocolate Chip Cookie Dough ice cream and red, puffy eyes. Maren was instantly flooded with memories of the girls lying together on the floor in Brooke's room, giggling maniacally while watching *Hannah Montana* reruns with two spoons deep in one carton of ice cream. She took a step backward and silently gestured for Brooke to come in.

Brooke hadn't set foot in their bungalow since Winnie had joined her at EBA for high school. Neither Maren nor Winnie was ever able to ascertain what had transpired to turn Brooke away from her long-term friendship with Winnie. After months of confusion and hurt feelings, they eventually gave up trying to figure it out and chalked it up to Brooke feeling threatened by Winnie's academic prowess, which probably made Brooke's inability to live up to her mom's high standards that much more painful. Brooke's icy distance even extended to Maren. Whenever Maren was at the Stones' house, Brooke primarily stayed in her room and communicated her requests to Maren by text. Maren hated herself for even thinking it, but as Brooke stepped through the doorway and looked around, it occurred to her that Alicia might have sent her daughter on a fact-finding mission. It didn't help that Maren felt like she'd been caught with her hands in the cookie jar, having impersonated Winnie to apply to Stanford a mere ten minutes earlier.

"My goodness, Brooke. You haven't been over here in forever. I'm guessing you heard about Winnie?"

Brooke nodded.

"Did you bring that ice cream for Winnie?"

Brooke nodded again and handed her the carton.

Maren was trying not to crinkle her eyebrows in concern, but Brooke still hadn't uttered a word. "Are you OK?"

Brooke let out a ragged sob and practically launched herself into Maren's arms. Apparently, the answer was no. She was shaking like she used to as a little girl, the wracking cries that only came from Alicia's disapproval all those years before, and suddenly Brooke was ten years old again, a pseudo daughter and sister to the Pressley girls. Maren led her to the couch.

Finally, Brooke spoke. "Is Winnie going to be OK? I've been the worst friend ever. I'm so sorry, Maren. You've never been anything but amazing to me, and I'm just the biggest asshole. Please tell me she's going to be OK?"

"She was pretty badly injured, but I think she's going to be all right eventually." Maren hesitated but had to ask. "Brooke, do you know anything about who might have done this to her? If you know anything at all, I beg you, please tell me so I can keep her safe."

Brooke shook her head and wiped her eyes with her sleeve before looking at Maren. "I really have no idea at all, Maren. I swear to God." She bit her cuticle, an old habit they'd worked on breaking for years at Alicia's behest. "But my mom is totally losing her shit over Stanford. I hate to even say this out loud. I mean, she is still my mom. But I don't know. I just don't know anymore. Every time I think there's a line she won't cross, she blows right through it."

Now it was Maren's turn to be silent.

"Can I see Winnie? I need to apologize to her. I've been so mean to her ever since she started at EBA. I need to explain why."

"No, honey, I'm sorry. Winnie needs to rest and can't be upset right now. She needs time to heal. You two can talk when she's feeling better."

"When I heard about Winnie's accident, I realized I've never had a friend as true as Winnie. And you've been more like a mom to me than my own mom." Brooke dropped her head into Maren's lap, a familiar position from a lifetime ago. "And I blew it all."

"There's always time to make amends in life, Brooke." Maren stroked her hair. "You just need to decide you're going to be your best self and do it. I believe in you. Always have."

Maren's pep talk brought about a fresh round of tears. "You know," Brooke sputtered, "I don't want Stanford. That's all my mom. I actually hope Winnie gets in and goes there. She deserves it, not me."

Maren stiffened. Was Brooke fishing for information? She hated having to be suspicious of this girl whom she'd loved like a daughter for so many years. "Well, listen, Brooke, you focus on what you want. If you don't want to go to Stanford, find another school you do want to go to and try your best. That's all any of us can do."

Brooke sat up and hugged Maren fiercely. "Thanks, Maren. Please tell Winnie I stopped by and I'd love to see her when she feels better. I hope she still likes chocolate chip cookie dough."

"Oh, she does," Maren assured her with a smile. "You take care of yourself. And please let me know if you hear anything I should know?"

"I will." Brooke nodded solemnly. "Maren? I know I've been a jerk and I've said some mean things to Winnie, but I really hope you believe that I would never physically hurt her and I didn't send that awful text."

"I know, Brooke," Maren said. "It's OK. I believe you."

PART
3

19

Kelly

NEWS OF WINNIE'S HIT-AND-RUN spread through EBA like a
stomach virus, and by Monday morning, the same parents who were
openly discussing the "Pressley situation" with relish were now eyeing
Kelly from the safety of their cars with shut mouths and narrowed eyes as
she made her way from the parking lot to the front door of the main building. Still peeved over the mean-spirited memes targeting her for the crime
of being a conscientious mom, Kelly decided it was time to give Ted Clark
an earful. As the PTA president, she'd become accustomed to relatively
unfettered access to the head of school, but today was not one of those
days. Ted's young administrative assistant, Ryan, must have been alerted
to her arrival when she signed in at the front desk, because he seemed to
be standing guard in front of Ted's closed office door. He stood erect with

an inscrutable facial expression. All that was missing was a military-grade rifle strapped across his chest.

"Good morning, Mrs. Vernon. What can I do for you today?" Ryan asked.

"Hello, Ryan, I need to see Mr. Clark," Kelly said in the sweetest voice she could muster. "It's very urgent."

"He's busy at the moment. Maybe you could—"

Kelly didn't wait for him to finish. "As I said, this is urgent." Kelly dodged past him with a hip check. When she thrust open the door, Ted was staring out the window. *Busy, my ass.*

Ted looked over at her, the intrusion taking him by surprise. "Kelly? Are you OK?"

Kelly was breathing hard, and her hands were curled into balls at her sides. "Did you hear what happened to Winnie? The accident? The threatening text?"

"Yes, I've been in touch with Maren."

"And? What do you plan to do about it?" She took a step closer to his desk. "What if Krissie's next?"

Ted motioned for her to have a seat. Kelly would have preferred to remain standing, but she acquiesced.

He leaned forward, lacing his fingers together in front of him. "We'll be sending out an email to the community later today."

"Are you beefing up security at school? You know I've been saying for years that we need to be doing more—more cameras, facial recognition at all the entrances, a security guard. What about all the rest of us who can't afford private security details at school for our kids? Come to think of it, I demand to know who else is applying to Stanford! How else can I be expected to protect my daughter from this monster?"

"Your vigilance on the topic of school safety is well documented." Ted leaned back in his chair. "Our students' safety is our highest priority. But we take our commitment to confidentiality seriously too," he said pointedly. "As I said, we'll be communicating more later today. The important thing is that we stay calm until we have more information."

He was talking to her in the voice people used to quiet a spooked horse, which really ticked her off. She would wager a year of college tuition that Ted would never dare be so patronizing to Alicia or Diana. "Stay calm? This is awful! I mean, who would do something like this? It certainly wasn't me, but you should see all the cruel things students and parents are posting on social media about me. How could anyone think I would do something like this after everything I've done for this school? Why aren't people pointing fingers at the Stones? I think we both know they're far more—" Kelly stopped herself midsentence. She was rambling. Ted had stopped listening. Kelly stood up. "Well anyway, I'm relieved to know you're taking this seriously. I look forward to receiving your communication. But please know this: if anything happens to Krissie, I will hold EBA and you personally responsible." As she turned to leave, her face smoldered with indignation.

———

Kelly brushed past Ryan's desk without a word and headed toward the conference room for the SST meeting. It wasn't scheduled to start for another half hour, but she wanted to be the first one there. The thought of the other SST mothers gossiping about her before she arrived was more than she could stand. As she walked down the hall, her skin prickled from the furtive stares cast her way by students and faculty alike. She didn't deserve this harsh treatment. She was a mother determined to support her daughter. Not a psycho killer.

As she waited for the other SST members to arrive, Kelly drummed her fingers on the conference table, trying to quell the anxiety that was searing her from the inside out. Beads of sweat dribbled down her back. At least she'd had the foresight to choose a moisture-wicking exercise shirt as her base layer, with the added precautionary measure of self-adhesive underarm sweat pads to avoid pitting out.

This group usually indulged in a boisterous round of college chatter as a warm-up the way athletes stretch before a workout. But today, when Augusta, Diana, Jennifer, Amanda, and Sarah arrived, they were quiet as they took their seats around the table. Kelly couldn't help noticing they were all holding identical to-go coffee cups from the independent Parisian-style café close to school where EBA mothers frequently hung out to kill time, gossip, sip their zero-calorie drinks of choice (black coffee or herbal tea, hold the milk, and God forbid no toxic sugar), and moan about how they were gaining weight that very second just from inhaling the heavenly scent of buttery, fresh-baked croissants. Kelly used to play that game too, but lately, she'd figured if she was going to gain the weight anyway, she might as well enjoy the goods.

She glanced at the clock. It was a few minutes after nine. No sign of Maren, but she couldn't stand to wait in the judgmental silence another second. "So! Shall we get started?" Her voice strained with nerves. "Lots to do today to get ready for Snowcoming." Kelly turned to Sarah, the chair of the Snowcoming dance. "Sarah, can you get us started with an update?"

"Oh sure, um, well, Maren's been handling most of it." Sarah flashed a sheepish smile at Kelly. "In terms of the dance itself, I think she—"

"Hey, ladies. Filling in for Maren today. Sorry I'm late," Bryan Stone said with a wink as he sauntered in doing his level-best imitation of a high school dude in cargo shorts and a rugby pullover. His flip-flops and the Ray-Ban sunglasses pushed up on his head completed the picture.

Kelly's relief that Maren wasn't coming today instantly gave way to annoyance. It was the beginning of November. Why was Bryan wearing shorts and flip-flops?

"Oh, Bryan, it's such a treat to have you here," Amanda said, touching his arm. "It's so rare that we have the male perspective when we're planning activities for the kids. This will be super helpful."

Jeez, was Amanda flirting with him? Amanda and her husband, John, had recently finalized their divorce, and she hadn't been shy about sharing details of her Tinder-driven sexual awakening. Kelly held back a dry heave. The Bryan Stone described in image pieces written about Alicia made him sound sophisticated and evolved, a man who "leaned in" to support his successful wife. That guy in no way matched the reality of the cocky man-child sitting across from her, legs spread wide like he was presenting his dick as a gift to be unwrapped by the lucky ladies of the SST.

"Can you guys believe what happened to Winnie over the weekend?" Bryan said. "Insane, right?"

His words were greeted with about the same degree of shock as if he'd taken a crap on the floor right in front of them. All eyes swiveled from Bryan to Kelly. "It's crazy. I mean, who would do such a thing?" she said, feeling her cheeks grow hot. "I went to see Ted Clark this morning, and he assured me that our students' safety is his highest priority and he will be sending out information to the community later today." She hoped the group would realize and spread the word that if she'd gone to meet with Ted Clark, she couldn't possibly be guilty.

"Alicia has her security team looking into it," Bryan said, scratching the stubble on his chin. "They're tracking down a lot of leads right now."

Kelly shuddered, wondering if Alicia's crack security team would be able to figure out what had happened to Winnie. She couldn't deny she was worried. "Has anyone heard how Winnie's doing?"

From the uncomfortable silence, it was obvious that none of the women had bothered to reach out to Maren with a supportive text. Herself included. They'd all been too focused on guessing whodunit and helping their kids finish their early admission applications. Kelly heard a story about one dad who was so obsessed with proofreading his son's application to Columbia that he had missed his uncle's funeral in Arizona.

"I just feel so horrible," Amanda said. "After everything Winnie's been through, I hope she gets exactly what she wants for college."

Yeah right. As long as it's not Duke? Kelly mentally challenged Amanda's pandering declaration.

"Oh, I know," Augusta said. "Bless their hearts. Maren and Winnie are so sweet."

"Actually, I woke up this morning thinking we need to set up a meal train," Amanda continued. "After that kind of scare, I'm sure they could use our support."

"That's such a great idea," Diana said. "Poor Winnie—and after she's worked so hard at EBA."

Kelly couldn't believe her ears. This was the same woman who only last week was calling for Winnie's expulsion. But Kelly figured she might as well follow the lead of all the other women eager to clear their names from the suspect list. "You know, I'm running to Costco tomorrow. I can grab something for the first meal train slot."

"That's awesome. I'll take the next spot," Sarah chimed in. "Honestly,

I can't believe no one ever warned us how brutal this whole college process would be. I for one can't wait for it to be over. And I hope *all* our kids get what they want."

"I think that's something we can all agree on," Kelly said. "Anyway, back to our agenda. I'm thrilled to announce Diana has been able to secure the use of a spectacular yacht on Lake Union for Snowcoming. Thank you so much, Diana."

Diana beamed. "My pleasure!"

Kelly continued, "So in light of the floating location, I thought it would be amazing for the kids if we made it a Noah's Ark theme. Maybe decorate the yacht with giant pairs of stuffed animals hanging from the ceiling?"

"Hmm, I don't think my friend would allow decorations to be attached to the interior," Diana said.

"Well, I'm sure Maren can figure out a way to do it without damaging anything," Kelly said.

"That's true," Diana said. "She's a magician, that one!"

Kelly tried not to barf right there on the table.

"Um, Bryan," Sarah said, tucking her hair behind her ear. "Maren didn't happen to give you an update on the celebrity for the big assembly?"

"Celebrity? Oh right, yeah, hold on." Bryan reached into his pocket and pulled out his cell phone. "Yeah, she sent me an email. I just gotta find it."

"Oh thank goodness," Sarah said, barely able to contain her relief, a feeling that was mirrored on the faces of the women around the table. Per usual, Maren had it all under control, and no one actually serving on the committee would be called upon to do the work themselves.

"OK, yeah, here it is," Bryan said, skimming the email and scrunching up his face. "Looks like it's in the works."

"In the works? That's it?" Kelly said.

"What's the big deal? I'm sure it will all work out." Bryan leaned back in his chair. "It's just a stupid announcement for a dance, right? Explain to me why there needs to be a celebrity?"

Now Kelly could see his legs splayed so far apart they were touching Amanda on one side and nearly reaching Sarah on the other. Was it still called manspreading when it crossed over into foreplay? "Well, Bryan," Kelly responded, fighting to maintain her composure. "It's called school tra-di-tion. Last year's SST got Russell Wilson to do it, and I do not want to be the one to disappoint our kids with a lame showing. In case you hadn't noticed, our kids have to work so hard to get into college that many of them are depressed, anxious, cutting, anorexic, and even suicidal. It's the SST's responsibility to plan activities to help reduce their stress and have a little fun. So hoping it all works out really doesn't cut it for this group."

"Wow, someone needs to Netflix and chill." Bryan chuckled, his eyes sweeping the room.

Unable to control themselves, the other women laughed out loud before quickly stifling their reactions. Kelly hoped that only she could smell her flop sweat. It wasn't hard to miss that everyone was avoiding eye contact with her.

"You know, I've been thinking." Diana's voice turned sassy. "Why should the kids have all the fun? We should have a stress buster for the parents while the kids are at their dance!" She clapped her hands together, applauding her own suggestion.

"Oh my God, that's the best idea!" Sarah squealed.

"It will be so fun! Maren can help me." Diana covered her mouth with her hand and let out a playful laugh. "Oopsy. Bryan, is it OK if I use Maren for this?"

Bryan looked up from his phone and shrugged. "Fine by me."

"Does that work for you and the SST, Kelly?" Diana asked.

If Diana wanted to spend her own time and money planning one of her infamous over-the-top parties, who was Kelly to stop her? Besides, it wasn't like parents could go to Snowcoming as chaperones anyway. After homecoming, the administration had sent out an email that parent volunteers would no longer be needed for school events, which was a polite way of saying they were banned. Apparently, the chaperones had been too busy gathering gossip and photographing the kids to notice the illicit drinking taking place under their noses. "Fine by me, Diana. As long as you're not counting on the SST budget to cover more than a few snacks. Anyway, I think we're done here." Kelly sprang to her feet and adjourned the meeting.

Amanda wasn't quite done though. "So, Kelly, just to confirm… you're doing the first meal train delivery for Maren and Winnie, right? Tomorrow?" She scribbled on the makeshift calendar she'd drawn on the backside of her SST meeting agenda. "Just want to make sure they know they have our full support."

"Yes, Amanda. I said I would," Kelly huffed over her shoulder as she tore out of the room and headed to the parking lot.

The second she reached the safety of her car, she ripped free the damp underarm sweat pads. They'd done their job and deserved a five-star Amazon review. But more disgusting than the used sweat pads now adhering to her dashboard was the way the entire room had sucked up to Bryan. Even worse, it was obvious that every single one of those women was now rooting for Winnie. Or at least pretending to be. What a difference a week made.

———

From: Ted Clark   Today, 2:55 p.m.

To: EBA Senior Class Parents,

Guardians, EBA Senior Class

Subject: EBA Community Values

Dear EBA Seniors, Parents, and Guardians,

As you may have heard, EBA senior Winnie Pressley was in a scooter accident over the weekend. Soon after the accident, she received a threatening text related to college. Winnie is recovering well from her injuries and is hoping to return to school next week. The police are actively investigating the accident and the text. If you have any information, please see me or contact the Seattle East Precinct directly.

Student safety is our highest priority. We have a security guard posted outside the school throughout the day, we have monitored cameras at all doors, and we've implemented a host of other tools, strategies, and emergency systems.

We understand that the college admissions process is a time of uncertainty, excitement, and high anxiety. However, it's critical that we never lose sight of EBA's community values. While what happened to Winnie is both extreme and abhorrent, it is far from the only instance of egregious behavior during this particular college admissions cycle.

We remind you of the following (especially parents and guardians, who have been the biggest offenders—by far—in each of these categories of misdeeds):

- Do not provide information, anonymous or otherwise, to the school about another student or, in the case of parents and guardians, about any student for whom you are not legally responsible. This includes information about a student's finances, ethnic and religious background, family, athletic résumé, cyberactivity, sexual orientation, sexual history, recreational drug use, moving violations, academic violations, and school attendance records. In case you are wondering, these are real examples of communications we've received about students this fall alone. This shall hereafter be known as the Golden Rule, EBA college edition.

- Do not solicit information about another student from the administration or faculty members.

- Do not contact any college or university with information about another student, whether anonymously or not.

- Do not monitor social media looking for damaging information about other students.

- Do not pressure students or parents to share college application plans, and do not gossip about who is applying where.

- Do not make judgmental comments about any colleges. It's

unkind and obnoxious—and makes all students feel unnecessary anxiety.

- Do not bring cookies, treats, or other gifts to the college counseling office.

- Do not come to the college counseling office without an appointment. Parents will no longer be allowed to loiter in or near the office after several suspected instances of eavesdropping.

- Do not lie in wait in the parking lot for college counselors. They will not talk to you about college outside the confidential office environment.

- Do not ask the college counselors how much money you should donate to X university to guarantee extra consideration for your child. There is no magic number, and if there was, we would not share it with you.

- Do not threaten violence or inflict bodily harm on an EBA student. Ever. Shaking my head that I even have to type these words. Yet here we are.

In case these rules are not clear or comprehensive enough, there is really only one question you need to ask yourself when considering any college-related action: *Might* this make me look like a gigantic elephant's asshole? If yes, just don't.

We have a wonderful senior class, and I have every hope and expectation that each student will find their best college fit.

Sincerely,

Ted Clark

Head of School

P.S. Please forgive my use of colorful language, but I've tried every nonprofane way I can think of to get these points across in previous emails, private conversations with parents and students, and impassioned remarks at assemblies. Here's hoping the message finally gets through. Because frankly, your EBA faculty and administration are all VFT (very fucking tired).

20

Maren

AFTER A FULL DAY spent catching up on paperwork and shuttling back and forth between the kitchen and Winnie's bedroom, Maren had just turned on the stove to heat up a carton of tomato soup for dinner when the doorbell rang. Tiptoeing to the door, she peered through the cloudy peephole. On the other side was the distorted face of Kelly Vernon, clearly trying to get a reverse glimpse through the looking glass. Until this fall, Maren had always thought of Kelly as an annoying but basically harmless ninny. But maybe she had underestimated Kelly. Perhaps she was more like those no-see-um bugs Maren used to dread as a kid when her parents took her to Florida on vacation—you barely noticed them until suddenly you'd been bitten a hundred times. Or your kid had been run off the road. All Maren wanted to do was eat her soup and go to bed, but instead, she smoothed her hair and straightened her back as she unlocked the deadbolt and opened the door. "Hi, Kelly, what a surprise."

"Hi, Maren. Amanda set up a meal train for you guys, and I took the first slot. Sorry for not texting first, but I brought you this Costco lasagna. How's Winnie's feeling? We're all so worried about her."

Kelly's face was studiously grim, her lips drooping awkwardly at the corners and eyebrows so pinched that the overall effect resembled an excruciating piece of performance art. But at least she came bearing free food. "Gosh, thank you. Do you want to come in?" *Please say no.*

"Oh! I don't want to intrude! But OK, maybe just for a minute," Kelly said, already several steps into the living room, which doubled as the front entry in their small but tidy home. Kelly took in the entire house with one glance, her eyes landing on the boot tray by the door with Winnie's and Maren's shoes neatly arranged. She appeared to be weighing whether she should remove her sneakers as Maren had seen her do so automatically at Alicia's house. "Oops—sorry about my shoes! I'll only stay a minute." She must have decided worrying about disgusting street germs was a luxury of wealth, sort of like buying organic.

"Thank you for thinking of us. Here, let me take that off your hands." Maren's arms almost gave way under the weight of the massive tray. "This will definitely come in handy, especially once Winnie is back to solid foods." She walked into the kitchen with Kelly at her heels and set the frozen tray of lasagna on the counter. It would never fit into Maren's freezer, and probably not even into her apartment-sized oven. But if she let it thaw a bit, she could slice it into serving size pieces and refreeze the extra portions.

"Oh! I didn't hear all the details of her injuries," Kelly said. "Did she break her jaw?"

"No, thank goodness. But the side of her face is covered in road rash and bruises, so she's really sore." Maren snuck a peek at the closed bedroom door and prayed Winnie would stay put. Four days after the accident, Winnie was still foggy and listless. She had a constant headache and struggled to find a comfortable sleeping position with her broken arm, the surgical site, and all the scrapes and bruises. Winnie was still in such bad shape that it might raise suspicion about whether she'd been able to apply to Stanford by the deadline of her own volition. The last thing Maren needed was to get hauled into EBA again for another Ted Clark interrogation.

"Poor Winnie," Kelly said. "It's just so awful what happened to her."

"I honestly never thought applying to college could be so dangerous," Maren said.

"Do you have any idea who could have done this to her? That threat was so terrifying."

"No clue." Maren shrugged but kept her eyes trained on Kelly's facial expressions in case she gave anything up. "I'm leaving that to the police."

"Oh right. Of course. I mean, I'm sure they're on top of it."

Maren nodded. Was Kelly's flustered reaction a sign of guilt? "At first, they thought there might not be enough evidence to pursue an investigation, but I guess the threat changed their minds. It sounds like the police will be poking around EBA and interviewing all the families with kids applying to Stanford for starters."

"You know, there's a rumor going around school that Winnie's planning to apply to every top-ten school," Kelly said. "I know for a fact a lot of people were really upset about it. Even though the threat talked about Stanford, really lots of parents at EBA might've had motive. I thought you'd want to know."

"That's quite a rumor," Maren said, not sure whether to believe Kelly. Maren wasn't born yesterday. Clearly Kelly had incentive to cast aspersions on other parents, given that she and her notoriously high-strung daughter were two obvious suspects. "You wouldn't happen to know how it got started, would you? Or if there's someone specific—"

"No, no." Kelly shook her head vigorously and opened her palms. "I mean, I really couldn't say. Your guess is as good as mine."

"Well, I'll be sure to pass that information along to the detective on the case. I assume he'll be contacting you for an interview soon."

"Yes, of course," Kelly said, clumsily backing out of the kitchen.

Maren cocked her eyebrow. Evidently, Kelly did not relish talk of police interviews and such.

"Well, listen, I need to run, but please let me know if there's anything else I can do to help. I mean it. Anything."

Maren was tempted to take her up on the disingenuous offer, just to see Kelly's crazytown reaction if Maren were to ask her for something that would really be helpful, like doing some of her own damn work for the SST. But alas, Maren called on her vast, ever-replenishing aquifer of willpower. "Thanks, Kelly. I appreciate the offer. I'll let you know if I think of anything." She ushered Kelly toward the entryway.

"Oh yes, please do. I mean it." Kelly seemed to be talking faster the closer they got to the door. "In the meantime, all you have to do is make a salad and bake some garlic bread and voilà—this should provide you with a few delicious Italian feasts."

It didn't escape Maren's notice that this bulk food offering included neither the salad nor the garlic bread. It also paled in comparison to the numerous elaborate, gourmet meal train deliveries Maren had helped organize at Alicia's behest or received on Alicia's behalf, most recently after Alicia's heartrending Facebook post last year (crafted by her PR team) about putting down their thirteen-year-old dog, Cardinal's father, Leland. Apparently, the less you had, the less you needed, or so went the logic of the wealthy.

Maren was just about to reach for the doorknob when Kelly, in an impressive feat of speed and agility, suddenly placed herself between the door and Maren and rested her hand on the wall. "So before I go...you mentioned UW a few weeks ago, but then with the rumors and the accident... I'm just genuinely curious. Where did Winnie end up applying?" Kelly stared expectantly at Maren.

And there it was. Maren suppressed a smirk. It came as no surprise at all to Maren that Kelly was choosing to ignore Ted's belated attempt to enforce EBA's community values. Maren briefly weighed the benefits of keeping up the UW smokescreen for a few more weeks. It was really none of Kelly's business where Winnie had applied. But Maren was way past her lifetime bullshit quotient. And she'd had it with Kelly especially. She ached to deal with her—and all these blasted EBA parents—head-on for once and put the speculation to rest. If Maren told Kelly the truth, the entire school community would know in about 8.6 seconds. The only thing holding her back was her fear of losing her job. She was bound to lose it at some point soon, but she didn't think Alicia would dare fire her right away, not when she was under such a cloud of suspicion because the threatening text had specifically mentioned Stanford. Her PR people were good, but they weren't magicians. Try as she might, Maren could think of no good reason why she should hold back any longer.

Pulling herself tall, Maren looked squarely at Kelly. "Actually, Kelly." Maren paused and took a breath. "Winnie applied early to Stanford. And Stanford is on the no-loan list, so if she gets in, she'll go for free. Isn't that awesome?"

Kelly's face flashed first with shock and then anger. With what appeared to be a great deal of effort, she settled her lips in the shape of a toothy smile that had all the emotional backing of an emoji. "Isn't that nice," she said in a tone that communicated the opposite. "And so very brave of you." Her nostrils flared as she took a final disapproving glance at Maren's modest home. "Well, I'll let you get back to your evening."

Maren opened the door. "Thanks again for the lasagna, Kelly!" Now Maren was actually grateful she didn't have to endure the awkward few seconds it would have taken Kelly to put her shoes back on. She watched Kelly waddle down the steps to her car before shutting the front door. Maren leaned back against the door, closed her eyes, and counted to ten before she let out her breath and slid down to the floor.

As Maren reflected on the latest rumor apparently making the rounds about her daughter, she could only shake her head. Applying to every top-ten school. Having just logged in to Winnie's application portal, Maren knew for a fact that was a load of crap. The viciousness of the EBA community had long ago ceased to surprise her. But perhaps Kelly had one decent point. Maybe the existence of this rumor meant she needed to expand her thinking about who might have had motive to be gunning for Winnie. Maren was still shuddering at that unnerving thought when Winnie flung open her bedroom door.

"Oh my God! Mom, is it true? Did you really apply to Stanford for me?"

Maren looked up at Winnie from the floor with a mischievous smile. "Well…you can't get in if you don't apply, right? Besides, you did all the work. All I did was push the button."

"But I figured that would be completely off the table after this." She waved her hand over her battered body.

"Then you have a poor opinion of me." Maren grabbed hold of the doorknob and pulled herself up. "I may seem like a pushover sometimes. I get that. I've had to make a lot of tough choices. But when the rubber hits the road, my friend? This girl's got tits of steel." Maren arched her back and pounded two fists against her chest.

"Really, Mom? I really applied early to Stanford?"

"Yup." Maren brushed a dust bunny off her pants. "I refuse to let those entitled pricks take away what you've earned without a fight."

Winnie's eyebrows furrowed. "But what threat were you and Mrs. Vernon talking about?"

Maren walked over to the kitchen junk drawer and pulled out Winnie's phone, which Winnie hadn't even asked for since the accident. Another sign of just how awful her daughter was feeling.

Maren had already managed to get the screen replaced at a repair shop she'd discovered last year after Brooke damaged her fifth brand-new iPhone in the space of six months (apparently phone cases looked too "basic"). "I'm going to show you something on your phone, but then it goes back into the drawer until you're better. Remember that the doctors said you have to rest your brain. But I need to explain what you're going to see." She led Winnie to the couch and turned to face her. "So listen. When you were in the ICU, I had your phone, and you received a text."

"What did it say?"

"In a nutshell, back off Stanford or whoever did this to you would finish the job." She pulled up the text and showed it to Winnie.

"Oh my God. This is insane." She dropped the phone down on the couch like it was radioactive. "And you still let me apply? Aren't you terrified?"

"Of course I am. But we can't let this stand in the way of your dreams." Maren took hold of Winnie's uncasted hand and paused for a beat before continuing. She looked deep into her daughter's wide eyes. "We—I—can't live in fear anymore. I promised myself when you were in the hospital that

I would stop being an obstacle in your path. I can't control everything, but I can at least do that. The police are investigating and said they'll keep an extra eye on our block. We will obviously need to take precautions. A lot of them. But please trust me. I'm not going to let anything else happen to you." Maren squeezed Winnie's hand.

"I guess if you say so…" Winnie said skeptically. Pulling her hand back, she looked out the window and inhaled deeply, as if a flood of oxygen would give her the strength to accept her mom's assurances.

As Maren watched her pensive daughter take in this new set of facts, she prayed she would be able to make good on her promise. And she renewed her private vow to do whatever it took.

After another few seconds, Winnie finally turned back to face her mother and nodded once. And then a smile, albeit a very crooked one, slowly grew on her face. "So I really applied to Stanford?"

"You bet your ass you did." Maren grinned back and then gingerly pulled Winnie in for a hug. As they relished this rare victory, Maren wished the moment would never end. She loved this girl with all her might.

"You know," Winnie said with a hint of laughter. "I don't think anyone has ever rendered Mrs. Vernon speechless like that. I wish I could have seen her face." Winnie tipped her head back and raised her eyebrows. "I bet that felt freaking amazing, huh?"

Maren nodded at her daughter, slowly and meaningfully. "You have no idea."

21

Alicia

ALICIA TOSSED HER STANFORD-BRANDED stress-relieving squishy ball back and forth between her hands as she listened to her COO wrap up the conference call. She squeezed the ball, thinking about Maren and Winnie's audacity. It hadn't taken long for word to reach her that Winnie had indeed applied to Stanford. But in light of the threat Winnie had received, Alicia's hands were tied. There was nothing she could do at this point other than wait for early admission day to arrive. Five weeks to go.

As the call ended and Alicia removed her headset, her assistant, Charlotte, knocked on the door and stuck her head in. "Got a minute?"

Alicia motioned for her to take a seat in one of the chairs in front of her desk.

The young woman perched on the edge and smoothed her skirt. "I hate to bother you, but that detective has called three times to talk with you about Winnie Pressley's accident," Charlotte said, biting her lip. "I keep telling him you're not available, but I get the sense he's getting really annoyed. I don't know how long I can put him off. What if he just shows up here one day?"

"Oh, Charlotte, you've been watching too much TV," Alicia said, batting away her assistant's worry. "I don't know why he's so eager to talk to me anyway. I certainly don't know anything. Email me his number, and I'll have my lawyer take care of it."

"Great. I'll do that right now." Charlotte stood up, her posture visibly relaxing. "Thank you."

"Can you close my door on the way out?" Alicia spun around in her chair and looked out over Puget Sound. What exactly was she supposed to tell the detective? That her husband and daughter were both furious with her that night and their whereabouts were unknown? That she was pretty certain her daughter had nothing to do with the accident because she couldn't give a shit about going to Stanford and had been doing everything possible to sabotage her own chances? That she herself had sent an email implying Winnie's last semester of EBA tuition was contingent on her not applying to Stanford? That her own husband recently threatened Maren's job if Winnie's application was ever submitted? To calm her worries about Bryan, Alicia had checked all five of their cars, not knowing which one he might have been driving that night. There was barely a ding or a scratch on Alicia's Mercedes SUV, Bryan's Range Rover, Bryan's Ford F-150, the Tesla Model X they all shared, and the Porsche convertible that Bryan only drove during the summer. Certainly nothing that screamed "hit-and-run." Thankfully, Brooke's new Range Rover was still pristine. But the detective was sure to ask where Alicia had been that night. Was she supposed to give him Professor Bejamaca's contact information and risk all the world finding out she'd hired him to write her daughter's college application essays? There wasn't a chance in hell that was going to happen.

Alicia shot off a text to her lawyer with the detective's contact information and explicit instructions to shut the whole thing down. Glancing at her watch, she realized Bryan would be arriving any minute. They'd invited a dozen couples to sit in the Aspyre box to see U2 that night. Part social, part business development. Diana and Michael Taylor were on the guest list. Alicia had been eyeing a company in Michael's portfolio, but Diana was the real reason she'd included them. As the self-appointed doyenne of the Seattle social scene, Diana was not someone you ever wanted to overlook. But Diana had canceled that morning, claiming she'd come down with food poisoning.

While she waited for Bryan, Alicia clicked open her personal email to check for any more last-minute cancellations. She deleted all the slick marketing efforts from her own company as well as Bergdorf Goodman, Avenue 32, Bluefly, Sephora, Amazon, and so many others. An alert from apairofgenes.com slid into the upper right-hand corner of her screen and caught her eye. The subject line read "Winnie Pressley Has a Message Waiting." This was maybe the fifth such message Alicia had received since uncovering the identity of Winnie's father. She'd assumed these were akin to the spam emails Aspyre's marketers sent out to entice users back to the site. In the interest of tidying up loose ends, Alicia logged back into apairofgenes.com to delete the account. Bryan walked in her office just as the actual messages waiting for Winnie appeared on Alicia's monitor.

She held up her hand, putting him off as she read the first message in disbelief—and then all the rest in utter horror.

Sent 18 days ago

Hi, Winnie,

My name is Naomi Alder. I'm married to your biological dad, Chase Alder. I have to be honest, we were shocked when your leaf appeared on our family tree a few days ago. We had no idea you existed, but we're trusting DNA doesn't lie. We've been on pins and needles hoping you will contact us. You can reply through the platform or email me at nalder2@alderfamily.com. We're excited to hear from you!

Naomi

———

Sent 16 days ago

Hi, Winnie,

It's Naomi again. We're guessing you're a senior in high school? You're probably pretty busy right now. We totally understand, but we really hope you'll reach out to us. We'd love to hear from you. And soon if possible.

Naomi

———

Sent 14 days ago

Hi, Winnie,

It's Naomi again. I know this is going to seem a little odd, but it's urgent we get in touch with you. I'm coming to Seattle tomorrow to try to find you.

Naomi

————

Sent 10 days ago

Hi, Winnie,

I thought I would hear from you after the accident. Are you OK? Maybe you don't remember, but I was there that night.

Naomi

————

Sent today

Winnie,

I'm back in Seattle. I need to meet up with you as soon as possible.

It's important.

Naomi

With her heart racing, Alicia reread the messages several times, trying to understand what had happened. All she'd done was click on Winnie's match list. As far as Alicia could surmise, doing so must have made Winnie's profile public and triggered a notification to people on her family tree. "Shit, shit, shit, God fucking dammit!" Alicia swore under her breath as she frantically scanned the website, looking for a way to undo her mistake. But she knew better than anyone this was not a mess that could be fixed by simply deleting the account or unchecking some box. Data lived forever.

"Leesh, what the hell's going on?" Bryan was sprawled on her office couch.

"Oh my God, oh my God, oh my God!" As Alicia processed the implications of what she'd done, her vision clouded, and her lungs constricted. Hyperventilation had always been one of those things that sounded so "drama queen," but she literally couldn't breathe. Bryan guided her over to the couch and repeatedly instructed her to drop her head between her knees. She obeyed his orders, since the alternative was apparently death by asphyxiation. As she held her head in her hands, her thoughts careened every which way. Even once her breathing slowed, her mind continued to race. She squeezed her eyes against the unusual prickle of tears. "I fucked up. I really, really fucked up."

Bryan rubbed her back and pulled her close. "You're OK," he said. "Now tell me what happened."

Alicia wanted nothing more than to bury her face in Bryan's chest and stay wrapped in his strong, protective arms, but this wasn't a scathing comment from a reporter where he could soothe her by calling the guy an asshole and cracking an off-color joke. She pulled back and searched her husband's eyes, trying to figure out where to begin. "Remember Brooke's eighth-grade science fair project a few years ago with those DNA tests?"

"Yeah…?" His brows knitted together.

"Winnie took one of the DNA tests too. When I set up her account, I pretended I was her mom. I guess I planned to tell Maren at some point, but it didn't seem like a big deal."

"So?" Bryan leaned back and spread his arms wide across the couch cushions.

"Remember when I got that anonymous text that Winnie was still applying to Stanford when Maren had been telling everyone she was going for UW? Well, the text also said that her first-generation college hook was bogus. I didn't tell you that part." Alicia picked at the cuticles around her thumbs. A nervous habit she'd never conquered. "I knew Maren didn't go to college, so it got me wondering whether there might be a dad in the picture. Maren's always been so secretive, I figured it was totally plausible." Alicia could sense Bryan was barely following her, but now that she was saying it out loud, she had to get it all out. "The company that we used for the science project, apairofgenes.com, added an ancestry option a couple of years ago. You know, where you can find relatives through matching DNA? All I did was peek at her DNA match list. Her biological father came right up. Once I had a name, it was easy to figure out he went to Yale."

"So she was lying about that too?" Bryan cracked his knuckles.

"Yeah, and the kicker was that it turns out I was mistaken all along about Maren never going to college. After I found out about the dad going to Yale, I talked to Ted and learned that Maren actually did attend college.

The background check I did on her when she first started with us must not have picked up that fact because she never graduated," Alicia continued. "So the anonymous text about the bogus first-gen hook actually had nothing to do with Winnie's father—it was always about Maren. If I had just called Ted to clarify the situation right when I got the text, none of this would have happened."

"I'm confused. None of what?" Bryan asked.

Alicia sighed deeply as she waded into the truly disastrous part of the story. "What I didn't realize was that by looking at Winnie's match list, I made her profile public. Winnie's biological father's wife, her name is Naomi, has been messaging me through the platform thinking I was Winnie. They never even knew she existed until I opened up her data for review." Alicia walked over to her desk, grabbed her laptop, and handed it to Bryan.

Bryan read Naomi's messages. "Oh Jesus, Leesh," Bryan said, running a hand through his hair. "Holy shit. She's in Seattle right now. They could meet and put all this together." He shut the laptop and set it on the end table.

"I know," Alicia said. "I can't believe this is happening. I don't know what to do."

"Does anyone else know about this?"

"No!" Alicia grabbed a tissue from her desk and dabbed at her eyes.

"Why is this woman so eager to find Winnie?" Bryan stood up and paced the room as they tried to figure out their next move.

"I don't know, but if I found out you had an illegitimate kid you never told me about, I would sure as hell want to find that little bastard and make sure she stayed far away from our family."

"She was in Seattle the night of the accident. Do you think she was involved?" He turned away from her and faced the window.

"Maybe?" Alicia said, willing it to be true. From her earlier research, she knew Winnie's dad lived in the Bay Area. Maybe he and his wife had somehow learned she was applying to Stanford and didn't want her living in such close proximity. That would fit with the threat Winnie had received about backing off Stanford. But even if this woman was somehow responsible for the accident, thereby exonerating Bryan and Brooke, Alicia could never prove it without revealing her deception.

Silence hung uncomfortably between them. One thing was certain: Alicia couldn't let this woman get to Winnie. There was no way the two of them could ever meet without exposing who had brought them together. No NDA was strong enough to protect Alicia in this situation. Thinking about the potentially far-reaching and humiliating consequences made the hair on her arms stand on end.

"Maybe you should call the lawyer?" Bryan suggested.

"And tell him what exactly? That I risked my livelihood and maybe our fortune trying to prove some poor high school girl was lying about the dad she's never met?"

"He might be able to fix this," Bryan shrugged. "He's helped us out of tight spots before."

Alicia shook her head. George Cox III might be excellent at drafting nondisclosure and nondisparagement agreements, writing threatening cease-and-desist letters, and paying off women to keep quiet about Bryan's indiscretions, but even he might draw the line here. "I think this is a whole different ball game. Oh my God," she moaned. "I don't know what to do."

The police were already sniffing around. She couldn't do anything to alert them to the existence of this apairofgenes.com account or she would become the prime suspect in Winnie's accident. Handling the situation on her own was her only option. Alicia grabbed her laptop and typed out a note, hoping it sounded like a scared and confused seventeen-year-old girl who regretted opening a Pandora's box.

> There's been a mistake. I never meant for any of this to happen. Please, I beg you, don't ever contact me again. Forget you ever knew I existed. I'll report you to the website. I'll do anything to make you leave me alone.

Alicia had never typed truer words.

"Jesus, Leesh." Bryan sat back down next to her and leaned forward with his forearms on his legs. "Do you think maybe you've kinda lost perspective? This whole Stanford thing has gotten totally out of hand."

Alicia bowed her head in shame.

Bryan gently rubbed her back. "Brooke told me at dinner last night she met with Ms. Barstow to start working on a backup list. If she doesn't get into Stanford, you have to let it go," he said quietly. "She chooses where she applies and what school she attends, and you have to get behind her."

Alicia nodded. What choice did she have? And anyway, even though Winnie had applied, Alicia was still confident Brooke would be accepted, especially now that Ted knew Maren had attended college, so what was the point of arguing?

"Come on," he said, pulling Alicia to him. "Brooke's a great kid. It's all going to work out. And I'm never going to let anything happen to you."

For once, Alicia was content to let someone else be in charge.

22

Maren

MAREN WAS STARTING TO wonder if she was suffering from PTSD. Most nights since Winnie's accident, Maren experienced the same vivid, bloodcurdling dream sequence: Winnie on the sidewalk laughing with friends and then turning to step off the curb directly into the path of an oncoming SUV. Maren down the street, trying to scream at Winnie to look left but unable to find her voice. No matter how hard she tried to engage her vocal cords, no sound emerged from her mouth. The instant Winnie's body was crushed under the tire of the SUV, Maren would wake up, her pajamas soaked with sweat and her throat on fire.

The less she slept, the more hypervigilant she became during the day. Her skin felt like a burlap sack, helpless to prevent the millions of raw nerve endings determined to poke out everywhere like straw; she could barely stand to have the softest of fabrics touch her. Worst of all, her heightened anxiety served as a disquieting reminder of her more distant past. As had become her habit since the accident, Maren checked her rearview mirror for any hint of someone following her. Seeing nothing out of the ordinary, she signaled a right turn before pulling onto the tree-lined EBA driveway.

The line of cars crawled toward the pickup zone. With her foot on the brake, Maren allowed herself a few blissful seconds to close her eyes and breathe. But it was as though that brief indulgence created an empty pocket of air into which an overwhelming exhaustion rushed. For the first time since Winnie was a little girl, Maren wondered how much longer she'd be able to keep her shit together. She was operating on zero sleep, working an unrelenting schedule, and tending to her daughter as body-guard/chauffeur by day and mom/caretaker by night. The concept of a "nervous breakdown" had always been mysterious to her, a malady that struck only the weak. But now she understood how someone both sane and strong might also reach that point of no return.

Indeed, it was only Thursday in a week she was beginning to think would never end. Thankfully, after nine days of convalescing, Winnie had been cleared by her neurologist to go back to school Monday. She was even feeling well enough to take the first tentative steps toward renew-ing a friendship with Brooke. Ever since the night Brooke had stopped by the house, she'd been texting Winnie daily with funny and heartfelt messages, asking for a second chance. She'd even come clean about the EBA entrance test being the reason she'd turned on Winnie in the first place and expressed relief when Winnie'd admitted she already knew what Alicia had done—and didn't hold it against Brooke.

On Winnie's first morning back at school, Brooke had been waiting to meet her in the drop-off circle with a sheepish grin and mochas and muffins from the café the girls used to love. Though a small part of Maren was still on guard, she couldn't deny that it warmed her heart to see the girls walking off to class together that morning, a scene Maren had once assumed she would witness throughout their high school years.

Word Winnie was back at school must have spread quickly, because by lunchtime on Monday, Diana had messaged Maren with her opening salvo in the text storm that now threatened to consume every spare second of Maren's life:

> **Diana:** Hey! I hear Winnie's back at school! Did you get the lasagna I left on your doorstep last night? Sorry couldn't say hi—was late for Homeless to Homefull meeting.

Maren recalled her disgust at answering her front door Sunday night to find Diana's meal train delivery—the third meat lover's lasagna from Costco that week. She knew for a fact Diana would never dare let a single bite of such processed slop pass the lips of a member of her family. Not only that, but instead of including one of those $10 cards she'd seen Alicia receive, Diana had scribbled "Get Well Soon, ♥ Diana" on the Costco receipt (in ballpoint pen that had malfunctioned on the glossy paper, to rather psychotic effect) and had thoughtfully pinned this note between the bottom of the lasagna tin and Maren's welcome mat. Even though Maren had known these wealthy EBA women for years, it was still startling to realize they all shared the same lack of imagination over what poor people ate. However, as Maren and Winnie still needed to eat and pay rent, Maren kept her thoughts to herself and continued the charade of gratitude she'd become so proficient at over the years.

> **Maren:** Yes, thanks so much. Will definitely keep us well fed.

> **Diana:** Oh good!

Diana: So now that Winnie's all better, hoping to get your help on my latest brainstorm! Bryan said it was OK for me to poach some of your time for the next few weeks. Hold on to your hat! I'm planning a STRESS BUSTER party FOR THE PARENTS on Snowcoming night! Isn't that the best?!!! After all, college application season is just as stressful for us as for them, amiright? 😉

Maren: Ah yes, true that. What do you have in mind?

Diana: I want it to be "off the hook" as the kiddos say!

Diana: I'm thinking Chihuly museum for venue?

Diana: Definitely catered with full sushi bar, oysters, etc.

Diana: Maybe for our sig drink we do a giant table-size replica of Puget Sound region with champagne for the water and caviar for all the islands?

Diana: Or wait, maybe caviar is too yesterday—how about alternating islands of imported matsutake mushrooms and Japanese Wagyu roast beef?

Diana: For music, maybe see if Dave Matthews is in town? Or even Macklemore—that would make the kids so jealous!

Maren's head was going to explode. She knew for a fact Bryan had zero authority to divert her attention from Alicia's endless demands. And she also knew the SST events budget, though ridiculously large given its mission to further coddle already overprivileged teens, would not be nearly enough to pay for Diana's parent party on top of the extravagant Snowcoming. So Maren was left to wonder: Was this parent party an SST event, a Diana side gig, or a highly unusual Alicia–Diana collaboration brokered by Bryan's idiocy? If it was anything but a Diana side gig, she was screwed. She'd never get paid for all her work. As always, the awkward burden of nailing down such bothersome details fell to Maren. This time, though, she needed the money too much to cave. Winnie's first hospital bills were already starting to pour in.

Maren: I'll be happy to start working on it. But just one question. I want to be clear on exactly who gets billed for my time?

Diana: Good question! I would say Alicia but don't want her to blow a gasket 😵

As Maren read Diana's blow-off nonanswer, her middle finger swooped and dove like an eagle zeroing in on its prey. If she wasn't careful, she might sprain her hand. She waited for a few more seconds as the typing bubbles waved at her before disappearing with no new text from Diana. She never made this sort of thing easy.

Maren: Haha. So I'll bill you then?

Diana: I guess. What's your hourly rate again? $20/hour?

Maren: Actually it's $40/hour.

Diana: Oh! Look at you all pricey now! I suppose that's OK.

Maren: It's actually a discount off my usual side gig hourly. And it's the same rate you've paid me for projects the past couple years. You know I love working with you, Diana!

Diana: Of course! TTYL!

Ever since that first text exchange, Maren had been forced to fend off Diana's latest "fun thought" roughly every ten minutes. Her texts had an almost rhythmic quality, like the thwack-thwack-thwack of baseballs smacked in a batting cage. Only it felt like Maren was stuck inside the cage, absorbing each line drive point-blank with her body. Diana's most recent idea, the one she just *had* to share with Maren the second it popped into her head (as if she had such a well-functioning filter all the other times), had been this award winner: "What if we call the party 'Snowgoing'! Get it? Snowcoming? Snowgoing?" *Yeah, Diana. Got it.*

Maren impatiently checked the dashboard clock. Already a quarter to four. She would barely have time to retrieve Winnie, drop her off at home behind the security of double-locked doors and windows adorned with alarm system stickers (in lieu of an actual alarm system, which was way out of her budget), and then hurry back to the Stones' to finish setting up Alicia's bedroom before her arrival home from her day trip to San Francisco. When Maren finally reached the front of the pickup line, she spotted Winnie talking to a woman who looked much younger than most of the EBA high school moms. She was probably one of the middle school moms who was always begging Winnie for her tutoring services. These moms paid Winnie a small fortune, but right now, Maren needed to get back to work.

She tried to catch Winnie's eye with a wave, but Winnie seemed focused on her conversation. As honking in the pickup line was forbidden, Maren gave up and tuned the radio to Winnie's favorite hip-hop station. Startled by a thump, Maren looked over to find Winnie banging on the car door with her cast. Maren jumped out to help load her fifteen-ton backpack into the car. "Now you're in a huge hurry?" she kidded.

"Let's go," Winnie said, thrusting her backpack at her mom with her good arm. "Now!"

"You don't have to be rude. I'm the one who's been waiting in this line for the past ten minutes."

"Sorry, I gotta get outta here."

Winnie was about to either burst into tears or start yelling, Maren wasn't sure which. What could that mom have said to rattle Winnie so badly? Maren turned, intending to shoot a death glare at the woman, but she was already gone.

Maren hurried back to the driver's seat. The second the door slammed shut, Winnie glowered at her. "What the heck, Mom? You know who my biological father is, and you didn't think that was information I might be interested in?"

"What are you talking about?" Maren locked eyes with Winnie. "That's absurd. Calm down. What's going on?" She checked the rearview mirror and put the car in Drive.

"*What's going on* is that woman I was just talking to…she's the one who was watching me on the bus the day before my accident."

Maren shuddered. "I don't understand."

"She just told me she's the wife of my *biological father*?" Winnie said. "How could you not tell me about this?"

"That's impossible, Winnie. I don't even know who your biological father is. I've told you that many times."

"Yeah, I know you have." She all but spat the words. "But is it the truth?"

"Yes, it's the truth! Of course it's the truth!" Maren slammed her foot on the gas pedal and peeled out into traffic.

"Well, that's what I told her. I said, 'I don't know what kind of twisted game you're playing, but it was a one-night stand, and we don't even know the guy's name.' But then she said, 'Winnie, don't you remember me from your accident? I'm Naomi.'"

"How did she know about your accident?" Maren was starting to panic and knew she should probably pull over, but she wanted to put as much distance between them and that woman as possible.

"How would I know? It's not like I can remember anything," Winnie snapped. "It was super creepy how she knew my name. And then when she said her name, she acted like I was supposed to know it somehow."

Maren wished she'd taken a closer look at the woman instead of just writing her off as a middle school mom. Dammit! How had she let this woman get to Winnie when she'd promised she would protect her? Maren should have been there waiting at school before the bell rang. She suddenly felt ill.

"That was when I saw you. She begged me not to go. Said she just wanted to talk and tried to convince me to go with her to get coffee. Of course I said no. I'm not an idiot. Then as I was leaving, she grabbed my arm and said, 'Please...it's critical. I have to talk to you.' She tried to press a piece of paper into my hand, but I ran off."

Maren swallowed hard. "Did she give you a last name? Anything else? Do they live in Seattle?" Her voice was thin with fear.

"Mom, do you think she had something to do with my accident? Why would she say she was there? I feel like there's something you're not telling me. I'm trying to work out what's going on, but my head hurts." Her voice quivered. "What does that woman want with us?"

"I have no idea," Maren said, her eyes fixed on the road. "But I promise I'm going to figure it out."

"Do you think you should call the detective and tell him about her?"

"Yes, definitely." Although what exactly she would say to the detective was an open question. The temperature outside was 50 degrees, but she was sweating like it was the middle of summer. She had to calm down. Maren reached over and squeezed Winnie's long, elegant fingers before grasping the steering wheel again with both hands. "Look, I haven't told you this, but when I met with Ted Clark a few weeks ago, he also said someone had anonymously tipped him off that you might be lying about your first-gen college hook because your biological father attended Yale."

"Are you kidding me? How could you not tell me that?"

"I thought it was baloney since there's no way anyone could know where your father went to college when I don't even know who he is."

"Yeah, so you keep saying."

"I swear. I figured it was just Alicia or Kelly or one of their kids making shit up. But something else is clearly going on."

"Ya think?" Winnie crossed her arms across her chest. She was not buying Maren's story. Which made sense, given how incomplete it was. Unfortunately, though Maren didn't have all the answers Winnie (or she) sought, the time had obviously come to tell Winnie the truth about her biological father. Maren's entire body tensed up. There was no way she could wade into this conversation and then go back to work for the afternoon like nothing had happened. As she swallowed the bile seeping into her throat, she resolved to tell Winnie everything she knew that night.

Ever since her own parents had betrayed her, Maren had sworn she would never put her own interests ahead of Winnie's. As she drove home from work later that night, she had to acknowledge that it had reached the point where Maren was protecting herself more than she was protecting Winnie, especially with that Naomi woman accosting Winnie after school today. Maren had stewed about it as she ticked through her long to-do list. In the end, she decided it would be cruel to break Winnie's heart without having concrete answers to the many questions she knew Winnie would have. After all, shouldn't Maren first try to fill in the gaps so she could reliably transmit the truth to her daughter? But the only idea she had that might provide some answers would require Winnie's help.

"Win? I'm home!" Maren shouted as she walked in the front door. "Everything OK?"

"Yep," Winnie called out from behind her closed bedroom door.

Maren popped her head in the bedroom. "Have you eaten anything?"

"Yep," Winnie said. "I made pasta. There's some extra on the stove."

"Thanks," Maren said. "So listen, I couldn't stop thinking about that woman."

Winnie glanced at Maren briefly and then looked back at her computer in icy silence. Permission to enter not granted.

"I feel like we're at a huge disadvantage if it's really true your biological father somehow knows who you are and we don't know who he is," Maren continued to speak from the doorway. "So I did some poking around, and I have an idea. I think if we have you take one of those DNA tests, maybe we'll learn something about that side of your, um, genetic family. It takes about six weeks to get the results, but the sooner we start the clock, the better." With no reaction, Maren figured she might as well press on. "Anyway, it's expensive, so I wanted to ask you if you'd be willing to take a DNA test before I buy it. No needles involved. You'd only have to spit in a tube."

"Yeah, I know what a DNA test is," Winnie said, her eyes still glued to her laptop screen. "I've done one before. With Brooke."

"What do you mean? That's impossible. I literally just read that section on the website. You're a minor. You would have needed my consent."

"No, I definitely did it," Winnie said, finally making eye contact with Maren. "I remember us spitting in a tube and laughing so hard about how disgusting it was." Winnie's tone turned wistful. "It was before Brooke started ghosting me… I think you were out of town setting up one of the Stones' new houses and I was staying with them."

The Del Mar beach house. It was the spring of eighth grade. "But why? Who gave you the tubes?"

"Alicia did," Winnie said. "She gave one to everyone in the house. For Brooke's science fair experiment."

"Are you kidding me?" She smacked the doorjamb with her open palm. "You're telling me Alicia took your DNA and never even bothered to ask my permission? But of course she did," Maren snarked under her breath. "It's one hundred percent something she would do." Why did that damn woman, who had literally everything, continually feel entitled to steal from her and Winnie?

Winnie nodded warily. "Do you think Alicia's the one who tried to sabotage my first-gen hook with Mr. Clark? It kinda makes sense, right?"

"I wish I could say no." Maren took a few tentative steps into the room and sat on the end of the bed. Her jaw clenched at the thought of Alicia running wild with Winnie's DNA, using it to snatch the college crown for her own daughter. Not only that, Alicia was potentially endangering Winnie in the process while also cracking open the one secret Maren desperately needed to reveal on her own timetable.

"I wonder if I already have an account set up on one of those sites." Winnie's curious mind was already starting to problem-solve. "That could be how this Naomi woman found me; that is, if she really is who she says she is." She flipped herself around so Maren could see her screen.

Together, they proceeded to search the websites of all three major consumer genetic-testing companies but struck out. It was Winnie who finally figured out why. "It says right here if a minor is tested, your account will be controlled by the parent until you turn eighteen. So it must be a subfolder of Alicia's account."

Maren felt the rage building inside her. "Looks like she pretended you're her daughter, *again*," she bit out. Winnie flinched slightly at the venom in Maren's voice.

"You have access to Alicia's computer, right?"

"Yes, I use the desktop in her office all the time to pay the family bills."

"Well then, I think you should do a little investigating, don't you?"

Maren hesitated for a moment. "I could get sued for that kind of invasion of privacy. This could end very badly for us."

"Yeah, but what Alicia did has to be totally illegal. We can't let her get away with this," Winnie said.

Maren took a deep breath. She reminded herself of her promise to leave fear behind; the least she could do was stuff it in her back pocket for a while. "You know what? You're absolutely right."

"But, Mom, you have to tell me what you learn. I have a right to know."

Maren bit her lip. She only wished she could satisfy Winnie's right to know without being forced to confront the truth herself.

23

Kelly

KELLY PARKED IN FRONT of the Seattle Police East Precinct. Wiping her palms on her pants, she smoothed her hair in the rearview mirror. According to the detective who'd contacted her, Ted Clark had passed along the names of the EBA families with Stanford applicants. Kelly wanted to appear helpful, of course, but now she was questioning her decisions not to tell Kevin and not to consult a lawyer. It wasn't as if they had a lawyer on speed dial, but she'd watched enough episodes of *Law & Order* to wonder if going into a meeting like this alone was the best idea. Especially given her suspicions about Krissie. But Kevin had been so irritated with her lately, and he'd been working day and night structuring a major client's acquisition for taxes and accounting, so she figured she would deal with this on her own.

Running a gauntlet of panhandlers, Kelly entered the precinct. "Can I help you?" the desk clerk intoned after ignoring her for a solid thirty seconds.

"Yes, thank you. I'm here to see Detective Davis. My name is Kelly Vernon," she said. "I have a ten a.m. appointment." She hoped that tidbit might move things along for her. The precinct waiting room was crowded and smelled like body odor.

The clerk made a quick call. "He'll be out in a few minutes."

Kelly took a seat on an ugly black plastic chair and placed her purse on her lap. She scrolled through her Twitter feed to avoid making eye contact with anyone, particularly the man with a tattoo on his face staring at her, but it was impossible not to eavesdrop on the conversations around her. She'd clearly left her safe little bubble where everyone sent their kids to private school, listened to NPR, read the *New York Times*, bought organic food, and only worried about which fabulous college their child would attend. Frankly, reality was a bit jarring.

"Mrs. Vernon?" A bold voice interrupted her listening in on a young couple who reeked of marijuana and were fighting about where to eat because between them they only had $3.02. She'd heard them laboriously count all their change. Three times.

"Detective Davis?" she said, standing to greet him.

They shook hands, and the detective led Kelly back to a large room buzzing with activity. "Thanks for coming in today," he said over the din. "We appreciate you taking the time to answer some questions." He pointed to a metal chair next to a desk covered with paper, folders, and what looked like the remainder of a breakfast sandwich. Kelly glanced around the room, intrigued by the chaos.

Detective Davis looked down at his notes. "So I understand your kids go to Elliott Bay Academy?"

"Yes." Kelly smiled. "My daughter Krissie is a senior. My other two children are in tenth and seventh grade."

The detective whistled. "Three kids at private school? That must set you back."

Because her kids went to private school, he assumed she was rich, which couldn't be more laughable, at least compared with most EBA families. How was she supposed to respond? "It's not easy, but our children's education is very important to us."

"Sure. So I spoke with Mr. Clark, the principal of the school—"

"He's actually the head of school," Kelly corrected.

"OK." He shrugged. "Anyway, he said you're pretty involved at the school. PTA president and chair of"—he looked down at his notes again—"the SST?"

"Yes, the Senior Send-off Team. It's the most coveted volunteer assignment at EBA." Kelly may have found the SST to be a gigantic pain in the ass, but she nevertheless enjoyed the status it conferred on campus. From the look on the detective's face, he was unimpressed.

Detective Davis cleared his throat. "People covet volunteer positions?"

"Um, yeah," Kelly said. "Our job is to plan surprise activities, parties, events, and stress busters for our overworked seniors."

"Oh, that's nice. My mom lives in one of those senior centers in Shoreline and loves when the young kids from nearby schools come to visit. Really cheers her up."

"Gosh, no, by seniors, I mean high school seniors—you know, our kids who are applying to college?"

Confusion clouded the detective's face. "EBA seems like a pretty fancy school. Is this for some of the underprivileged students on scholarship who work after-school jobs and such?"

"Um, no. It's for all the seniors—they work really hard in their classes. Lots of honors and AP courses, and many of them play highly competitive sports and compete in bands, orchestras, chess competitions, math Olympiads, and the like. It's such a rat race to get into college these days, you wouldn't believe it. These kids have zero downtime. They're so programmed and stressed out. And all that is on top of having to take tons of standardized tests to get into college."

"Tons? My kids graduated from UW and Western, and I only remember them taking the SAT. There are other tests?"

"Yes, well, the Ivy Plus schools all require not just the SAT achievement test but also SAT subject tests in both humanities and STEM fields, unless of course your kid takes the ACT, in which case many of the Ivy Pluses will waive the SAT subject test requirement," Kelly said, well aware she was rambling, but she'd never been interviewed by a police detective before. He seemed to be listening intently to everything she said. She sat up a little straighter, pleased to be helping the investigation. "And most kids take both the SAT and the ACT to see which one they perform better on, and then they take their preferred test at least one and sometimes two or three more times after months of private tutoring."

"And Ivy Plus is?" His eyes narrowed.

"Ivy League schools plus Ivy League–equivalent schools like Stanford, MIT, schools like that," Kelly spouted. He sure had a lot of questions. Was this part of his detective process, or did he really not know anything about good colleges?

"Got it. Sounds pretty intense," he said, leaning back in his chair and folding his arms. Detective Davis rubbed his chin. "So your daughter Krissie? She also applied to Stanford? Like Winnie?"

"Yes, Krissie's a double legacy. Both my husband and I attended Stanford. Alicia Stone's daughter, Brooke, applied too. There may have been other students who also applied?" Her voice rising at the end invited the detective to spill the names of any other students he may have come across in his investigation.

Detective Davis didn't take the bait. "Do you think Winnie's accident had something to do with Stanford only taking one more student?"

"I'm not the detective," Kelly said with a smile. "But you should know there was a rumor going around that Winnie was applying to the top ten colleges in the country just to see if she could get into every one of them. Lots of parents were very upset that she would try to take spots she had no intention of using. Maybe that had something to do with the accident?"

"I see," Detective Davis said, jotting down a few words in his notebook. "So after word spread, there were a lot of memes on social media featuring you. I assume you're aware of them." He cocked his eyebrow at her.

Kelly could feel her cheeks burning. "Yes, I've seen them."

"Interesting that so many people thought you had something to do with it, don't you think?"

Kelly shifted in her seat and stared down at her hands, which were fiddling with the straps on her handbag. Taking a deep breath, she looked Detective Davis square in the eye. "I think people are jealous of me for my commitment to my children. My daughter is quite extraordinary, and I'm sure many people would like nothing more than to see both of us fail. Frankly, I'm scared Krissie might be the next victim. Do you have any idea who went after Winnie?"

"Where were you the night of the accident?" he asked, tapping his pen on his desk.

"You can't be serious." Kelly's eyes grew wide. "But for the record, I was home with my entire family having dinner and watching a movie."

"What movie?" he pressed.

"*The Princess Bride*," Kelly said without hesitation.

"Love that one," he said, smiling at her. "So I'd like to ask Krissie a few questions. Is there a time you can bring her down?"

Kelly froze. Short of directly posing the big question to Krissie, Kelly had tried every which way to ask her daughter whether she'd had anything to do with the accident. But each time, Krissie had blown her off, in much the same way as she dismissed Kelly's concerns about her lack of eating, her constant workouts, and the hair plugging up her bathroom sink. Her mental state was already so fragile, how could Kelly possibly subject her daughter to a police interview? And then she'd have no choice but to tell Kevin. Kelly had to put Detective Davis off at all costs. "We would love to help, we really would, but I'm very concerned about my daughter right now. She was diagnosed with trichotillomania, and now we're worried she's becoming anorexic. And anyway, I don't even know what she can tell you because she was home with the rest of our family watching *The Princess Bride*."

Davis pushed back his chair and looked at his watch. "I'll be in touch then. Maybe after some of this college stuff calms down? I understand Stanford's early admission notification date is December 15?"

Now he knew something about college? "Oh, well, OK," Kelly said, disappointed he wasn't giving Krissie a pass entirely. At least she'd bought them some more time.

"Is there anyone else who you think I should be talking to?"

"Alicia and Bryan Stone," Kelly said without hesitation. "My daughter overheard their daughter, Brooke, bragging that her mom hired a big shot college professor to write Brooke's application essays. And word on the street is they donated $15 million to Stanford to pave the way for their daughter's admission. They certainly have a lot to lose, don't you think? Obviously, you didn't hear this from me."

The detective nodded and scribbled another note. "Thanks for your time, Mrs. Vernon." As Kelly stood up, Detective Davis added, "Actually, if I might make one observation?"

"Sure." Kelly hesitated. Had she gone too far pointing the finger at the Stones? But at least what she'd said about them had the benefit of being the truth.

"Sorry if this is out of line, but I wonder: Has your SST group considered ways to reduce the stress your kids are under all the days they *aren't* attending your stress busters? It just seems like everyone—parents and kids alike—might be happier."

Kelly's jaw dropped. Was he serious? Given his line of work, Kelly was surprised that he didn't grasp the concept that all this parental college stress was about making sure their children had opportunities and didn't end up like the derelicts in the waiting room. She worried constantly about economic inequality and feared her kids faced a binary future— they would either succeed spectacularly or fail miserably. Without the safety net of a trust fund (which so many kids at EBA seemed to have), Kelly felt that she had no choice but to strategize over every aspect of her children's lives. The truth was Kelly had engaged in this anxiety-fueled opportunities arms race in large part because she knew admission to an elite college like Stanford would be the stepping-stone to a top grad school, a prestigious career, and, ultimately, financial success. With the stakes so high, she wasn't about to be the schmuck who fell down on the job. "Thanks, Detective," Kelly said, turning back to address him. "That's excellent advice." She didn't want to risk contradicting him, even if he was clueless.

24

Maren

IT WAS LATE AFTERNOON by the time Maren finally arrived at the Stones' after finishing a mile-long list of errands. She perused the other cars in the massive driveway. The dinner chef, the housekeeper, and Bryan were all home, but no Brooke or Alicia yet. This was as good a time as any to access Alicia's desktop. She walked in the front door, greeted Cardinal with her usual sweet talk and pointed knee, and hollered out her routine arrival announcement. Bryan's golf clubs were in the front hall. Excellent. His post-golf routine was to grab a beer from one of the four taps on his kegerator (because the six beers he drank on the golf course were not enough) and then head to the shower. From there, Maren chose not to imagine the scene. She padded upstairs and slowed at the door to the master bedroom. As she suspected, the shower was running.

She entered Alicia's study and sat in the chair behind her large mahogany desk, an activity that was hardly out of the ordinary. Maren was normally required to log in with her own unique username and password. Today, she logged in with one of Alicia's go-to passwords and quickly gained access. When she pulled down the bookmarks menu, "A Pair of Genes" was at the bottom of the list. Maren almost laughed out loud at Alicia's sloppiness when she realized she wouldn't even need to guess the account username and password—the computer browser automatically supplied them for her. She clicked on the subfolder for Winnie, and a dashboard appeared. "You have multiple family connections. See your Family Tree here." Click. Boom.

Her hand quivered as she swiped at the tear on her cheek that appeared out of thin air. It was an out-of-body experience taking in the name that appeared above Winnie's leaf, connected to her daughter's name with a thin green line. Chase Alder. A name she didn't recognize at all. What the fuck? Who the hell was this guy? But she had no time to delve deeper. Very shortly, Bryan would emerge from the bedroom dressed in his usual home lounge attire—gym shorts and, well, that was all. Just gym shorts.

She clicked on the Messages folder and watched as several messages from Chase Alder's wife, who Maren noted was in fact named Naomi, appeared one after the other on the screen. With no time to read the messages, let alone fully absorb their meaning, Maren whipped out her cell phone, snapped photos of each screen, and then jumped out of the chair and took one photo from a distance in case she ever needed to prove the computer in question was in Alicia's office. She made sure to capture in the background of the photo the *Vogue* magazine cover featuring Alicia in the World's Most Powerful Women issue, which Maren had framed and hung on the wall for her. And then, finally, one more click back for a snapshot of the family tree.

Thankfully, she hadn't yet gotten to the to-do item of applying WD-40 to Alicia and Bryan's bedroom door hinges, so she heard the door swing open. Time was up. Maren logged out and then reflexively hid behind the open office door, waiting for Bryan to pass. She listened as he thumped down the stairs like an elephant. Nothing about that man was subtle. When the coast was clear, she went down the hall to the master bedroom to finish her chores for the day, blazing with fury at everyone. At Alicia for such a massive invasion of privacy; for stirring up a past that Maren badly wanted to keep buried; and for dragging Winnie into this, forcing Maren to finally have *the conversation* with Winnie not on her terms but on Alicia's. At this Chase Alder, whoever he was, for the heinous, life-changing thing he'd done to her. At his wife for having the balls to approach her daughter at school. At Bryan because, well, just because he was such a pig.

Maren's seething anger gave her the energy she needed to attack her work. And as she did, she made a plan. First, she would go home and do some online research on this Chase Alder asshole, and then she would try to work out what all this meant for Winnie's safety. The question of how to extricate herself from this abusive relationship with Alicia was no longer theoretical; she resolved to keep her eyes peeled for the first available off-ramp.

Unfortunately, no amount of planning could drown out her dread of the impending conversation now looming over the one and only relationship on earth that mattered to her.

———

A few blocks from home, Maren pulled over on a side street, threw open the car door, and spewed the contents of her stomach onto the road. She wiped her mouth with a half-used Starbucks napkin the consistency of sandpaper and then tossed the rapidly disintegrating material into the puddle of vomit before finishing the drive home. If finding out the name of one's rapist wasn't a reasonable excuse for littering, then she would accept the punishment without complaint. As she continued home, her hands squeezed the steering wheel with such force that their continued trembling seemed almost to defy the laws of nature. Maren was neither physically nor emotionally ready to have this conversation with Winnie.

When she got home, she was relieved to see that Winnie's bedroom door was closed. She pulled a loose strand of hair back behind her ear only to find it was wet. Instinctively she lifted her fingers to her nose. One sniff of her own vomit and she almost threw up again right there. She raced down the hall to the bathroom, peeling off her clothes as she moved, and jumped into the shower.

The blisteringly hot water ran down her body. She prayed the whooshing noise made by the water slapping against the fiberglass shower-surround would drown out the sound of her weeping in the same way the water itself was washing the evidence of her tears down the drain. Though she tried to keep her mind fixed in the present—on the hot water, the slippery soap, and the repetitive action of scrubbing her scalp with shampoo—her willpower was no match for her psyche, which was apparently determined to dredge up the past.

———

The last time she'd cleaned herself with such violence was eighteen years and three months before. Maren vividly remembered waking up on the Kickapoo Country Club golf course in the wee hours of the morning, curled up in a ball and crying. As she lay there, she had the odd sense her mind was trying to recall what had just happened while simultaneously attempting to blot it out forever. But all she could think about was fluid. Sweat, a sticky sensation, and the golf course sprinklers spraying her with rhythmic precision. She reached her hands down to explore the aching sensation in her vagina and came up with the torn remains of her underpants. And that was when she noticed the blood.

The only crystal clear thought she had for the next twenty minutes was that she had to get home and shower. She pulled herself up from the sand trap she didn't remember entering and stumbled toward the pool house to find her best friend, Jane. She was almost there when Jane came running toward her. Thank God.

"You slut!" Jane screamed as she got closer. "How could you do that to me!" Jane's hands were clenched.

"Jane!" Maren started bawling. "I think someone raped me! Please help me! I need to get home. Please!"

"Raped you? Maryanne saw Charles pick you up on the pool deck and carry you off to the golf course. She said you were giggling. When Charles came back, he told the whole party that you begged to have your cherry popped before you went to college."

"Look at me!" Maren stared down at her once-beautiful white dress that was now ripped up the side and dotted with a mix of sand, blood, and water. "Do I look like someone who did this on purpose? I don't even know what happened!" She felt like she was screaming, but her voice came out in a whisper.

Jane was crying now too, black mascara streaming down her cheeks. "You're such a fucking liar," she spat. Over Jane's shoulder, Maren could just make out Charles's silhouette along with a few other boys clustered together.

"I swear! If that's what he said happened, he's the liar. You have to believe me."

"Just go home," Jane sneered. "Oh, and here's a hot tip: don't screw any guys your friends like at college. It's the opposite of cool."

Maren fell to her knees sobbing as Jane, her best friend since third grade, turned her back and returned to the waiting group.

————

Maren had no idea how long she'd been in the shower when her mom forced her way into the bathroom, but her fingers were wrinkled like raisins, her skin was bright red from the scalding water, and she'd long since taken a crisscross seated position over the shower drain. She was also pretty sure she was still bleeding; she was definitely still crying.

"Maren! What in the world is going on? The water's been running for over a half hour. Our water bill is going to be a fortune." Her mom whipped open the shower curtain and stood with one hand on her hip, glaring down at her daughter.

Maren hugged her knees to her chest and whimpered, "I think Charles Brown raped me."

"What do you mean you *think* he raped you," her mother said, stepping forward and turning off the water. "That's impossible. He's a nice boy. He goes to Harvard. Did you tease him?"

"No! You don't get it." Maren sobbed uncontrollably as her mother held open a towel and looked away while she climbed out of the tub.

"Maren, have you been drinking?" Her mom sniffed the air, disappointment writ large on her face.

"It's not what you think! I don't know exactly what happened, but I know it was bad. Really bad."

"Well, no one would ever believe you in your state," she said. "Anyway, what would you have me do? Tell the president of the Kickapoo Country Club that his son may have raped my daughter, but she can't be sure because she was too inebriated? We'd be the laughingstock of the club in five seconds flat. I'd never be able to show my face in church again."

"But shouldn't we call the police?"

"And tell them what exactly?" her mom said. "No, you're going to get yourself cleaned up, say your prayers, go to bed for a few hours, and start your new life at IU tomorrow as planned. Whatever may or may not have happened tonight will be a distant memory before you know it." Maren's mom motioned toward the door.

"I can't."

"Why not?"

"I have my period. I think the tampon is stuck. I can't even feel the string. That's bad, right?"

Maren's mom was such a prude she'd barely acknowledged the onset of puberty. The day almost-twelve-year-old Maren had first gotten her period, she'd been sure the brownish fluid on her underpants meant she had some horrible disease. After assuring Maren she wasn't dying, her mom had disappeared and returned a half hour later with a brown paper bag from the drugstore and told Maren to take it to the bathroom. No instructions, no advice. Just a bag with pads and tampons for Maren to figure out on her own. Sex had never been a conversation between them either, other than she was not to do it out of wedlock. All Maren knew was what she'd learned from the developing bodies book she'd borrowed from the library out of desperation. But now, her mom sprang into action as though her entire life depended on it. "Sit on the edge of the counter. Come on. Let's go."

"What are you going to do?"

"Just do as I say, Maren." Her nostrils flared in disgust.

Fifteen minutes later, after more attempts than Maren could count, untold exhortations to try harder to relax muscles Maren hadn't known existed, and even at one point the careful use of dull tweezers, her mom finally fished out the tampon from Maren's insides. "There," her mom punctuated the moment. "Now off to bed."

It was the last time Maren would ever use a tampon in her life. She remembered hoping her mom was right that she would be able to put this whole thing behind her once they dropped her off at college the next day. Little did Maren know she'd be back home for good at Thanksgiving with an even bigger problem.

———

"Mom?" Winnie's voice penetrated the bathroom door. "Are you OK?"

"I'm fine, honey." Maren turned off the shower and reached for a towel. "I think maybe I picked up a stomach bug. Don't come too near me, OK?"

"OK, but did you find out anything at the Stones'?"

Maren steadied herself against the bathroom sink and tamped down another wave of nausea. "No, not yet. Everyone was home this afternoon. I'll figure it out tomorrow though." She just needed a little more time.

"Well, that sucks. I guess I'll just hang out in my room for the rest of my senior year," Winnie snarked at Maren through the door before her footsteps retreated down the hall.

"Beats any plan I can think of," Maren muttered.

A few minutes later, she'd toweled off, put on her pajamas, and slid under the covers with her laptop and phone. She breathed in and out several times and tried to accept the inevitable. Thanks to her unscrupulous boss, Maren had no choice but to finally confront the truth about who this Chase guy was, aside from the cruel architect of her long-term misery and the partial creator of her greatest joy.

Maren started with a garden-variety Facebook name search and struck gold immediately. What kind of an arrogant asshole rapes a woman and then maintains a public Facebook page? According to his "About" page, he worked for Williamson, McKinnon, and Goldberg, LLC, a San Francisco law firm specializing in torts and civil rights claims. He'd studied at Northwestern School of Law and—there it was—Yale University for undergrad. Seeing that Chase had attended Yale confirmed that it had to have been Alicia or another member of the Stone family who'd snitched about Winnie's supposedly educated "father" to Ted Clark. Other details quickly came into view. He lived in San Mateo, California, and was married to one Naomi Alder. But his birthday, or rather his birth year, was the real shocker. He was only thirty-three years old, which would mean he had only been sixteen years old when he'd raped her. What kind of monster does something like that at such a young age?

Maren clicked on the photos tab and squinted at the screen. At first glance, Chase didn't look familiar, but there was one close-up that sparked a glimmer of recognition. Nothing concrete though; more like a vague sense that she might have laid eyes on him once. She looked at more photos. The most recent one was from more than a year and a half ago— of him and his wife with two little kids, a boy and a girl. The pictures looked like they could have been lifted straight from a J.Crew catalog.

Maren swallowed over the lump in her throat and then zoomed in on his wife, Naomi. With a start, Maren realized that Naomi resembled the brown-haired woman with the Nike cap who had been in the ER while she'd waited for word about Winnie. What the heck was going on? Had she caused the accident?

She continued digging, but the sparse Facebook page didn't answer any of her questions, including the one that had been eating a hole in her gut since she first saw his name: How had Chase Alder ended up at Kickapoo Country Club that night, with his penis forcibly thrust inside her? But really, what had she expected? A series of tell-all posts chronicling his life as a violent sex offender who hid in plain sight dressed as a Brooks Brothers model?

She was just about to give up when she saw an old picture of what looked like a large family reunion. Chase had been tagged by someone: "Missed you (again) at Kickapoo, cuz." Maren sat up in her bed and strained to make out the faces in the picture. Her heart skipped a beat when she realized she was looking at none other than Charles Brown and his extended family. And just like that, she remembered where she'd seen Chase. He was Charles's younger cousin. Different last names, but it would explain the hints of Mrs. Brown's face and languid body movements that Maren tried hard not to notice in Winnie from time to time.

Maren thought harder. Maybe she'd seen Chase at the pool earlier that fateful day—she remembered that Charles's cousins occasionally visited from California in the summer—but she had no recollection of him at the party that night. She wiped the curtain of sweat off her face. So she had been at least partly right. Charles might not be Winnie's father, but his cousin was. And given what her ex-best friend Jane said that night, Charles had something to do with her rape. But what?

Maren was reeling. She'd operated all these years under the assumption that Charles was her rapist, but with no memory whatsoever of the actual act, she could never truly be sure. If it wasn't him, she'd assumed it had to be one of the other four boys who'd been at the party that night. Boys she'd grown up with, swimming and sledding and dining at Kickapoo Country Club. An unforgivable betrayal, but somehow the knowledge that she'd known her attacker had become an integral stitch in the fabric of her story—a story she'd slowly and agonizingly come to terms with. But now to discover she'd actually been raped by a virtual stranger? It was as though her entire narrative had unraveled in her lap, and to knit it back together, she had to experience every excruciating detail once more.

But this time, she didn't have the luxury of eighteen years to make her peace with the new version of the story. Winnie was possibly in grave danger, and it might have nothing to do with Stanford. Maren had to tell her everything—and soon. The heartbreaking conversation she'd feared since the day she'd first nestled Winnie in her arms was coming at her like an asteroid. She buried her head under a pillow to muffle her crying and tucked herself into a tight ball to smother her shaking. Would this nightmare never end?

A familiar darkness soon engulfed her. She was so tired. Not in the normal superficial way, but tired in her marrow, wrung out on a cellular level. If a five-alarm fire were to rage through the house in that moment, Maren knew she might not summon the will to save her own life. But she would do anything to save her daughter. Somehow, she needed to find the strength to protect Winnie.

With her stomach rumbling, Maren forced herself to set down the laptop and go to the kitchen for a fortifying snack. She nibbled on a cracker, but the thought of any more food in her stomach was revolting. Instead, she reached deep into the cabinet above the fridge for her emergency vodka bottle. Foregoing the glass entirely, she downed several gulps straight from the bottle. The vodka burned going down, but it eventually numbed her nerves a degree or two, enough for her to continue her quest for information.

Back in her bedroom again, Maren pulled up the photos she'd snapped of the apairofgenes.com correspondence on Alicia's computer. The messages had started about ten days before the accident. Her heart skipped a beat as she read them in order and put together that Naomi had been in Seattle more than once over the past few weeks. Not only was Maren correct that she was the woman from the ER, but it was now clear she was also the woman who had stalked Winnie on the bus the day before the accident and who had accosted Winnie at school just yesterday. Why was her rapist's wife so hell-bent on finding Winnie? Maren flipped to the final screenshot. Naomi's most recent message was sent just last night, mere hours before Maren discovered Alicia's handiwork. Maren read in utter disbelief.

Sent 1 day ago

Winnie,

It's Naomi again. I'm sorry if I'm scaring you. You obviously don't remember me from your accident, but I was the one who called the medics and waited with you until help came. I know you don't want to hear from me anymore, but I have to explain our situation because we are racing against time. I'm begging you to just read this email. Please.

Chase and I have been married for eight years. We live in San Mateo, California, with our two children. I've uploaded a photo so you can see your half sister, Olivia, who is six years old, and your half brother, Eli, who is three. We also have two golden retrievers called Mac and Cheese (named by Olivia and Eli) and a cat called Candy.

A year and a half ago, when Eli was eighteen months old, he was diagnosed with acute lymphoblastic leukemia, a type of fast-growing cancer. Eli went through chemotherapy, but six months later, the cancer returned. More chemo, more hospital stays, and another remission. Three months ago, the cancer returned again. Now we're told he needs a stem cell transplant to survive. Statistically, our best chance for a match is a blood relative. None of our close family matched. I went on apairofgenes.com to try to locate more relatives in our quest to save Eli, but so far, we'd failed to turn up a match. And then your name popped up.

Eli is the sweetest little boy. He loves trains, balls, animals, and Spider-Man. He's been so brave. Winnie, we are running out of time and options, and we are absolutely terrified of losing our little boy. We know it's a huge thing to ask of you given that you don't know us, but would you be willing to be tested to see if you are a match with Eli?

Naomi

Given that you don't know us? That was the reason it was a huge ask? Not, say, given that my husband raped your mom when she was only seventeen and you were the result of his violent act? Maren had no clue if this woman was part of some elaborate con designed to draw Maren and Winnie out or whether she was, as she claimed, truly the mom of a little boy with cancer who was married to a rapist and either didn't know or didn't care. All options felt equally absurd. And even if she was telling the truth about her boy, a child who may or may not be Winnie's half brother, Maren couldn't help her harsh gut reaction: Why should the fate of her rapist's son be any of Maren's or Winnie's business, let alone their responsibility?

She felt ugly admitting that to herself, but she was helpless against the anger swelling inside her like an abscess. As far as she was concerned, they could all rot in hell. She might not be able to put him in jail after all these years (she'd long ago researched the statute of limitations for sexual assault in Indiana), but she could send him to a different kind of purgatory. And after everything he'd taken from her, was it wrong that she thought she could probably live with that?

Alicia's final message back to Naomi posing as Winnie suggested that on this point alone, she and Maren were aligned:

I'm sorry about your son, but I have no interest in getting tested. Stop harassing me or I will go to the police. This is your last warning.

What a callous woman. At least Maren had a justifiable reason for withholding help for this little boy, whereas Alicia's cold response was obviously motivated by very different (self) interests. But still, Maren didn't love the notion that regardless of the reason, she'd landed on the same morally questionable stance as Alicia.

At a loss, Maren searched Naomi's name. Unlike Chase, Naomi maintained updated pages on nearly every social media platform from

Instagram to Facebook to LinkedIn. A quick perusal of her accounts revealed a mom on a desperate mission to find a stem cell donor for her terminally ill son. In the most recent photos on Instagram, Eli was bald, and Chase and Naomi sported stoic smiles and raccoon eyes that bore witness to intense grief. There was no way Naomi could be faking Eli's illness. Her public social media presence stretching back for years all but confirmed that. As a mom, Maren felt awful for Naomi, she really did. And that darling little boy. Dear lord, was she becoming a monster too? There was no doubt her anger was righteous and justified, but was that enough to turn her back on an innocent child?

And then there was the matter of Winnie's accident. Had Naomi really been the one to call the medics? The doctors had told Maren that Winnie likely would have died on the parking strip that night if she hadn't been found in time to stop the brain bleed. She supposed it was possible Naomi was lying about the SUV, but if Naomi had been the one to cause Winnie's accident, at the very least it wouldn't have been on purpose. She would hardly have been able to harvest stem cells from a dead minor. Maren didn't owe Chase a damn thing, but might she owe Naomi a karmic debt for saving her daughter's life?

Maren pulled her hair back into a rubber band. If Naomi wasn't the one who ran Winnie off the road, then Maren was back to assuming the hit-and-run really had been the by-product of EBA's deranged college frenzy. She shook her head to clear her thoughts. As distressed as she was, she couldn't afford to get distracted. Above all else, she had to figure out who was behind Winnie's hit-and-run.

All through the evening, Maren's erratic emotions came at her from every direction, like bullets slicing through the air as she ducked and dodged. She would tense up with rage and then be overcome by a wave of shame and then, again, sympathy. She wiped away her tears, swearing at herself to get it together. After hours of this epic internal battle, Maren couldn't shake the worry that Winnie might never forgive her if she didn't come clean.

The only thing that could break Maren forever would be if she lost her daughter. The thought of being estranged from Winnie the way Maren had been from her own parents was unbearable. For most of her adult life, she'd yearned for a road map to survival. Instead, she'd been forced to travel uncharted terrain. While far from perfect, Maren was proud of the hard work and ingenuity she'd applied to the effort. At some point in the past few years, she'd even begun to dream she might finally outrun her past and do more than merely survive; she might actually learn to thrive alongside her remarkable daughter. But ever since Winnie's star-crossed dreams of Stanford had taken center stage, Maren's tenuous grasp on everything she valued seemed to be slipping. Not only did she still have to contend with her overarching terror that Winnie's attacker was still at large, but on top of that, she was left to fret about what Naomi might do next, now that Alicia had thrown cold water on her plan to save her son. As Maren well knew, a desperate mom could be unpredictable. It was time for Maren to take the plunge and tell Winnie the truth.

25

Alicia

ALICIA AND ERYN, THE member of Aspyre's social media team sent to take photos of her at the SST meeting, pulled up to EBA. As Eryn unclicked her seat belt, Alicia put her hand on Eryn's arm. "You know, I think maybe I better go in alone. The moms will probably get all weird about you being there because I didn't clear it ahead of time. I'll text if I need you." The social media team might want content showcasing her good works in the community, but Alicia had her own agenda to get through first.

For starters, her lawyer had been stonewalling Detective Davis, and Alicia was desperate to know if there had been any developments that would point the finger at someone other than her family. Asking Maren herself was out of the question, but she was willing to wager that good ol' Amanda Russell would be more than willing to stir the pot with Alicia, Kelly, and Maren all in the same room. None of this was gossip she wanted people whispering about at Aspyre.

Alicia took off her sunglasses and gazed at her reflection in the mirror Eryn was holding so she could reapply her lipstick. No amount of injectable filler and expensive concealer could hide the dark circles under her eyes. Ever since she'd read Naomi's last email about her sick son, Alicia had been unable to sleep. Every night, she tossed and turned, trying to push the photo of Olivia and Eli Alder she'd seen in the apairofgenes messaging thread out of her mind. They both had Winnie's big piercing blue eyes. The face of the dying little boy haunted her, but it was Olivia on whom she was most fixated. The little girl wore a Sleeping Beauty princess dress in the picture Naomi had attached. Her long blond hair fell around her shoulders, and a huge smile revealed several missing teeth. But it was Olivia's arms wrapped protectively around her little brother, who was bald with no eyelashes or eyebrows, that gutted Alicia. What would happen to this little girl if her brother died? While Alicia had been much older than Olivia, losing her own brother had fundamentally altered the course of her own life. And not in a good way.

After Alex died, a suffocating sadness had descended over Alicia and her parents that seemed to either scare or repel people. When school had started that fall, Alicia's teachers, her friends' parents, even her friends had treated her differently. They hadn't known what to say. They wouldn't make eye contact. She was no longer Alicia, the sophomore at Grosse Pointe High School. She was the dead swimming star's sister. A constant cautionary tale of the dangers of drinking and driving.

Alicia had started eating lunch alone in the school library and reading the *Detroit Free Press*. One day, she'd come across an article about the twentieth anniversary of President Kennedy's assassination that captivated her. For months afterward, she'd retreated to the library stacks, plowing through book after book on the Kennedy family, inexorably drawn to the multiple tragedies they'd suffered and somehow survived. Alicia couldn't help but wonder what would have happened to John F. Kennedy if his older brother, Joe, hadn't been killed during World War II. Joe had been the one their father was grooming for greatness.

Alicia didn't think her father had ever dreamed Alex would be president of the United States, but he'd definitely had big plans and high expectations, starting with an NCAA title and the 1988 Olympics in Seoul. She'd imagined that as the cloud of Joe Kennedy Sr.'s grief lifted, he'd transferred all his hopes and dreams to John. That was how Alicia felt when she was changing sides during a high school tennis match that spring and noticed her dad, for the first time, sitting on the bleachers next to her mom.

Though Alicia was not a particularly strong tennis player, every time she won, her parents got excited. A small reprieve from their intense unhappiness. They weren't delusional enough to envision a tennis scholarship to Michigan in Alicia's future, but they thought a #4 Singles State title sure was. One day, Alicia was playing a girl from another top team in the state. A pretty blond. Every game went to deuce many times, a real battle. When they switched sides at 4–3 and were each taking a drink from their water jugs, Alicia looked the other girl up and down and said, "You're not as fat as everyone says you are." Alicia smiled, put her water jug down, and went to her side of the net to return serve. She didn't lose another game.

During other matches, sometimes Alicia switched the score and lied about it. Sometimes she called close balls out on purpose. There were whispers, of course, but who was going to accuse the girl whose brother had died of cheating? Alicia won the #4 Singles State title that year and for the next two years using the same tactics. All that mattered was winning so her parents would be happy. When she was in her early thirties, a therapist finally helped Alicia understand that she had been dealing with immense anger about Alex's death and that inflicting pain on other people had made her feel better. But by then she'd acquired an appetite for winning, and the lying, cheating, and manipulating had become a tough habit to break.

Alicia pushed the negative thoughts from her mind, blotted her lips, and took one last look in the mirror. Promising to take an Insta-worthy photo, she slammed the car door behind her. The moms would be assembling one hundred Giving Thanks care packages to be delivered to the seniors before they left for Thanksgiving break next week. According to Kelly's reminder email, this year, the SST had decided to add a philanthropic twist to the annual event by making another hundred care packages for one of Diana's pet charities, Homeless to Homefull, the downtown homeless shelter for women and children.

After Diana's food poisoning the other night, Alicia had called her, but Diana hadn't yet returned the call. Not only that, but Diana hadn't responded to any of Charlotte's emails sent the week before the concert to schedule their traditional lunch for Diana's birthday. Alicia had no idea what social infraction she'd committed to warrant Diana's disappearing act. Maybe if she posted a picture from today's meeting tagging Homeless to Homefull for her nine hundred thousand followers, Diana would stop avoiding her.

As she pulled open the door to the Taylor Family Conference Room, Alicia steeled herself, knowing she was about to come face-to-face with Maren for the first time since Alicia had discovered Naomi's emails to Winnie on apairofgenes.com a couple days ago. While she hoped Naomi had gotten her stern message and given up trying to contact Winnie, Alicia knew better than to underestimate a mother running out of options.

"Alicia, what a treat to have you join us," Kelly said, clapping her hands together and giving her a smile so big it bordered on cartoonish. "The custodian is bringing in the Giving Thanks supplies from my car."

Alicia flashed Kelly a tight smile in a half-hearted attempt to hide her annoyance that the supplies weren't set up already. When the door opened again, the custodian entered with several boxes balanced on a dolly, followed by Maren with an armful of bags. Alicia smiled at Maren and then busied herself setting down her bag and jacket on a chair before joining the other mothers who were standing around the table chitchatting. As soon as Maren started opening the boxes and placing their contents on the table, Kelly, Amanda, Sarah, and Jennifer began arguing over the most efficient way to arrange the items. Alicia rolled her eyes but saw an opportunity to corner Diana while the others spent the next ten minutes reinventing how to fill bags assembly-line style.

"I hope you had a great birthday," Alicia said, settling into the chair next to Diana. "I'm so sorry we weren't able to find a time for our usual lunch."

"No worries." Diana shrugged and flipped her beautiful blond hair over her shoulder. "I'm so over big birthday celebrations."

Yeah, right. For her fiftieth birthday last year, Diana had flown fifty friends (Alicia and Bryan included) on a private jet to Paris, rented out an entire floor of the Four Seasons Hotel George V, and hosted her birthday dinner in the ornate Gallery of Battles at the Palace of Versailles.

"Well, anyway, I brought you a little something," Alicia said, dangling a small gift bag containing the $300 Alexander McQueen silk scarf Maren had picked out.

"Oh, you didn't have to do that," Diana said, taking the handles of the gift bag between her fingers as if she were holding the tail of a dead rat.

Alicia watched her tuck the gift bag into her large Stella McCartney tote without opening it. "It's too bad we didn't get a chance to catch up at the EBA Leadership Circle cocktail party last week."

"Oh, you mean the rich people's affinity group?" Diana whispered behind her hand.

Alicia smothered a laugh. Maybe she'd been blowing Diana's recent flakiness out of proportion if she still wanted to share an inside joke. At the beginning of the school year, EBA's Diversity Task Force had announced via email a series of parent affinity groups—LGBTQ+, Pacific Islander, African American, Hispanic, Muslim—to help build a greater sense of belonging in the community. Diana had texted Alicia wondering what affinity group they were supposed to join. Moments later, they'd both received email invitations to the EBA Leadership Circle cocktail party. An exclusive event with the head of school for EBA's largest donors. Coincidence? "Oh, Di—"

"How's Winnie?" Amanda's voice rose up through the chatter.

"She's doing well, thanks," Maren said without looking up from the box of granola bars she was unpacking.

"Is there any news about the accident?" Diana asked, trying to appear helpful by exuberantly adjusting the piles others were making.

A pregnant silence swept through the room. All at once, every woman around the table was in motion. Piles were straightened, boxes were opened, eyes shifted, and heads drooped, waiting for Maren's answer. Alicia could sense several women in the room stealing peeks at her and Kelly.

"Winnie doesn't remember much." Maren shrugged as she pulled handfuls of socks from another box. "The police are still in the process of interviewing people and collecting evidence."

Alicia glanced at Kelly. She was playing with the pendant on her necklace and appeared to be eating one of the granola bars intended for the homeless. After all the memes posted on social media, Kelly had to be their top suspect.

"Alicia, did your security team learn anything?" Amanda asked. "Bryan said at the last meeting they were working on it. He was so sweet."

All eyes in the room turned to Alicia. She swallowed. Hard. The only directions Alicia had given her team after the accident were to beef up Brooke's security, but she wasn't about to admit that her husband lied to the SST. Out of the corner of her eye, she saw Maren. Staring at her, waiting for a response.

Alicia tucked her hair behind her ear. "Unfortunately, my security team didn't come up with anything." Alicia contorted her face (or at least as much as the Botox would allow) into her best disappointed grimace.

"I can't believe no one's come forward," Sarah said. She was pulling EBA-branded earbuds out of a box.

"With all the security cameras these days, you'd think one of them would've picked up something," Augusta said.

"Have you thought about offering a reward?" Diana asked Maren.

Maren looked uncomfortable but didn't say anything.

"That's a brilliant idea, Diana!" Alicia leaped at the opportunity to deflect suspicion over the accident, simultaneously rescuing Diana from an embarrassing silence. "I'd be happy to put up a reward. I'll talk to that detective. Anything to help." But the moment the words tumbled out of Alicia's mouth, she regretted them. She'd been avoiding contact with the detective at all costs, and now she'd just publicly committed herself to reaching out to him. What the hell had she done? Had she spent years honing her poise and judgment in boardroom battles only to crack under the pressure of a goddamn SST meeting?

26

Maren

AFTER YEARS SPENT ANTICIPATING Alicia's every need, Maren had slowly but surely chiseled a tiny peephole into Alicia's soul. Unfortunately, looking through the peephole was like trying to see the rocky bottom of a glacial crevasse—the kind that regularly swallowed mountain climbers whole—through a drinking straw. As if Maren needed any more evidence of Alicia's corrupt soul, her Oscar-worthy performance at the SST meeting today had provided it. Her ability to pose as an altruistic philanthropist and compassionate employer while secretly allowing a young child to die in service of her own ambition made it all but official: Maren was working for a sociopath.

On her way back to school to retrieve Winnie later that afternoon, Maren stopped at the grocery store to stock up on bread and butter in anticipation of the difficult conversation to come. One of the few traditions she'd carried over from her childhood was the comforting magic of hot, heavily buttered white toast. Like Wonder Bread white. The intense gnawing sensation in her gut indicated that today would be a full-loaf encounter. Maren headed straight for the toaster the second they arrived home.

A few minutes later, Maren entered the living room with a plate piled high with toast, buttered all the way out to the edges just the way they both liked it, and sat down next to Winnie.

"Wow. Must be serious," Winnie said, glancing up from her phone. "That's, like, half a loaf right there. Let me guess. Today's toast topic is my dad?"

Maren nodded grimly. "I need you to promise to just listen for a little bit, OK? This is going to be upsetting, and I'm sorry."

"OK…" Winnie said, chucking her phone down on the large, rectangular ottoman that doubled as a coffee table.

Maren had her attention now. She tucked one leg under her and faced Winnie. "So you know how I've always told you I didn't know who your father was and that you were my gift from a one-night stand?"

"Yeah?"

"Well, that wasn't a lie…but it wasn't the complete truth either."

"What do you mean?"

Maren took a deep breath. She felt like a little girl standing at the end of the high dive for the first time, working up the courage to jump. She closed her eyes and leaped. "I was raped, Win. Your father was the man— or boy, I guess—who raped me." It was a relief to finally say it out loud, but she was suddenly chilled to the bone. She reached for the throw blanket behind her and wrapped it around her shoulders.

"What do you mean by raped?" Winnie's eyes were bugging out. "Like date rape? Was this, like, an ambiguous consent situation?"

Maren knew there was a whole vocabulary around sexual consent and assault these days. In many ways, she wished she'd come of age in today's world. But then she might have aborted Winnie. Maren's life would have been easier, but she wouldn't trade Winnie's bright light for any alternate journey in the time-space continuum.

"No," Maren responded, her eyes already tearing up. "I mean raped, as in I was passed out drunk, and I never knew who did it to me."

"Oh my God," Winnie said and reached for her mom's hand. "What happened?"

"Well…I was seventeen, basically your age, and it was the night before I was leaving for college. It happened at a late-night party at my parents' country club. It was by far the worst, most traumatic night of my life. I'm so sorry," Maren said, grabbing a tissue from the side table and drying her eyes.

"Why are you apologizing?" Winnie said.

"I don't know. I don't know," Maren repeated while staring down at the mountain of toast in front of her, unable to meet Winnie's eyes. "My mom made it even worse by not believing me. She blamed me for drinking too much. Ordered me to go to college and forget about it. I think I've carried so much shame and pain over this for so long it's like I can't separate what really happened from whether it's somehow my fault."

"Oh my God. I'm sorry I keep saying that, but just, like, oh my God. Then what happened?"

"When I came home for Thanksgiving a few months later, I thought I was just depressed and fat, but my mom figured out right away I was pregnant, and my parents totally freaked. I was too far along to consider an abortion—not that my parents would have allowed that anyway. Long story short, they ended up driving me to Wisconsin at the end of that weekend and leaving me there at a creepy home for unwed mothers that was straight out of the 1950s. All my parents cared about was making damn sure no one at their precious country club or church ever found out their daughter was a slut. The plan was for me to give birth to you and then hand you over to a 'nice Christian family,'" Maren air-quoted.

Winnie's doe eyes were breaking Maren's heart. She'd known this would be tough, but it was wrenching to watch her daughter internalize that she was not just unwanted but actually forced upon Maren. "Anyway," she said, waving her hand in the air, "obviously I couldn't go through with it. What I need you to understand is that even though you were conceived without my consent, I knew by the time I was in my third trimester that I was meant to be your mom. I did what I had to do to keep you. And sadly, that meant running away from everything and everyone I had ever known."

"So my grandparents didn't die in a car crash when I was a toddler?" Winnie looked stunned.

"No, they didn't. My dad died of a heart attack when you were five. My mom is still alive, and I send her a card once a year with your picture," Maren said. "But she's never responded."

"I can't believe she doesn't want to meet me. I can't believe you lied to me." Staring straight ahead, Winnie hugged a pillow to her chest.

"I only hid the truth to protect you until you were old enough to handle it." Maren reached out for Winnie's hand, but Winnie pulled her arm away. "End of story. I wanted you to feel normal, wanted, and loved— because you are all those things. None of this was your fault."

"But half my genes are from a horrible person." She turned to Maren with tears freely flowing. "Tell me the truth: Do you ever look at me and hate me?"

"No, sweetie, no! Of course not," Maren said, again reaching for

Winnie's hand. This time, Winnie didn't resist. "I hate the man who did such a hideous thing to me, but I love every single cell of you. You've never been anything but perfect to me from the second you were born."

"Wait..." Winnie said, wiping away her tears with the back of her hand. "So that Naomi woman outside school really is married to my dad? I mean, your rapist?"

Maren nodded. "You were right about the account Alicia set up a few years ago with your DNA sample. I found it yesterday. My guess is she logged back in to try to find your dad with the hope of ruining your first-generation hook, not that it would matter what his education level was when you've never even met him, so don't ask me what her thinking was there," Maren said, reaching for a piece of toast and taking a bite. "But because of all this, I learned the name of my rapist for the first time. I always thought it was this one entitled creep I'd grown up with, but I was wrong. It was a name I didn't even recognize, which meant I'd been raped by a complete stranger."

"Oh my God, Mom! That's awful."

"It turns out it was the entitled creep's younger cousin." Maren brushed the crumbs from her lap into her hands.

"If that woman hadn't come to Seattle, would you ever have told me any of this?" Winnie asked.

"I always told myself I would tell you when you were eighteen." Maren looked down at the half-eaten piece of toast in her hand. "But if I'm being completely honest, the closer you got to eighteen, the less I could imagine it. The thought was just too painful. I guess with DNA testing everywhere these days, though, I would have told you eventually, but no mom ever really wants to tell her daughter she's the product of rape."

As they sat side by side, each consuming a piece of toast, Maren could all but hear the gears turning in Winnie's head, trying to weave together the new threads of her life story. Winnie's initial shock and anger had been expected, but Maren took it as a good sign that Winnie hadn't stormed off to her bedroom or grabbed the car keys. Unsure what to say next, she waited for Winnie to make the first move.

"What do you think his wife wants from me?"

Maren almost wished Winnie had more questions about the rape or her grandparents. Anything to avoid humanizing her rapist and his wife. But she owed Winnie the truth. "Apparently their three-year-old son has leukemia and needs a stem cell transplant. They seem to be hoping you might be a match."

"Wow." Winnie slumped back into the couch. "I feel like I just walked into the middle of a soap opera. So that's what the woman meant when she said it was critical that she talk to me. That little boy is my half brother, right?"

"Genetically speaking, yes," Maren said, starting to worry about where the conversation was headed.

"Will he die if he doesn't get the transplant?"

"It sounds like he might," Maren acknowledged. "It's sad, but sometimes people get sick and die."

"But there's a chance I might be able to save him?"

"There's a chance, yes. But it's not without risk. You just had brain surgery for God's sake. You could get an infection. You yourself could die."

"Like you just said: it's sad, but sometimes shit happens."

"That's not exactly what I said." Maren was definitely regretting Winnie's tenure on the award-winning EBA debate team right now. "But regardless, that doesn't mean you have to *ask* for shit to happen, as you put it. Not when you have another option."

"Like letting my half brother die? No thanks. Even if his dad is a terrible person, that's not his fault. Any more than it's my fault, right?"

"You may want to help the boy, but what about me? I'm a victim here too."

"I get that, Mom. I really do. But what about the part where you got me out of the deal? Doesn't that count for something? And also, I don't think this is the sort of revenge that would really make you feel better."

"Oh really, then what would?"

"I don't know. Maybe getting a life?" Winnie said, her tone softening. "You've spent the past eighteen years all alone holding onto this awful story, letting it define you."

"I have a life." Maren looked away. "I have you. I have my job." Her voice sounded hollow, as though she were ticking off items on a grocery list.

"Come on, Mom. You have a job you hate, working for a total bitch who pushes us both around. You have me, but I'm going to college soon. And I always thought you didn't have time for friends or dating since you're a single mom and all, but that's not really the problem, is it?"

Maren avoided her daughter's perceptive eyes.

"Don't you think it's time for us to figure out how to let this go and help you move on?" Winnie asked gently.

"Maybe, but it kills me that he'll never rot in prison for what he did to me."

"I know," Winnie said.

"Can I at least kick him in the balls until he turns into a soprano?"

"Sure. I promise I'll hold him down for you, OK?" Winnie said with a brief chuckle, but then her brow furrowed with her telltale determination. "I just want to meet them and see if there's any way for me to help the kid."

Maren massaged her temples. "I wish it were that simple. If we meet with them, you'll probably learn some things that will be so upsetting you'll wish you'd never asked."

"If there's more, can't you just tell me now?"

"There are some things only my rapist knows. And there are other things I can only say out loud once. Please don't ask more of me. I'm strong, but I'm not superhuman." From the concerned look on Winnie's face, Maren thought, or maybe hoped, she'd pushed back hard enough that Winnie would reconsider asking for the meeting.

"I think we should email them now. We'll feel bad if we wait too long and something happens."

Maren had obsessed for so long over telling Winnie the truth about her origin story, but she'd never thought for a moment to envision a meeting with her daughter, her rapist, and his wife. This was beyond soap opera; it was more like an episode of *The Jerry Springer Show*.

Maren sighed. "How did I raise such a good person? Right now, I wish you were a little more selfish and callous. But listen, even though you think you're so smart, you're still a minor for a few more months. So we're going to do this my way. Let's not forget, you had brain surgery a couple of weeks ago, and your arm is still healing," she said, pointing to Winnie's cast, "and we don't even know who did that to you. For all we know, they could have something to do with it. Naomi said herself she was there. I'll arrange the meeting, but if you change your mind at any time, all you have to do is say the word and we're outta there."

Winnie nodded her assent.

"One more thing. When we meet him—"

"Wait, I don't even know his name," Winnie interjected.

Maren was loath to say her rapist's name out loud for the same reason she didn't allow Winnie to name the stray cats that appeared at their back door every so often. She feared Winnie would become attached to something she couldn't have. "Your sperm donor's name is Chase Alder."

Winnie nodded, and Maren continued. "I need him to come clean about everything that happened that night if I'm ever going to get closure. I need you to respect me on this. If he refuses to be honest, we walk. OK? I don't care how cute or innocent his kid is, that boy's blood will be on his father's hands, not yours, if he can't treat us with the decency we deserve after what he did."

"I can live with those terms. And, Mom? This wasn't your fault. I'm really sorry for everything you went through." Winnie laid her head down in Maren's lap.

"I'm sorry too." Maren stroked Winnie's silky hair. "About everything except you."

———

From: Maren Pressley   Today, 9:45 p.m.
To: Naomi Alder
Subject: My Daughter

This is Maren Pressley. You are under the mistaken impression you've been communicating with my daughter through apairof-genes.com, but someone else has control of that account. Please cease all messages through that platform immediately.

I will give you and your husband one chance to meet my daughter and me to explain yourselves. Your husband must accompany you or the deal is off. Meet us at the Four Seasons Hotel restaurant in downtown Seattle tomorrow at 5 p.m. Bring medical records proving your son's condition. Be prepared to tell the truth about everything. I am making no promises other than to hear you out. If I get even a whiff that either of you is holding back information about ANYTHING, I will physically drag my daughter home, and you will never see her or her stem cells again.

From: Naomi Alder   Today, 9:47 p.m.

To: Maren Pressley

Re: My Daughter

We will be there. Thank you so, so much.

The next day, Alicia flew out early for a board dinner in NYC, and Bryan was picking up Brooke early from school and taking the family jet to meet Alicia in "The City" for the weekend. Never one to miss an elite golf opportunity, Bryan had finagled an invitation from one of Aspyre's investment bankers to play Winged Foot, an exclusive golf course in the Hamptons. While Bryan would be occupied golfing and drinking, Brooke and Alicia would be busy shopping with the personal stylist Maren had hired to help them find dresses for Snowcoming and the Parents' College Stress Buster Extravaganza, or whatever the hell Diana was currently calling it. With the Stones on the opposite coast, Maren had a bit more time to prepare for the meetup with the Alders.

Maren was no stranger to the accoutrements of power, having served Alicia for so long. Just as Alicia did when she was preparing for a television interview or public speaking event, Maren forced herself into an ice-cold shower to invigorate her mind and body. Though she rarely put effort into her own hair and makeup, she did Alicia's all the time. Rummaging through Winnie's makeup drawer, Maren moisturized and then applied foundation, mascara, eyeliner, sun-kissed powder, and lipstick. She selected the outfit from her wardrobe that most telegraphed competence and control—black slacks and a red blouse. An updo twist completed the don't-fuck-with-me portrait of power she sought. Satisfied with her appearance, Maren headed to EBA to pick up Winnie from school at three p.m. sharp, and from there, they drove straight downtown.

Though it would be only a small win in the confrontation that was about to unfold, Maren was fixated on arriving and being seated at the table well before the Alders. The thought of walking into the restaurant knowing Chase would be watching her body move through the tables toward them was more than she could bear. She needed to have control of the entire interaction, and that started with her appearance and the initial greeting. She figured Winnie might as well do some homework and get a fancy meal out of the ordeal; Maren fully intended to stick the Alders with the bill.

There weren't enough flowers in the world to create an atmosphere of warmth in the marbled hotel lobby of the Four Seasons, although clearly the staff had been ordered to try. The pungent fragrances did little to soften the harsh clicking of women's heels on the hard floor or the thrum of rich people demanding their due, but at least the dim lighting didn't further aggravate the pounding headache she'd awoken with that morning. As they wound their way toward the empty restaurant and chose a table in the back overlooking the waterfront Ferris Wheel, Maren congratulated herself on her first tactical victory.

As always, Winnie was ravenous after school. She glanced at Maren, silently confirming and reconfirming permission, before placing her order for a $25 organic grass-fed burger with fries. Maren couldn't help herself. "She'll also have a shaved vegetable salad on the side."

Winnie shot her a dirty look.

"What?" Maren shrugged. "I'm not an idiot. You think I'm going to pass up a chance to stuff you full of organic produce? If you're this smart growing up on pesticides, just think what a genius you'd be if I could have afforded clean food." She turned to the server and added, "I'll have a bottle of sparkling water with a lime, please." She hoped the expensive bubbly water would settle her roiling stomach.

As they waited for their food, Winnie worked on her AP Physics homework. It was a stunning day, and Maren looked out the window at Puget Sound, the nearby commuter islands, and the majestic Olympic mountain range. The natural beauty of the scene was an incongruous backdrop for the ugly conversation Maren was anticipating. "Mom, look." Winnie kicked her mom under the table, her voice interrupting Maren's musings.

Maren looked to her right and saw the server coming toward them with a large round tray. For a second, she didn't see the couple trailing the server. And then her rapist was standing before her. Her throat turned dry and scratchy, and she felt the first telltale itching of her palms. She reached into her purse for two Benadryl and tossed them into her mouth. She would not give him the satisfaction of watching her break into hives.

"Hi, Maren. Hi, Winnie. I'm Chase Alder," he said, with Naomi standing by his side. Both appeared exhausted and tear-stained, as though crying was their default mode. "This is my wife, Naomi." Naomi looked about as awful as Maren felt, with stringy hair, wrinkled clothes, no makeup, and dark, almost purple-hued circles beneath her bloodshot eyes. Maren was pleased she'd had the foresight to dress up for the meeting, though a small part of her felt sorry for the woman. *As for Chase*, she thought, *let him suffer*. At least he knew better than to extend a hand in greeting to Maren or Winnie.

Maren kept her face blank as Chase caught her eye, but it was only for an instant; he looked away red-faced as soon as propriety permitted. However, he couldn't resist the pull of the familiar features of his offspring. Maren and Winnie were similarly drawn to his face. It was lost on no one that Chase and Winnie had identical blue eyes and the same small dimple in their chins. Clearly, the DNA test had not issued a false result.

"May we sit?" Chase asked politely.

Maren waved her arm in invitation to take the seats opposite her and Winnie. "I trust you don't mind footing the bill for Winnie's meal today."

"Of course! Order anything you want, Winnie. I mean, both of you, of course," Naomi babbled. "Winnie, do you want an ice cream sundae?" Chase glanced at his wife with raised eyebrows but stayed quiet. Maren immediately glimpsed the strong physical resemblance he bore to his hateful cousin Charles Brown, the man she'd erroneously blamed for all these years.

Winnie squinted at Naomi, and Maren predicted her daughter's snarky comeback, something like, "No, I don't want an ice cream sundae. I'm seventeen, not seven." But instead, Maren heard Winnie's actual response: "Yes, please," she said. "Can I have it with whipped cream and a cherry but no nuts?"

"That's exactly how my kids like theirs," Naomi said softly, her eyes wide.

Maren's stomach sank. Was she going to lose her daughter's undivided love and affection to these people when all was said and done? There was no way she'd endured so much to end up alone. "You're here early," Maren remarked, as much to divert her own thoughts as to clip the small talk.

"I know, " Naomi said. "We figured we'd come straight here from the airport and have some coffee while we waited for you. We didn't want to risk being even one second late."

"As long as we're all here, we might as well get this done." The sooner Maren could push her way through this surreal meetup, the sooner she could go back home to her comfy couch and her soft blankets—and pretend this entire scene was a product of her imagination. She looked directly into Naomi's eyes. "Before we go any further, I need you to first explain why you were in the ER the night of Winnie's accident. I know I saw you there. Did you cause the accident? And remember: the truth or we walk."

"Please don't leave. I'm begging you. I'll tell you everything," Naomi said.

Maren stared at her and waited. The one revelation she'd had in the wee hours of the night that still held water when she'd forced herself out of bed in the morning was this: Maren was and would always be Winnie's mom first and a rape victim second. No matter how sympathetic this Naomi might appear, Maren could not allow herself to soften or she might miss a crucial clue about Winnie's hit-and-run.

"I swear I told the police everything I saw. I was driving a ways behind a dark SUV that seemed to be closely following Winnie when I saw her fly off her scooter onto the parking strip. The car sped off without stopping or even slowing down. I was the one who called 911, and then I waited with you until the medics and police arrived," she said to Winnie. "You don't remember that at all?"

Winnie shook her head in response.

"I didn't see any other identifying details of the car or driver," Naomi continued. "It was dark, and it all happened so fast. Please believe me, I would never try to hurt your daughter. I went to the ER to make sure she was OK."

"Is that so? But you didn't tell the police everything, right?"

"No. You're right. I didn't tell the police that I knew who Winnie was. I'd actually been following her since the night before, trying to work up the nerve to talk to her. But I promise I didn't cause the accident."

"And tell me again what exactly you wanted to talk to Winnie about?" Maren raised her eyebrows in question.

"Like I wrote to Winnie in my apairofgenes messages—although after Winnie seemed to have no idea who I was yesterday at her school and after your email last night, I'm totally confused about who I was communicating with…" Naomi's voice trailed off briefly. "Anyway, according to her DNA test, she was my husband's biological daughter. I was only trying to get a good look at her and figure out where in Seattle you lived so I could ask you both for help. I was desperate to have Winnie tested to see if she's a stem cell match for our son, Eli. Obviously, I didn't know at that point what Chase had done to you, Maren. I hope you can believe me—I had no clue until he told me everything last night."

"Wow. That must have been a real shocker, learning the father of your children is a rapist. Welcome to my life," Maren muttered. And then, into the stunned silence, she continued. "So, about that night…" It was the moment of truth. Maren turned to look at Chase and pushed through the catch in her throat. "Chase, I have this funny feeling we've met once before. Can you please refresh my memory?" Maren knew her words sounded sardonic and glib, but it was the only way she could handle the weight of this moment without falling apart. She could feel her nerves shake and her windpipe constrict, threatening to silence her.

Chase recoiled and seemed to shrink in his chair, as though it was just now dawning on him that he would be confessing his sins to his victim, his wife, and the daughter he was meeting for the first time. He looked like he was going to throw up right there on the table.

Maren took a centering breath and summoned some steel to her voice. "And please, don't leave out a single detail. I demand total honesty or you will never see us again. I know you don't know me, but take my word for this: I never make idle threats." She stiffened her back and stared him down. This man had stripped her bare once before; she wouldn't let it happen a second time.

"Chase?" Naomi elbowed her husband, who looked like roadkill at the moment of impact. "You need to start talking. Now."

"Uh, yes. OK. Sorry. I just… Well. OK," he stammered. "First, let me say I am so incredibly sorry for what I did to you that night. I can't imagine how terrible the past eighteen years have been for you. I mean, other than you, Winnie. Of course." Chase ran a hand down his face.

Maren said nothing. Winnie was playing with a french fry. Naomi was crying. The server walked toward the table, probably to ask how Winnie's burger was tasting so far, but he took one look at the body language around the table and astutely turned back. She hoped Chase was a good tipper.

"So, yeah, that night. I was sixteen, and my family was visiting my cousin's family, the Browns, for a week of tennis and golf at their country club. Which was also your country club. Kickapoo?"

"Yes, I'm familiar with it." Maren forced a smirk, her insides lurching. "Please continue."

"As you know, obviously, there was a big party at the club that night, but my family was leaving early the next morning, so we didn't go. At about midnight, Charles came back to the house and woke me up to drag me out to the after-party. He said it was on fire, and he was going to help me get lucky. I was still a virgin and had made the big mistake of admitting that to Charles earlier in the week. I didn't want to go, but he called me a pussy and all sorts of other things. He'd already finished a year of college, and I was only going into my junior year of high school, so I gave in. While we walked back to the club, he made me pound tequila. I know it's no excuse, but I really hadn't partied that much, and I didn't realize how hard straight tequila would hit me. Before I knew it, I was wasted.

"When we got to the after-party in the pool house, everyone was dancing, and he told me to look around and pick the hottest girl. I had seen you at the pool earlier in the week. It was an easy choice. I still had no idea what he was up to though. I just thought he was going to get you to dance with me."

"Jesus," Winnie whispered.

Everyone looked at Winnie.

"Your cousin roofied her, didn't he?" she said.

Maren watched in disbelief as Chase nodded at Winnie and then turned to Maren and locked eyes with her for the first time since he'd arrived at the table. "I'm begging you. You have to believe me. I had no idea what Charles was up to. I didn't even know what a roofie was back then. He handed me the tequila bottle and told me to keep drinking, and then he went to the punch table and filled a cup. He gave it to you and danced with you while you chugged it."

Chase took a sip of water. "After that, he came back over to me and told me you thought I was cute and wanted to do me on the golf course." His head was bowed like he was relating the story to the flatware on the table. "I honestly couldn't believe my luck. I was horny and drunk, and a beautiful girl wanted to have sex with me. Charles told me to take the tequila bottle and he'd meet me on the twelfth hole in a few minutes.

"But when he got there with you, you were so drunk you were barely conscious. He was actually carrying you fireman style. I remember telling him this didn't feel right and trying to leave, but he swore to me over and over that you told him you couldn't wait to have sex with me."

Maren could barely swallow. Or think. She felt like she might pass out. She lowered her head and covered her ears.

"Mom? Are you OK?" Winnie tapped Maren's shoulder. "Mom? Here, drink this." She placed the glass of sparkling water in Maren's hand. Maren robotically obeyed her daughter. "OK. Keep going," Winnie said harshly to Chase. "My mom needs to hear the rest."

Chase nodded once. To Maren, his eyes looked as far away as she felt. She realized with a start that they were both back in that life-altering moment, sand rubbing on bare skin, only he was supplying the memory for both of them. "I remember him laying you down in the sand trap and pulling up your dress. Charles spoke loudly to you and said, 'Mare-mare, here's your boy. Ready for him?' Your head moved up and down, but deep down, I think I knew he was moving it for you. You never had a chance to consent. Then he ripped off your underwear and told me to get to it. I was so drunk by then and, to be honest, terrified, that I almost couldn't, um, you know, physically do it, but then Charles was taunting me. Said he'd tell everyone I was a cocksucking faggot—that was the worst insult to a teenage boy back then. So I did it. Afterward, I remember Charles saying, 'Man, those roofies are like magic, huh?' All I could think to do was stumble back to Charles's house, puking the whole way.

"I knew it was wrong. So wrong. I was raised to respect women. I couldn't believe I'd done such an evil thing, but then I just wanted it to go away. I figured if I never spoke of it again and never saw Charles again, maybe it would somehow disappear. But now, I have to confront what I did. I can't imagine all the suffering I caused you. I want you to know I have never and will never forgive myself. I know it's far too late, but I'm so sorry, from the bottom of my heart. And I want to make amends to you."

Maren was crying, tears of agony but also of relief. The one piece of the puzzle she'd never understood: she'd been drugged. It made so much sense she was surprised she'd never suspected it. Even though she hadn't recalled drinking nearly enough that night to black out, she'd always accepted her mom's accusation that she all but asked for it. Of course, Maren was enlightened enough these days to know that even if she hadn't been roofied, it still wouldn't have been her fault. But rational thought had never been enough to shake the suffocating shame she'd internalized long ago as a seventeen-year-old girl whose parents believed she was a drunken floozy who'd had it coming.

"Mom, it's OK. See? It wasn't your fault. It wasn't your fault at all." Winnie looked up at her biological father. "It was his fault. And his cousin's fault. Not yours."

"She's right," Chase echoed Winnie. "It was my fault. And not that this makes it any better, but I want you to know a few more things. First, I've never seen or spoken to Charles since the morning after. As I was about to get into my parents' car, he threw his arm over my shoulder and whispered in my ear, 'No worries, bro. I got your back. Told everyone at the party it was me who popped her cherry. Told them she was crying after cuz she didn't realize it would hurt so much the first time. No one will ever know.'" Chase shook his head in disgust.

"On the long drive back home," he continued, "I swore to myself I would do everything in my power to make up for what I'd done, to be a better man. I didn't want to be anything like that pig. So I hit the books hard junior year, determined to get into the best college I could. I ended up at Yale and was one of the few men there to major in gender studies. I learned all about sexual harassment, assault, consent, and justice. Then I went to law school. That's where Naomi and I met. Naomi was the first and only woman I had relations with after, um, that night. And I hope to keep it that way forever." He looked at his wife, who glared back at him with an expression as hard as marble. "Now I work in San Francisco for a law firm where I primarily represent victims of sexual harassment in Title IX cases. I know this is all probably cold comfort to you, but I want you to know I was a stupid kid who made an immoral and illegal decision, but I'm not a monster."

"That's a sweet story," Maren said with a deadened voice. "But you never sought me out to apologize or see if I was OK, did you? Or turn yourself in to the authorities? You were able to keep control of your narrative the entire time, accountable only to your own quaint ideas of what it means to 'be a better man,'" Maren air-quoted.

Chase looked down at his hands.

"And you never thought it was important enough to tell your own wife."

"Believe me, the past few weeks have been hell for me."

"You've got to be fucking joking. Are we supposed to feel bad for you?" Winnie bit out, her voice tense with rage.

"No! I'm sorry. Of course not. That's not…that's not what I mean," Chase stammered. "It's just once I found out about you, I was so torn. On the one hand, I never wanted anything more in my life than for Naomi to find you so we could have a chance of saving Eli. But I'm ashamed to admit that another part of me hoped you'd be unreachable since I knew finding you would blow up my entire life. I was such a coward. I didn't tell Naomi at first on the off chance she might never find you. Like she said, I didn't tell her until last night when we got your email. We stayed up all night before heading to the airport this morning." He paused and looked over at his wife with tears in his eyes. "I honestly don't know if our marriage can survive this, but I'll do absolutely anything to save our little boy."

Maren glanced at Winnie. Winnie's face was still twisted with resentment, but her eyes were brimming with tears. "We will consider—and I'm not promising more—but we will consider getting Winnie tested if you are truly ready to take full responsibility for your actions."

"What do you want me to do? Child support in arrears? Pay for Winnie's college? Whatever you want. Just name it. I'll do anything. Please." Chase pulled out a checkbook from his sport coat pocket.

Maren took a deep breath. She couldn't deny that after two decades of financial struggle, the offer of restitution was highly tempting. All night long, Maren had wrestled with the question: What exactly was her endgame today? Was it a revenge fantasy à la *The Girl with the Dragon Tattoo* in which she turned the tables and tormented her attacker? Was it to provide Winnie with her unvarnished origin story now that she was on the cusp of adulthood and poised to make her own life decisions? Or was it as simple as finally being allowed to speak her truth out loud? As with most multiple-choice questions, the correct answer was the catchall Option D: all of the above. Did money fit into the equation at all? Maren sighed. The answer was no. Profiting off the pain of her past would not help her heal.

But after all she'd endured, she deserved to know if this man was willing to publicly acknowledge the consequences of his actions the way she had been forced to for years. On the way to the hotel, she and Winnie had discussed what this might look like. Now, Maren cast a glance at Winnie, who nodded slightly in return. "You have Instagram, right?" Maren asked Chase.

"I do," Naomi answered for him. "I've been trying to spread the word about Eli."

Winnie took over. "How many followers do you have?"

Naomi pulled out her phone. "About fifteen hundred."

"OK, that'll do," Winnie said. "Chase—take a picture of me with Naomi's phone."

Winnie posed for the camera while Chase obeyed and took the picture.

Winnie said, "OK. Now type this caption. Ready? 'Hi, this is Naomi's husband, Chase Alder. I want to introduce everyone to my biological daughter, Winnie. I viciously and violently raped her mother after she'd been roofied when I was sixteen and she was seventeen. I never knew Winnie existed until a few weeks ago. I am so sorry to everyone who trusted me and believed in me. And especially to Winnie's incredible mom. I hope someday she can find it in her heart to forgive me. She's raised a spectacular young woman all on her own, and I deserve to be in jail.'"

Chase looked like a dead man walking, but his thumbs dutifully pecked away at the keyboard. He shoved the phone over to Winnie for her approval.

"Perfect," Winnie said.

"Now post it," Maren ordered.

Chase winced, but he lowered his index finger to the phone. An instant before he made contact with the screen, Winnie dove across the table and snatched the phone from his hand. "On second thought,

I don't think I want to be known to the world as your daughter. I'm good with just my mom." Winnie whipped out her own phone and took a picture of the draft post, with Chase and Naomi in the background. "But we'll keep this photo just in case we ever change our minds." She cocked her head. "It really sucks knowing someone else controls your destiny, huh?"

Chase and Naomi nodded, their faces a matching shade of gray.

"Well, my mom's had to live that way her entire adult life, so you'll just have to deal with it." Her voice trembled with emotion.

Maren placed a hand over Winnie's clenched fist. It was both a silent thank-you to her daughter for the gift of her empathy and a gesture of comfort she hoped would help Winnie weather the rest of this painful conversation.

Maren closed her eyes to gather her strength. She stole a cold french fry from Winnie's plate and, finding it lacking, waved down their waiter and ordered an expensive bottle of wine. Finally, she broke the silence as she locked eyes with Chase again. "Now I think it's your turn to listen to the avalanche of pain and hardship you set off with your little joyride."

———

Before launching in, Maren visualized all the burdens Chase had saddled her with traveling like a bolt of lightning from her chest to his. She watched him physically shrink under her withering glare. Let him suffer under the weight of his own carnage. Let him experience waking up in the middle of the night gasping for air with the desperation of a person being buried alive. Let him know her pain.

With a deep breath, she took the first tentative step toward setting herself free. "I suppose the most basic things I need you to know are: one, you stole my virginity that night, and two, you literally shredded my insides." Her voice was hoarse. "It took me more than a month to heal physically. A month in which every time I peed, it felt like I was soaking in acid. A month of pain whether I was sitting or walking. Weeks of itching as my fragile tissue healed. And every single twinge of pain or discomfort threw me headlong right back into the worst minutes of my life when I woke up on the golf course disoriented, bloodied, and covered in sand, with no fucking idea what had happened to me.

"The morning after you raped me, my parents drove me to IU to start college. I was supposed to rush a sorority and try out for the cheerleading squad. And I'd been over-the-moon excited to study literature. All summer, I practically slept with the course catalog, planning out my four years of study. But in those few minutes, you also stole my education from me. I was so depressed when I got to college I barely left my dorm room except to eat. By the time my parents came to pick me up for Thanksgiving, I'd gained an ungodly amount of weight. I didn't know it then, but that was the last time I would ever set foot on a college campus as a student. My mom, who refused to believe I was raped in the first place— she told me I must have asked for it—quickly figured out I was pregnant."

Maren paused when the waiter appeared at the table to pour her wine. She took a few sips in silence and continued in a trancelike state. "My parents were religious, so they wouldn't consider an abortion. And anyway, I was already in my second trimester by that point, and no clinic in Indiana would have performed one. But just imagine being Winnie's age," she said, glancing over at Winnie, "not quite eighteen, and realizing you had to spend the next six months carrying your rapist's baby to term and then going through childbirth. Now imagine not knowing for sure who did this to you because you had zero recollection of the act itself. How about you, Naomi? Can you imagine that?" Maren leaned forward and narrowed her eyes at Chase and Naomi. "Can either of you imagine your sweet little daughter going through that in, what, about ten years or so?" Their faces were hollow with a small sliver of the terror Maren had experienced. *Good.*

"My parents were mortified. What would they tell their country club friends and fellow churchgoers? The solution they came up with was to send me off to a massively fucked-up home for unwed mothers. This place—it was called Greatest Gift Estate—had developed an entire business model around coercing attractive white girls like me to give up their babies for adoption. They offered free 'luxury' lodgings," Maren air-quoted, "and medical care—unless the babies weren't delivered for adoption at the end of it all. If the birth mother kept her baby, the inflated costs were charged in full.

"The problem was, by the time I was in my third trimester, Winnie was already mine in my heart, and I knew I had to protect her from these conniving people who wanted to take her from me. I escaped when I was eight months pregnant. All I had were the clothes on my back and the babysitting and lifeguarding savings I'd presciently taken with me the day my parents dumped me at that dystopian hellhole. I left in the dead of night, hitchhiked, bought a bus ticket out west, and eventually ended up in LA, where I gave birth to Winnie. I naively figured my parents would eventually come around, but I badly miscalculated. After I left, they were charged more than $100,000 for my four-month stay. Their anger at being stiffed, coupled with my alleged whore-like behavior, were more than enough justification to make good on their promise to disown me.

"So you see, you also robbed me of my safety net and my family that night. I actually had to find out about my dad's death from an online obituary." Maren wiped a tear from her eye. "When Winnie was little, we bounced around between homeless shelters and unsavory shared living situations. We were all alone. We were desperate. There are things I did to survive and keep Winnie safe. Things I won't even say out loud. That's how bad it was." Maren cast a sheepish glance over at Winnie to see if she was catching the meaning behind her veiled words. But of course she was. Winnie was intelligent and perceptive, and Maren had raised her to be street smart. "There were times I thought we might not make it. The only thing that kept me going was this amazing girl right here, who I loved with my entire being from the moment I first held her."

"I love you too, Mom," Winnie whispered and traced a heart on her mom's palm.

Maren lovingly brushed a wayward lock of Winnie's hair behind her ear. The ice cream sundae that had been wordlessly delivered by their waiter several minutes earlier sat untouched in front of Winnie, a melted puddle. "The last thing I need you to hear is this: in my entire adult life, I've never made love to anyone," she said, wringing her hands. "All the things you two have taken for granted in your own lives—romantic love, intimacy, companionship? I lost them all," she said softly, her eyes fixed on Chase. "You stole those from me too."

A sidelong glance at Winnie's pale face told Maren she'd probably shared enough for one day. "But lucky for you, I got Winnie. It's only because of my fierce love for her that I'm even willing to sit here in this restaurant today and hear you out. But if you were me, knowing all this, tell me: Why the hell would you ever help the person who had done this to you and gotten away scot-free? Why shouldn't I make you pay the ultimate price?"

Both Naomi and Chase were openly sobbing now. Chase kept looking over at Naomi, trying to catch her eye, which she studiously avoided. No, it wasn't at all clear their marriage would survive this deep wound. Maren tried to see that as a victory, but Naomi's desperation made Maren sad in spite of herself. It was Naomi who first gathered her emotions enough to speak.

"Maren. Winnie. I'm almost speechless. I can't even begin to tell you how sorry I am for the traumas you suffered because of Chase. There's no excuse for his actions. None whatsoever." Her mouth twisted in disgust, but she kept her eyes trained on Maren. "But even though I know I have no right to ask anything of you, I'm begging for mercy, mom to mom. For my little boy."

Naomi reached into her tote bag and pulled out an overflowing manila folder. "These are some of Eli's medical records, like you asked for." She nudged the folder toward Maren. Stapled to the outside of the folder was a frayed snapshot. "And this is Eli. He's three, and he's dying of leukemia, and Winnie may be the only person who can save him. It was like a gift from above when I received a message from apairofgenes.com that we had a new family connection and it turned out to be Eli's half sister. Please don't let him be collateral damage."

Naomi's eyes contained the distinct combination of love and pain only a mother could know as she ran a finger over the picture of Eli. "Just look at my sweet boy," she said. "You're obviously a loving mom. Try to imagine if this were your child."

Maren didn't have to imagine though. She'd felt that same cocktail of emotions only a couple weeks earlier in the ER. The little boy's smile in the picture looked just like Winnie's when she was a little girl. Maren tore her eyes away and tried to coax her facial expression back to ice, but she was pretty sure her glassy eyes betrayed her.

"Eli's just a baby. He's already had months of chemotherapy, and nothing's worked." Naomi was talking fast, like the sands of the hourglass were running out. "If he doesn't get a stem cell transplant soon, he'll definitely die. I swear to you, we—both of us," she said, giving Chase a look more injurious than a swift kick to the groin, "will spend the rest of our lives trying to make this up to you."

"Please," Chase croaked, his head cradled in his hands. "Please. I'm so sorry. Your anger at me is totally justified, but please don't take it out on our son. And on Naomi. She's the best woman I know. I don't deserve her. Never have. Please. I'm begging you."

"I think we need to sleep on it," Maren said. "We'll get back to you in the morning."

"No, Mom. I'll do it. I'll get tested," Winnie's broken voice interjected.

"Are you sure? You don't have to say yes right now. You can take some time to think about it."

"I can't have this little boy's death on my hands. He's a victim too, just like us."

"The first step is just a blood test, right?" Maren asked Naomi.

Naomi nodded in response.

"OK, I'll consent to the test. But just so everyone is clear, Winnie can back out at any time. Even if she's a match. We're only agreeing to the test. Text me the information, and we'll take it from there." Maren took out a pen and scrap of paper from her purse and scrawled her phone number on it.

As Naomi reached across the table for the paper, she and Chase spoke over each other. "Thank you, thank you so much."

Maren and Winnie rose to leave. Chase and Naomi stood too, but both remained rooted in place, as though they'd come upon a nest filled with eggs and were afraid to disturb it.

"Just one more thing," Maren said. "At least until Winnie is eighteen, I'm in control here. You do not have my permission to communicate directly with her. Everything goes through me. Or the deal is off. And as I said in my email, no messaging through apairofgenes. Ever. You have my cell phone. Text me."

"Yes, of course," they said in unison, practically falling all over themselves to placate Maren.

"Maren?" Naomi said. "Can I ask you one question about that?"

"About what?" Maren asked.

"About the account. What's the deal? Who's been getting my messages if it wasn't you or Winnie?"

"I'm not at liberty to tell you who my boss is, but suffice it to say she's a world-class sociopath. Winnie and her daughter both applied to Stanford. She stole Winnie's DNA and tried to use information about Chase's educational background to damage Winnie's application."

"Seriously? That sounds completely insane," Naomi said.

"Just wait until your kids are in high school," Maren said. "You'll see."

"What kind of person would do that?" Naomi asked.

"Alicia Stone, that's who," Winnie blurted.

"Winnie!" Maren scolded. "I'm bound by an NDA!"

"Who cares?" Winnie said with a shrug. "It's your NDA, not mine. And it was my DNA. So whatever."

"I guess that's fair." Maren smiled ruefully. Honestly, there really wasn't much else she could say in response to that logic.

"*The* Alicia Stone? CEO of Aspyre?" Naomi asked, her jaw slack. "All my friends idolize her. I can't believe it."

"Well, as I'm sure you now see, some people"—Maren pointed her chin at Chase—"are not at all who they present themselves to be." She put on her coat and nudged Winnie toward the door. But then she stopped and turned back to face Naomi. "Regardless of how this testing business turns out, I wish you the best of luck with Eli. Mom to mom, I'm truly sorry for your pain. And also, thank you for calling 911 for Winnie and for staying with her."

In a sweet act of protectiveness, Winnie put her arm around Maren as they walked the block and a half to the car in silence. By the time they arrived, Maren's body was rigid with the effort of keeping her composure. Without a word, Winnie retrieved the keys from Maren's purse and guided her into the passenger's seat. As Winnie turned the key in the ignition, the insignificant rumble of the engine coming to life was what finally broke the dam. Maren cried nearly two decades' worth of tears on the three-mile ride home.

27

Kelly

FOR THE PAST SEVERAL years, Kelly had dreaded family gatherings with her parents and siblings, which took place wherever her older sister, Elizabeth, dictated based on her kids' arbitrary youth sports schedules. This year, with Kelly's nephews both in college, her mom insisted on returning to the family tradition of Thanksgiving at their Connecticut home. But when Kevin added up the cost of five airline tickets and a rental car, he balked. Ashamed to admit to her family the real reason they wouldn't be coming east, Kelly lied that Kaleb's fall fencing league required all seventh-grade competitors to be in Spokane for a Thanksgiving weekend tournament. After all, if her sister could play the youth sports card to run roughshod over the family for a decade, why couldn't Kelly use the same excuse?

Unfortunately, Kelly's mother then decided everyone should journey to Seattle instead for an early Thanksgiving. In a sick power play, Elizabeth and her family elected to skip the holiday festivities altogether and go to the Bahamas, effectively thumbing their noses at the rest of the family who had bent over backward for years to accommodate them. At first, Kelly was royally peeved that Elizabeth was blowing off their makeshift Sunday-before-Thanksgiving celebration, but maybe it was just as well. Kelly's sister was married to a successful hedge-fund manager, had a rockin' bod from working out two hours a day, and was a college snob to boot. Not exactly the person Kelly was dying to spend several days with. At least her younger brother, Simon, a high-priced lobbyist in Washington, DC, and his wife, Monica, had agreed to the change in coast and were bringing their precocious little boys, Jake (age five) and Trevor (age three).

With the average age of the family gathering skewing younger, Kelly hoped that maybe this time, every conversation throughout the pseudo holiday weekend would not automatically segue to test scores, internships, job opportunities, and the college choices made by the grandchildren of her parents' friends (and all their friends' friends' friends). However, as soon as her family appeared on her doorstep, it became apparent Kelly wouldn't be catching a break.

"No, Kelly. The *wooden* spoon!" her mother directed, glass of chardonnay in hand, from the kitchen island where she'd parked herself because her sciatica was acting up from the long flight. "Where was I? Oh yes, our new neighbors, the Bergers? Their older son went to Cornell and got a job at Goldman. They're insufferable. Can't stop talking about him. I don't see what the big deal is. Cornell is basically a state school masquerading as an Ivy."

With her back turned to the island, Kelly rolled her eyes at her mother and snuck a square of dark chocolate she'd stashed in the spice drawer. Kelly's father had gone to Harvard for undergrad and law school.

Her mother had spent one semester at Radcliffe before dropping out to get married, but her Mrs. degree entitled her to share in her husband's attitude that Harvard was superior. In everything. Elizabeth graduated from Harvard and married Dan, a Harvard man, and now both their boys went to Harvard as well. Listening to her mother belittle Cornell, Kelly experienced a post-traumatic flashback to the day, long ago, when she'd broken the news to her family that she would be attending Stanford rather than their alma mater. Her parents had been so appalled they'd openly discussed not paying her tuition.

"We see the Bergers' younger son coming out of the house in the middle of the day all the time. He went to some college I've barely heard of. Where did that younger Berger boy go to college, Marty?" Kelly's mom called out to her husband, who was watching football in the family room. Kelly's kids were in no way huge football fans, but today they were glued to the TV right along with Grandpa, Kevin, and Uncle Simon. Anything to avoid a Grandma Nancy inquisition replete with comparisons to their overachieving cousins who were currently basking on a beach.

"Gettysburg," he yelled back.

"Oh right, but anyway, I think he's living at home and plays video games all day. I don't even know if he graduated. They never talk about him," Nancy said, lowering her voice as if she were describing a young man with some ghastly disease. "Kelly, why aren't you using the PAM? And why even bother with a school like that? What a waste." Her mother broke off a tiny corner of a cracker and touched it ever so slightly to the fig spread before taking a nibble. "Did Elizabeth tell you Tanner has four job offers for when he graduates in the spring? I think he's narrowed it down to UBS and a hot tech start-up. Kelly, why are you putting so much butter in the potatoes?" Nancy paused to take a large sip of wine. "And

I'm sure you heard Taggart has an internship at Google in New York this summer?"

Kelly added another large dollop of butter to the potatoes. Why did her mother feel the need to update her about her own goddamn nephews? But then again, her mother seemed mystified that Seattle had running water and was still befuddled by the three-hour time difference despite Kelly having lived on the West Coast for thirty years.

"It's really too bad Krissie isn't being recruited for a sport like Tanner and Taggart. Did your admissions people give you a sense of how many students Stanford is going to take?" her mother asked, wrinkling her nose at the mere mention of Stanford, even though it had surpassed Harvard as the most selective school in the country years ago. "Kelly, aren't you going to zest that lemon for the green beans?"

"We're not sure." The last thing Kelly wanted was for her mother to know Stanford was only taking one more EBA student. They'd eviscerate her for throwing away Krissie's early admission opportunity on Stanford when she could have also played a legacy card at Harvard. But to Kelly's relief (and amazement), Krissie hadn't been interested in Harvard.

"I met a man on the plane who works for Amazon. He said their recruiters are using a drop-down menu of fifteen top colleges to screen job applicants. Kelly, you should get ahold of that list," Nancy said, refilling her wineglass again. "I'm sure Stanford's on it, but you should cross-check it with Krissie's backup schools. You don't want her to pick the wrong school and not be able to get a job when she graduates."

"I'll be sure to track it down." Kelly pasted on a smile and slathered a cracker with fig jam and a hunk of goat cheese.

Nancy recoiled as Kelly shoved the entire cracker into her mouth. "What schools is Krissie looking at out east?"

"You know, Mom, EBA says students are deserving of their privacy when it comes to college, so they ask us not to talk about our kids' lists," Kelly said, completely exasperated. "It's up to each student what they want to share. Maybe you should talk to Krissie yourself." Kelly left her mom alone in the kitchen and headed upstairs for a moment of peace. That morning, Kelly's mother had actually followed her into the bathroom to finish telling her about the SAT score of her manicurist's daughter.

All in all, by the time Kelly and her family had filled their plates and taken their seats around the holiday table, Kelly was bone-tired and more than a little ticked off that nobody had offered to help her. This was not at all what she'd signed up for. Surveying her modest, adequately decorated table, sprinkled with the pine cones and twigs her nephews had gathered from the backyard, she tried not to think about what Diana Taylor's "tablescape," as she referred to it, would look like on actual Thanksgiving Day in her stately dining room overlooking Lake Washington and the Cascade Mountains.

With minimal ceremony, Kelly's father announced, "This looks great. Let's eat." But before he could complete his first fork-to-mouth delivery, five-year-old Jake shrieked, "Stop! Grandpa Marty, stop!" And then, in his best imitation of a disappointed adult, he said, "Silly Grandpa. Don't you remember about silent grace?"

The entire family stopped and stared at Simon and Monica. Grace, silent or otherwise, was not and never had been part of their Thanksgiving family tradition. Monica tried to wave off her young son with a subtle head shake and a frantic "It's OK, honey," but Jake was not to be deterred. They *had* to do silent grace.

After a crummy day, Kelly felt herself buoyed as her latent mischievous big-sister streak rose from the ashes. She sent a sideways smirk toward Simon and then turned to her nephew. "Why, Jakey, I don't think we've ever done silent grace before. Can you show us how?"

Simon tried to muffle a groan with his napkin.

Jake nodded his head. "First we all hold hands like this," he said, grabbing ahold of his neighbors' hands. "Then we all put our heads down like this and say thank you to God for our food. But not out loud. You say it silent."

Kelly shot all her kids a silent glare, distinguishable from a silent prayer by its ominous tinge, as they all clasped hands around the table and waited until Monica broke the silence with a breezy thank-you to Jake.

Grandpa Marty raised an eyebrow toward his own son as if expecting an explanation, and a good one at that, but Simon ignored his father's entreaty. Grandpa Marty promptly resumed his turkey-destroying mission. He was a serious and focused eater.

Grandma Nancy never could resist a controversy though. So she posed the question that was on everyone else's mind. "What in the world was that all about? We don't say grace!"

Simon tilted his head toward Monica, begging for a rescue. But it was Jake who answered his grandma's question. "Grandma, we're Quakers now," he proclaimed.

Kelly choked on her pinot noir and watched in slow-motion horror as it sprayed out of her mouth first and then her nostrils (and, was it possible, even her eyeballs?) onto the white tablecloth in front of her.

"Gross, Mom!" Katherine said.

Kelly noted her middle child's mortified expression, saw a vision of Quaker Oatmeal cylindrical boxes, and burst into hysterical laughter. When she came up for air, she peeked over at Simon. He hadn't looked this uncomfortable since that time in high school when she'd barged into his bedroom and interrupted a tube-sock moment. "Well, Si, care to enlighten us?" Kelly sputtered.

"Quakers? Quakers?" Nancy repeated. "What on earth?"

Monica sat up a little straighter in her chair. The whole family was agape. "We might as well tell you. Our family has made the decision to convert to Quakerism."

"Yes, so we've heard," Kelly's mom said, a glazed look in her eyes. "But I don't *understand*."

"What are you talking about? That's ridiculous." Grandpa Marty waved his fork through the air, uncomfortably close to Kaleb's head.

Monica cleared her throat. "Well—"

"It's so I can go to the friendly school!" Jake piped in.

"What's the friendly school, Jakey?" Kelly coaxed.

"It's the school I went to play at one day. I want to go there again cuz the playground's so fun, but Mommy says the kids who get to play there are Quakers. So now we're Quakers, so maybe I can go there, and then after that, Mommy says I can go to a good college like Hanford."

"It's called Harvard, Jake. Not Hanford. Remember?" Monica snapped at her son.

Jake's bottom lip quivered. "Sorry, Mommy. I always forget."

Kelly watched as the puzzle pieces she'd already put together in her mind snapped into place for the others around the table. Simon had called Kelly last spring to confide that Jake had been rejected for prekindergarten at the prestigious Oakley Friends School, a private school rooted in the Quaker tradition. Monica was of the belief that the only road from DC to Harvard went through Oakley Friends and had been more enraged than Simon thought possible. Apparently, she feared Jake's rejection would damage not only his future but his younger brother's as well. At the time, Simon had told Kelly they intended to have Jake reapply for kindergarten. Monica had evidently decided to leave nothing to chance this time around.

"Wait, are you saying you guys actually switched religions to get your kids into kindergarten?" Krissie's mouth hung open. "Wow. And I thought my mom was obsessed."

"Easy, Krissie," Simon said, cocking his head toward the mini provocateur of the Thanksgiving table. "And anyway, it's not just kindergarten. It's entry into the best school in the mid-Atlantic."

"That's messed up." Kaleb threw some side-eye at his uncle as he scooped another helping of mashed potatoes onto his plate.

"Look, you have to do whatever it takes these days to get a leg up on the competition," Monica said. "I won't apologize for being a conscientious mom."

"Monica, do not apologize," Grandma Nancy said. "I think it's genius. Pure genius. Reminds me of when Elizabeth—anonymously, of course—ratted out that cheater who was higher on the Harvard tennis recruiting list than Taggart. Of course, one can never be sure, but we always suspected that was why Taggart got off the waiting list."

"Are you kidding me? I never heard that story," Kelly said, incredulous.

As the conversation meandered through the next hour of the not-quite-holiday dinner, Kelly pondered the constantly shifting line between conscientious and outright nutcase. If her mom, her sister the snitch, and the Quaker fakers at her table were any indication, Kelly had substantial room to maneuver without tumbling over the precipice.

After she loaded the last dishes into the dishwasher, Kelly quietly stole upstairs. For some reason, she'd been unable to throw away the disposable phone she'd used last month to text the made-up rumor about Winnie's college plans, instead hiding it in her sexy-time lingerie drawer. No doubt the least-frequented place these days in their entire house, so she'd been confident no one would stumble across it.

As Kelly powered up the phone, she mulled over the salacious nugget from Maren's past she'd uncovered in the background check she'd invested in a few weeks earlier. She hadn't for the life of her been able to figure out how to use it to Winnie's Stanford detriment. Brooke was another story altogether. Kelly had the goods on her, but she kept holding back from going after her directly because Alicia was so damn powerful. But what kind of mom was Kelly if she didn't have the backbone to go all out for her daughter? Admission decisions were less than three weeks away; it was now or never. Kelly punched in the phone number she'd committed to memory. At the sound of the beep, she spoke in the deepest voice she could muster and anonymously reported to the Stanford Admissions Office the fraudulent essays submitted by one Brooke Stone of Elliott Bay Academy.

28

Maren

THE FLIGHT ATTENDANT SET down the elaborate celebrity-chef-created meals on their linen-lined tray tables. Maren could still scarcely believe they were sitting in first class on a plane to San Francisco, complete with spacious seats, bowls of nuts fresh from the oven, and free cocktails served in heavy-base lowball glasses. "Don't get too used to this," Maren said to Winnie.

Winnie grinned from ear to ear in response, unable to speak with her cheeks stuffed full of gourmet chocolate.

Their packed Thanksgiving weekend itinerary was even more mind-blowing. Tonight: check into a five-star Palo Alto hotel. Tomorrow: guided tour of Stanford. Thursday afternoon: Winnie's solo visit to the Alders' home in Berkeley to meet her half sister Olivia and Chase's father, who had already sent an email to Maren expressing his eagerness to meet Winnie. Thursday evening: Thanksgiving buffet dinner for Maren and Winnie in the hotel restaurant. The Alders had invited them to join their family Thanksgiving dinner, but that was a "hell no" for Maren. Then, on Friday morning, Winnie would check in to the children's hospital where Eli was currently getting slammed with chemo to prepare for his transplant of the stem cells the doctors would extract from deep inside Winnie's bones. If all went smoothly, Maren and Winnie would be home by Sunday evening, and no one in Seattle would ever know the details of their excursion, which would surely top the list of most bizarre college visit weekends in history. Eli's fate would take longer to determine.

The Stones were spending Thanksgiving week in Telluride, so Alicia had reluctantly acquiesced when Maren asked for time off to take Winnie camping on the Washington coast. Normally, Maren would be busy over the long holiday weekend taking care of Cardinal and her eight additional canine clients around town, but a young tech at Cardinal's vet was thrilled to step in for Maren and earn a little extra money. And Maren's industrious daughter had taken it upon herself to send Naomi a spreadsheet detailing the financial hit they would take by leaving town. Naomi had responded with a Venmo payment three times the quoted amount.

Maren's leg jiggled. For most of her life, whenever she'd let down her guard, she'd ended up regretting it. Worrying had become part of her armor, like a garlic necklace to ward off the evil spirits. It was exhausting living this way, but she couldn't seem to stop. What if something went wrong with the procedure? Had she asked the doctors enough questions?

Due to Winnie's acute epidural hematoma only a month earlier, the doctors were reluctant to use a more current stem cell harvesting procedure that involved repeated but relatively painless blood draws. As it was explained to Maren and Winnie by the pediatric oncologists, there was a slim but real risk to Winnie's recovering brain associated with possible changes in pressure with that procedure. However, given the gravity of

Eli's condition, they offered Winnie the alternative of using an older surgical method for collection involving dozens of bone marrow aspirations in her pelvic bones. Winnie would need to be under general anesthesia for the brief procedure. The doctors said her lower back would be sore for a few days, but as long as there were no complications, Winnie would be back at the hotel by dinnertime the same day.

Maren had once again pressed Winnie to consider calling off the stem cell donation; the thought of Winnie enduring the more painful procedure for Chase's benefit was almost more than Maren could bear. She had even urged Winnie to think about whether her schoolwork might suffer, thus jeopardizing her grades for this all-important senior fall. But Winnie would have none of it. She worked ahead in all her classes just in case and insisted she could handle a little discomfort to save someone's life. So the plans had moved forward, with Maren equal parts proud of her brave daughter and terrified.

Maren shook her head in disbelief at the current state of her life. Before the blood test, she had sworn to support whatever decision Winnie made. Once they'd learned Winnie was a near-perfect match to Eli, Winnie was determined to go through with the stem cell harvest. It wasn't like Maren wished the poor little boy would die. She was damaged, for sure, but her heart still had a warm beating center even if it was encased in a protective shell. Selfishly, though, Maren had hoped a negative match would end their association with the Alders before they could sink their teeth into Winnie and form an independent relationship with her. Maren wanted desperately to hate them all. But if she was having trouble sustaining such feelings after what Chase had done to her, then what were the chances Winnie would remain immune to their considerable charms?

On Wednesday morning, Maren and Winnie awoke to a basket from the Alders delivered to their hotel room filled with fruit, chocolate, popcorn, directions to everything, and gift cards to nearby coffee shops and restaurants. Maren and Winnie used one of the cards to devour a locavore breakfast at a diner near the Stanford campus. The Stanford tour, delivered by an enthusiastic, backward-walking, lightning-fast-talking sophomore, reconfirmed for Winnie that this was where she hoped to spend the next four years. Even Maren had to admit it seemed perfect. Great weather, Nobel laureate professors, a beautiful, fountain-filled campus.

As she lay in bed in the dark late that night, Maren watched the peacefully sleeping form of her exhausted daughter in the bed opposite hers. Her logical brain was pleased she'd submitted Winnie's application in the wake of the accident, and she hoped for Winnie's sake she would be admitted. But there was something about that place with its shiny facade and laid-back vibe that screamed fake to Maren, as though underneath all the practiced smiles, there existed a seething underbelly of competition and privilege, much like EBA. Perhaps it just appeared to Maren more country club than institute of higher learning? Anyway, there were no guarantees Winnie would get in.

But what if she did? This was no longer a theoretical question. A flood of adrenaline washed through Maren's irrational brain and swept into every corner of the hotel room, forcing all hope of sleep out the door. Early admissions decision day was only two weeks away. Even covered in the luxurious warmth of the hotel's silky down duvet, Maren's entire body shivered. If Winnie won the spot, would a competitor target her as a scapegoat for their own disappointment? Or might they catch a break at long last, with the madness of this fall finally lifting once decisions were delivered and outcomes settled? Maren tried to quell her anxiety with a deep belly breathing exercise, to no avail. All she wanted was for Winnie to realize her dreams, but as decision day crept closer, so did a familiar sense of dread—and a vexing awareness that there had to be more to the picture than she was currently able to see.

———

Maren had done everything she could think of to pass the time while Winnie spent Thanksgiving afternoon at the Alders'. She took a walk through downtown Palo Alto, window-shopped at the local bookstore, sipped coffee, and even went for a swim in the hotel pool. As she toweled off after her shower, she wondered for the hundredth time how the visit was going. It was a peculiar, deeply aching kind of loneliness for Maren, knowing Winnie was off meeting new family members to whom Maren would never feel connected. She thought this must be how divorced parents felt when their kids went off to celebrate holidays with their ex's family, only about ten thousand times more alienating.

At five p.m., Winnie's card key finally unlocked the door, and she burst in, her eyes bright with excitement. "Oh my God, my half sister, Olivia, is so incredibly cute. She looks just like pictures of me when I was her age. That sounds kind of obnoxious, huh?" She laughed at herself as she did a full body flop onto her beautifully made bed. "I must have seemed familiar to her, too, because she took one look at me and decided I was her new best friend. She sat in my lap or held my hand the entire time." She turned onto her side to face Maren's bed. "She was so sweet, but she misses Eli, and every five minutes, she would tell me how she can't wait to play doggie—that's their favorite make-believe game—with him when he gets home from the hospital. It was so sad. Every time Olivia talked about Eli, Naomi would go into the other room for a minute, I think to try to stop crying."

"You're doing such a good thing, sweetie." Maren said, setting her novel down beside her. "I'm really proud of your strength in all this. It's not easy."

"I know it's the right thing to do. But I am a little scared."

"I know, honey. You're tough though. And I'll be right by your side for as long as the doctors will let me."

"Thanks. I know this sucks for you. I get it. I really do. But I wish you could see. They're a really nice family." Winnie had a faraway look on her face. "I met Chase's dad. He was the nicest man. He gave me a huge hug and said, 'Granddaughter, I've dreamed of meeting you every second of every day since I found out about you. I'm sick thinking of all the years I've missed with you.'"

"Sounds welcoming. Was your, um, his wife there too?"

"Nope, she died last year. He said he was so sad that she missed the chance to meet me. He told me she would have smothered me with love but that knowing what Chase had done would have broken her heart."

"I bet. It's hard to imagine being a loving mom and learning your son had done something so awful," Maren said.

"Yeah...the whole day was so sad and happy at the same time. I guess the definition of bittersweet?" Winnie continued. "I asked Chase's dad what I should call him, and he was so cute. He said, 'I hope you'll call me Grandpa, but if not that, then Jack will do for now. You can call me whatever you like, just don't call me late for dinner!'"

Maren shook her head. Her dad used to make that same bad joke when she was a kid. "Was anyone else there?"

"No, it was just Chase, Naomi, Olivia, and Jack. Mom—would it bother you a lot if I called him Grandpa? I've never had a grandpa. It felt kinda nice."

"Winnie, listen to me," Maren said as she moved across the gap between the beds and covered Winnie's hands with her own. "I've had you all to myself for your whole life. But for so long, it was devastating to me that I couldn't provide you with more of an extended family. I trust your judgment here, and I can live with you pursuing a relationship with them. I just don't want you to be disappointed if their interest in you wanes after tomorrow's procedure. I've learned the hard way that people can be pretty awful. I hope for your sake that's not the case here. But just do me a favor and keep your guard up a little while longer?"

Winnie teared up. The emotion of the day was overwhelming, and now Maren had just thrown a bucket of cold water on her optimism. Why couldn't Maren just let Winnie have her moment in the sun? "But look, there's no harm in hoping for the best. Don't let me drag you down. How about we go have ourselves a feast downstairs and be thankful for everything we do have. Deal?"

"Deal." Winnie fist-bumped Maren. "I'm starving. Let's eat!"

———

Maren and Winnie arrived at the hospital at half past six on Friday morning for check-in and pre-op. The past couple weeks had been harrowing, not the least from an insurance perspective. Shortly after Winnie had decided to go through with the procedure for Eli, Naomi had texted

Maren for their insurance info. Maren promptly set up a phone call with Naomi and Chase to break the news that she and Winnie were among the ranks of the uninsured. It wasn't Maren's fault, she knew, but the sting of embarrassment pricked at her as though she'd failed an important mothering exam.

"But what about Obamacare?" Chase had asked.

"Sorry to break it to you, Mr. Golden-Haired Man of Privilege, but even with Obamacare, the cost is prohibitive. Welcome to my reality." What a dickhead.

"Sorry, I just didn't realize," Chase said. "Shit."

"But you work for goddamn Alicia Stone!" Naomi said. "Are you kidding me? You mean to tell me…oh Jesus, what a stingy bitch! I still can't believe I actually held her in such high esteem all these years!"

"It's not ideal," Maren said, "but when your focus is survival, you figure out how to make things work, and you don't complain. And also I'm bound by a strict confidentiality and nondisparagement agreement, so please don't ever repeat that to anyone, OK? She will absolutely crucify me."

"Of course," Naomi said. "I promise. Chase, we gotta figure out how to get Winnie's procedure covered. Eli started chemo prep yesterday. Poor little guy feels so crummy. I don't know how much more his tiny body can take."

"I got this," Chase jumped in. "Don't worry about insurance. I'll take care of it. We're gonna get both of you insured—and keep you that way after this is over. I meant what I said. I can't erase what I did to you, Maren, but I will do everything in my power to help you going forward and see that my, um, your daughter is taken care of."

We'll see about that, Maren thought, thinking of the seven medical bills she'd already received and stuffed in a drawer in the few weeks since Winnie's accident. She still had no idea how she'd pay them without going bankrupt. But for the time being at least, she'd take whatever leg up the Alders were offering.

———

Winnie had been taken to the operating room at eight thirty a.m. Maren had been directed to the surgical waiting room for the duration of the procedure. She checked her phone again for the time. It was nine thirty a.m., and still not a word. The doctors had said they would let her know as soon as the thirty-minute procedure was over and Winnie was in recovery, but she had no way of knowing whether the procedure had even begun. The last time she sat in a hospital waiting room, less than a month ago, the rage she'd felt toward the driver who'd caused Winnie's accident had kept her company through the night. Today, if anything were to go wrong, she would have only herself to blame. Why had she agreed to let Winnie do this? Maren put her head between her knees to tamp down her nausea.

"Can I get you a cup of water or coffee, dear?" A deep, soothing voice interrupted Maren's misery.

"No, thank you, I'll be fine," she said to the stranger who had taken a seat beside her.

"You must be Maren," he said. "I'm Chase's father, Jack. It's good to meet you."

Maren croaked out a hello and put her head back down, hoping to put an end to Jack's overture before he got going. By design, Maren had yet to come face-to-face with Chase and Naomi. She assumed they were in Eli's room with him.

"I'm sure you're worried about Winnie. We all are. She's an absolute angel to do this, especially under the circumstances. I assume I have you to thank as well." He paused but continued when Maren didn't respond. "I know there's probably never a right time to say this, but please let me apologize for my son's wretched behavior. If I'd known about it back then, I would have hauled him to the police station myself. No one deserves what he did to you."

Maren tried to shove the tears down, but her emotions were too on the edge. She did not want to deal with this right now. "You know what, Jack? There may not be a right time to talk about this. But there's definitely a wrong time. And while my daughter is having holes drilled in her bones to help the son of my rapist? Well, there's probably not a worse time to have this chat, wouldn't you agree?"

"Yes, I suppose you're right. That was insensitive of me," Jack said gently, seemingly unfazed by her harsh tone. "It's just, I don't know, you looked so lonely sitting here, and I thought maybe you could use some company. But I didn't feel right talking to you without first acknowledging the reason we're all here."

Maren peeked up at him. He had a full head of silver hair, a lanky body, and a patrician nose. At first glance, she didn't detect a resemblance to Winnie, which was a relief, although she wasn't sure why. "What's your relationship to the Brown family anyway?" Maren asked flatly. "Are you the blood relation? Or your wife?"

"My late wife was Charles's mom's sister. For the record, I never liked that family. For years, Evelyn and I scratched our heads trying to figure out what her sister ever saw in that pompous jackass she married. And it was clear Charles was an utter piece of garbage from his toddler years on. None of that excuses my son's behavior, but I just thought you might be interested to know we've had as little to do with them as possible over the years, especially once Chase started refusing to visit them years ago." He scratched his head. "And now I finally understand why."

"I'm sorry for the loss of your wife," Maren said, remembering what Winnie had told her about her "grandmother" passing away. Dammit, why couldn't she help being civil to these people?

"Thank you. Ovarian cancer is a rough way to go. But I'm glad she never learned what Chase did to you, although she would have adored getting to know your lovely daughter." He smiled at Maren. "Winnie really is delightful. Your parents must be so proud of you for overcoming such hardship and raising a wonderful girl."

Maren's head snapped up, once again thrown back on her heels. Her voice came out laced with steel. "I guess Chase forgot to mention the part about my parents blaming me for the rape and disowning me when I refused to give Winnie up for adoption?"

Jack's eyes widened in surprise. "No, I'm sorry I didn't know that. Chase has been too upset to tell me the whole story. Said he'd give me the rest of the details after Eli was out of the woods. I've never seen my boy so broken up. First Eli gets sick, then his mom dies, and then he has to confront what he did to you. I think he's starting to fear this is his karmic retribution. The only silver lining has been getting to know Winnie."

"Poor baby," Maren muttered but then instantly berated herself for acting so juvenile. "Sorry, I don't mean Eli. I can't imagine how hard that would be. But forgive me if I don't shed too many tears over your son's suffering."

Jack nodded somberly. "I'm a professor of law at Berkeley with a master's in philosophy, and even I can't adequately answer the question of whether someone who's done such an evil thing can ever be considered 'a good person,' but I do believe he's a far better man than he was that day.

He may not be good, but he's at least become decent. And if I've learned anything over the years, it's that one can never have enough decent family. I hope with time you'll be able to figure out a way to let us be part of your and Winnie's family."

"I highly doubt you'd be inviting us into the family fold if you knew everything I had to do to get here." Maren looked away.

"Try me."

Maren narrowed her eyes. She knew men like this. From their privileged perches, they had no problem being magnanimous, and they could talk a big game about tolerance too. They were the men who would donate a million dollars to a homeless charity but couldn't bring themselves to make eye contact with the homeless people begging outside their highrise office buildings. "OK, fine, but you might want to pop a blood pressure pill first, Gramps." She looked at the clock on the wall before glancing back at him to gauge his reaction. He was just sitting there, politely waiting with an open expression on his face.

"Look," Maren said. "Suffice it to say, I kept us mostly sheltered, fed, and safe the first couple years of Winnie's life in LA by working as an exotic dancer, and then later, when I had the chance to make even more money with far less time away from my baby girl, I took it." Recalling that brief chapter of her life always sent a chill down her spine. Every single second had been torture. "On my third date, I got caught up in a sting and was convicted for being an unlicensed escort. I was locked up in county jail for two weeks. It gave me an arrest record, and I almost lost Winnie. I quickly figured out it wasn't the life for me long-term, but I can't erase the past. And frankly," Maren said with a defiant gaze, "I'll never apologize to anyone for keeping my daughter safe. The people who take advantage of young women in my situation—desperate and destitute single moms—they're the ones who should feel ashamed. I did what I had to do to survive after your son destroyed my life.

"So anyway," Maren said, her eyebrows raised at Jack in open challenge, "still want us to join your nice polite family? Or maybe we're a little too lowbrow after all? I mean, borrowing a few stem cells is one thing, but putting the formerly homeless ex-prostitute and her offspring in the family Christmas card is another thing altogether."

"Yes."

"Yes what?"

"Yes, I still want you as part of this family," Jack said. "Full stop."

For the love of God, when was this surgery going to be over? Maren looked skyward in exasperation. "We'll see about that." It was all she could say.

"I'll take that," Jack said. "Now, even though I'm grateful as all get-out that we learned about you and Winnie, what that Stone woman did to you by taking Winnie's genetic material without your consent? That was not decent. And I'm quite certain it was also illegal. You could probably press charges, you know."

"Yeah right." Maren rolled her eyes. "That would not end well for me, I can guarantee you. Do you have any idea the resources that woman has at her disposal?"

"Stranger things have happened. Bernie Madoff got what he deserved. That Elizabeth Holmes fraudster did too."

"Yeah, but your son didn't. Charles Brown definitely didn't. Brock Turner didn't, and that one gives me nightmares given Winnie's determination to go to Stanford. I sometimes worry I'll be sending her to the wolves if she gets in there like she hopes. The rich and powerful always get their way in the end."

"Not always, but I see your point. Anyway, if you ever change your mind and want to go after her, let me know. I'll help. And also I think you should consider having Winnie apply to Berkeley. It's just as good as Stanford but with far less arrogance. I promise to look after her."

"Thanks," Maren said. "I'll definitely keep that in mind."

"Keep what in mind? Pressing charges? Or Berkeley?"

"Berkeley. To be honest, Stanford doesn't seem right to me. It feels, I don't know, a little too perfect."

"And how about pressing charges?" Jack said.

"That I will not keep in mind. There's no way I'd be that crazy. It would be a suicide mission."

"Mrs. Pressley?" A nurse in scrubs approached Maren. "Good news. Your daughter is in recovery. The procedure went smoothly, and she's starting to wake up now. I can take you back to see her."

"Oh thank God!" Maren jumped up.

Jack stood with her. "Excellent!"

"And the stem cells are being filtered as we speak. Eli should receive his transfusion within a few hours." The nurse looked at Jack. "You're Eli's grandpa, right?"

"Yes, and Winnie's too."

Maren shot him a look.

"Maren, think about what I said about family, OK?" Jack said with a wink. "Can I come see Winnie in a bit?"

"Man, you are really persistent, I'll give you that," she said. "Fine—OK, you can come see her. That's all I'm promising for now."

He grinned at Maren. "I'll take it."

As Maren followed the nurse down the hall, she couldn't help shaking her head. That Jack was some character. A little smile fought its way onto her face, threatening to take up long-term residence.

29

Alicia

THEIR DRIVER PULLED AWAY from the house, and Alicia sighed as she stared out the window. The week skiing in Telluride for Thanksgiving, followed by a week in Europe visiting all the Aspyre offices and meeting with key investors, had left her exhausted and stressed. Detective Davis was fed up with her lawyer's delay tactics and had given Alicia and Bryan until Friday, December 18, to sit for an interview or he would haul them in for obstructing an investigation. The one piece of good news—or at least no news taken as good news—was there had been no more messages for Winnie on apairofgenes.com after Alicia's threat to go to the police if that Naomi woman didn't cease contact.

It had been a Herculean effort to coax herself off the couch and out of her sweats to get ready for Diana's vanity party at the Chihuly Glass Museum, but there was no way she could bail and risk alienating Diana with their relationship still on shaky ground. Alicia stole a glance at Bryan. With his head tipped back against the leather headrest, she could see his eyes were closed and his face looked relaxed. No wonder, since he'd stood out on their porch smoking a joint while waiting for the driver. Alicia had refused when he'd offered her a toke. Marijuana might be legal in Washington, but it was not sanctioned for Aspyre employees. She didn't need to add whispers of drug use to her mounting problems, even if it might make the evening a little more tolerable.

As the car meandered toward downtown, Bryan said, "Hey, wanna see Brooke's new college list?"

No, Alicia thought, *what I want is confirmation that Brooke is Stanford's chosen one.* After Ted Clark's scathing "community values" email, she had ceased pinging Ted for reassurance and instead tried to lean on Stanford's director of admissions. But they must have been screening his calls, as she was she never able to get through. After four unreturned calls, his assistant left Alicia a message letting her know she'd receive a courtesy call several hours before admission decisions were posted online for all applicants. But with only ten days to go, playing along with Brooke's new college list was easier than pissing Bryan off. The new list would be moot anyway once Brooke got into Stanford. "Sure," she said with fake enthusiasm.

"Brooke asked me to go to her meeting with Ms. Barstow before Thanksgiving break, and my golf game was canceled last minute, so I went. This is the list they came up with. Just so you know, Brooke seems pretty excited about a few of these schools." He handed Alicia his phone.

Alicia sighed. "And you're just telling me?"

"Gee, Leesh, I don't know. You've seemed pretty preoccupied lately," he said with a pointed glance.

Alicia chose to ignore the jab and pulled her reading glasses out of her handbag. As she scanned the list, she kneaded her forehead like it was one of those squishy Stanford stress balls she kept in her office. She expected underwhelming, but this list was downright disorienting. Colorado College, NYU, Santa Clara, Lewis & Clark, Whitman. At least USC and Emory were included. She knew a few CEOs who had sent their kids there and lived through the humiliation.

"Jesus." Alicia groaned. "I honestly don't think I've ever brought someone in for a job interview from a single one of these schools. Maybe USC?"

"Brooke loved Lewis & Clark. We did a little road trip while you were out of town last week."

Alicia tossed his phone on the seat between them. How had those two managed a college visit without even telling her? "Please tell me that's not the stoner school Steve Jobs went to."

"No—you're thinking of Reed College. That's southwest of Portland. Lewis & Clark is just north of the city. It took us less than three hours to get there. It's close to home but not too close."

Bryan grew animated as he extolled the benefits of this school Alicia had barely heard of and had definitely never entertained her daughter attending. When she'd actually needed his help with Brooke's essays, he'd been nowhere to be found. At this point, she wished he would just stick to screaming from the sidelines at her soccer games. "Hmm" was about all she could muster.

"Ms. Barstow said most of the schools on the list are still a stretch."

Alicia turned her head to Bryan, her mouth hanging open. "These are a stretch? Are you fucking kidding me?"

"But Brooke's a development priority, so she's in a different category. It probably makes sense to write a $1 million check to each one. It's only—" He paused, counting the number of the schools on the list. "It's only $7 million."

"Only $7 million," Alicia muttered, which looked like a bargain after the $15 million she'd forked over in Aspyre stock to Stanford. Early admissions decision day couldn't arrive soon enough. They'd delete this embarrassing emergency fallback list and never speak of it again. They rode the rest of the way in silence.

When they arrived at the museum and stepped out of the car, Bryan said, "Come on, babe. Let's forget about college for one night and try to have a little fun." He kissed her cheek and threw his arm around her. She tried to smile back. As they entered the party in a room filled with the most exquisite glass sculptures on earth, it was hard not to ponder the fragility of it all.

30

Kelly

THEY'D ONLY JUST ARRIVED, but the Elliott Bay Bellini—the signature cocktail offered by smartly attired waiters at the entrance to the party—was already packing a wallop on Kelly's empty stomach. She gazed around the room at what had to be the most elaborate parent "stress buster" in history. Kelly had starved herself all day to save room for what she knew would be a menu to die for, having already sampled some of it at the last SST meeting. Her first order of business was to hit the appetizer buffet for a nibble. Four steps into her quest, a trio of EBA dads hailed Kevin over. "I'll catch up with you later." He winked at her.

It was just as well that she was on her own for a bit. Kevin needed to network, and she needed to eat. *A win-win.* As she surveyed the glittering glasshouse, she gave herself permission to be swept up in the glamour of the night. She did a perfunctory scan of the crowd but was distracted by the abundant food artfully placed throughout the massive room, not to mention the intricate salmon-and-blue (EBA colors) ice sculpture inspired by one of Chihuly's famous installations. Her eyes lit up, and she floated over to the nearest tower of delicacies.

Seattle's latest James Beard Award–winning chef had curated a veritable showcase of the Pacific Northwest's finest cuisine: Dungeness crab leg cocktail, Salish Sea spot prawns and Hood Canal oysters, Wagyu beef sliders on brioche buns smeared with what had to be a crack-laced pickled pepper aioli, salmon poke in sesame cones with a note card thoughtfully clarifying that the salmon used in the poke was not the species preferred by endangered orcas, curried chicken bites served in Skagit Valley winter greens, and Kelly's personal favorite—bite-sized balls of fried Beecher's macaroni and cheese with a hint of truffle oil, the most obscenely delicious thing she had ever tasted. "Oh my God," she gushed aloud. Her taste buds were exploding with pleasure.

Her moment of bliss ended abruptly when she tuned in to Amanda and Sarah talking a few feet away from her. They were urgently discussing the rumor that Ethan Martin raised his ACT score from a 25 to a 33 using some incredible new tutor from the Bay Area. Kelly had heard this same rumor a few days earlier and was furious. An eight-point jump was practically unheard of.

Amanda and Sarah had already spotted her, so Kelly had no choice but to join the conversation. For once, she had no stomach for college gossip. "Can you believe this spread? Diana really outdid herself, huh?"

"Amazing!" Amanda agreed. "We were just talking about Ethan's incredible new test score. I know the Martins and the Stones are good friends. Do you think Alicia used the same tutor for Brooke? If so, you might have even more competition for that spot than you bargained for!"

"I want the guy's name for my next kid," Sarah said. "I spent $10,000 on tutoring, and Hannah's score only went up three points."

Kelly smiled. She wasn't about to reveal that she'd spent far more than that on tutoring and boot camps to secure Krissie's 34 on the ACT, and she definitely wouldn't ever tell a soul how she'd ratted out Brooke for cheating on her essays. So with nothing of consequence left to say to these women, she hoisted up her empty glass like a mime and chased down a server with a tray of Bellinis.

Across the party hall, Kevin appeared to be working the room with the effortless charm that had made him a rainmaker at his firm. He was in his element. Why ruin a good thing? Scanning the crowd again, this time, her eyes landed on Diana, Augusta, and Alicia chatting near the photo booth, dressed to the nines.

Augusta was stunning in navy silk artfully draped over her curvy figure, setting off her auburn hair. Alicia wore a sophisticated dark-gray number with blouson sleeves and ruffle cuffs. And Diana wore a drop-dead-sexy winter-white gown with a plunging neckline and a slit to high heaven. Everyone greeted Kelly politely, but she was self-conscious in the black empire-waist maternity cocktail dress she'd found packed away in the basement, which had looked passable in the mirror of her dimly lit bedroom but now read a little shabby under the luminous canopy of blown glass and gave off the faint scent of mothballs. She touched her ear, nervously seeking security in her diamond studs, but pulled her hair forward to cover her ears when she glimpsed Diana's gigantic gem-encrusted earrings. "What an incredible party," Kelly exclaimed to the group. "Diana, this is amazing! Thank you so much for pulling it all together."

"I think we all deserve it after this fall." Diana smiled, declining to share any of the credit with Maren, who Kelly knew probably took care of 99 percent of the event logistics and was passing a tray of hors d'oeuvres at this very moment. But then again, Diana had agreed to foot 99 percent of the bill.

"Cheers to that," Alicia said, raising her glass to Diana.

As they all clinked their glasses together, the gorgeous Summer Kendrick, owner of Seattle Spirit, the exclusive health and beauty concierge experience accessible only through equity membership, shimmied into the circle in an exquisite emerald-green cocktail dress and received a warm welcome. Kelly admired how Summer could move in a way that seemed graceful, effortless, and humble—all at the same time.

"So I have some fun college news to share!" Summer shot Diana a glance that seemed to seek permission to continue, like a nervous habit. Diana's monthly spending at Seattle Spirit probably covered Summer's mortgage payments, which made Summer eager to keep her best customer happy.

"Oh?" Diana asked. "What's that?"

"Juni committed to row at Brown!" Summer squealed.

A chorus of strained enthusiasm greeted Summer's shocking announcement. It was obvious Kelly wasn't the only one trying to reconcile this somewhat astonishing news. Juni was a nice girl who did pretty well in school but didn't take many AP classes. And Brown was one of the hottest Ivies right now. All heads turned to Diana, since everyone knew her daughter, Tenley, had applied for early admission to Brown.

Diana sported a smile as she fiddled with her five-carat diamond ring. "Wow, Summer. I thought Juni committed to row at UW?"

"She hadn't signed her letter of intent yet. The Brown coach saw her at a race over the summer and really pursued her." Summer seemed bewildered by her daughter's good fortune.

"I can't believe you've never mentioned this," Diana said. "Will it be difficult for her to balance such rigorous coursework with rowing?"

"The coach said they provide tutors for every subject." Summer shrugged. "I mean, college is college. How hard can it be?"

Diana seemed to deliberately retrain her features back into her usual winning smile. "Well, good for Juni. Now, you all must excuse me. I think our special guests for the evening are ready to take the stage." She winked at Kelly.

When Diana had texted Kelly the name of the band she'd lined up for the evening's entertainment, Kelly's jaw nearly hit the floor. This was a parent stress buster, for God's sake. Diana had also asked the band to do the on-campus Snowcoming announcement for the seniors. And they'd said yes! Kelly wondered how much that had cost Diana. Maybe she'd sweetened the deal by promising to help get someone's kid into EBA?

"Welcome, EBA parents!" Diana's voice reverberated in the mic as she stood on the empty stage at the front of the room. "While the kids are having a blast at their Snowcoming dance, Michael and I just wanted to tell you how absolutely ecstatic we are to host this special parent event. We've all worked so hard and sacrificed so much for our children to reach this point. It's such a stressful time for all of us right now with early admissions decisions coming out soon. So tonight, we owe it to ourselves to relax and have some fun!" Diana thrust her wineglass high up in the air. Calling for a drumroll, Diana introduced the hired musicians for the night—just a little local band called Pearl Jam.

The band joined a gleeful Diana onstage and launched into their set. The first song was one of Kevin's favorites. He was an excellent dancer, and Kelly knew he'd be looking for her. However, she couldn't bear the thought of jiggling around on the dance floor in full view of all the svelte EBA moms, so like a middle school wallflower, she slinked off to the refreshment table instead. A few minutes later, she spotted Kevin dancing with Amanda right up at the front of the stage in a crush of drunken parents. Amanda looked like she'd borrowed one of her daughter Audrey's "un-dresses," as Kelly liked to call the teenage fashion trend of dresses that barely concealed the girls' butt cheeks. And to Kelly's dismay, Amanda was pulling it off thanks to the wonders of her divorce diet.

The next song took everyone by surprise. Instead of playing one of their own songs, Pearl Jam started riffing on Bob Dylan's "Rainy Day Women No. 12 & 35." It was a perplexing choice, at least until they reached the famous chorus—"everybody must get stoned"—and a team of servers, full of pomp and circumstance and with impeccable timing, rolled out a cart filled with gourmet cannabis desserts to the center of the dance floor. Pot desserts at a quasi-school-sanctioned event? Kelly was momentarily thankful Diana had failed to mention the cannabis cart to her. Plausible deniability. But really, what did it matter? Double Ass would never risk scolding Diana and Michael Taylor.

Kelly continued watching as Kevin and Amanda danced wildly for a few more songs before Kevin led Amanda over to the chocolate fountain. Dipping a pretzel into the cascading waterfall of bittersweet chocolate, he offered it to her with a flourish. Amanda closed her eyes, threw her head back, and indulged in the luscious treat.

Kevin had always been a bit of a harmless flirt, but was this something more? Kelly really couldn't imagine it. She'd always taken comfort in the solidity of their relationship. They'd certainly had more arguments the past couple years, but Kelly attributed that fact to the strain of money, Krissie's approaching launch, and college craziness in general, not some global issue with their marriage. But then what middle-aged wife did see an affair coming down the pike?

Barely holding back tears and not wanting to make a scene, Kelly took off in search of the bathroom. She realized she must have taken a wrong turn when she found herself outside the Chihuly Theater. Having visited the museum before with the kids, she remembered sitting through a film about the artist that ran on a loop. She was 100 percent certain the heated voices she heard on the other side of the cloth curtain were not from the film.

Indeed, it was immediately clear she was listening to an exchange between Bryan and Maren. She would know their voices anywhere. Kelly clasped her hand over her mouth to stifle her surprise. She could hardly believe her luck. Was it possible she was overhearing a lover's quarrel? EBA moms had speculated for years whether there was anything going on between the two of them. Bryan's wandering eye was legendary, and Maren was young and obviously beautiful despite her attempts to cover up with her "plain Jane" style. If Kelly could obtain proof of an illicit relationship, Lord knew she could put that information to excellent use. All she had to do was stand still and avoid detection, and Bryan and Maren might unwittingly reveal all their secrets. She leaned closer to the curtain.

31

Maren

"JEEZ, BRYAN—YOU'RE SO wasted," Maren said. "This theater is off-limits to party guests. Why don't you go find Alicia? Or I can call you an Uber?" She was clinging to her last shred of patience. *Would this goddamn stress buster never end?*

When Maren had reported for duty three hours before the party, she was informed by the museum liaison that Diana had committed her to doing periodic sweeps of the Chihuly Theater in case the large "Do Not Enter" sign at the theater entrance wasn't persuasive enough. So now, on top of everything else necessary to meet Diana Taylor's exacting party standards, Maren also had to play bouncer to a steady stream of overstressed parents looking for a quiet place to snort or screw away their college admissions worries. She'd just shooed out one disheveled duo—a dad and mom who were in flagrant violation of the old adage "dance with the one that brung ya"—when Bryan stumbled into the darkened theater.

"I don't wanna go home," Bryan said with a pouty face. "At least not with her. She's so nasty all the time."

"Well, Bryan, I'm afraid that's not my department," Maren said, trying to keep it light. "But I do need to clear this room, so why don't you head on back to the bar?" She pointed her finger toward the exit, since he seemed even more slow-witted than usual.

Before she could react, Bryan's hand darted out and grabbed ahold of her outstretched arm, and he yanked her into his chest. "There, that's better," he slurred as he groped her butt.

"Let go of me! Now!" Maren hissed as she wrestled out of his grip. He lunged toward her again, but this time, she saw it coming. She jumped back out of his reach but ended up falling to the floor in a heap, having forgotten all about the wooden viewing bench behind her. Her heart was pounding with terror. He'd always been a nuisance, but she'd never felt she was in danger until this moment. If she had, no amount of money or security could have coaxed her to stay with Alicia. "Bryan, don't. Please!"

Standing over Maren, he paused for an excruciating few seconds. Like the dog who finally caught the squirrel but had no idea what to do with it. "You know what's funny?" he said, pointing at her lying on the ground. "You and Winnie are both clumsy. Like mother, like daughter." He started to fumble with his belt buckle.

Maren's blood ran cold, but it was his words that were even more chilling than his actions. "What are you talking about?"

"I just thought I'd scare her a little. My car never touched her. How was I supposed to know she'd be such a klutz? But hey," he said, raising his hands, "I didn't send that batshit text afterward. I dunno who did that."

"Oh my God. It was you." Maren spoke in a whisper. She almost couldn't believe the words coming out of her mouth, but her hushed voice paradoxically seemed to scare him more than her yelling. He startled and stepped back, affording her the opportunity to scramble to her feet. As she did, she pulled a corkscrew from her apron pocket and held it in her closed palm. She would be ready if he came at her again. Every fiber of her being screamed at her to flee, but she had to get the rest of the story out of him. "What kind of monster are you?" she baited him in a low, guttural voice.

"What? What are you gonna do, call the police? They'd never believe trash like you over me. I'm Bryan fucking Stone."

Maren was seeing red. "You've known Winnie over half her life. She was like a sister to Brooke. How could you do this? And then to not stop and help her? She nearly died."

"Riiiiight. How would that have looked?" Bryan sneered. "I'd been drinking, and the goddamn girl who beats my daughter in everything has an accident right before the Stanford deadline? I don't think so."

"You fucking assholes and your college obsession," Maren said.

"Hey, I don't give a shit about college. I just wanted some peace in my goddamn family. That night when I saw Winnie on her scooter, it hit me how much easier everything would be if we'd never met you two. You're always teasing me with your smokin'-hot body. Alicia's always riding Brooke to be more like perfect little Winnie. And I'm just the house idiot who my poor daughter takes after, according to my own wife." His volume rose. "Well, fuck that. You're an ungrateful bitch. After everything we've done for you and Winnie, she just couldn't stay in her lane. Oh hey—get it?" Bryan chuckled.

The venom in her eyes must have told Bryan the rules of the game were about to change. Without another word, he turned, shoved the cloth curtain to the side, and stormed out of the theater. "Well, if it isn't Kelly

Vernon," Maren heard Bryan scoff. "They should hang a cowbell around your neck. I swear to God, if you say one goddamn word, I'll fucking ruin you and your loser husband."

"Oh my God! Oh my God!" Kelly responded. "I was just on my way to the bathroom. I didn't hear a thing!"

Maren didn't even bother following Bryan out, as she knew there wasn't a chance in hell Kelly would ever come to her aid. Every muscle in her body quivered in the wake of Bryan's assault and shocking confession. She perched on one of the wooden benches and tried to collect herself. She needed to get back to work, but her swirling thoughts pinned her in place. Now that she finally knew the truth, Maren allowed herself a fleeting moment of vindication. She'd been right all along: Winnie hadn't been run off the road by accident, and the incident was at least tangentially connected to the Stanford skirmish.

But the truth was even uglier than she'd imagined. Her daughter had almost died because someone she'd known, someone she'd trusted to some extent, someone she'd relied on for their very survival, had decided one night on a whim that his life would be a little easier if Winnie no longer existed. It hit her like an anvil to the head: Through the prism of their unparalleled (and, at least in Bryan's case, unearned) privilege, Bryan and Alicia viewed her entire life—everything she cared about, including her beloved daughter—as little more than a disposable item to be used and discarded at will. But it was the sting of Bryan's cavalier laughter that really put her over the edge, as if this was all just a gigantic joke to him.

Maren could no longer ignore the incessant pinging coming from her phone tucked in the pocket of her catering uniform. No doubt Diana needing her help with yet another bullshit problem at this bullshit party. As she pulled out her phone and Diana's texts unfurled, the words on the screen blurred, and Maren was once more transported to that night at Memorial Hospital pacing in the ER. She could have lost her *daughter* that night. And from the moment the detective had brushed off investigating EBA's rich and famous for the alleged hit-and-run, Maren had been fixated on how to convince him to overcome his reluctance. Deep down, she had known someone at EBA was at fault. She had known *someone* had attacked her precious girl. And even that night, up against the faceless culprits hiding behind their money and privilege and power, Maren knew that the only way to ensure that no one would touch Winnie again was to make sure the police were watching. And the only way to get the police to watch was to lie.

That awful morning when her daughter was barely conscious in the ICU, Maren had taken her first step toward fighting back when she bought that burner phone and texted the "Back off Stanford" threat to her own daughter's phone. Maren would forever feel guilty knowing she had made Winnie fear for her life these past weeks. But her gamble had paid off. She had forced everyone around her to finally pay attention. And now, she would have to do it again.

Hauling herself to her feet, Maren smoothed her uniform and returned her cell to her apron pocket. She knew that Bryan's confession to her—without corroboration—was useless; the police would never take her word over his. But there had to be *something* she could do to make him pay. Walking down the dark hallway toward the loud, thumping music, the situation started to come into focus. Maren grew stronger with each step. She might not be able to nail Bryan for what he'd done to Winnie, but there was more than one way to get justice.

32

Kelly

"HEY, YOU AWAKE?" KEVIN said. "I thought you might need a caffeine assist this morning."

As the words penetrated, a hand gently shook her shoulder. The sensation resonated through her nauseated body, which was coiled protectively in the fetal position. With a whimper, she pried open her goopy eyes and rolled over toward the sound of her husband's voice. There was Kevin, standing next to the bed, offering up a giant, blessed mug of coffee. She couldn't remember the last time he'd brought her coffee in bed. A sign of guilt?

Her mind was blank. This had to be her worst hangover in decades. "Thanks. I feel like crap. What happened last night?" She gazed out the window at the dreary, overcast December morning.

"Well, for starters, the cannabis cart happened," Kevin teased.

"Oh, no." Kelly grabbed a pillow from Kevin's side of the bed and pressed it to her face. "Please tell me I didn't." But the pillow couldn't shield her from the list of all she'd consumed. The last thing she clearly remembered was standing at the cannabis cart. Though the always responsible mother in her had called for restraint, the steady stream of Bellinis earlier in the night may have compromised her resolve. Kelly was pretty certain she'd eaten only one "pot" de crème. Though it was possible she also tried a few nibbles of the coconut giggle nuggets and maybe just a taste of a caramel cannabis cupcake.

Suddenly, she remembered the reason she'd taken refuge at the cannabis cart in the first place. Images of her husband and Amanda furiously gyrating on the dance floor and Amanda suggestively devouring the sweet-and-salty pretzel floated into her consciousness. Quickly followed by the fight she'd overheard from outside the Chihuly Theater—and Bryan's unbelievable admission. Once again, she was overcome with intense relief that it hadn't been Krissie who'd run Winnie off the road. Peeking out from under the pillow at Kevin, now sitting on the side of the bed waiting for her to complete her trip down memory lane, Kelly said, "It's all coming back."

"Pearl Jam at a school event. That was something else, huh?" He sipped his coffee.

"Yeah," Kelly countered, "so was Amanda's dress."

"Oh come on, that was nothing. I looked for you."

"Well, actually, maybe it all worked out for the best." Kelly wrapped her hands around the warm mug.

"What do you mean?"

"I saw you flirting with Amanda, and I got really upset." Kelly blinked to keep the tears down. "I was looking for the bathroom, but I got lost and ended up outside the Chihuly Theater. I heard an argument, so you know me. I stopped and listened. It turned out it was Bryan Stone and Maren."

Kelly hesitated. She had no doubt Bryan wouldn't think twice about following through on his threat, but how could she not tell Kevin? This had already gone too far. "I know this sounds completely insane…but I heard Bryan bragging to Maren. He was the one who ran Winnie off the road."

"Are you kidding me?" Kevin said. "That can't be right."

"No, it's true. I swear. This happened before I found the cannabis cart," Kelly said.

"Why would he do that? And then why would he admit it to Maren? That makes no sense."

"I don't know. He was really drunk. And obviously thinks he's untouchable."

"What a raging asshole." Kevin shook his head. "And then to send that death threat afterward? That's just sick."

Kelly's right eye twitched. If the tables had been turned, she would have been livid with Kevin for keeping such a huge secret about one of the kids. "The thing is," she said, taking a sip of coffee to steady herself, "Bryan said he didn't send the threat."

"Then who did?"

Kelly stared into her coffee cup. "I'm worried it might have been Krissie."

Kevin took a moment to register Kelly's words. "What are you talking about?"

Her head was pounding. She was wholly unprepared for this conversation, but what choice did she have? "I don't know for sure." Kelly's hand wobbled as she set the cup down on her nightstand. "Remember that night she heard us talking about how Winnie was lying about UW and still applying to Stanford?"

"Yeah?" His brows furrowed.

"Well, I didn't want to alarm you, but after that, I discovered she started pulling her hair out again. She even got extensions to hide a bald spot and didn't tell me. And she stopped eating and was working out at least twice a day." Kelly nervously smoothed the covers over her lap. "I was hoping once she submitted her application, she might calm down, but then the accident happened. I just had this gut sense she was involved somehow, like maybe she cracked under all the pressure."

"That's a pretty big leap from pulling out her hair and not eating to potentially mowing down another kid. Or making that threat."

"You probably don't remember, but the night of the accident, everyone was home for dinner, and then we watched *The Princess Bride*. Krissie got up in the middle of the movie and left to go work out. Her route to the health club would have taken her down the street where the accident happened."

"If you were so worried, how could you not say anything to me?"

"I don't know." Kelly grabbed a tissue off her nightstand and blew her nose. "I felt horrible even thinking she might be involved, let alone saying it out loud to anyone."

"I'm not just anyone, I'm your husband. I'm Krissie's father," Kevin growled. "I had a right to know all this."

"I know. I should have told you."

"You're damn right." Kevin ran his hand through his bedhead, causing his hair to stick up even straighter in the air.

"But at least now we know she didn't go as far as I thought. Bryan was clear as day about that."

"Have you actually talked with Krissie about any of this?" Kevin asked.

"I tried, but of course she denied it," Kelly said, biting her lip. "There's more."

"More? What do you mean more?"

"Ted Clark gave my name to the detective investigating Winnie's accident. I didn't want to worry you, so I went down to the police station a couple of weeks ago by myself. He'd seen all the memes about me, so of course he asked where I was the night of the accident. I said we were all home for family dinner and a movie. But I left out the part about Krissie taking my car to work out. But now he keeps calling me to schedule a time to bring Krissie in for questioning. I've been putting him off because I'm so worried about her, but I think he's running out of patience."

Kevin stood up and paced. "Is that everything?"

"No." Kelly looked down at her plum-colored nails from the manicure she'd splurged on for the party. "I never told you how I found out Winnie was lying about UW and her first-generation college hook." She paused and then finally looked up at Kevin and spoke softly. "Or what I did with that information."

Kevin stopped moving and stared down at her, his expression impassive but the color of anger creeping up his neck.

Kelly took a deep breath. "I overheard Winnie's college counselor in a coffee shop. After lots of phone calls, I figured out Maren had enrolled at Indiana University. I used a disposable phone to text some EBA moms, including Alicia, that Winnie was lying about her first-generation hook. I also made up a rumor that Winnie was planning to apply to every top-ten school just to prove she was the best. And then after Thanksgiving, I used the same phone again to leave an anonymous voicemail for Stanford Admissions that Alicia had hired a professor to write Brooke's essays." Kelly collapsed back into her pillows.

Kevin sat back down on the bed and held his head in his hands for what felt like several minutes. Kelly didn't dare speak.

When Kevin finally lifted his head, he didn't turn around to face her. His voice was low and tense. "When I read Ted Clark's email about EBA's community values, I actually laughed out loud that people would resort to all those things. But, my God, it sounds like he was talking directly to you." Kevin stood up and turned to face his wife. "That night when Krissie was crying about not being able to compete with all these people lying to get into Stanford, I told our daughter to hold her head up high. That we weren't cheating and cutting corners like those other families. And you just sat there eating your ice cream. You didn't say a goddamn word."

Kelly shrank into the covers as she absorbed his contemptuous glare.

"But no matter what you did, the bottom line is Bryan Stone is an adult responsible for his own actions. I'm no lawyer, but the threat that we don't even know for sure Krissie sent wasn't the cause of Winnie's injuries. Christ, that poor girl."

Kelly sat up straighter in bed and nodded, relieved by Kevin's cogent analysis of the situation.

"You shouldn't have lied to the police though. That's dangerous business. The last thing we need is to get tangled up in their investigation, but it sounds like Krissie might not have a choice. Now I'm going to have to find us a lawyer." Kevin's voice was quiet and cold as ice. "What you've done has crossed so many lines. And now you've dragged me into your bullshit."

He paused for a moment. Dead silence. In two decades of marriage, she had never seen this particular look on his face, a barely controlled anger simmering just under the surface.

"I mean, Jesus Christ, Kelly," he spat. "You're so consumed with EBA, micromanaging the kids, and fucking college. What the hell happened to you? You were really willing to risk everything? Our daughter's mental health? The well-being of another child? Breaking the law? Our family's reputation? And for what?" Kevin ran his hand down his face and shook his head. "Just so we could say our daughter got into the most selective college in the country?" He stared out the window. "I honestly don't know how much more of this I can take."

"I know exactly how you feel." As Kelly had counted down to early admissions day, it dawned on her that she would have to go through this process two more times with Katherine and Kaleb, an exhausting thought. "But the EBA moms who've been through it before say it's easier the next time around because you know what to expect. And what are the odds of this Stanford situation happening again?"

Kevin's jaw dropped. "No, Kelly. I don't think you do," he said, taking two long strides toward the door. "By this, I meant us. Or to put a finer point on it—you."

As he pulled open the bedroom door, Kelly begged, "Wait! Kevin! Please just give it a few more days. Once Krissie is accepted, things will all go back to normal. I promise!"

Kevin slammed the bedroom door behind him in answer, and the wave of nausea Kelly was barely holding at bay surged inside her. Dashing to the bathroom, she was a mere three feet shy of the toilet when she doubled over and puked up the remnants of her gluttonous night all over the tile floor. It was a steaming unholy mess, far too symbolic of her life.

33

Maren

Hi, Diana,

Thanks for the Venmo this morning. However, I noticed you called it a final payment, but several outstanding invoices remain.

1. We agreed on a $40 hourly rate for party planning, and I worked 80 hours up to the day of the event. By my calculation, your "final" payment covered only 28 hours. I'm attaching my invoice (again) with a detailed accounting of my time.

2. I'm also attaching an additional invoice for my hours on-site the day/night of the party. These hours included decorating, setup, overseeing the caterers and janitorial staff, managing special requests from guests during the party (e.g., I sent a bartender out to a liquor store to pick up a $1,000 Japanese whiskey on Michael's orders and told them to add it to the catering bill), and reuniting forgotten items with their owners. FYI—still remaining in the Chihuly lost-and-found are nine women's coats (four fur), seven designer handbags, three IPhones, fifteen men's suit jackets, two prescription pill bottles, and, oddly, three pairs of men's underpants, two women's thongs, and one lace bralette. Perhaps you can account for the unequal number and type of undergarments, but I'll leave it at that.

3. Last week, I sent you yet another reimbursement request for the $5,000 down payment for party rental equipment. As you will recall, I had to use my personal credit card because you said you were too busy to read me your card number over the phone. I need you to reimburse me immediately so I can use my card for groceries again. My daughter, for one, will very much appreciate this.

4. Finally, I am also invoicing you $10,000 for hazard pay. I did not agree to serve as a chaperone for parents stumbling wasted into forbidden areas of the museum. And I most definitely did not agree to being repeatedly hit on (this is a polite

phrase for the inappropriate behavior I endured) by seven EBA husbands, yours included.

Regards,

Maren

————

From: Maren Pressley   Today, 10:45 a.m.

To: Jack Alder

Subject: On Second Thought

Dear Jack,

Remember your offer in the hospital waiting room to help me? I'm in.

Maren

————

From: Jack Alder   Today, 10:50 a.m.

To: Maren Pressley

Re: On Second Thought

Dear Maren,

That's excellent news. After we spoke at the hospital, I did some legal research and consulted (off the record, of course) a friend in law enforcement in hopes you might decide to defend yourself and Winnie against this egregious overstep. I will be in touch tomorrow to discuss a plan of action in more detail.

You are one courageous young woman.

All the best,
Jack

P.S. Any thoughts about the family question yet?

34

Alicia

From: EBA College Counseling   Tuesday, December 15, 6:30 a.m.

To: EBA Senior Class Parents and Guardians

Subject: Sensitivity during College Decision Season

Dear Senior Class Parents and Guardians,

As colleges begin to release their early admissions decisions, we ask that you please keep in mind this is a sensitive time for many students. Many will receive a rejection from at least one school over the course of the admissions season, and some will be rejected from several top choices. While we understand you may feel invested in your student's college journey, remember that come fall, their dorm room will not be big enough to accommodate you or your ego. This is a solo flight, Amelia Earhart–style.

While you may express your pride in the privacy of your own homes, we ask that you be mindful of our community values and beg you to refrain from: (1) public boasting about your student's accomplishments, (2) gossiping about other students' results, and (3) making value judgments on various schools. Never forget— one student's safety school is another student's dream.

We are confident that all our seniors will end up at very fine institutions of higher education. Please be the adults in the room.

The EBA College Counseling Team

P.S. Our office will be handing out treats to seniors this week (Chocolate Hugs & Kisses, Smarties, Nerds, Good & Plenty, 100 Grand bars, Starburst, Sour Patch Kids, Now and Later, etc.—you get the idea). All will be nut-free. Please do not complain to us about giving your kids candy. Trust us: sugar will be the least of your concerns next year when your students are navigating daily life without your helpful guidance.

———

Pacing around her office, Alicia repeatedly checked her phone to make sure the volume was turned up and that she'd turned off Do Not Disturb mode. Her eyes lit on the red bag with the giant Stanford "S" sitting on the conference table. Festooned with matching tissue paper, ribbons, and bows, the bag had been filled by her assistant, Charlotte, with nearly every item offered on the Stanford University Bookstore website in anticipation of Brooke's acceptance. Maren never would have assembled such a garish-looking gift, but it would have crossed the line to delegate this task to her longtime personal assistant.

When her phone finally rang and displayed the magic 650 area code, her heart raced. "Hello, this is Alicia Stone." She hadn't been this eager since the day she'd walked into the Aspyre boardroom knowing she was about to receive the offer to become CEO.

"Mrs. Stone, this is Pauline Danforth. I'm the assistant to Assistant Provost Martin at Stanford University."

Why was Stanford's version of Double Ass calling her? She'd expected the call would come from the director of admissions or even the president. Not some low-level secretary. Maybe her job was to get Alicia on the line. "Hello, Pauline, how are you?"

"Fine, thank you, ma'am. I'm calling today about your daughter Brooke's application to Stanford," Pauline said.

"Great," Alicia said. Was no one else getting on the phone?

"OK. Stanford received more applications than ever for next year's incoming class. This is by far the most diverse group of applicants coming from all fifty states and nearly seventy countries. We are looking for students who will bring their diverse experiences, backgrounds, and cultures to our university."

Was she reading from a goddamn script? "Pauline, can we just skip ahead to the part about Brooke?"

"I'm sorry," Pauline said. "I was told I have to read everything in a certain order."

"Fine." Alicia slumped over her desk with her phone pressed to her ear while Pauline recited the rest of the boilerplate admissions mumbo jumbo.

"OK, here's the part you've been waiting for," Pauline said. Alicia could hear her opening an envelope. "Brooke is a remarkable young woman. She was certainly a unique applicant, and it was our pleasure to get to know her through the admissions process."

Alicia pressed her lips together in anticipation.

"However, at this time, Brooke's application has been deferred," Pauline read. "Including scholar athletes, Stanford will be accepting several Elliott Bay Academy students as part of the early admissions process. Should any one of these students choose not to enroll at Stanford, the university would be pleased to offer that spot to Brooke."

"Are you kidding me?" Alicia exploded. "After everything I've done for Stanford, this is how my daughter is treated? This is how I'm treated? You're going to let in a bunch of dumbass athletes but not the daughter of a trustee who's given the school a massive donation? This is completely unacceptable. I demand to talk to the director of admissions."

"Ma'am, I can pass your message along. Best of luck to you and your daughter."

Alicia opened her mouth to argue, but she heard the telltale three beeps. Whoever this Pauline was, she'd ended the call. Dashing to her private bathroom, Alicia slammed the door and proceeded to let rip every single expletive she knew, but her profane vocabulary was inadequate to the task. She stared at her crazed reflection in the mirror. How was this fucking possible?

———

Alicia sat atop her bed to watch the maelstrom unfold firsthand in a secret EBA Facebook group set up as a supposed parental "safe space." Like a lion hunting her prey, she waited for the lucky Stanford winner to reveal her good fortune.

EBA PARENTS SECRET FACEBOOK GROUP

This is a SECRET group, for parents of EBA seniors ONLY. Share your college results here! Acceptances, rejections, questions, final decisions all welcome! DO NOT invite any EBA faculty to this page...we don't want to get busted!

Robin Riley: OK EBA Moms! I'll start the ball rolling! No big surprise because Alexis received her likely letter from Harvard months ago, but it's official! She's still not 100% sure crimson's her color, so she might end up tossing in a few more applications for regular decision. Who knows!?! I highly recommend D1 recruitment! Makes the whole college process so much less stressful.

COMMENTS:

Donna Peterson: Congrats! What a superstar! Between Alexis and Winnie, hope there'll be a few spots left at top schools for the rest of us poor schmucks 😉

Barbara Jackson: Jason got into Tufts! If Alexis goes to Harvard, they can meet up in Beantown!!!

Robin Riley: Congrats to Jason! It's a trek from

Cambridge to Tufts, but maybe they'll be on the same flights to Boston?

Barbara Jackson: Jason should be so lucky

Sarah Silver: Did anyone else get into Middlebury? Hannah's hoping she'll have some buddies in Vermont!

Laura Simms: I heard Scottie Chapman got rejected from Princeton. Too bad—he's a great kid. His parents must be super bummed with both of them alums and all. Gotta be an athlete to win the big prizes!

COMMENTS:

Robin Riley: Well…a SCHOLAR athlete anyway!

Sarah Silver: Ha! Touché! I forget—did Alexis take AP math & science or just regular? Just want to know what's possible for kid #2

Amanda Russell: OMG! OMG! I was so sure Audrey wouldn't get in anywhere that I went a little crazy! We spent a fortune visiting 15 schools—most of them twice! Once to get a feel and show early interest and the second time to do the full-court press, meeting with classics professors, orchestra program heads, interviewing, etc. So proud of how hard we worked on her cello supplement—it was a masterpiece! Even after all that, I was still certain she'd get in nowhere (or be stuck going somewhere like Boston College or Occidental—not that they're bad schools, they're just not a fit for Audrey). Silly me! She got into Duke! We are just beyond shocked and thrilled!

COMMENTS:

Holly Strong: Rockstar!

Sarah Silver: Anyone know if Greer Wagoner got into Vanderbilt?

COMMENTS:

Augusta Wagoner: Bless your heart for being concerned, Sarah. As a matter of fact, Greer did get into Vanderbilt and will carry on the Wagoner family tradition. #soproud

Jennifer Tan: Lily got into Wash U! We're so excited!

COMMENTS:

Amanda Russell: That's amazing! Where is Wash U again? Is that in eastern Washington?

Jennifer Tan: No, St. Louis. It's Washington University in St. Louis.

Sarah Silver: Oh! Is that dangerous? Isn't that near Ferguson?

Amanda Russell: Jeez, Sarah! Is Yale too dangerous? Or Columbia? What's wrong with you?

Sarah Silver: Oh, good point! Congrats to Lily!

Amanda Russell: Breaking news! Brooke Stone just posted on Instagram she was deferred by Stanford.

"What the fucking hell?" Alicia said out loud to no one in particular. Bryan was in bed next to her with headphones on, watching a Netflix show and not interested in hearing any of the comments that were so backhanded and cutting they belonged on Centre Court at Wimbledon.

Livid, Alicia threw back the covers and stomped down the hall to Brooke's room. "Are you fucking insane?" she yelled at Brooke, who was in bed typing away on her phone. "What were you thinking posting our most humiliating news on social media?"

Brooke snorted. "It's only humiliating to one of us."

"We're going to get you in there one way or another. When we do, do you really want the whole goddamn world knowing you got in off the waitlist?" Alicia gripped the doorknob. "Delete that Instagram post. Now. Or I'll have my IT team shut down your account."

"Go for it," Brooke said with a smirk. "Wish them luck finding my Finsta."

"What are you talking about? What's that?"

Brooke just grinned.

Alicia slammed Brooke's door, returned to bed, and hit Refresh.

Diana Taylor: Tenley is going to Stanford! Hooray!!!! So proud of my beautiful girl!!

COMMENTS:

Peggy Wainwright: Holy crap! Congrats! But I thought Tenley applied early to Brown?

Diana Taylor: Changed her mind at the very last minute. Crazy!

Kelly Vernon: WTAF!!!!! DIANA YOU'RE SUCH A BACK-STABBING BITCH! YOU LIED TO EVERYONE ABOUT BROWN! RESPECT THO—YOU PULLED OFF THE COLLEGE HEIST OF THE CENTURY. CAN'T BELIEVE I MISSED IT! FUCK YOU!

Maren Pressley: Congrats to Tenley, **Diana Taylor**! Must have been two spots after all. Winnie got in too!

Kelly Vernon: OH FUCK NO! CAN'T BELIEVE WINNIE GOT AWAY WITH LYING ABOUT A FIRST-GEN HOOK. EVERY-ONE KNOWS YOU FUCKING WENT TO COLLEGE, **Maren Pressley**. GO HOOSIERS!

Kelly Vernon: WHAT ELSE DID YOU LIE ABOUT??

Kelly Vernon: OH WAIT…LET ME GUESS

Kelly Vernon: DID YOU WAIVE YOUR USUAL ESCORT FEE FOR THE STANFORD ADMISSIONS DIRECTOR IN EXCHANGE FOR WINNIE GETTING IN?

Kelly Vernon: LOOK AT THIS CUTE LAPD MUGSHOT I FOUND! WAS IT JUST LIKE ORANGE IS THE NEW BLACK?

Tenley Taylor: Hey lovely ladies…this site isn't as secret as you think

Tenley Taylor: Gee, I wonder if this had anything to do with me getting into Stanford: Taylor Family Foundation Donates $30 Million to Stanford Center for Entrepreneurial Studies

Tenley Taylor: Thanks, Mom and Dad, for gifting me a school I didn't even want to go to

Tenley Taylor: Come to think of it, all you parents suck. Don't you agree **Ted Clark, EBA Senior Class**?

Ted Clark: I order this page to be taken down immediately. **Kelly Vernon**, you and your family are hereby referred to the EBA disciplinary board for possible expulsion pending review of multiple egregious violations of EBA community values.

"FUUUUUUCK!" Alicia yelled. "There were two spots, and Brooke didn't even get one of them?"

"What?" Bryan pulled out one earbud.

"Tenley got into Stanford!" she sniped.

"I thought she applied to Brown?" he said.

"That scheming, underhanded, calculating bitch," Alicia said, clicking on the link Tenley included in her post. "Brooke blabbed to Tenley about my $15 million donation. I saw it in a text. Diana must have found out and bought the fucking spot right out from under me for $30 million. No wonder she's been avoiding me."

"No shit," Bryan said.

Bristling at the tone of respect in her husband's voice for Diana's brazen move, Alicia pushed her reading glasses up on her head and slammed her laptop closed. "By the way, Winnie got in too. What a massive fucking betrayal after everything I've done for them."

Bryan didn't register the Winnie news. Or maybe he didn't care at this point. He had already put his earbud back in and returned his attention to the screen balanced on his knees. Alicia was pleased she'd at least refrained from posting something embarrassing in the online melee like Kelly, thus averting a PR disaster, but that was about the only silver lining.

Sliding out of bed, Alicia crossed the hall to her office quaking with anger at Diana and Maren. That idiot Stanford Double Ass had said one of the EBA kids would need to decline their offer for Brooke to get a spot. Even if Tenley didn't want to go to Stanford, Alicia knew better than to think Diana and Michael would give up the spot after spending $30 million. Sitting at her desk, Alicia forced herself to focus on Maren. Winnie taking Brooke's spot was a bridge too far. As much as it would turn her own life upside down and risk bringing further police scrutiny, without a doubt, this was the end of the line for her long and useful relationship with Maren. And Maren had only herself to blame. But before Alicia shit-canned her, she needed Maren to give up Winnie's spot, and she knew exactly which buttons to push to make that happen.

———

After ten years of ceding her daily life management to Maren, Alicia stayed up all night trying to sort it out. It was a little scary realizing just how much she relied on Maren. To her credit, the woman was meticulously organized. Color-coded binders that included maintenance records, inventories, and warranties for every car, home, and appliance they owned. Online folders with holiday card mailing lists, packing lists, grocery shopping lists, gift lists, preferred vendor lists. Even a file with photos of every outfit Alicia owned, including when and where she'd worn them. Calendar reminders for everything down to when to change the filters in each refrigerator. As the sun came up, Alicia sent her security team and IT specialist emails notifying them to block Maren's access to the house and their internet server later this afternoon as soon as Alicia sent word, and she emailed her lawyer to draw up an eviction notice. Her last email was to Ted Clark, alerting him she would not be paying for Winnie's final semester at EBA.

Before getting in the shower, Alicia texted Maren:

Here's a link to a good article about organizing. Says you should have backups of all your favorite things. Check your email for a list. Please plan to pick up all these items this morning. And let's meet at Vital at noon for lunch. We need to celebrate Winnie's success.

35

Maren

"I'LL SEE YOU AT three," Maren said to Winnie as they pulled into the drop-off zone at school. "Try to steer clear of any college conversations if you can." It was the morning after early admissions results, and emotions would be running high on campus.

"Not a problem," Winnie said sardonically.

Maren touched Winnie's shoulder. "Don't forget what we talked about last night. Kelly is nothing but a pathetic, vindictive loser. She's the one who should feel ashamed. Not me, and definitely not you. Don't let anyone make you feel bad today."

"Don't worry about me. I'll be fine." She opened the car door. "Good luck with Alicia. Love you, Mom."

"Love you too, sweetie," Maren replied. As she put the car in Drive and checked her side-view mirror, she heard a loud knock on the passenger side of the car. She looked up, and there was Kelly Vernon pounding her fist on Maren's window. Standing there in the rain, Kelly looked like a rabid coyote. Her eyes were bloodshot and swollen, hair wet and pasted to her face, and Maren could have sworn that was a pajama top peeking out from the collar of her puffy coat.

Maren leaned across the seat and cranked the window down a smidge. She didn't have time for Kelly's next-level bullshit. Nor was she about to let the inside of her car get soaked on account of this woman.

"I'm so sorry for what I did last night," Kelly said, crying. "I was so drunk. I totally lost my mind."

"Yeah, I've heard that one before. I don't get it. What were you trying to accomplish by publicly humiliating us? It wasn't going to change Krissie's Stanford result. Did it make you feel superior? Is that it? But to pull my daughter into this is unforgivable."

The car behind Maren honked, which was not in keeping with the EBA parent code of conduct. Then again, Maren was currently violating at least three different drop-off procedures. The backup of cars behind her stretched out as far as she could see. She needed to get out of here. *Pronto.* As far as Maren was concerned, this little chat was over. But before she could pull away, Kelly practically threw herself onto the hood of Maren's car.

"No, please, I'm so sorry!" Kelly hollered at the windshield. "Isn't there anything I can do to make it right?"

"Why? So you don't get kicked out of EBA?" Maren yelled back.

Kelly's silence said it all.

"Fuck off, Kelly." Maren prepared to inch the car forward, with or without Kelly attached to her hood, but then reconsidered. Ignoring the growing chorus of horns behind her, she rolled down her own window. "Actually, you know what? There is one thing. Tell me exactly what you heard Bryan say at Chihuly."

"I heard everything," Kelly said. Suddenly eager to rat on Bryan, she came around to Maren's window. "I heard him try to assault you, and I heard him confess to running Winnie off the road. It was awful."

Maren was seething. So Kelly really had heard the whole exchange. How could someone stay silent after hearing an adult admit to nearly killing an innocent teenager? But today, Maren was fixated on one goal and one goal only. She would not be distracted by her outrage. If Kelly could help her achieve her aims, Maren would use her without a second thought. "Fine. If you want to make amends, meet me at Vital at noon and sit in the far corner away from me—and make sure Alicia doesn't see you. When I wave to you, come over and only answer the questions I ask. Got it?"

Kelly was nodding her agreement when a commotion nearby caught their attention. A fistfight was under way between two dads. What had been a honking insurrection only a minute before was suddenly a silent rubbernecking assembly. All Maren could hear was the word "Yale" being grunted between punches. She watched as Ted Clark sprinted from the admin building to break up the fight, suffering a glancing blow to the side of his face in the process.

An instant later, Ted must have spotted Kelly standing at Maren's car. He immediately approached, grim with purpose. "You need to leave the school grounds now, Kelly." Ted pointed toward the parking lot. "I have far more important things to deal with today. And don't come back until your disciplinary hearing."

Kelly, for once, did as she was told.

Then Ted leaned down to Maren's window and with one hand pressing on his cheekbone said, "Are you OK?"

"I'll be fine, thanks," Maren said, trying hard to suppress a highly inappropriate smile. "I've dealt with worse. How 'bout you?"

"These fucking parents," he muttered. Then he caught her eye and shot her a crooked grin that gave her goose bumps as he waved her car on.

———

Maren sat in the corner of the crowded acai bowl café Alicia had designated as their celebration spot, her limbs fidgeting with nervous energy. She scanned the room and briefly marveled at the dozen or so diorama-style boxes hanging on the walls. They hung vertically, like paintings, and featured square dividers similar to those in Alicia's jewelry drawer. But instead of being filled with necklaces and earrings, they were filled with soil that somehow defied gravity and live succulent plants that grew outward from the boxes, enveloping the room in a lush green hug. Maren actually found herself reaching a hand toward the wall and rolling one of the succulent leaves between her fingers to confirm that the plants were real. With that mystery solved, she fixed her eyes again on the front door of the café. For fuck's sake, this woman would be late to meet Michelle Obama.

Maren played with the napkin in her lap as she attempted to slow her galloping heartbeat. After more than ten years answering to Alicia's every whim, Maren usually knew what Alicia would ask her for before the thought occurred to Alicia herself. So she had not been surprised by Alicia's text in the wee hours of the morning professing an out-of-the-blue but unquenchable desire to stock up on her inventory of personal essentials—immediately. And neither did Maren harbor any mistaken notions about Alicia's plans for this unusual midday meeting. In a few minutes, Maren would be relieved from her duties and cast from the Stones' lives for good. For the past several hours, she'd dashed from one store to the next, like a hostage suffering from Stockholm syndrome, vacillating between wondering how in the world Alicia would ever manage life without her and realizing that what was about to happen would render that question irrelevant.

Maren heard the bell on the café door jingle and looked up to see Alicia marching in with the untouchable confidence of a superhero floating miles above the pedestrian worries that plagued mere mortals, even top-one-percent mortals. Maren watched as Alicia unwound her scarf and sat down in front of the acai bowl and bee pollen smoothie Maren had ordered for her prior to her arrival. Smiling tentatively at Alicia, Maren handed over two giant shopping bags with the makeup and various other cosmetics she'd purchased for Alicia that morning. Sort of like a last supper, but for Alicia's face.

"From what I hear, congratulations are in order." Alicia's smile was brittle, even a little sinister.

"Thanks, Alicia." Maren spoke softly, attempting to disguise her jitters. "I'll pass that on to Winnie." Maren allowed her gaze to take in the hunched-over form of one Kelly Vernon, who had shown up as promised. She hoped Kelly would stay tucked away in her corner until Maren was ready for her.

"Yes, well. No child gets into Stanford completely on her own. There's always a parent in the background pulling some strings, no?"

Maren leaned back in her chair. "I wish I could take some credit for this. But really, Winnie did it all on her own. She wanted Stanford more than she's wanted anything her whole life. You know she's always idolized you."

"If only my own daughter felt that way," Alicia said.

"Brooke's a good kid, Alicia. Just give her time and a bit of space. You'll see."

"About Brooke…as everyone knows, she was deferred. But I've been assured that if anyone from EBA declines their spot, Brooke will be admitted." Alicia stabbed at a piece of fruit in her bowl like she was imagining it was one of her husband's testicles. Or maybe Maren was just projecting. "I can see to it Winnie gets into a different Ivy Plus school, and I'll pay all her expenses—if she declines Stanford."

"Thanks for the generous offer, Alicia. But I don't think that's going to work for us."

"Do I need to remind you that you've worked for me, Alicia Stone— Fortune 100 CEO, Top Ten Reviewed TED Talker of all time, bestselling author and feminist icon—for the past ten years? If I fire you without a reference, there isn't a person of means in this country who will hire you. Or perhaps you're prepared to go back to your previous profession?"

That didn't take long. "Winnie has her heart set on Stanford. At this point, it would take a lot more than threats to talk her out of it."

"Fine. I'll also write you a check for a million dollars. So we have a deal?"

Maren tapped a finger on her chin. "Tempting, but no. You see, Winnie's still a tad upset over your little genetics stunt."

Shock flickered on Alicia's face, but she expertly transitioned to her trademark PR smile. Maren doubted anyone else would have noticed the momentary slip, but Maren knew Alicia's facial tics better than anyone.

"I tried to tell her not to sweat it," Maren continued, "but she's just so oversensitive since learning her father's identity. Come to think of it, we're both pretty pissed off about that."

"Did you snoop on my computer? I could have you thrown in jail, you know. And what do you mean you didn't know her dad's identity? How's that even possible?"

Maren stayed silent.

Alicia shifted in her seat and took a measured sip of her smoothie before continuing. "Anyway, I didn't do it to hurt Winnie. I adore her. I meant to get your permission for the DNA test but just forgot. It's not like you would have refused. And it was years ago. No big deal," Alicia said, waving her hand through the air.

"That's debatable," Maren said. "But then you decided last month to access the DNA account again—this time to dig for dirt on Winnie's father, didn't you? And you still didn't tell me about the account."

"You left me no choice, Maren. After all these years, I know almost nothing about you other than the escort conviction I found on your criminal background check when I first hired you, which as you know I agreed to overlook and keep secret all these years. But when someone texted me that Winnie's first-generation hook was a lie, how else was I supposed to figure out if you were lying to EBA and Stanford—and me? For all I knew, maybe you've been conning me this whole time. And I've trusted you with everything—my work, my daughter, my husband, my life. All I did was run Winnie's genetic information through a database and peek at her family tree. It was harmless. Stop overreacting."

"Alicia," Maren said, shaking her head, "I have to know. Do you feel even the slightest remorse about withholding information that could help save Winnie's half brother's life? You put an innocent child's life at risk."

"That's all nonsense, and you know it," Alicia snarled. "I didn't cause that boy's illness. I just chose not to help. There's no law compelling some-one to be a Good Samaritan." To her credit, Alicia blanched ever so slightly before recovering her equilibrium. "Maren," she said sternly, "do I have to remind you that you are bound by the strict NDA you signed years ago?"

"Oh right, you mean the one you had me sign after you stole my eleven-year-old's identity and made her take the SSAT exam under Brooke's name to cheat her way into EBA?"

"Lest you forget, I paid for Winnie's entire education at EBA after that."

"True…" Maren said. "But only because I caught you. And then you reneged on the college part of the deal."

"I see what you're angling for," Alicia smirked. "Greedy, greedy girl. Two million dollars for Winnie's Stanford spot. And I'll sue your ass to kingdom come if you ever breathe a word to anyone in violation of our agreement. My lawyers will tear you to pieces."

Maren reached into her purse and pulled out her phone, making a show of opening up her Notes app. "Hmm…interesting. According to my research, there's something called a public policy exception to NDAs when they're used to cover up criminal activity."

Alicia's eyes narrowed. In a move clearly designed to regain the upper hand, she took her time spooning a bite of acai mush into her mouth, swallowed, and said in a calm, low voice accompanied by a smile, "You conniving little bitch. You don't know the game you're playing."

"I wouldn't be so sure about that." Maren smiled back. "After all, I learned from the best."

"Three million. That's my final offer."

"Or what?" Maren looked up and waved Kelly over. She waited the few seconds it took Kelly to appear at their table. "Or you'll sic Bryan on Winnie again so he can finish the job he started when he nearly killed her?"

Alicia rolled her eyes. "As if. You don't know it was him. I don't even know it was him. But really, who knows what he's capable of? We both know he's such a fucking moron, anything's possible." Now Alicia was mopping her brow. And her upper lip. And her chest.

Maren turned to Kelly. "OK. Here's your big shot at redemption, Kelly. Tell Alicia exactly what you heard Bryan say to me at the stress buster party."

Kelly took a deep breath and let it rip. "He said he was the one who ran Winnie off the road. I heard him say he did it because he was sick of having perfect Winnie in his life always outshining Brooke. He saw the opportunity to scare her and took it."

Alicia waved a hand through the air again like she was swatting flies. "Oh, please. That's hearsay. Besides, no one would ever believe you two with your track records. It's your word against his."

"We'll see about that," Maren said.

Apparently not done with her star turn, Kelly continued, "Also, you should know…Bryan said he was drinking that night, and that's why he didn't stop to help Winnie. I couldn't believe my ears."

"Just tell me this," Alicia said to Maren. "Why would someone like you be so fixated on one specific college anyway? Isn't any college education for Winnie a giant leap? I mean, I get why *she's* so obsessed with Stanford," she said, sneering at Kelly. "At least she and her husband went there. But why Stanford for Winnie? Brooke's the one who really needs Stanford. I thought you cared about her. She's devastated, you know."

"Of course I care about Brooke. I practically raised her." Alicia reared back like she'd been slapped. "But let's be honest—Brooke isn't the one who's devastated about Stanford. You are." Maren raised her eyebrows. "Especially once word gets out that your personal assistant's daughter got in when your own daughter got rejected."

"The nerve of you. I'm a good mom. Fine. Five million."

"Five million what?" Kelly interjected.

They both ignored Kelly. In that moment, over Alicia's right shoulder,

Maren spotted several black windbreakers swarming in through the door of the café and moving toward them, like a beehive had been smashed open. Alicia's back was to the door, and she hadn't yet noticed the hush falling across the room. With a smirk, Maren said to Alicia, "Are you really a good mom though? Because from where I sit, you're nothing but a hateful shell of a person who's about to get what she's had coming for so damn long."

Alicia must have finally heard the footsteps. She swiveled her head to see what the commotion was about. Whipping her head back to Maren, Alicia's eyes betrayed a combination of wild panic, total disbelief, and utter contempt. She opened her mouth to say something, but for once, she was speechless.

"Alicia Stone, I'm Federal Agent Danforth. Pauline Danforth. We spoke yesterday about your daughter's application to Stanford? You're under arrest on suspicion of the crimes of federal mail fraud and wire fraud in connection with stolen genetic material. Please stand up slowly with your hands in the air." Agent Danforth briefly glanced at Kelly and then added to Alicia, "Looks like we'll also be referring your husband to local authorities for prosecution for his involvement in an alleged hit-and-run."

Alicia sat paralyzed in her seat with a look of helplessness Maren had never seen before.

"Ma'am? Stand up please. You have the right to remain silent. Anything you say can and will be used against you in a court of law."

"Jesus Christ—I know my fucking rights. You're making a huge mistake." She stood up and barked over her shoulder at Maren. "Call Bryan and tell him to contact our lawyer. Now!"

"Really?" Maren leaned back in her chair. "By the way, I have to confess. I lied to you. Winnie didn't get into Stanford. She was deferred just like Brooke." With her eyes glued to Alicia's, Maren unbuttoned the top two buttons of her blouse, ripped out the wire taped to her chest, and threw it on the table.

"So only Tenley got in?" Alicia said as the FBI agent handcuffed her.

"Yup," Maren said.

"Wait, what?" Kelly asked bewildered.

Maren turned to Kelly. "You can go now."

"But what's going on?" Kelly persisted. "I don't understand. Is she being arrested because of that professor she hired to write Brooke's essays?"

"She wasn't up until now." Agent Danforth's ears perked up. "But that sounds like another potential federal crime. You wouldn't happen to know the name of this professor, would you? Stanford reported an anonymous tip to this effect, but without the professor's name, we had difficulty corroborating."

Alicia looked at Kelly with pure hatred.

Kelly tore her eyes away from Alicia's and sheepishly shook her head. "I don't know his name. I wish I did. I'm sorry."

"Wait, but I think I do," Maren said, searching her memory from the night she'd stopped by the Stones' just before Winnie's accident. "Bejamaca. Professor Bejamaca from Boston."

Agent Danforth nodded at Maren. "Excellent. We'll be following up on this."

Alicia emitted a shocking noise resembling Maria Sharapova's infamous tennis grunt. The agents took that as their cue to escort Alicia out of the café, with Alicia vigorously protesting for the duration of the delicious perp walk that she'd done nothing wrong, or at least nothing worse than all the other parents at EBA were doing. Maren couldn't help the shit-eating grin that forced its way onto her face as she turned on her heel and followed the agents, leaving a slack-jawed Kelly behind, hopefully forever.

When Maren emerged from the café, she was pleasantly surprised to find that the morning rainstorm had given way to rare December sunshine. Squinting in the bright light of the afternoon, Maren waited for her vision to adjust. Finally, her gaze landed on its target. Grandpa Jack was waiting for her outside the FBI's unmarked van. Overcome with emotion, she crossed the street and collapsed onto his chest.

"Perfect execution, my dear," he said, wrapping his arms around Maren. "There should be more than enough on tape to lock Alicia up in a federal penitentiary. In fact, my law enforcement contacts tell me the U.S. attorney for Seattle is champing at the bit to use this case to establish precedent for applying the federal criminal code to theft of genetic material and identity. It's been happening more and more, and the state criminal codes aren't equipped to tackle this twenty-first-century problem. And they may even have enough evidence to charge Bryan. It's a long shot given the lack of physical evidence, but your brilliant stroke bringing that Kelly woman to the sting should at least provide fodder for a full investigation. You should feel good. Your work will help prevent a lot of innocent victims down the road."

Maren didn't know exactly what road she'd be traveling from here, but at least it would be her hands on the wheel navigating her future from this point forward. As for Winnie, Maren was confident she'd raised a resilient daughter who was well-equipped to forge a life on her own terms. She may not have been a perfect mother, but she'd gotten that part right. And for now, that—and Winnie and Gramps—was more than enough.

EPILOGUE

EBA PARENTS SECRET FACEBOOK GROUP

Amanda Russell: Hi all! Now that we're all recovered from our temporary college insanity, I'm reactivating this old secret Facebook group from last year (this time, I got the privacy settings right, I promise!). I miss you all since our kids graduated and was thinking it would be fun to reconnect. See my Facebook event invite to make care packages for the kids as they study for their first college finals!

COMMENTS:

Sarah Silver: Thanks for bringing us all together again, Amanda. You're so amazing! Totally count me in! Sadly, I still have a raging case of parental college mania—I don't recommend having back-to-back seniors applying to college! 😔

Diana Taylor: Thanks for the invite, but I won't be coming. Tenley dropped out of Stanford last month and is traveling in Europe.

Sarah Silver: Oh no! You must be so devastated! Do you want us to set up a meal train for you and Michael?

Augusta Wagoner: Hey y'all. I'm afraid I have to miss the fun. Greer has a mother-daughter sorority event at Vanderbilt. xoxo

Augusta Wagoner: P.S. I'm guessing Alicia won't make it either?

Amanda Russell: I don't think she's up for early release for at least another nine months. Were you all glued to the news reports about her trial over the summer too? It sounds like the judge really threw the book at her after she put up such a fight in court.

Robin Riley: Did you guys listen to the wire tape recording they played at the trial? I mean, wow! No wonder Bryan dumped her. The whole world heard her call her own husband a fucking moron! Too bad they weren't able to make a case against him. I heard the prosecutor didn't want to go forward with just a he said/she said/ she said case without any physical evidence. I thought for sure Bryan would have been just arrogant enough to save the phone he used to send that text as a souvenir, but I guess the police never found it.

Augusta Wagoner: Why do the biggest pricks always manage to get off? Oops. Hahaha

Donna Peterson: I guess Brooke doesn't need a finals care package since she didn't end up going to college, poor girl.

Peggy Wainwright: Poor girl? Brooke's doing just fine. Her tell-all has been on the NYT bestseller list for weeks!

Amanda Russell: Has anyone been in touch with Kelly Vernon? Wanted to invite her, but she seems to have dropped off the face of the earth ever since her family was asked to leave EBA. Deleted her social media accounts, deactivated her cell.

COMMENTS:

Jennifer Tan: Actually I ran into Kelly a couple of weeks ago and didn't even recognize her. She lost 25 lbs. and looks fantastic! She started a test prep nonprofit for low-income students. Krissie spent the summer at a wilderness therapy program in Colorado for anxious and depressed teens and apparently came back a new person. She even managed to enroll at Tulane on schedule and loves it there, and she's not doing STEM anymore. Kelly's other kids are at public school, and she said they're super happy. Sounds like she and Kevin are finally in a good place after a bumpy road. All those memes that circulated for months after Alicia's trial starring Kelly as the hero of her own pathetic, shitty story were pretty rough on the family, but it sounds like they made their peace with the help of A LOT of therapy. Will send you her new number.

Sarah Silver: That's incredible! Kelly should market her diet plan. Leave EBA and lose 25 lbs? Sign me up! Sigh…

Amanda Russell: Did you all see Brooke's book dedication? "To Maren and Winnie—the truest friends." I guess they patched everything up. I hear Maren enrolled at the University of Washington?

COMMENTS:

Maren Pressley: The rumor is true. I am officially a UW Husky studying literature. I also adopted a rescue dog, spend my free time volunteering at a homeless shelter for women and children, and am happier than I've ever been. Winnie is loving UC Berkeley. As a bonus, she's reconnected with some long-lost family in the East Bay, including two adorable little kids. The little boy recently survived a battle with leukemia, and Winnie's close relationship with him has inspired her to go pre-med.

Holly Strong: Maybe you should write a book like Brooke. Or a screenplay. I bet you have some unbelievable stories from all those years working for Alicia

Maren Pressley: Sorry to disappoint, but no tell-all or movie will be forthcoming. Signed away all my rights when I settled my civil suit with the Stones. $$$

Sarah Silver: I'll tell you this...the SST isn't the same without you this year. We're a total mess!

Maren Pressley: Somehow that doesn't surprise me!

Amanda Russell: I heard Ted Clark took a job with the UW School of Education after he quit EBA. Have you run into him there?

Maren Pressley: As a matter of fact, I have 🖤

Amanda Russell: Will everyone's kids be home next summer? Duke's on-campus recruiting program is the bomb! Audrey already has summer job offers from Amazon, Goldman Sachs & Morgan Stanley... #decisionsdecisions!

AUTHORS' NOTE

The shenanigans portrayed in our fictional Elliott Bay Academy and parent community are exaggerated representations (*we hope!*) of the temporary insanity that overtakes many high school communities across the country every year during college admissions season. Further, our characters' sometimes-egregious value judgments regarding various colleges and universities are intended to illustrate the dark underbelly of parental competition fueled by rankings, hooks, gossip, and fear—and are not in any way representative of our own views about these schools or the students who attend them. We're positive all the colleges and universities mentioned in *Girls with Bright Futures*—and for that matter, those not mentioned—offer outstanding educational and life experiences. After all, college is what you make of it. *Right?*

READING GROUP GUIDE

1. When we enter the novel, Maren and Winnie are having a tough conversation with the Elliott Bay Academy college counselor regarding the Stanford early admissions process. What do you glean from this conversation? How is this conversation different from how the other moms and their daughters learn about the Stanford news? What does this say about schools like EBA, their politics, and how they operate?

2. Maren and Winnie planned to emphasize Winnie's first-gen status as a "hook" for college admissions. What would college admissions look like without this and other hooks such as athletics, legacy, or development priorities? Are any aspects of this system fair? Is there an argument for scrapping the whole system? If the system were 100 percent merit based, do you think parents would be any less manic about college?

3. When Maren compares herself to Alicia, Kelly, and the other
    EBA parents, she struggles to feel like a well-connected pro-
    vider. Even Kelly, who is wealthy by every reasonable stan-
    dard, feels inadequate in comparison to Alicia. How do
    Maren and Kelly handle these negative self-comparisons?

4. The three women in this book are vastly different from one
    another. However, they share a common goal—securing
    what's best for their child. What do you make of the dynamic
    in which each character's actions seemed to push another
    character to go to further lengths to achieve her goals?
    Where and why do you think they crossed a line? Is there
    any justification for their manipulations?

5. There are moments of humor throughout the novel that
    speak to the ridiculous lengths the characters will go to in
    order to get ahead. What was one of your favorite moments
    that made you think *I can't believe they did that*? Have you
    ever encountered a person or situation that mirrors the EBA
    parents' behavior?

6. Throughout the novel, Maren struggles with the trauma
    in her own past and Winnie's origin story. If you were in
    Maren's position, would you have consented to a face-to-
    face meeting with Chase and Naomi? If you were in Winnie's
    position, would you have taken the donor match test to see
    if you could help Eli?

7. Maren's life is fundamentally altered by Chase's criminal assault, whereas Chase suffers few consequences. Do you believe someone who commits such a heinous act can be redeemed through future good behavior? How do you feel about Chase by the end of the novel? Does he have more or less integrity than Alicia? How about Kelly?

8. Discuss the role of DNA testing in the novel. Have you ever taken a consumer DNA test or allowed your child to be tested? What are some of the positives and negatives associated with widespread use of this technology?

9. *Girls with Bright Futures* ends with details about where the families are in one year. How do you think the mother-daughter relationships will evolve over the next few years? Will the mothers remain as involved in their daughters' college lives, their decisions about jobs or graduate schools, or even their romantic relationships?

10. Ultimately, what do you think *Girls with Bright Futures* says about how privilege, opportunity, and ambition cycle through our society? Do you see any parallels between the novel and our current culture? To your own life experiences? Are parents today more amped up about college competition than in previous generations? If so, why? Are there any obvious fixes that would lessen the intensity?

A CONVERSATION WITH
THE AUTHORS

Girls with Bright Futures follows three mothers as they fight for their daughters' futures. Of the three lead women, did you have a favorite to write? Did you have any challenges finding their unique voices?

Would you ever confess to having a favorite child? We loved writing each of our leading ladies, but that doesn't mean we weren't rooting for one of them (cough, cough—rhymes with SPAREN). We started with a pretty clear vision of what we wanted to accomplish for each of the women vis-à-vis the Stanford competition, but their individual voices took a lot of work. We spent a ton of time creating elaborate backstories for each of our main characters, much of which never made it into the novel, but this exercise helped reveal their voices organically. People always ask how we write together, and this is a key element. We leverage the fact that there are two of us, so we each take primary responsibility for different characters to start. We'll never reveal who writes what, because in the end, we edit absolutely every word together, but dividing

things up really helps us more quickly and easily discover and individu-
alize our characters' voices.

What research did you have to do to bring the EBA community to life? How did you delve into the complicated world of college admissions?

Between us, we have four kids ranging in age from thirteen to twenty-three. Although *Girls with Bright Futures* is not autobiographical and the EBA parent community is wholly fictional, you could say we've been "conducting research" for nearly twenty years while our kids attended various schools, participated in numerous sports and extracurriculars, and, of course, applied to college. One of the things we were struck by during the college admissions process was the existence of what we refer to as the "college admissions industrial complex." This complex, which didn't exist when we were applying to college, feels designed to prey on parents' insecurities and anxieties. By the time kids reach high school, they and their parents become the targets of sophisticated market-ing campaigns from, for example, colleges and universities looking to increase their applicant pools; standardized testing services looking to build their market shares; and private consultants selling services (usu-ally expensive ones), such as test prep, résumé building, essay writing, far-flung service trips, college-tour planning, and athletic recruitment. In the face of such overwhelming "opportunities," parents worry: Are we doing enough? Maybe we need another six-hour package of tutoring for the ACT? Or maybe we need to find a way to send them to one of those summer programs at [insert name of selective university]? One of our favorites was an email from a test prep company admonishing ninth graders to set up their LinkedIn profiles to showcase their awards and honors. We had a good laugh over that one, especially since one of us (who shall remain nameless) still had not figured out how to make her own LinkedIn profile.

In addition to anecdotal experience, we devoured newspaper and magazine articles and several nonfiction books about the college process. Two of our favorite books in this vein were *Excellent Sheep: The Miseducation of the American Elite and the Way to a Meaningful Life* by William Deresiewicz and *Where You Go Is Not Who You'll Be: An Antidote to the College Admissions Mania* by Frank Bruni. We were actually completing the first draft of our manuscript when the Operation Varsity Blues college admissions scandal broke, and suddenly, this world we'd been depicting was all anyone could talk about. We found it validating on some level that our chosen topic was clearly part of the zeitgeist. And like most people, we were shocked by the extent of the criminality. What we were not surprised by was the parental anxiety component.

As coauthors, what does your brainstorming and writing process look like? What's the best part of working as a team?

By far the best part of working as a team is having another person who is equally invested in every single aspect of the book...and all the laughter. We have a really good time, and at least one of us is usually able to remember why we made a certain decision or changed a particular detail. Our best brainstorming happens on long walks or over text late into the night. We typically write side by side and spec out all plot points chapter by chapter. One of our favorite moments is sharing a new chapter with each other and the surprise of seeing how our partner creatively accomplished each goal.

When writing the suspense aspect of *Girls with Bright Futures*, how did you map out all the twists and turns? Did you know "whodunit" going into the project?

We are both laughing right now hoping that the other one remembers how we mapped it all out! As a writing team, we are plotters out of necessity, so we figured out the major twists and turns before we started writing. We had poster boards with color-coded sticky notes all over them spread across Tracy's dining room table and floor for months as we tried to keep track of what each character knew and what the reader knew at any given point in time. As we got further into the writing and editing process, our characters added a few twists and turns of their own, further complicating our storyboards. And then our fabulous editor, MJ Johnston, had great suggestions for heightening the suspense. We had a strong sense from the start about "whodunit" and why, although we did play around with a few alternate ideas before eventually coming back full circle to our original plan.

If you had a child attending EBA, which character would you avoid at the SST meetings?

All of them! Just kidding! But seriously, we intentionally amplified the crazy in the SST meetings and at EBA in general to show the very real temporary insanity that seems to overtake so many of us during the stressful college admissions process, which can affect friendships and even our self-worth as parents. It's a very insecure time for all involved. The truth is that like anywhere, some people are truly awful no matter the situation, and some people are absolute saints, but most of us fall somewhere in between, and the college madness makes people act in ways detrimental to all types of relationships. We are only seeing a snapshot of these SST women during the height of anxiety. Some of them may have been lovely, normal people before the toxic college race, and they may go back to that after. But during, the general rule is "steer clear!"

Girls with Bright Futures is a fantastic blend of suspense twists with a lighter, often-comic look at the absurdity of one elite community. How did you strike a balance between the darker, more suspenseful scenes and the levity of the EBA parents and their hijinks?

Our natural tendency veers toward humor, but we wanted to write domestic suspense, so it was definitely a balancing act. We approached striking that balance the way we used to make mix tapes (or in today's parlance—a playlist). You need to vary the speed and tempo to keep things interesting. We intentionally juxtaposed suspenseful and emotional scenes with the more comedic EBA parent scenes as a way of heightening the drama but also to further emphasize the absurdity of the college madness.

Do you have similar reading lists?

Rarely does a day go by that we are not talking about books, movies, TV shows, and articles over our morning coffee. We constantly add to our shared reading list and divide up who reads what and then make recommendations to each other.

ACKNOWLEDGMENTS

Girls with Bright Futures was born out of the pressures of modern motherhood, a mutual desire to collaborate on something creative, and most of all, our recognition of the value of unconditional friendship while navigating life's peaks and valleys. After countless brainstorming sessions (about the book—but also, if we're being honest, about what the heck to make for dinner, *again*), writing retreats, editing draft upon draft, supporting each other through life-altering events, and working side by side in our kitchens for several years, our friendship is stronger than ever, and our partnership pushes us to be the best versions of ourselves in work and life. So we must start by thanking each other for the gift of this thriving, challenging, and fulfilling KatznDobs enterprise. However, we are abundantly aware that without the help of so many others, we would never have achieved the indescribable thrill of holding this debut novel in our hands. We have many people to thank, so please hold your applause to the end!

To Carly Watters, our brilliant literary agent: we are forever grateful to you for betting on us. Your guidance made us better writers, and your industry expertise helped bring our dream to fruition. Thank you a million times over! Our gratitude also extends to Curtis Russell and the P.S. Literary team.

To MJ Johnston, our editor at Sourcebooks Landmark: your lovely, collaborative style coupled with your keen eye for storytelling and pacing made this book so much better and made our first publishing experience both enjoyable and educational. Thank you to Jessica Thelander, our production editor; Karin Kipp, our copy editor; Sabrina Baskey, our proofreader; Nicole Hower, our cover design lead; Holli Roach and Jillian Rahn, our page designers; Molly Waxman and Kirsten Wenum, our marketing leads; and the entire Sourcebooks team for believing in and supporting this book.

To our film/TV agents, Addison Duffy and Eni Akintade, at UTA: it's impossible to convey how much your enthusiasm for our manuscript's adaptation potential, even before we had a book deal, meant to us.

To Crystal Patriarche and the BookSparks team: thank you for playing such an integral role in our debut launch. We are grateful to have you on our team!

To Taryn Fagerness: thank you for all your efforts on our behalf.

To our meticulous beta readers: thank you for your insightful comments, for your willingness to drop everything and read our latest drafts, and for not laughing us out of the room in the early days—cringe! In particular, giant thanks to Lisa Caputo, David Fallek, Spencer Grayson, Joanne Kennedy, Anne Rees, Katherine Slack, and Margaret Slack. Many thanks also to the people who generously welcomed us into the publishing industry: Sarah Burnes, Carol Cassella, Ming Chen, Wah

Chen, Dan Donahue, Andrea Dunlop, Elizabeth Egan, Coralie Hunter, and Kim Scott.

One of the many complicated aspects of writing as a duo is how to thank the loads of additional friends who've supported us in so many ways through this journey. Our love and immense gratitude go to: Vibha Akkaraju, Sarah Alsdorf, Michele Bosworth, Mackenzie Caputo, Mark Caputo, Amy Carter, Charlie Carter, Dan Covitz, Lynn Engle, Barbara Fielden, Sally Frankenberg, Terri Fujinaga, Susan Gibbons, Michele Godvin, Salina Gray, Erika Grayson, Lisa Hales, Matt Harris, Alice Hauschka, Barb Herrington, Libby Hill, Gena Hocevar, Jeanne Hoppe, Catharine Jacobsen, Hank Kaplan, Neen Koenigsbauer, Clark Lombardi, Anne Lyons, Vilma Plantz, Naomi Runkel, Lili Sacks, Jennifer Schorsch, Eve Stacey, Sally Swofford, Kristen Sycamore, Ayala Thomas, Effie Toshav, Susie Wertheimer, Maria White, Kevin Young, and Karen Zucker. Special shout-outs to our awesome and ever-available legal consultants, Van Katzman and David Fallek, and our expert medical consultants, Dr. Jonathan Drachman, Dr. Jeoffrey Stross, and Margaret Slack. Finally, around the time we embarked on this second act, our dear friend was setting out to become the first pediatrician ever to serve in the U.S. Congress. To U.S. Congresswoman Kim Schrier: your courage is our inspiration.

Last but not least, we wish to thank our families. For once, this is something we cannot do together.

Tracy: I am grateful for my incredibly supportive and loving extended family across the country, including: Mom and Dad Dobmeier; "Sis" Amy Funke & "Bro" Fred Funke; stepmom Rhonda Friedman; awesome niece and nephews, Anna, Luke, and Nathan; and the Melman/Schwartz clan.

To my sister, Carrie: I love you always and wish we didn't live so far apart. To my wonderful dad, Barry Friedman, and my late and forever-missed mom, Sandy Friedman: thank you for raising me with boundless love and the high expectations that I still try to live up to every day. To my sons, Ben and Matty: I am overflowing with pride and joy for the exceptional young men you have become. My love for you is unshakeable. And finally, to my husband, Eric: my biggest champion, my inspiration, my best friend, and the love of my life—I would be (Wendy, can I buy an adverb?) *utterly* lost without you.

Wendy: A heartfelt thank-you to my sweet and endlessly supportive husband, Van. James Taylor has always said it best for us: "They were true love written in stone." To my kids, Jack and Carly: always have the courage to try. I am incredibly proud of you both and love you forever just the way you are. A huge thank-you to my wise and inspiring parents, Jeoffrey and Ellen Stross, for your unwavering love and support to pursue this dream and every other. To Jonathan, you're contractually obligated to be my brother, but I'm so lucky to also call you my friend. To my loving extended family—the Katzmans, Levines, Roberts, and Team Strong—your encouragement means the world to me. Thank you in memoriam to my grandpa Oscar Schwartz, who instilled the mindset of being a lifelong learner.

ABOUT THE AUTHORS

Photo © Kristen Sycamore Photography

After supporting each other through two decades of motherhood, Tracy Dobmeier and Wendy Katzman thought: "Let's write a book and *really* test the friendship." Several years later, their friendship is not only still intact, but they would even go so far as to grade it an A+. With such a perfect GPA, maybe *they* should apply to Stanford? Just kidding! They would never leave Seattle where they live (not together, though it often feels that way) with their husbands, pets, and last remaining school-age kiddo. You can find them at dobmeierkatzman.com and @katzndobs on Instagram. Or in Tracy's kitchen.